THE RIDDLE OF THE STORM

Book One

GLENLOCK

By: R. L. Snyder

Apart from any use permitted under U. S. Law, this publication may not be reproduced, stored, or transmitted, in any form, or by any means, without permission in writing from the publisher or the copyright holder.

Printed in the United States of America

Copyright © 2022 By: R. L. Snyder

ISBN: 978-0-9995179-9-4
     979-8-9875247-1-8

This book is a work of fiction. Names, characters, businesses, places, events, and incidents are either the product of the author's imagination or used in a fictitious manner. Any resemblance to actual persons, living or dead, or actual events is purely coincidental.

Cover Design and Formatting by 100 Covers

Published by: MECROSS Publications LLC

P.O. Box 1061

Gorham, Maine 04038

Also by R. L. Snyder

The Branwen Saga
Branwen

The Riddle of the Storm
The Valley of the Storm
Glenlock

The Shadow War
The Blocker
First Dragon
Oathsworn

Watch for more at www.robertsnyderwrites.com

To the soldiers of the 402nd Special
Operations Detachment, 10th Special
Forces Group. It was an honor
to have served in your company.

FERNWEH

(German)

A feeling of homesickness for places you have never been.

Contents

Cast of Characters..I
Prologue..1

Chapter 1: The Package..13
Chapter 2: Maggie...22
Chapter 3: The Mountain...37
Chapter 4: Outside the Valley of Storms...........................45
Chapter 5: Glenlock...56
Chapter 6: Treason..61
Chapter 7: Sir Hal..69
Chapter 8: The Making of a King...................................79
Chapter 9: Kyūdōda Yumi...84
Chapter 10: Discovered..93
Chapter 11: Titles Count...103

Chapter 12: Edwenna 112

Chapter 13: The Bloody Meadow 117

Chapter 14: Eldon 125

Chapter 15: Lost Children 132

Chapter 16: Daemons 144

Chapter 17: Tilden 150

Chapter 18: The Battle of Eldon Hill 159

Chapter 19: Awakening 174

Chapter 20: Eleanor 183

Chapter 21: Legionaries 191

Chapter 22: A Wedding 200

Chapter 23: Ambush 205

Chapter 24: The King's Chamberlin 211

Chapter 25: Astrid 216

Chapter 26: The Messenger from Cyneburg 227

Chapter 27: Sir George 232

Chapter 28: What to Do with the Wounded? 237

Chapter 29: Plan of Attack 244

Chapter 30: The Fort 257

Chapter 31: The Chamberlin's Message 266

Chapter 32: Carnage 273

Chapter 33: Revelations 281

Chapter 34: An Ally 287

Chapter 35: The Road to Tilden 292

Chapter 36: A Meeting on the Hill 297
Chapter 37: Sacrifice...308
Chapter 38: Arrival..313

Epilogue..327
Definitions..331
Authors Note...333

GLENLOCK

ERISTA

EAMON SEA

THE GREAT SEA

CENT

ANTUS

SOUTHLAND

CAST OF CHARACTERS

Harold (Hal) Bennet: Government Agent
Pam Fuller: Sister of Hal
Mike Fuller: Pam's husband
Micky Fuller: Hal's nephew
Miyamoto Musashi (Mike): A martial arts instructor from San Francisco
John Lackland: King of Cent
Henry Lackland: Crown Prince of Cent
Edwenna Lackland: Princess of Cent, Henry's sister
Eleanor Lackland: Princess of Cent, Henry's sister
Sir George Williamson: Chamberlin and friend to King John
William Eyre: Clerk to King John
Bartholomew Eyre: Clerk to King John, brother to William
Francis Appleby: Sir George's captain
Steven Longarm: Sir George's man
Billy Thatcher: Sir George's man
Dick Franklin: Sir George's man
Harry Millerson: Sir George's man

GLENLOCK

Sam Millerson: Harry's son
Fredric King: Friend of Harry
Johnnie Casher: Friend of Harry
Patrick Allgood: Friend of Harry
Thomas Clinton: Friend of Harry
Bruce Son-of-Bruce: Henry's man
James Longbow: An archer
William Quick Arrow: An archer
Colby Three-Fingers: Sergeant-of-the-Guard
Irwin Mercier: Baron of Tilden
Sir Marlowe Mercier: Son of Irwin
Sir Jamie Mercier: Son of Irwin
Sir John Mercier: Son of Irwin
Sir Walter Mercier: Son of Irwin
Marjorie Mercier: Daughter of Irwin
Brian Mercier: Son of Irwin
Priscus: Healer
Richard Ainsworth: Sir Jamie's man-at-arms
Franklin: Sir Jamie's man
Osborn Kennington: Duke of Sandford
Oswald Kennington: Son of Osborn
Sir Ainsley: Knight of Sandford
Sir Ealdwine: Knight of Sandford
Kenneth: Sir Ealdwine's Squire
Abernathy: Sir Ealdwine's Sergeant
Humphrey: Healer
Sir Robert Beckett: Knight of Sandford
Sir William Beckett: Son of Robert
Darwin Benton: Earl of Burke
Clyde Huddleston: Baron of Endell
Sir Philip Huddleston: Son of Clyde
Randolph: Sir Philip's squire

Sir Edwyn Benton: Son of Darwin

William Benton: Son of Edwyn, squire to Sir Jamie

Peter: Sir Edwyn's squire

Ramsey of Wairdell: Sir Harold's man-at-arms

Bailey: Ramsey's son, Sir Harold's squire

Irwin: Man-at-arms

Sir Randel of Eudell

Bascom: Sir Randel's squire

Caesar Aurelias: Emperor of Lantus

Augustus: Son of Caesar, Imperator of the Sixth Legion

Celsus Aelius: Centurio Primus Pilus. Senior Centurion of the First Cohort of the Sixth Legion

Antonius: Decurion of Scouts

Ianuarius: Senior Decurion, Commander of Cavalry, First Cohort

Felix: Legatus, Lantusian ambassador to Cent, son of Caesar, brother of Augustus

Paulus: Cousin of Felix

Lucius: Senior Decurion of Cavalry escort for Legatus to Cent

Marko: Decurion of a Turmae, assigned to Felix

Brutus: Decurion of a Turmae assigned to Felix

Artorus: Legionnaire

Titus: Decurion of a Turmae assigned to Felix

Sabinus: Healer

Aeric of Ingibjörg: King of Southland

Astrid Leofric: Daughter to Aeric, Princess of Southland

Knut Leofric: Son of Aeric, Heir to the throne

Oelig Thirrussib: Huscarl, Bodyguard to Astrid

Frigg Daggerblood: Shield Maidan

Leif Sijvidottir: Cousin of Knute and Astrid

PROLOGUE

Off the coast of the Dark Forest

The cold spray broke over the bow of the single mast drakkar, her red sail snapping in the wind like a clash of thunder. Knut Leofric smiled as he watched the water drip from the jaws of the dragon's head seated above the prow as it soared once again above the waves.

"Hungry, my friend? You will feed soon, I promise."

"Knut!"

He turned to the stern. Eric One-Eye waved with one hand while keeping the other on the steering board. He pointed larboard and Knut scanned the shoreline of the nearing coast. Seeing nothing new, he worked his way back to his helmsman.

"What see you, old man?"

Eric smiled and adjusted the leather patch over his left eye. "I may have but one eye, Jarl, but it sees what needs to be seen. Near the shore lie four vessels."

Knut stared and as the ship rose on a swell, he saw them.

"Found you."

He turned to Eric and slapped him on the shoulder. "As usual, a true tracker of the seas. Thank you, my friend. Now it is time for retribution."

Knut called to the men sitting on their sea chests in the longboat's belly.

GLENLOCK

"Drop sail. Steep the mast."

He turned to Eric. "Signal the others to come alongside."

Knut stood with his legs spread wide, rocking with the movement of the boat as he waited for the other dragon ships. He looked down at the activity taking place on the deck of Serpent's Breath, his father's flagship. Eighty warriors opened the hole covers to prepare for pushing the eighteen-foot oars in place. Each man adjusted his sea chest to be used as a rowing bench.

As the other five ships came alongside, Knut looked at his boat captains. Sibbe Brodirsson, Leif Sijvidottir, Kaetil Hjarrandissan, Magnus Skulidottir, and the youngest, Ulf Firesoul. Skilled warriors all. Handpicked by the king himself to seek the cowards that had killed so many of their people and taken their children.

"Their vessels lie offshore of the Dark Forest." he called out. "Four massive ships. I don't know how many are aboard. We take them first. Then we go ashore and see what we can find."

"Magnus, Sibbe, you take the two to port. Ulf, you and Kaetil, take those that lie starboard. Clear their decks with your archers if you can then board. Look for the children. Lief and I will wait in case you should require aid."

"What do we do if they yield?" Ulf asked.

Knut stared at the young man for a moment. Then shook his head. "Make sure they don't. Any other questions?"

"Do we burn them?" Magnus asked.

"The ships or their crews?" came the voice of a young woman from Ulf's crew.

Knut laughed. "Frigg Daggerblood, do what makes you most happy. Far be it from me to try to tell you what to do."

Laughter from all the crews, accompanied by several comments, agreeing that trying to tell Frigg to do anything that did not suit her was tantamount to suicide.

"Signal when they are secure. If you need help, push off and we will come. If all goes well, I will see you on the beach."

Knut turned towards his crew as the other boats moved away. "Prepare for battle, my friends." He pointed to the beach. "There lies our quarry."

There was no cheer as the warriors of Serpent's Breath readied themselves, opening their chests and withdrawing the sleeveless chainmail shirts favored by raiders. When he felt all were ready, he shouted, "Oars out!"

They pushed twenty-five of the long oars out through the holes on each side of the longboat. Thirty men kneeled between them, ready to cover the rowers with shields if needs be or to take an oar if a man should fall or tire.

Leif Sijvidottir brought the Devilfish and her crew of sixty to a safe distance on the starboard side of Long Serpent. Knut was pleased to see that the young captain had placed four archers in the bow.

"Nickolas, call the pace, if you will."

The man Nickolas, one of the thirty kneeling between rowers, climbed to his feet and began to chant, slamming the hilt of a spear on the deck to keep the beat while his long mustachios, braided and tied, swung in cadence.

"Dip those oars then raise them high,"

The rowers cried out, "Dip, pull. Dip, pull."

"Draw them back and make us fly,"

"Dip, pull. Dip, pull."

"From bow to stern above the waves,"

"Dip, pull. Dip, pull."

"Let them see what comes their way."

Eric's voice rose above the chant as they worked their way closer to the beach.

"Hold!"

The rowers dropped their oars into the sea and held them steady. The boat ceased its forward movement two hundred yards from where the waves broke upon the black sand. Knut turned to his helmsman.

"Eric, keep us steady. We wait for the others. If the children are not there, we head for the beach."

The big man nodded and called to the ships' boys, "prepare the lines."

The drakkar bobbed in the uneasy water as Knut and the others watched while over two hundred raiders threw grappling lines and worked their way up the sides of the massive ships. He turned at the twang of a bowstring. Leif shrugged his shoulders.

"Someone looked over the rail."

Knut smiled, then returned his attention to the enemy vessels. They were massive things. Near as tall as the defensive wall of a steading. Three tall masts aligned evenly along the deck; their sails tied to long crossbeams sitting near thirty feet above the deck. No steering board, but a massive rudder similar to the ones he had seen Lantusian traders. Strange sea creatures adorned the hull from bow to stern, the waterline to the gunnels high above, all painted in brilliant colors.

Nickolas approached and whistled. "No hiding that. Seems like they want to be seen."

Knut laughed. "Not too good for raiding."

"Look," Nickolas said, pointing to the nearest boat. Sibbie was along the rail waving his arms. He cupped his hands to his mouth and called out.

"The ships are abandoned. No one is aboard."

"And the children?" Knut inquired.

Sibbie shook his head.

"They must have taken them ashore. Signal the others to meet us on the beach."

Sibbe nodded and turned away.

"Let's get underway, Nickolas."

The big man resumed his position in the boat's belly.

Knut called to Leif. "We head to the beach. Be careful. No crew aboard and ships this size could carry a lot of men."

"Then let us go get them," Leif laughed. He turned to his men. "It is time to show the prince what the Dragonfish can do. Up oars."

Eric chuckled. "I do believe he intends to beat you to the beach, Jarl."

"Nickolas," Knut shouted. "Do not allow that to happen."

"Aye, Jarl. All right, you sea rats, it is time we put that pup in his place."

The men cheered as they pushed the oars up towards the bow. Water dripped from the flat panels of the oars while the men waited for the command to drop them into the sea.

"Now dip and pull, you bastards! Put your backs into it. You let that boy and his children beat us to the beach and you will walk home."

They dropped fifty oars into the sea, and the boat began to move. Nickolas started banging his spear on the deck.

"Attack speed!"

As the boat picked up speed, Knut moved forward. He leaned his hand on the neck of the carved figurehead and watched the beach.

"Where are you?"

He scanned the shoreline and then the forest less than a hundred yards from the surf. Nothing.

"How did they get to shore?"

Knut did not see when they passed Dragonfish, focused on the coastline ahead.

"Prepare to come about." He heard Eric call.

Eric closely watched the dragon's head on the bow, waiting for the right moment to give the command.

Knut picked up his round shield and drew his sword.

"Scouts, to the stern."

"Now! Portside dip and hold. Starboard up oars," Eric commanded and leaned into the steering board until the ship swung around. Then he lifted the steering board as the stern gently ground to a halt in the sand. Ten men jumped into the surf and worked their way to the shore, where they formed a small defensive shield wall. The ship's boys leaped over the side, ran up the beach, and pounded long metal stakes deep into the sand. Removing the ropes wrapped around their torsos, their ends attached to the boats, they cinched them tight, securing the ships to the shore.

"Oars in," Nickolas called.

They pulled in the starboard side oars.

"Raise oars."

The fifty oars stood tall above the deck, looking like an orchard of leafless trees.

"Down."

The men carefully lowered and stacked the oars on the deck next to the mast, then recovered their shields from the outside of the gunwale.

"Over the side," Knut yelled as he lept over the stern onto dry land. "Scouts out."

He turned when he heard Devilfish beach itself. The men of both boats rushed forward of their prince and waited, shields and weapons ready.

Leif walked up beside him.

"Someday I will get to shore before you."

"Someday, cousin," Knut said, slapping him on the shoulder and sporting an affectionate grin.

"Now what?" Leif asked.

"We wait for the other boats and the scouts to tell us what lies beyond those trees."

"How did they come ashore?" Leif asked, looking around.

"Look there." Knut nodded towards the trees where several small boats rested covered with branches.

Leif shook his head. "Piss-poor job hiding them." He turned and looked at the massive ships resting offshore. "I have never seen anything like them. They are so damn tall it is a wonder they don't tip over. And three masts."

"I admit they are strange," Knut said. He stood and watched as his people dropped into their boats.

"Trouble?" Leif asked.

"I don't think so."

"Wait, smoke. They have fired the ships."

"That was fast."

"Sibbe said they found no one aboard."

"And the children?" Leif asked.

"Not there. Get your men organized and join me here. Quickly."

"You see something?"

"No. I feel something."

"Have you ever landed here before?"

Knut stared at the forest. "I know of no man that has landed on this cursed shore. None that have ever returned."

Leif stared at the trees.

"What do you think lies within that forest?"

"I do not know. And have no desire to venture in to find out."

One hundred and thirty men formed a loose arch around their prince and waited for the other boats.

When the captains arrived, Knut asked, "What did you find?"

Sibbe looked at the others and shrugged. "Nothing. Only one guard and he was in the sea with an arrow in his chest before we climbed aboard."

Knut turned to the wall of thick trees. "We wait for the scouts, then move inland. I intend to find these bastards before we lose the sun."

A shout made them all turn in time to see two of the scouts burst from the trees. One stumbled in the loose sand of the beach. He quickly regained his feet and tried to flee back towards the others. He had only gone a few yards before he crashed back to the sand, the long shaft of a spear quivering in his back.

"Run! Back to the boats!" the other scout screamed. He stumbled and three of Knut's warriors rushed to his aid. But before they could reach him, a storm of long arrows fell upon them.

"Shield wall!" Knut yelled, and the warriors rushed together, creating a wall of wood a hundred warriors wide.

Minutes went by and no one appeared from the forest.

"What are they waiting for?" Frigg asked, twisting the handle of her ax nervously.

Leif adjusted his shield as he turned to her. "You in a hurry?"

"My ax is hungry."

"Quiet, you two," Knut said. "Listen."

From the trees came a sound reminiscent of a stampede of cattle.

"What's that?" Björn Arnbidsonson asked.

"I don't know," Knut said.

While the second rank lifted their shields over those of the first, tightening the wall, the others lifted theirs over their heads.

The sound of movement stopped. Then a strange yell echoed from the dark woods and a wave of warriors appeared sprinting towards them at an unnatural pace.

"Oden save us," Frigg said. "There must be thousands of them."

Knut grabbed Leif by the shoulder. "Take your crew and get to your boat. We will hold them as long as we can. Take Ulf and the ship boys with you."

"I will not leave you."

"You will do as I say. Tell my father what has happened."

"But..."

Knut smiled. "No buts, cousin. If we all run, they will kill us all before we cast off. Maybe we can slow them long enough for you to get to sea. My father must know."

Leif stared at him for a moment, then grabbed Knut's forearm. He turned and pushed his way back through the lines.

"Devilfish to me! Ulf, you come too."

"What?" the young man said.

Knut turned to him. "Go with Leif."

Ulf stared at him for a moment, then returned his attention to what was racing towards them. "I stay with my crew."

Knut looked at him, then smiled. "I am sorry for suggesting otherwise. Leif, go. Ulf stays."

Leif Sijvidottir nodded and moved towards his boat. As the warriors of the Devilfish fought their way out of the wall to join him.

Knut felt someone push a shield into his back. He turned.

"Frigg, what are you doing?"

She smiled. "Did you really think I would leave my Jarl? What would my mother say?"

Before he could answer, the enemy struck the wall of wood. Their attack was so powerful that it pushed the defenders back nearly two feet. But the wall held, and the slaughter began.

Leif looked back, and seeing the power of the hoard as it struck the wall of shields, realized his crew was in danger of being overrun as the enemy encircled the defenders.

"Run! To the boat!"

Seeing what was happening, his helmsman had already cut the anchoring ropes and pushed the boat off the beach. Twice, he lost sight of the crew as the enemy closed around them. Each time they broke through, there were fewer of them.

He called to the boys in the other boats. "Grab your bows and join me here. Quickly!"

He picked up a bow and launched arrow after arrow into the enemy, doing what he could to help the crew reach the boat. The boys from the other boats joined him as they climbed aboard.

Finally, Leif tumbled over the side. Twenty of the crew followed. Only twelve were able to recover oars. The boys tended to those too badly injured to help.

When it was too deep to follow, the enemy finally ceased their pursuit.

When the helmsman realized they were far enough from the shore that they were no longer within range of the enemy arrows he called, "hold! Get the mast up and raise the sail."

Leif grabbed him by the arm. Blood flowing from several wounds. "We wait," he gasped.

He stood at the gunwale and watched the drama unfolding on the beach. It did not take long. He dropped his head, his chin on his chest as tears flowed down his cheeks.

"Take us home."

Ten miles north of the Valley of Storms

The day was warm, the power of the sun unopposed by any cloud. The rolling fields of rich grass were devoid of trees or bushes, which worked well for the sheep, but not so much for those that tended them.

Eight-year-old Nathanial Treecher worked his way under a small outcropping of moss-covered rock. He smiled as he crawled into the shallow hollow, knowing that his brother was too big to seek the shade of the granite shelf. Sometimes being small had its advantages. He leaned back and closed his eyes. It did not take long before he began to doze.

A frantic shout from his brother interrupted his slumber. He jolted awake, banging his head. Rolling out from under the rock and climbing to his feet, Nathanial rubbed the quickly growing knot on his head. He squinted as his eyes adjusted to the light. Fearing wolves were at the sheep, he reached for the sling hanging from the rope he used to keep his ragged britches from falling. Picking up one of the round stones from the pile he had collected, he placed it in the sling. Although young, his aim was steady and the power of the sling deadly.

"Forget that!" His brother called as he drew near. "Run!"

"From what?" Nathanial asked, looking around.

"Daemons!" Matthew gasped, catching his breath. He grabbed his young brother by the sleeve. "From the valley. We need to warn the village."

"Daemons? What do you mean daemons? There is no such thing."

"They're real, Nate. I've seen them. Daemons, creatures from nightmares. Just like the ones Gran told us about."

Matthew looked behind him quickly and then pushed his younger brother. "Come on, Nate. Run!"

Never had Nathanial seen his brother show any kind of fear. Even when they encountered one of the big silver wolves that occasionally ventured from the forest. Four years his senior, Matthew had always been his protector. Whether a bully in town or a wolf in the meadow, Matthew was there. Nathanial was terrified to see his brother show fear.

"Come on, you need to run. As fast as you can."

Matthew took a breath and, seeing the fear in his brother's eyes, did his best to calm himself.

"Tell you what, I'll race you." He pushed him. "I bet I can beat you. Now, go!"

Nathanial raced toward home. He was no fool. He knew what Matthew was doing. So, he ran faster than he had ever run before.

The older boy lagged a few feet behind, acting as a buffer between him and whatever followed. Down the slope, across the lea, and up the next hill, they ran. As they reached the apex of the hill, Nathanial was relieved to see the village not more than a half-mile below and stopped to catch his breath.

"We're almost there, Matty."

"Nate!" Matthew called out, grunting in pain.

Nathanial turned and saw his brother on his knees, a very long arrow sticking out of his back.

"No!" he screamed as he ran to him. He stared at the arrow, not knowing what to do. Catching movement from the corner of his eye, he saw several figures crossing the open field towards the hill.

"They're coming. Get up, Matty, I'll help you. We need to go. We need to get help."

Grabbing him by his shirt, Nathanial pulled and tried to lift the bigger boy to his feet. Matthew cried out in pain and Nathanial let go.

"What do I do, Matty? Tell me what to do."

Matthew grasped his brother's arm and, as a trickle of blood seeped from the corner of his mouth, he whispered, "Leave me, Nate. You need to run. Warn Ma. Please. Save them."

"No, Matty. I won't leave you."

"You have to. I'll be okay. Da will come back for me."

He smiled, then arching his back, he took a deep breath and looked up at the clear sky. A long sigh escaped his lips, his fingers released their grip, and he fell onto his side, his eyes staring at nothing.

"Matty?" Nathanial said as tears streamed down his face. "Don't go! Please. I need you!"

Nathanial looked down the slope. Six men stood at the base of the hill watching him. Each one armed with a longbow. No, not men, something different, something not right. Matthew's daemons. One notched an arrow. They began to climb the hill. Toward him. He could hear them speaking casually to one another as if nothing had happened.

Scrambling to his feet, Nathanial began to run. Halfway down the hill, he could see people moving about in the village below and he shouted, even though he knew he was still too far away to be heard. An arrow suddenly found purchase in the ground ahead of him. He veered to his left. Another landed in his path, and he changed direction once more. Arrow after arrow fell until he could go no farther. He stopped, stooping over while catching his breath. He stared at the things with a combination of hate and fear as they casually walked toward him.

When only a few yards away, they stopped. One of them pointed at him. They spoke to each other using words that had no meaning for the boy.

"You killed my brother!" Nathanial screamed through his tears. "Why would you do that?"

He reached for his sling and realized he had dropped it when Mathew had grabbed him back at the rock shelf.

The things stared at him as if surprised he had spoken. One of them handed his bow to another and approached, pulling the shafts from the ground, and tossing them aside as he worked his way closer. When only a foot separated them, the not quite-a-man stopped. It was so close Nathanial could smell its breath. It reeked of death.

He wiped the tears from his eyes. Straightening to his full height, he looked up and screamed.

"He was my brother! And you killed him!"

Balling his fist, he suddenly swung with all the power his small body could generate, striking the thing. It was like driving one's fist into a tree.

"You killed him! You killed him!" He screamed over and again as he plummeted the monster with his fists. Out of breath and with his knuckles bleeding, he fell to his knees and sobbed.

"Why?"

The daemon looked down at him and then, seeming almost amused, it raised its hand and struck.

CHAPTER 1

The Package

The chime of the doorbell alerted the young boy that a new adventure was about to present itself. Abandoning the Matchbook truck, he was using to complete the demolition of a skyscraper of wooden blocks; he jumped to his feet and darted to the door. Before he could grab the knob, the voice of his mother made him freeze in his tracks.

"Mikey! What have I told you about opening the door to strangers?"

The young boy turned to his mother and threw his arms out, palms up, shoulders hunched.

"But, mom, it may not be a stranger."

Exasperated by her five-year-old son's ability to rationalize his misbehavior, she stepped between him and the door.

"But you don't know that. For all you know, it could be a bear."

"Ah, mom. Bears don't ring doorbells." He laughed. "They knock."

Chuckling, she pushed him back and opened the door. A FedEx delivery man waited with an amused grin.

"Got twin girls about the same age. Always got an answer," he said.

"They certainly do. Twins. You poor man," she said with an understanding smile.

"Sometimes." He held out a clipboard. "Mrs. Fuller?"

"Yes."

"Need you to sign." He handed her the electronic signature device.

She scribbled her name, and he handed her a large white envelope.

"Thank you. You have a nice day," she said.

"You're welcome. You do the same." He smiled at Mikey. "Good luck."

"To you as well."

Pam closed the door and glanced at the return address. Harold Bennet, Augusta, Maine.

What are you doing in Maine, big brother?

"Who's it from?" Mikey asked, barely able to control his curiosity.

"It's from your Uncle Hal."

"What's in it?"

"I don't know."

"Is it for me?"

She looked at him and raised an eyebrow. "Not everything my brother sends is for you."

"Ah, Mom."

But it usually is, she thought as she sat on the couch. Mikey jumped up beside her, watching eagerly as she tore open the flap.

"Sorry, honey. Not for you."

"Okay."

He jumped down and headed for the discarded pile of blocks. It always amazed her how quickly he accepted that not everything had to be for him. She hoped he never outgrew that.

Hal must be back in the states. But why Maine?

She wasn't sure where he was most of the time or what he did. Something for the government, he told her once, a job he did not like to talk about, but she suspected it to be with one of the three-letter organizations. When Hal left the army, he was hired almost immediately. She was never sure if it was because of his language skills or Special Forces background. Whatever it was, it took him out of the country a lot. She worried about him.

They were close once, before the army. Her mother died shortly after she was born. Their father did the best he could, but he was a soldier, which meant that every three or four years they moved. Long-lasting relationships were hard to establish, let alone to maintain.

When their father deployed, they would stay with Aunt Jackie, his sister, who was a member of the U. S. State Department stationed in Japan. She was a little older than their father, unmarried, and strongly independent. But she loved them, and they returned the feeling.

A helicopter crashed somewhere in Central America and killed their father shortly after her fourth birthday. Aunt Jackie became their permanent guardian.

She did her best, but she too worked a lot. Hal was older by two years and took his job as big brother very seriously. Her dating years were hell. After she married, they drifted apart with him either overseas or on the east coast while she and her family lived in California. She would hear from him on birthdays and holidays, but they did not see one another often.

Hal had worshiped his father and as soon as he finished school, followed in his footsteps and enlisted in the army. His superiors recognized his skills and offered him the opportunity to go to OCS. Two years later, he volunteered for Special Forces.

At first, he was excited, happy. It was as if he had found a home. He loved the men he worked with. But that all changed after his second tour in Afghanistan. He got out after that. He never explained why.

They both spoke fluent Japanese. Hal had a knack for languages and studied Mandarin and Farsi. Skills she was sure were at a premium in today's world.

She removed a manila envelope from the shipping package and undid the string that secured it. Inside was a sheaf of type-written papers. There was a note attached with a paperclip in one corner of the top sheet. It was dated, August 14, 2021. Two weeks ago.

>   *Pam,*
>
>   *I think I'm about to do something really stupid. Big surprise, right? But this may be more than my normal idiocy.*
>
>   *Something happened to me last year. Something I could not share with you. My last assignment had not gone well. I needed time alone to think, to unwind. So, I took leave and found a place far away from Washington. That's when it happened.*
>
>   *What I'm about to tell you is going to sound crazy. Sometimes I even doubt it myself. But I promise you this did happen. I have not been able to stop thinking about it. It's driving me nuts. I wrote it all down, thinking it would*

make more sense if I looked at it at a later time. Made no difference. Reading it now, I realize I must have jotted everything down so that I could show it to you someday. You're the only person I trust with this. You're the only person who might believe me. Take a look at it. And try to keep an open mind.

 Your brother,
 Hal

She picked up the first typewritten page and began to read.

In August of 2020, I rented a cabin in Aroostook County in Northern Maine. That's way up near the Canadian border. What the locals call "The County". I have no idea why, but it is about as far from civilization as you can get on the east coast. Nothing but mountains and trees.

After returning from my last assignment, I needed time to unwind. Things had not gone well. Some people died. My people. Everyone says it wasn't my fault, but they were my people.

It was my boss that suggested I take time off. Smart lady. She knows me well and although she would never admit it, cares what happens to me. She knew I was hurting.

The cabin was listed as being rustic and isolated. Exactly what I was looking for. The only amenities being the doors and windows closed. The bed was an old military cot, OD green nylon stretched over an aluminum frame. No electricity, water was from a well outside, and cooking was done on a cast-iron stove fueled by wood (not included). The owner provided an ax.

The facilities were outside in the back. You know, one of those small houses with a wooden seat sporting a hole.

I brought supplies for a week. The guy I rented the cabin from told me to bring my own TP. Good advice.

The first two days were nearly perfect. I was starting to relax. I even dozed off once or twice during the day while listing to the water splash over the rocks in the creek. It was nice, peaceful, and non-threatening.

I even caught two good-sized trout with a simple bamboo pole I found covered in cobwebs in a corner of the cabin. Fat worms were at a premium under the damp leaves of the forest.

I had visitors too, a large raccoon that did not seem to be concerned about me watching him, and a porcupine that was way too friendly. The damn thing wanted to rub against my leg like a cat. Called the raccoon Ricky and the porcupine Spike. Original, I know. I'm very creative. I found out you can scratch the head of a porcupine without disturbing any quills if you're careful. He seemed to like it.

Everything was peaceful, and I was beginning to unwind until the night it happened.

The evening began quietly enough. I had finished a nice dinner of trout and corn chips and went outside to enjoy the cool of the evening. I settled into the comfortable old wooden Adirondack chair on the porch and sipped a Coors Light that I had kept cool in the stream.

My two companions amused me while they wandered in the open area to the front of the cabin looking for morsels I may have "accidentally" dropped. I know you aren't supposed to, but they were good listeners. Better than a bartender. Kept their thoughts to themselves. They deserved a tip.

Clouds moved in near the end of the day. It looked like it might rain, so I went inside to read. I was trying to finish the latest James Rollins novel I had picked up at the airport in Portland. Pretty good. About Catholic vampires.

I heard a few drops strike the metal roof and went to the door to look outside. Ricky and Spike had gone home as the first drops fell. Smart guys and they knew I didn't allow visitors in the cabin.

At about nine, I decided it was time to turn in. I tucked the automatic I'd brought with me under my pillow. Some habits are hard to break, and after 9/11, Federal Agents were required to be armed at all times.

I worked my legs into my open sleeping bag. The zipper was jammed halfway down, and it wasn't worth fighting with. Besides, it was warm.

I was out within minutes, and of course, the nightmare started.

Rapid-fire weapons sounded outside the old stone building with the intermittent concussion of explosions jarring swaths of plaster from the walls. Dust floated in the hallway as the warm air danced in the beams of sunlight, giving a feeling we were between worlds.

Bruce hugged the wall as he slowly worked his way down the hall, his assault rifle held at the ready, his eyes darting from side to side. The kid was new, a recent release from the Air Force PJs. He insisted on taking point. Said he had worked with the

GLENLOCK

5th Group on his last deployment. I should never have agreed, but he insisted, wanting to prove to the team that the Air Force knew how to train special operators, too.

He gave me a quick grin and a thumbs-up. Nodding, I turned and checked on the others. Three of my guys followed while another two waited outside at the back door. As I returned my attention to the newbie, I saw the wire crossing the floor.

"Freeze! Booby-trap!"

The explosion shook the cabin. I rolled off the cot and got caught in the sleeping bag when I hit the floor. Panic gave way to frustration as I remembered where I was and tried desperately to free myself from the bag. Another massive burst of mind-numbing sound announced that the gentle rain had escalated into a raging storm. The wind outside roared like a jet engine as it beat against the walls of the small log cabin. The rain plummeted, the metal roof sounding like gunfire. I was beginning to wonder if it was a sound idea to be surrounded by hundred-foot pine trees.

Finally, free of the bag, I worked my way to the door and, cracking it open, peeked outside. It was like looking into a waterfall that someone had dropped an electric toaster into. I couldn't see anything but a wall of water and the intermittent bolts of electricity flashing across the sky.

The wind swept the porch clean, blew the Adirondack chair into the mud to the side of the cabin, ripped the tarp off the woodpile and scattered the dry wood I had stacked earlier on the porch.

Visibility was limited to just a few feet beyond the edge of the porch. I couldn't even see the trees. But even over the howl of the wind and the crash of thunder, I heard them creaking and clacking as the constant gusts buffeted them. How they remained standing, I had no idea.

A sudden gust of wind did its best to force the door open. I had to lean my shoulder into it to get it closed. I dropped the wooden locking bar in place and stepped back. The violence of the storm surprised me. It was like being trapped inside a hurricane. There was an old portable radio in the cabin, and I turned it on. Nothing. It was strange. I knew it worked because I had been picking up country-western stations from Canada all day. With a storm, this violent there should have been something, some kind of alert.

Nothing I could do about what was going on outside, so I straightened the cot and recovered the bag. I worked my way inside, hoping to get back to sleep, which seemed unlikely, but I decided I should try.

The cabin conspired to keep me awake, however. The rain continued to beat down on the roof. I buried my head in the pillow and worked at getting my heart rate under control. Some people say rain falling on a tin roof is a soothing sound. I'm not one of them.

It didn't take long for me to realize that sleep was no longer an option. I got dressed and was lacing my boots when the rain abruptly stopped. I don't mean it slowed down; it stopped. It was as if someone had turned it off. The wind too. The sudden silence was complete and unnerving. Like some massive beast had come along and simply eaten all the sound in the world. I experienced a typhoon once in Southeast Asia. As the eye passed over us, I remember the same effect.

I stepped to the door and listened. Nothing. I cracked it open. It was pitch dark. No rain, no lighting. Not even in the distance. It was like the storm had just vanished. But there were still clouds, for I could see no stars nor the moon, which should have been near full.

I picked up an electric lantern and turned it on before cautiously stepping onto the porch. The humidity was stifling, making even taking a breath a challenge. And the smell. Not that of wet things, but burned things. Like the aftermath of an electrical fire.

I stood listening. I think I stopped breathing for a moment. Nothing. No birds, no frogs, no insects, nothing. Not even the gentle thud of water dripping onto fallen leaves. Then a sound reverberated beneath my feet. Like fingernails scraping across a chalkboard. My heart pounding, I stepped back just as a small head peeked out from under the steps.

"Damn, Spike! You almost caused me to have a stroke."

He waddled onto the porch and looked up at me like he was seeking forgiveness. I was about to offer to get him a blanket when the forest exploded in sound. Howls and barks, hoots, and screeches. It was like every animal in the forest decided to speak all at once. Spike looked up at me and began making high-pitched chirping sounds. He seemed scared.

I retreated toward the door, keeping my back to the cabin, watching the forest. Spike didn't move but continued to stare into the dark as if looking for something. I still couldn't see clearly beyond a few feet in front of the porch. But there was movement nearby. Shadows. Some were small, some not so.

I was about to step inside when I glimpsed a faint beam of light appearing from the sky, casting a diffused shaft of illumination upon the trees like a spotlight in heavy fog. As it grew wider, shadows danced within the confines of the light, making the trees seem alive. Dark clouds appeared, and the light moved around them, looking like fast-moving water striking rocks in a strong current. Then the clouds started to move. Slowly at first but quickly increasing their momentum, rippling like the tail of a kite caught in a brisk wind.

As the sky moved, the animals stopped talking. Even Spike seemed to have lost his voice. It became incredibly quiet. The temperature dropped. I could see my breath.

Suddenly, the ribbon of gray light became a sheet that filled the sky. Ripples of electricity rolled and flowed like whitecaps on a turbulent sea. Then a loud crash, the sound like hundreds of peals of thunder merging all at once. I was thrown to the floor. Spike rolled like a car had hit him and fell off the edge of the porch. He got to his feet and disappeared under it.

Then it was gone. The gray light, the lighting, everything, gone.

I pulled myself to my feet and looked at the sky, trying to make sense of what I had just witnessed. Then the storm started back up. The rain, the wind, the lighting. I ran inside and dropped the door's locking bar in place. I leaned against it to catch my breath.

In just those few seconds, I had gotten soaked. I took off my wet things and dumped them in the steel sink. I dug out a set of sweats and, after drying myself, got dressed.

Luckily, I had brought some wood inside before the storm. I started a fire in the fireplace and draped my wet clothes on the hearth to dry. The icy rain had chilled me to the bone.

I knew there was no way I was going back to sleep, so I kindled a fire in the stove and put the kettle on to make coffee. I put a coffee bag, kinda like a tea bag but bigger, in my cup and waited for the water to boil. When ready, I poured the steaming water into the cup and sat down in an old wicker rocker that came with the cabin. It was peaceful, just rocking in front of the fire, listening to the rain on the roof, and sipping my cup of Folger's. I remember thinking this would make a great commercial.

I finished the coffee and decided to fix another. Just as I got to my feet, someone began banging on the door. Not a knock but the door rattling thud associated with someone slamming their open palm upon the surface.

CHAPTER 2

MAGGIE

I dropped my cup, fortunately; it was one of those plastic camping types, so it didn't break. I rushed to the cot and recovered my gun.

"May I come in, please? Hello in the cabin. Anyone there?"

I stood staring at the door and popped the safety off.

"I would appreciate it if you would invite me in. It is quite unpleasant out here."

Invite? Not may I come in or let me in. Invite. I know this sounds stupid, but at that moment I had a ridiculous thought. I'm in the middle of nowhere, in a storm, in Maine, and someone bangs on my door asking to be invited in. I think I watched too many horror movies as a kid or Mr. Rollins's book had gotten to me. Of course, I knew there was no such thing as a vampire, but I must admit the thought crossed my mind.

"Please let me in," the voice said. "I assure you, I mean you no harm."

Like I hadn't heard that line before.

"Who are you?" I called out to the closed door. Closed and locked.

"I am Henry," the voice from the other side said. "Henry Lackland."

"Step back and do not try to open the door until I tell you to."

"I will do as you request."

I lifted the bar and quickly stepped to the side of the door. The side opposite the hinges. I've kicked open enough doors to know what happens if you're on the wrong side of the hinges. I told him to open the door.

The hinges complained as it slowly opened. Just like in all those old movies. I remember thinking that I should have never read Salem's Lot.

I kept my weapon trained on the shadow of the man standing on the threshold. He took two steps into the cabin, holding his hands out to his sides.

Not a vampire.

The stranger was dressed in black from his high-topped boots to the mesh hood on his head. Mesh—steel mesh, as in chainmail. Black chainmail. A chainmail shirt, or jacket, or whatever the hell it was called, covered him from his shoulders to his knees. On his hands were gloves, the backs covered in mail, and the uppers in steel plates. No wonder it was so loud when he knocked.

"Who are you?" I asked, keeping the gun leveled at his chest, almost afraid of what he was going to tell me.

"As I have said, I am called Henry."

"I mean, what are you doing here?"

He looked around and smiled. "To be perfectly honest with you, sir, I have no idea. I suppose I am lost."

The wind shifted and blew rain into the cabin.

"Close the door and step into the light," I told him.

Pushing the door closed by leaning his back against it, he kept his hands where I could see them. He took a step into the flickering light generated by the fireplace. I almost shot him. The son-of-a-bitch had a sword. A big one hanging at his side.

"Drop the blade!" I shouted.

He reached down with one hand and undid the buckle to the thick leather belt. It hit the floor with a clunk.

"I assume that the thing you are pointing at me is some kind of weapon," he said calmly.

"It is," I said, surprised he had to ask. "Why are you dressed like that? What are you doing wandering around the woods dressed as a medieval knight? There a renaissance fair nearby?"

"I know not what you mean by medieval, but a knight I am," he said calmly. "My father dubbed me himself in my seventeenth year."

"Your father?"

"Yes."

"And who is your father?" I asked.

"John."

"John," I said. All I could think of was he better not tell me what I thought he was going to tell me.

"Yes, King John. I am Henry, his firstborn."

He did. "You mean John, brother of Richard, as in the Lion Heart?"

"That is correct. Although my father did not approve of that name. My uncle awarded himself the title. As you may have heard, there was a brief disagreement about who should assume the crown upon my grandfather's passing. I believe my uncle was posturing to gain the support of the nobles. He was the younger brother and therefore not next in line to the throne."

I had not heard that. And I thought John was the younger brother.

"May I step closer to the fire? I am quite chilled," he asked politely.

I remember thinking about what he said. Did not approve, not, does not approve. I wondered what happened to the uncle.

Henry was shivering and appeared to be no threat. Nuts maybe, probably, but he seemed a peaceful nut. I lowered the barrel of my gun but held on to it. "Go ahead," I told him, pointing to the fire.

I didn't know who this guy was, but there was little doubt that his elevator was stuck between floors. I mean, come on, King John. He didn't even get the history right.

As he stepped towards the fire, I kicked his sword away. I had no idea where this guy could have come from. There were no mental hospitals nearby that I was aware of, but you never know how far a nut can run. But he didn't act like he was crazy. I know people. I can read them and am rarely wrong. Kept me alive so far. I knew this guy was no threat, and that he believed what he was saying.

"You might want to take off those wet things," I told him. "I'll get you something to wear."

He turned and smiled at me. "You are most kind, sir. Thank you. Do you mind if I ask your name?"

"It's Hal. Hal Bennett."

"I thank you for your hospitality, Hal Bennett."

A long rumble of thunder made the cabin shake. He chuckled. "I am sure you did not expect company on a night such as this."

I smiled. "Sure didn't."

He pulled the hood off and I watched, fascinated, as he grabbed the mail by the bottom and pulled it over his head, bending until he was almost touching his toes. The thing slid off him onto the floor and hit the wood with a loud thud. Under it, he wore a thickly padded vest tied in the front with leather shoestrings. Under that was a black shirt that came down to his mid-thigh. The neck was open almost a foot and held together with another leather shoestring. Wide leather stitches attached big billowy sleeves through little metal rings. Not the sort of attire found at any of the major clothing outlets I was aware of.

When he dropped the shirt, I took in a deep breath. This dude had scars. Long cuts and pucker marks, almost like bullet wounds, but bigger and oddly shaped. He had been in some nasty fights.

"What were you doing before you became lost?" I asked, regaining my composure.

"Looking for my cat."

"Your cat?"

"Yes, Maggie. Have you by chance seen her? She is a long tooth."

"I'm afraid not. Sorry." Never heard of a long tooth. Must be one of those designer cats.

"She is normally good at taking care of herself, but I am concerned about her being caught in this storm."

"Nasty, isn't it?" I observed, not sure what else to say.

"I have never seen the like. My squire calls it a daemon storm."

"Your squire?"

"John. Good lad. Sir Jamie's younger brother. Been training him since his twelfth summer."

"Training him?"

"For knighthood."

"Naturally." This guy's delusion was detailed. "Have you had your cat long?" I asked, trying to show interest.

"Since she was a kitten. Sometimes I think she believes she adopted me and that I am her responsibility. You know how cats are."

Nope. Dog guy. Always thought cats were too uppity. "Sure," I said, trying to sound like I meant it.

Henry sat on the hearth and pulled off his boots, and sure enough, they had little spurs. Gold ones, or at least gold colored. Then he pulled off his leather pants. He definitely didn't have any concealed weapons. My inclination was to turn away. I bet that wet leather chafed, but I reminded myself that delusional or not, with scars like the ones displayed on his back, this guy had not been living a quiet life.

I looked at him in the flickering light. He appeared to be of a similar age to me, maybe mid to late twenties. His dark beard was well-trimmed close to his handsome face while he wore his hair long, coming to his shoulders and cut square. It reminded me of Prince Valiant from the comics.

Without turning, I reached into my bag with my free hand and threw him a pair of black nylon sweats. My last set of dry clothes. He caught them and sat for a moment, feeling the material.

"This cloth is unusual. It is not wool nor linen."

"Nope." I wished he would hurry.

He pulled the pants on. "These are pleasant against the skin."

I bet they were. He slipped the jacket on and stared at the zipper. I was going to explain how it worked when he asked me a question that caught me off guard.

"Are you a hermit, Hal Bennett?"

"A hermit? No, why do you ask?"

He waved his hand over the expanse of the cabin. "This does not strike me as a place that receives many visitors."

I smiled. "True. It is isolated. I came up here to be alone."

"From where?"

"D. C."

"Deecee? Is that a nearby village?"

"You have never heard of Washington D.C.?"

"I am afraid I have not. In what kingdom does it reside?"

"Kingdom? The United States." I reassessed my earlier opinion. This guy's elevator wasn't caught between floors. It had grown wings and flown away.

"I am not familiar with that kingdom." He thought for a moment. "Are you in hiding?"

"No. Just needed to get away for a while."

"I envy you. There have been many times I wished I could get away from my duties."

"Duties?" I asked.

"As my father's enforcer. It can prove distasteful work. He can be a cruel man. Especially since the death of my mother."

He stood and turned his back to the fire. "What type of profession do you practice if I may be so bold as to ask?"

I thought for a moment about how to explain what I did.

"I'm a sort of policeman."

"I am not familiar with the term."

"I stop people that wish to harm those of my ... ugh ... kingdom."

"Like a shire-reef."

"I suppose." I had no idea what a shire-reef was, but it kinda sounded like a sheriff, so I agreed.

"A difficult and noble profession you practice, Hal Bennett," he said with a sincerity that was a little unsettling.

"There are times."

Reaching down, he recovered his clothes and spread them out near the fire. They smoked as the heat reached them.

Another blast of thunder rocked the cabin, and we both looked at the window.

"I do hope Maggie has found shelter," he said.

"I'm sure she has." Actually, I was sure the poor thing was gone. No way a domestic cat could survive this storm.

He picked up his mail shirt. "Have you something I might use to dry this? And maybe some oil?"

I pulled a towel from my bag and threw it to him.

"Sorry, no oil."

"Thank you. This will do." He sat cross-legged on the floor and started to dry the metal shirt.

"I will have John sand and oil it later." He looked up and smiled. "If I can find him, of course."

"Of course."

I sat in the rocker and watched as he worked. Neither of us spoke. I realized that I still had the gun in my hand. I pulled my bag a little closer, flicked the safety, and laid it on top, ensuring I could reach it quickly if it became necessary.

"I hope that means you no longer consider me a threat," he said, nodding at the gun.

"Let's just say I don't want to shoot you right now," I said, forcing a smile.

"I thank you. I have never seen a weapon such as that. Is it deadly?"

I thought about my last assignment. "Very."

"Interesting."

He looked around the cabin while he rubbed the material of the sweats between his thumb and finger.

"I do not know what is happening, Hal Bennet. Everything seems so similar, but yet different. These clothes, your weapon. It is most confusing."

"I'm going to be honest with you, Henry. I'm more than a little confused myself. This has been one crazy night."

I looked out the window. "It looks like the storm is slowing down. If you want, I will help you look for your cat."

"That would be most kind of you, Hal Bennet."

"The name is Hal. Just Hal."

He smiled. "Then Hal it is. And I thank you."

"For what?"

"Your hospitality. Your offer of help. You appear to be a noble man."

There was a time, maybe. Now, I wasn't so sure.

"I have been called many things in my lifetime. But I think you are the first person ever to refer to me as being noble."

"More's the pity, for there is little doubt that you are such a man," he said.

Embarrassed, I walked to the window and looked out. Once again, someone had turned the storm off. Although I was fairly sure Henry was not what he claimed to be, an honest-to-God knight, I decided to help him with his quest. Finding his cat. What could it hurt? I reached into my duffle and pulled out a pair of loafers and slipped them on.

"Those look to be comfortable footwear," he said. "I have never seen their like. From what type of beast are they made?"

I looked down at what was in effect lace-less sneakers, rubber soles, and all. Something like a deck shoe.

"I have no idea. Picked them up at Walmart last week."

"Wall Mart?"

Obviously, bulk shopping was not a thing where he was from.

"A marketplace."

"I see."

I walked to the door. "Shall we take a look?"

Stepping onto the porch, I waited until Henry put his boots on and joined me. He looked silly with those high boots over the dark sweats with the double red stripe down the outside of the leg. I did my best not to smile. The jacket was still unzipped.

"Want some help with the jacket?" I asked, assuming being a medieval knight would not be familiar with a zipper.

He gave me a questioning look, and I ran mine up and down a few times to show him. I undid the fastener and showed how that worked as well. He tried and then, with a big grin, ran it up and down.

"Remarkable," he said.

I returned the smile, thinking of the horse I saw on TV once. It enjoyed playing with a zipper. I was beginning to like Henry. Nut or not.

The night was still. No noise except for the sound of water dripping off the trees. The air was heavy with moisture and the smell of burned insulation. One thing I was thankful for was that all the bugs seemed to have taken the night off.

"It is very quiet," Henry said, joining me as I stepped off the porch into the mud, which came up to my ankles. I suddenly envied Henry those boots. He raised his hands to the sides of his mouth and called out.

"Maggie!"

I wasn't sure he would have heard the cat if it answered, meowed, mewed, whatever cats said when called to let you know they heard you. Now a dog you could hear. Nothing like a good bark to let you know where it was.

We walked side-by-side towards the trees. He called several more times with the same result.

"Henry?" I asked.

"Yes, Sir Hal."

"Just Hal."

He smiled. "Someone else's mistake."

"Why don't you have a British accent?"

He stopped and looked at me. "British?"

"You know, the language they speak in Britain. Where I assume you're from."

"I am from the Kingdom of Cent, Hal. Where my father is king. I have told you thus. I speak Glenlockian, as do all the civilized peoples of Tera. As do you."

"As, do I? I'm speaking English. American English. I've never heard of Glenlockian."

He stared at me for a moment and then looked around. "Where am I?"

"Maine."

"Maine?"

"The state of Maine. In the USA. Just south of the Canadian border. These names mean nothing to you?"

"I have heard stories. I never believed them," he said, staring at me.

"Stories?" I asked.

"About other worlds. Worlds like mine, but different. As a boy, my tutor told me such tales. Stories about the possibility that many versions of Tera might exist. Where things are the same, yet different. He was a learned man but want to flight of fantasy. Or so I believed. Now I am beginning to wonder."

I was almost afraid to ask, but my curiosity was piqued. "What was the name of your tutor?"

"Alfred Winghead."

Thank God. I thought he was going to tell me it was Merlin.

"He believed that these other worlds would have people such as us, but they would live different lives. Many of his stories assumed this is where daemons existed." He chuckled. "You do not seem to be a daemon, Sir Hal."

"Thanks," I said. Though some might not agree, I kept that to myself. And I decided to ignore the title.

"Some scientists believe that there are infinite versions of our world." I shook my head. "Or other worlds." This was getting ridiculous.

"If that is so," he said. "The question that needs to be answered is, am I on your world, or are you on mine?"

I pointed to the colorful sweats he was wearing; I shrugged my shoulders. "Pretty sure we are on mine."

Looking down, he chuckled. "A valid point." He turned towards the trees and called out again. "Maggie!"

Although the dawn was not far away, the shadows of the forest blanketed the world in near-total darkness. Pulling my cell phone from my pocket, I activated the flashlight app. Henry looked at the device but did not comment. He touched the zipper of his jacket. He smiled and shook his head.

"Your world."

"Why don't you tell me what you were doing just before you knocked on my door. Maybe it will help us get a better idea of where to look," I said.

"Very well.

" My father had tasked me to determine the reason a group of farmers failed to appear with their tithe on tax collection day," he began. "Were they in trouble, or had they willingly failed to show? I had been forced to do things like this before. It was distasteful work. The taxes are not excessive, and most of the monies are used to benefit the kingdom. We do not grow rich by the toil of others.

"The penalty for refusing to pay, however, is severe. I have had to enforce the law before. Even though I did not wish the farmers ill-luck, I was hoping there was good reason for their absence."

He stopped at the edge of the trees and called out, "Maggie!"

I shined the light ahead of us, thinking of some of the things I'd done. "Doing what needs to be done can be tough, but often, it's making the hard calls that keep everything from falling into chaos. At least that's what I tell myself."

"Does it help?"

"Sometimes," I said, the words coming out softer than I had intended. I decided to change the subject. "Maggie!" I called out, knowing that the odds were against hearing a reply.

He smiled and as we stepped deeper into the darkness; he continued with his story.

"My father insisted I take but a small conroi. Just enough men to discourage brigands."

"Conroi?" I asked, never having heard the word before.

"A small force of knights and fighting men," he explained. "I did not wish to bring soldiers, so I selected a group of friends to accompany me. We had been comrades for some time and had fought side-by-side. Sir Jamie, Sir Randel, James Longbow, William Quick Arrow, Bruce son-of-Bruce, our squires John, William and Randolph, and, of course, a half dozen servants."

"Of course."

Fought who I wondered? I stamped my feet to get some of the mud off my soaked shoes and give myself time to gather my thoughts. The leaves on the floor of the forest had offered some respite from the quagmire, but not enough.

"At the first village," he continued. "We were told of strange things being seen near the Valley of Storms. When asked what they meant, one of the charcoal burners told of seeing daemons.

"If strangers, not daemons, of course, were seen in the kingdom, it was my responsibility to ensure they were not a threat. I decided we needed to investigate. We were near to the coast, and I was concerned about raiders.

"Two days out, the weather took a turn. I had camp prepared to wait out the coming storm near the mouth of the valley and set out with two of my archers and my squire to seek our evening meal. Of course, Maggie accompanied us as she was wont to do. She loved the hunt. It was not long before William Quick Arrow had taken down a good-sized doe. I told the others to take it back to camp. Maggie preferred to hunt alone and had left us a short while past. She had not yet returned, and I wished to wait for her. My men did not like leaving me without a guard, but I insisted. They laughed when I told them Maggie would provide me with whatever security I might need. Reluctantly they returned to camp, John saying he would keep an eye out for Maggie, and I ventured deeper into the valley to look for her.

"It was not long before I reached the leading edge of the forest at the far end of the vale. My horse would go no farther, so I turned back into the valley.

"It was then it began to rain. Just a shower at first, but shortly it became a torrent. The sky changed color, and the air was full of strange odors. I called for Maggie, but with the roar of the wind, I was sure she would not hear me. Knowing she had enough sense to seek shelter if the storm worsened, I decided it was time to return to camp.

"I looked up and what seemed like daemons danced within the clouds. My horse required little urging to leave the valley. I was having difficulty keeping her head when we were struck with an explosive clash of thunder so intense it nearly drove me from my saddle. Rearing in terror, my horse jolted into a gallop. I could not regain control and before I knew it, I was tossed onto the valley floor.

"Dazed, my vision blurred, I looked up and saw Maggie fighting the elements as she tried to reach me. I reached out for her as another blast of thunder drove me to the ground. That is the last I remember before waking and seeing your hut."

There was a lot in Henry's story worth exploring, most notably the whole "demons or daemons" thing, but before I could ask for clarification, the sky changed. The clouds were beginning their dance again.

"We best hurry, Henry. I think the storm is about to revisit us."

He looked up. "I believe you may be right." He pointed. "And by the looks of it, the daemons are back as well."

The strange beam of light had returned.

He cupped his hands around his mouth and called out, "Maggie!"

The wind picked up, and the air became thick, making it difficult to breathe, like being trapped in a sauna. No rain yet, but it was coming. I could smell it. I experienced a tornado once outside of Chicago. This felt the same.

We continued our trek into the trees, and I called out for the cat. I doubted we would find the poor thing, but I had grown fond of Henry in the short time I had known him and wanted to help.

The rain started. Slowly at first, but then with a vengeance. The wind again howled, and it was hard to stand upright. We leaned into the gale and continued as best we could. The heavy rain, lack of natural light, and the wind reduced visibility to almost nothing. Realizing the futility of continuing, I grabbed Henry by the sleeve and yelled.

"We need to go; there's no way we're going to find her in this! I'm sorry, Henry. We can try again later."

He nodded. Without saying a word, he turned and started back to the cabin. I didn't think it was possible, but the storm got worse. It was the massive streaks of lightning and the deafening crashes of thunder that numbed the senses. Concentrating on reaching the cabin, I missed a stray root and lost my footing. I dropped the phone as I fell, losing it in the mud and leaves. Searching the ground clutter, my hand touched it just as an intense flash of lightning illuminated the forest. I froze.

Standing in front of me, only a few feet away, was something that could not exist. Should not exist. Not in Maine or anywhere else on Earth. Not in today's world.

I didn't move as the creature stared at me. It was terrifying and magnificent. A thing of majestic beauty with a tawny brown coat similar to that of a cougar highlighted with a series of dark stripes. A stubby tail like a bobcat's flicked back and forth nervously.

It must have weighed three or four hundred pounds and stood over four feet at the shoulder, but it was the teeth that were the focus of my attention. Two long, thick, slightly curved canines extended a good foot and a half from its upper jaw.

Henry rushed forward and reaching the animal wrapped his arms around her. I climbed to my feet and stared at the two of them like a man in a trance.

"She is well, Hal. I have found her. My Maggie."

The cat looked at me and I was surprised at the intelligence I saw in her eyes. It took me a few extra heartbeats to find my voice.

"She is beautiful, Henry," I yelled.

"Hal is a friend, Maggie," he said, and the cat nudged me and purred. A rumble of sound sending shivers down my spine.

The rain lessened for a moment and the temperature dropped several degrees. I looked up at the sky. A strange greenish light materialized within the clouds, pulsing like something alive. I saw that the waving gray ribbon was back flowing between the borders of the light. I pointed to the strange cloud.

"Henry, we need to go! Bring Maggie."

I looked to ensure he had heard me. Henry had stepped back a few yards and was yelling something and pointing at the sky, but I couldn't make out the words. An emerald mist suddenly enveloped him and Maggie, clinging to them. I thought at the time that should not have been possible in this wind. Little darts of electricity danced around the mist encircling the two.

Henry fell to his knees, and the cat raised her head to the sky. Her mouth opened as if calling, the deadly curved fangs seeming to draw a small burst of lightning to them. A crash of thunder knocked me to the ground. When I regained my feet, I was alone.

I searched the area but could not find them.

Accepting that they were gone, I fought my way back to the cabin. The storm was in full force and the only thing I could think of was returning to the relative safety of the small building.

My phone wasn't working. It's time in the mud and wet had been too much for it. I struggled through the mire that had thickened near the structure where the ground had been cleared, finally making the steps to the porch.

Spike stood near the edge of the steps sheltered on the porch, watching as I worked my way back. Almost like he was waiting for me. Foolish, I know, but it made me feel good to think so.

I looked back toward the forest and stood for a moment. I don't know, maybe I was hoping to see them once more. I finally turned to the door and, opening it, looked down at the small animal at my feet. Spike was looking up at me.

"Okay, buddy. How would you like to come inside? I could use the company." He waddled in and lay down near the fire.

Removing my wet clothes, I rang them out in the sink, then placed them by the fire. I picked up those I had placed on the hearth earlier; they were dry.

Putting the kettle on, I threw a few more pieces of wood into the fireplace, trying not to disturb Spike, who looked up at me. I have no idea how smart porcupines are, but I thought I could see trust in the little guy's eyes.

I sat in the rocker and did my best to allow my muscles to relax. I looked at the cot and the disheveled sleeping bag. It would be easy to dismiss the events of the evening as a bad dream, or maybe a hallucination. A byproduct of what I had been through in the last few months.

A log fell in the fireplace, resulting in a burst of sparks and flame, drawing my attention to what lay on the hearth. Next to my little friend was a small pile of metal. I got up and walked over. Reaching down, I picked up the chainmail shirt. I'd been right; it was heavy. I carried it to the table and put it down before noticing the sword belt near my cot.

Picking it up, I partially withdrew the blade from the scabbard. There was the symbol of a lion and words etched into the metal. I took it closer to the fire to better see what was there.

HONOR AND JUSTICE

A note in Hal's handwriting was attached to the last page.

This did happen, Pam. I know Henry was real, as was Maggie. His clothes, chainmail, and sword prove it. I have not been able to stop thinking about it. Why did this happen? Where did they come from? And why was it that it was my cabin Henry showed up at?

Two weeks ago, I called the guy that owns the cabin to see if I could rent it again. He said he would love to, but no one has been able to get to it for almost a year now. A week after I left, a terrible storm began. It was unusual in that it was confined to the mountain. It has not stopped. Not moved. The owner told me that a group of scientists had come to study it, but the storm was so bad they could not get up the mountain. They tried to set up their equipment at the base, but the winds nearly destroyed it. They left and have not returned.

I think it is the same storm, Pam. I think it is there for a reason. As crazy as it sounds, I think it is waiting for me. I need to go back. I can't help feeling I have to. I believe there is something in the storm waiting for me.

By the time you get this, I hope to have reached the cabin. I don't know what is up there, what is going to happen. But I feel that if I don't go back, I'll go mad.

I love you, Sis. Try to understand. Tell little Mikey and Big Mike I said hello. If all goes well, I will see you at Christmas. If I don't call by then, well, maybe the storm took me to see Henry and Maggie.

Love,

Your brother, Hal.

Pam placed the last page atop the others on the table. She stared at it.

"Oh, Hal, what have you done?"

Tears filled her eyes. She stifled a sob when she felt a small hand take hers.

"Are you all right, Mommy? Don't cry."

She looked down at her son and wiped the back of her hand across her eyes.

"I'm fine, sweetheart."

He climbed up on the couch beside her. "What's wrong?"

She pulled him to her and kissed the top of his head.

"It's nothing. Your Uncle Hal is going away again, and it makes me a little sad, that's all."

"Uncle Hal will come back. He always does."

She did her best to smile. To reassure the boy that all was well.

"Yes, he does."

But this time, she wasn't sure.

CHAPTER 3

The Mountain

Hal Bennet sat staring at the rain as it plummeted the hood of the Jeep, bouncing like wet ping-pong balls. He had asked the lady at the airport car rental counter for something with four-wheel drive, hoping to be able to navigate the road up to the cabin. She said the only thing she had was a 2010 Jeep Liberty she kept for the local rangers. It wasn't new, but she was sure it would do the job. Seems she was wrong.

He entered the storm as he approached the base of the mountain. The drive up from Portland had been sunny and then... wham. He had seen nothing like it. It was as if the storm was alive.

The sign he used to find the mountain road last year was gone, but he didn't need it. There was no doubt he had reached his destination. Although the road itself was gone, nothing but mounds of mud and debris. The break in the trees on either side told him he was in the right place.

He turned off the ignition, realizing there was no way he was going to drive up the mountain.

"You know you are insane, Hal," he said out loud just to make sure he wasn't trapped in a nightmare.

Pulling his Detroit Tigers baseball cap down tight on his head, he cinched the hood of his Gortex jacket, leaving only his face exposed. Picking up a pair of green aviator gloves from the side console, he slipped them on. Then he tried the door. It didn't budge. Leaning his shoulder against it, he pushed, the wind doing its best to keep him inside as if warning him to go back home. The door finally opened wide enough for him to squeeze through, and he jumped out of the way as it slammed shut, almost removing his fingers.

"Shit. I'm damned well not going to get that open again."

He worked his way around the hood of the Jeep to the other side, where thankfully it worked as a windbreak. Afraid the tailgate would be blown from the vehicle, he decided to try the back door. It opened with no resistance, and he reached inside. He had put the seat down to accommodate his supplies, so he was able to reach the large military-style backpack.

Ensuring the long waterproof case attached across the top was secure, he pulled the heavy bag towards the door and propped it up as he worked his arms through the straps. Taking the weight of the rucksack on his shoulders, he adjusted the straps and fastened the waistbelt.

Slamming the door, he pressed the key fob and locked the Jeep. He smiled. "Who the hell is going to take it?"

Wiping the rain from his eyes, he looked up at the mountain and shook his head. "Yep, no doubt about it. You are fricking crazy, Hal Bennet. Certifiably insane."

He stepped around the car and was almost knocked off his feet as the full force of the wind hit him. Going around the remnants of the road, he slogged his way through the clinging mud until he reached a rock ledge at the base of the mountain. Keeping his head down, he took a deep breath and began to climb, zigzagging almost parallel with the slope as he worked his way slowly upward, using bushes and small trees as handholds to keep his balance. Thankfully, the thicker trees acted as a buffer against some of the wind and the stinging rain. But not much.

I should have brought goggles.

He froze when he heard a crack quickly followed by a thump as a large limb struck the soggy ground less than twenty yards ahead. He stared at the wood partially embedded in the soft soil.

"Yep, fricking mad as the Hatter."

He resumed his climb, splitting his attention between his precarious footing and the clacking branches of the trees above him. Several times he slipped, the mud threatening to take him back down the side of the mountain.

After close to an hour of climbing, he fell to his hands and knees in exhaustion, the large rucksack causing him to almost lose his balance and tumble back down the treacherous slope.

Leaning against the thick trunk of a monstrous pine, he closed his eyes as he tried to regain his breath and quiet his heart rate. His arms felt as heavy as lead and his thighs burned like hot coals were embedded in the tissue.

Worse than Ranger School and the Q course combined.

Pulling up the sleeve of his jacket, he looked at his waterproof Rolex watch, a gift from his aunt on his eighteenth birthday. He remembered remarking at the time that it was not self-winding. His aunt laughed and told him time was not to be taken for granted.

It was almost ten in the morning and yet the sky was dark and cast deep shadows that made him feel like he was traipsing through one of the haunted forests in a Grimm's Fairytale.

Reaching into a waterproof pocket of the jacket, he pulled out a zip-lock bag of gorp, a trail mix of peanuts, cereal, and chocolate. He took a fistful and popped it into his mouth, quickly closing the bag to keep the contents dry. He chuckled to himself as he remembered the gorp his sister used to send him while he was stationed in Afghanistan. The guys on his team teased him that it was officer's gorp because she used cashews and Reese's pieces instead of peanuts and chunks of Hershey's chocolate. They were good people. He missed them.

Working his way to his feet, he resumed his climb. For the next hour, his world became a constant ritual of climb, rest, then climb some more accompanied by increasing amounts of pain and exhaustion, but he kept going. He had to. Something was waiting for him. Driving him on. He didn't know what, but knew he had to reach the cabin.

Eventually, it became too much, and he collapsed, falling on his face in the mud, the incessant rain soaking him through the waterproof jacket and pants.

Cold, shivering, his muscles unable to function while screaming in pain, he had reached his limit. There was nothing left. He could not go on. He closed his eyes, and everything went black.

He was dreaming; he knew he was, remembering the fear he felt on his first scout swimmer night mission. Ten kilometers of open ocean with nothing to keep you on track but a compass. He could feel the cold water seeping in through the neck of his wetsuit as he swam. Kicking while lying on his back and dragging his ruck behind him, he kept looking around for his teammates. Worrying about losing sight of the others and swimming out to sea. His imagination went wild as he felt something strike his leg.

He threw up his arms and screamed, pushing away the cold gray snout of the tiger shark. Burning pain as it drove its teeth into his hand brought him awake with a start.

Wiping the water from his eyes, he focused on the shadow standing in front of him. Tiny black eyes staring from a dark face surrounded by a halo of needles.

"Spike?"

Looking at his injured hand, he shook his head. Sticking out of his palm like a small flagpole, was a porcupine quill. Knowing it was barbed, he took a good grip and pulled, crying out as it broke free of the skin.

"Damn, Spike, those things hurt."

He worked his way onto his knees and looked around, blinking to clear his vision. There, like some fairytale cottage come to life, stood the cabin.

With the last of his strength, he pushed himself to his feet and stumbled towards the sanctuary from the storm. When he reached the stairs, it became too much to keep on his feet and he fell to his hands and knees. Crawling up onto the porch, he discarded his pack and, placing his hands on the wall, inched himself to his feet, then tried the door. It flew open, and he fell to the wooden floor. The last thing he remembered was Spike running past him.

He did not know how long he was out. Painfully gaining a sitting position while every muscle in his body screamed, he looked around the cabin. Spike lay asleep on the hearth of the cold fireplace; the rest of the cabin was draped in shadow. Stray beams of light lay upon the floor like the bars of a jail cell.

Daylight.

He checked his watch.

Nine. AM? Must have been out all night.

He checked the porch and saw that his rucksack remained where he had dropped it. The incessant rain continued, but the wind had slowed down to something almost normal and there were breaks in the clouds, allowing some light through.

Getting carefully to his feet, he grabbed the strap of the ruck and dragged it into the cabin. He closed the door and looked around. Everything was as he had left it. The rocker, the pile of firewood stacked in the corner, even the box of coffee bags he left for the next occupant.

With an effort, he removed his wet rain gear and rummaged in the ruck for dry clothes. He started fires in both the fireplace and the wood stove, trying to drive away the chill that threatened to sap his remaining strength. Pouring water into the dented copper kettle, he put it on the stove to boil.

Lowering himself into the rocker, he waited for the cabin to warm, and the kettle to whistle.

Spike was curled up on the hearth, enjoying the dry warmth. Hal shook his head, wondering how the little animal had remembered him after a year. Maybe porcupines are related to dogs. That made him think of Maggie.

A long tooth. And I thought it was a house cat.

When the kettle whistled, he gingerly worked his way to the stove and fixed the coffee. Before returning to the chair, he rummaged around one of the many pouches of the backpack and withdrew a bottle of acetaminophen. Thinking about downing the entire bottle, he decided to begin with a mere two.

Watching the fire and sipping the coffee, he considered what he was doing. It made no sense. By nature, he was a cautious man. To risk his life climbing the mountain in this weather was not the action of a rational man. Was he losing it? Was it PTSD? He knew of guys that had genuine issues dealing with reality after coming back. After two tours with the army and all the shit he had experienced since joining the Company it was possible, he supposed. But he never seemed to have any issues before. Tired, yes, nightmares, yes, but hallucinations, no. So, what was driving him to return here? And why now?

The warmth of the cabin, the gentle rocking of the chair, and his exhaustion soon lulled him to sleep. No dreams. No nightmares. Just blissful oblivion.

When he woke, Spike was still asleep. The little guy seemed to do a lot of that.

Hal stoked the fire in the fireplace and rekindled the stove. Shaking his canteen, he cursed. Empty. Looking out the window, he could see the rain was still coming down. Pulling on his jacket, he picked up the kettle and canteen, intending to take them to the pump and fill them.

As he opened to door Spike dashed out.

"Where you going, buddy?"

The little porcupine ran down the steps, squatted for a moment, then rushed back through the open door.

"Okay. Well, I appreciate that. Never expected you to be housebroken."

He filled the kettle and his canteen and returned to the warmth of the cabin. Putting the kettle on the stove, he removed the jacket and his shirt, rolling his shoulders to loosen up the sore muscles. He dropped to do a few pushups and felt a stab of pain in his hand. Remembering the quill, he got up and looked at it. It was red and a little inflamed. Recovering a tube of ointment from his bag, he worked it into the wound.

Hal continued with stretching exercises while waiting for the water to boil. Once the old metal kettle began to shake, he pulled it from the stove and poured it over the coffee bag. Reaching into the cargo pocket of his military-style trousers, he withdrew a packet of cinnamon oatmeal and dumped it into the plastic bowl he had taken from the cabinet.

Stirring a little hot water into the mix, he took the oatmeal and coffee and walked to the rocker. Spike suddenly appeared at his feet, looking longingly at the bowl. Hal took a couple of spoonfuls and then lay the bowl on the floor. Spike quickly ate what was left.

"Hungry?"

The wind suddenly picked up and the rain hitting the tin roof sounded like hail. The trees began clacking against one another, sounds he remembered from the last time he visited the cabin.

Finishing his coffee, he walked to the window. He smiled. "None of your demons, Henry. Not yet, anyway."

Looking at the ruck, he checked the contents were dry and serviceable. He had taken a lot of time deciding what to carry. Clothes, food, a medkit (not everything in it was standard or easy to acquire. Or legal), a small dob kit with a solar-powered electric razor, a toothbrush, and the other odds and ends of field grooming. These were easy to plan for.

The special items took some time to get. Not everything was available on the open market. Planning for the unexpected was nothing new to him. But the unexpected he might face was something different.

Deciding he needed another cup of coffee, he reached for the kettle when a brilliant flash of light followed immediately by the explosive reverberation of thunder drove him to the floor. Ear's ringing, and blinking his eyes, he looked around, afraid the cabin had been struck.

Nothing, thank God. No damage and, more importantly, no fire. Climbing to his feet, he looked out the window. It was dark. No longer was any light getting through the clouds.

The ringing in his ears finally subsided. There was no noise. He was beginning to think the crash of thunder had rendered him temporarily deft until he heard a squeak from under the table. Spike looked at him, terrified. It wasn't that he was deft. There was no sound. No rain on the roof, no thunder, nothing.

He opened the door. The smell of burned electrical wiring greeted him as he stepped onto the porch.

Spike took up a position near his foot. He sat there and stared up at Hal.

"Never could get over how funny that looks."

Streaks of light worked their way through the dark clouds, striking the trees and casting long shadows across the open ground in front of the cabin.

He wrinkled his brow. Something was not right. The clouds didn't move, and the beams of light looked like lines on a chalkboard. The whole thing resembling a painting or a photograph.

Stepping back into the cabin, he recovered a holstered Sig Sauer 365XL, 9 mm semi-automatic pistol with a twelve-round magazine. He drew the slide back a little to ensure a round was chambered, giving him thirteen. Checking it was on safe, he fastened the holster to his belt and slipped the pistol in.

Donning his Gortex jacket, he zipped it halfway up, then tugged his baseball cap snugly on his head.

Making sure the pack was once again watertight, he picked it up and lay it on the table, then slipped his arms through the straps. He tightened them down, pulled his gloves from a pocket, and pulled them on before snapping the waist belt closed.

Something bumped his leg, and he looked down.

"Sorry, buddy. I think I'm going to have to leave you again. Not sure if I will be coming back. I'll leave the door open. Cabin's yours for now. Take care, little buddy."

The wind picked up as he walked out onto the porch. The rain started again and quickly poured down; the wind driving it so hard the drops were painful when striking the bare skin of his face.

Crashes of thunder and flashes of lightning heralded the full fury of the storm. Hal looked back at the little porcupine staring at him from the doorway.

Going to miss that little guy.

He took a deep breath and stepped down into the mud, and slogged his way toward the trees. To the spot, he had last seen Henry and his cat.

"What the hell am I doing?"

A crash of thunder made him look up, and it did not surprise him to see the flowing odd-colored clouds begin to push together. Electrical charges worked in all directions, up, down, horizontal, zigzagging across the sky, looking like something from Doctor Frankenstein's laboratory.

The colored clouds began to sink and twirl. As they did, they drew together, thickening almost into a solid force, all of it working its way toward Hal.

He could not move, not from fear, although he was terrified, but as if something had wrapped around him, preventing him from doing so. And then the pain began. The pressure in his eardrums increased until he became afraid they might burst. The light becoming so bright his eyes cried out for the shelter his eyelids could not provide. The muscles in his back contorted and seized in excruciating pain. When he felt he could no longer take it, he blissfully lost consciousness.

CHAPTER 4

OUTSIDE THE VALLEY OF STORMS

"Don't make no sense to me."

"What makes no sense, Franklin?"

Stepping from the shadows, a man in his mid-twenties with shoulder-length blond hair and a corresponding well-trimmed beard finished cinching his baggy brown trousers.

"The storm, Sir Jamie. I mean, we hear it, we see those damn dark clouds, the lightning lights up the sky, but it never leaves the valley. It ain't right."

Throwing the twig, he had been chewing into the fire; the man sitting next to Franklin rose to his feet and looked around.

"I can't say it bothers me all that much. At least we don't get wet."

"True enough, Richard, but it just ain't natural," Franklin said. "We been here a whole nine days, and that storm has been sitting there, never moving. It don't stop, it don't move, and it don't never let up. It's giving me the shivers is all I'm saying."

Jamie looked down at the grizzled soldier and smiled. "Would you rather it moved closer, Franklin?"

Franklin, a man in his early thirties with greasy brown hair and a scraggly beard, shook his head. "No. But it is a bit spooky is all I'm saying."

Jamie looked at the raging storm. "I must agree with you there. It does seem to be counter to nature." He turned to Richard, his man-at-arms, and tutor in the art of war. He was older than the others, but unlike Franklin, he was well-groomed and athletically built. His hair was shorn short, and his light brown beard worn tight to his face.

"Going to check the lines?" asked Jamie.

"Yes, milord. There has been no sign of wolves, but I know they are out there. Heard them last night. The horses seem a bit skittish, so I thought I might walk around a bit. Maybe bring them in a little closer to the fire."

"Good idea," Jamie said. He turned to Franklin. "While he is doing that, you should do a walk around before we settle for the night."

Standing, Franklin stretched his back and nodded. "As you wish. Need to stretch my legs a bit. Been sitting here too long." He chuckled. "My ass is asleep, and I need to wake it in case the wind I felt in my britches carried with it something more."

Jamie laughed. "Well, take a spear. Wolves are sly beasts. No need in taking chances. And check your trousers." He sniffed. "You may be right."

Franklin sniffed and smiled before walking to a stack of long spears resting against a nearby boulder. Jamie looked down at the dozing young man remaining seated at the fire. He nudged him with his foot.

"William, go with Franklin."

William Benton, Jamie's fourteen-year-old squire, jumped to his feet and rubbed his eyes. "Sorry, Sir Jamie. Just resting my eyes."

Jamie chuckled. "I'm sure you were. Go with Franklin. Have a look around, then come back and get some sleep. Your father will be here sometime tomorrow, I expect, and I don't want him to think I abuse you."

William smiled. "He would never think that, Sir Jamie. I think he feels you are too soft on me."

"He may be right," Richard said. "Maybe I need to lengthen the number of hours you train a day."

"I'm good, Richard. No need for that," the boy said, holding up his hands. He started to follow Franklin when Jamie called out.

"Spear."

Rushing to grab one of the long, deadly shafts, William hurried to catch Franklin.

Richard nodded toward the retreating squire. "He's a good boy, Sir Jamie. Going to make a fine knight someday."

"That is several years away yet, Richard," Jamie said as he recovered a water skin and brought it to his lips. He shook the leather bag and dropped it. "We will need to get water tomorrow."

"How is his training progressing? Is he as difficult as I was?"

"Not nearly, begging your pardon, sir." He smiled. "Truth be told, he reminds me a lot of you at that age. His swordcraft is coming along well enough, but he still has trouble remembering that his shield is a weapon too. Uses it fine to defend but just cannot seem to get the knack of using it offensively. If I remember right, you had to learn the hard way how to use it properly."

"Oh, I remember well the number of times you knocked me nearly senseless with that wooden staff of yours."

"Bruises heal. Sword strikes do not. Your father always told me I was too easy on you."

"Easy!"

Richard smiled. "That is what the baron said."

"I am sure he did. Well, keep at it. He must learn. I would feel better if I knew he could properly defend himself."

"You expect trouble?"

Jamie looked again at the distant valley containing the storm. "I always expect trouble. The Frisians have been quiet for too long. You know what they are like. So, yes. I expect trouble."

Rubbing the scar that ran along his face from his left eye to his jaw, Richard nodded. "Aye, sir. I know exactly what the sneaky bastards are like."

"I hope we are both wrong. Is there any ale left?" Jamie asked.

"There is always ale." Richard walked to the dwindling pile of supplies stacked near the spears and, recovering a leather bag, shook it. "It is well that tomorrow is our last day. Sir Edwyn should be here by midday if he left on time, and not a moment too soon. This is the last of it."

"Really?" Jamie asked with a smirk.

Richard grinned. "Well, maybe not the very last."

He handed the bag to Jamie, who pulled the cork and took a strong pull. Handing the bag back, he nodded his thanks. "I'm going to take William at first light to the edge of the valley. We shall watch until midmorning, then return. Have everything readied so we can depart as soon as Sir Edwyn arrives. I am in a hurry to leave this place. I agree with Franklin. That storm is not natural. It makes me feel...uneasy."

"Did the prince say what we are watching for?" Richard asked.

"Only that we are to watch the storm and report if there are any changes."

"Never in my life have I witnessed a storm that has lasted this long or never moves. A year it's been sitting there like some evil thing is controlling it."

The young knight looked at the raging storm but did not respond.

"Sir Jaimie!" Franklin called.

Jamie jumped to his feet when he saw the bloodied spear in Franklin's hands.

"What has happened, Franklin?"

"The boy. William. He's hurt."

"How?"

"We were attacked."

Jamie grabbed his sword. "By what? Wolves?"

"I don't know. But it weren't no wolves. It, I mean they, came out of the dark. One of them struck young William. I heard him cry out and saw the shadowy figure of a man standing over him. I threw my spear and struck whoever it was, and he ran."

Richard grabbed a spear and fell in beside Jamie. "You said they, Franklin. How many?"

"I don't know. Three, maybe four. They stayed in the shadows."

"Take us to William. Why did you leave him?" Jamie demanded, worrying about his young squire.

"I was afraid to move him, sir. Too dark to see how badly he was hurt. He's alive, I know that. I checked him before I come to get you. He groaned but did not speak. I waited until I heard the attackers run off. Once sure they was gone, I felt it would be best to get you."

He reached for a torch and lit it in the fire. "This way. I am sorry, milord."

Jamie drew his sword. "You did the right thing, Franklin. If you both had fallen, we would not know of the danger. Now let us hurry."

Franklin led them to a small clearing lying in the deep shadows of a thick grove of oaks. William lay unmoving at the far edge. Jamie rushed to him, and dropping his sword, kneeled beside the boy. Richard and Franklin kept a guard on either side of them, facing the trees.

"I need more light," Jamie said.

Franklin held the torch over the still form of the squire, and Jamie searched for wounds.

William groaned.

"Are you all right, lad?" Jamie asked.

William looked up and suddenly screamed, his eyes wide. "Devils! Daemons!"

He collapsed and went limp. Jamie rose to his feet with the boy in his arms cradled like a babe. He nodded to his sword. Richard recovered it and stood beside him, holding it at the ready in one hand, the spear in the other.

"Back to camp. You two. Watch my back," Jamie said.

They moved quickly but carefully back to their camp.

"Build up the fire, Franklin. Richard, bring the horses in closer. I want to be able to see them."

"Should I saddle them?"

"Not yet. Let us see what the evening brings."

As Franklin added fuel to the fire, bringing it to life, Jamie lay his squire on the ground close enough to see but not close enough to burn. He began to feel and look about his body.

"Help me turn him over, Franklin."

As they rolled William onto his side, Jamie let out a gasp. The full length of the boy's shirt had been laid open from shoulder to waist, the edges covered in blood.

"Water, quickly. And rags. Get my spare shirt and tear it into strips. And bring the vinegar and honey from my saddlebag. Hurry."

Franklin returned with a bag of water and Jamie's saddlebag. He ran to the knight's bedroll and grabbed a linen shirt and tore it into strips.

Jamie gently washed away the blood. "Not too bad. Thank God his spine is intact. Looks worse than it is. Get the vinegar."

Franklin rummaged through the leather bag and retrieved a small clay bottle. He pulled the stopped, sniffed, then handed Jamie the jar, who poured a little vinegar onto a strip of the torn shirt and washed the wound.

"Honey."

GLENLOCK

Richard pulled the jar from the bag and handed it to him. Opening it, Jamie smeared honey onto the wound, then covered it with pieces of the shirt.

Richard gently covered William with a wool blanket. "I should have been with the lad."

Standing, Jamie picked up his sword and returned it to its scabbard. "There is nothing you could have done, Richard." He turned to Franklin. "Tell me everything that happened."

Franklin took a deep breath. "We walked together listening for wolves. When we reached the lea, I started towards the trees to my right while Master William moved across to the trees on the far side. I thought I heard something in the brush and went to check when I heard him cry out. I ran back and saw someone standing over him. I threw my spear. I think I hit him, and he disappeared into the trees. I ran to the young master. He was breathing, but I could not see where he was hurt. I called to him, but he did not answer.

"I checked the trees nearby and heard what sounded like several men moving quickly away from us towards the stream. That's when I decided it was best for the boy if I come for help and to warn you. "I am sorry, Sir Jamie. I shouldn't a let the lad go on his own."

"He is my squire, Franklin. A man near grown, no longer a child to be watched over. He is a part of our company and was doing his duty. You did nothing wrong. And you did the right thing coming for us. If there were more of them in the forest, they could have taken you, and Richard and I would have had no warning."

"You said you saw a man. Are you sure?" Richard asked.

"It looked like a man. I mean, it ran like one."

"A man. Where did he come from, and why would he attack you?" Jamie asked.

"Sir Jamie," Richard whispered. "I hear movement."

"Where?" Jamie whispered.

Richard towards the glen, "There."

They listened. The creatures of the night had stopped chattering. All was quiet. The horses moved nervously. Jamie placed his hand on the neck of the closest beast. It snorted and looked at him, the large brown eyes of the worried animal staring in fear.

"Shush. Be still. I am here," he said, stroking the horse's nose. The animal calmed and Jamie whispered to Franklin, "Stay with William." He drew his sword.

Franklin moved back to the still figure, his spear raised, ready.

The subtle sounds of a disturbed leaf and the cracking of a stick were the only sign that something, or someone, was nearby. Then the sounds began to fade away. Whoever had approached seemed to have changed their minds and were retracing their steps back towards the meadow.

When they could no longer hear anything, Richard turned to Jamie. "I think they are gone. Do you wish me to check?"

"Quickly. And be careful. You see or hear anything, you come right back. Do not try to face them on your own."

Richard nodded and moved quietly away from the camp. Franklin and Jamie waited anxiously until Richard returned.

"Whoever it was is gone. I heard the night creatures of the forest speak. Nothing disturbs them."

Jamie nodded. "I think we could all do with some of that ale now, Richard."

Nodding, the big man walked to his saddle and retrieved the bag of ale. He sheepishly handed it to Jamie. "I was keeping it for an emergency."

"I believe this is such an occasion," Jamie said with a grin. He took a long drink and handed the bladder back. Richard offered it to Franklin.

"Who do you think it was, Sir Jamie?" Richard asked.

"I have no idea. We have been here for over a week and have encountered nothing larger than a rabbit. I know not who attacked Franklin and William, nor can I think of a reason why."

"Could it be Frisians?" Franklin asked.

"This far south. I think not. More likely outlaws. Although I have never heard of them working this close to the valley."

"The young master said it was a devil. A daemon," Franklin said nervously.

"I have encountered neither and doubt they exist. It was merely a man. Men," Jamie said.

Not convinced, Franklin tightened his grip on the spear. "As you say, milord."

Jamie put his sword away. "One of us will remain on guard while the others sleep. We will do two-hour shifts. I will go first. Franklin, I will wake you." He looked up at the moon. "The clouds have moved on and the moon is bright. I doubt anyone could approach without us seeing them or disturbing the horses. But keep your spears nearby."

"I will lie near young Master William, Sir Jamie," Franklin said. "I will keep him safe."

Jamie nodded. "Thank you."

As the other two settled in their bedrolls, Jamie stood at the edge of the camp, a spear resting on his shoulder. He stared into the darkness and listened. He turned and looked at the nearest horse. "You keep your ears open, my friend. I am counting on you."

When the sun was full, and the fog of the morning had burned off, Jamie opened his eyes and looked around. He sat up. "Why did you not wake me?"

"You needed rest."

"But…"

Richard hung a tin pot over the fire and checked the oatcakes cooking on a flat stone.

Jamie shook his head and smiled. "Thank you."

"Kettle is on, tea soon and the cakes are about ready," Richard said, as if he did not hear him. "Sorry, gentlemen, but I used the last of the bacon yesterday and there are no drippings to soften the biscuits. But it is good Lantusian tea. And there is honey."

Jamie stood, stretched, then walked over and kneeled next to William. He placed the back of his hand on his brow.

"How's the lad doing?" Richard asked.

"Still asleep. Doesn't feel too warm, which is a good sign. Hopefully, there is no corruption. I am a little surprised he has not awakened, however."

He placed his hand on the boy's shoulder and applied pressure. "William?"

There was no reaction.

Franklin walked into camp carrying three full and dripping leather bags. "The horses are fed and watered, Sir Jamie, and I have filled the water bags."

He put them down and looked back towards the creek. "Saw no one, but there were plenty of fresh prints in the mud. Near a dozen, I would guess. Strange things they were."

"Strange in what way?" Jamie asked.

"Ain't normal. Not for a man. Whatever made them prints wore no boots and only had four toes. Looked like they were human except for that. One big, three little."

"All of them the same? Four toes?"

"I checked both sides of the creek. The same and I was right. I did hit one of them. Looked like they dragged something with them. Left a trail of blood. Must have got him good."

"You are sure they are gone?"

"Pretty open ground around the creek. If they was nearby, I'd a seen em. They was moving north, away from the valley."

"Tea is ready, Sir Jamie," Richard said.

Jamie walked over and Richard handed him a tin cup. He blew on the steaming hot liquid and took a sip. "Franklin, saddle my horse. I am going to the valley. Richard, help me with my hauberk."

"I will go with you," Richard said.

"No. I need the two of you to remain here and watch over William and wait for our relief. If they should arrive before I return, tell Sir Edwyn all that has happened."

"But what if them things are still about?" Richard asked.

Jamie smiled. "Then I shall slay one of William's daemons. What a story the bards could make of such an encounter. Do not fear, Richard. I shall be vigilant. Once past the creek, the way is open ground and there is no place for an ambush. I will be fine."

"Sir Jamie."

"What is it, Franklin?"

"The valley. The storm. It stopped."

They looked towards the valley.

"Strange," Richard said.

"Spooky," Franklin added.

Jamie returned to lacing up his padded gambeson. "Hurry with my mail, Franklin. I need to see what is happening in the valley. The prince will want to know."

Jamie bent at the waist and held up his arms as Franklin slipped the chainmail over his head and shoulders. He stood and the thirty pounds of metal fell to just above his knees, split on either side, allowing him to sit a horse. He settled the coif over his head, then buckled on his sword belt, which helped to settle the weight.

"Your helmet, Sir Jamie?" Franklin asked.

He thought for a moment and then shook his head. "I do not believe I shall need it."

Richard helped him into the saddle, then lay his hand on Jamie's foot. "Let me go with you."

"No, Richard." He smiled. "I shall be fine. After all, I was trained by the greatest weapons master in all of Cent. I will look and quickly return. I give you my word. If there be danger, I shall turn and flee.

"Now, hand me my shield and a spear."

Franklin offered him a spear. Jamie took the eight-foot staff and settled it over the cantle. He then handed him his long kite shield, and he slid it over his shoulder.

Richard looked at him.

Jamie smiled. "I promise, Richard."

Richard watched as his knight, a man he had trained from a boy, a man he loved as a son, rode towards the unknown.

Jamie looked around as he walked his horse towards the opening in the hills that led to the valley. It was quiet. Too quiet. There was no birdsong, no buzz of an insect, not even the gentle rustle of the leaves in the trees. He couched his spear and moved cautiously forward. A sudden crack like the breaking of a large limb echoed from the valley, quickly followed by another.

Jamie shifted his shield to his left arm and urged his mount forward.

As he entered the mouth of the valley, he was surprised to see a lone figure near the center of the meadow that lay between the rock walls of the valley. The oddly dressed man stood staring at two unmoving figures lying in the grass. He looked up as Jamie approached.

"They attacked me," the stranger said. "I had no choice."

Jamie halted his horse a spear's length away and looked at the forms in the grass. Each wore a boiled black leather cuirass. Two deadly-looking curved swords lay beside them. No boots covered their four-toed feet.

Staring down at the stranger, he lowered the tip of the spear; the point centered on the man's chest. "whence do you come, stranger?"

The man looked up.

"Maine?"

CHAPTER 5

GLENLOCK

Hal turned his head as the bright sunlight penetrated his eyelids. He slowly opened his eyes and squinted. As the light hit his unprotected eyes, a sudden attack of vertigo caused the world to spin uncontrollably, resulting in severe nausea. He rolled to his side and emptied his stomach.

Once his head stopped spinning, he propped himself onto an elbow and looked around. He was in a valley. Red rocks and scrub brush climbed the steep slopes on either side while lush green grass covered the bowl itself, looking like someone's well-maintained lawn. No trees or brush marred the surface of the plain. A narrow pass concealed what lies outside to what he assumed was the east based on the location of the sun. Then again, it could be the west since he had no idea what time it was here. Wherever here was.

He looked at his watch. Nine AM. Of course, that was assuming time worked the same way here and that the sun rose in the east and set in the west.

The wide mouth on the farther side of the valley opened onto a forest of old pines, tall oaks, and white birch.

He worked his way to his feet and took inventory. No broken bones. His hearing had returned, and his vision cleared. And most important, his stomach had settled.

Working out of the straps, he dropped the ruck before rolling his shoulders to loosen them up. Turning his head from side to side and pushing his chin into his shoulders normally helped ease the stiffness in his neck. But there wasn't any stiffness. Or any pain. He looked at his hand. Nothing. No redness, no soreness from Spike's quill. It was like it was never there.

His clothes were wet, even under the waterproof. Strike that, water-resistant, rain gear. Unzipping the jacket, he checked to ensure he had not lost the pistol. It, too, was a little damp. He lay it on the grass beside him. Removing the rain gear, he stripped off his wet clothing. As warm as the air was, he still felt a chill.

Unbuckling the long case from across the top of the ruck and setting it to the side, he undid the straps securing the top flap and withdrew a towel and dry clothes. Fatigues from his time in the service and a pair of lime-green canvass deck shoes he had picked up in the Bahamas.

He rolled the sides down on his tan desert boots, allowing them to dry in the sun. Pulling a plastic canteen from the side of the bag, he took a long drink.

"I hope to God this is your home, Henry. I'm going to feel damned foolish if it isn't."

He leaned down and ran his hand through the grass. Dry. That's weird. Was the storm only on my side?

He looked around. Nothing. No sign of life. A field like this would be great for deer or maybe rabbits. But nothing. Not even the shadow of birds flying overhead or the insistent sound of insects buzzing around.

Is there something wrong with the valley? Some kind of toxin in the air or the grass?

He began to wonder if this was the same valley Henry had described.

I know he said one of his men killed a deer. And he said Maggie had been hunting. But there is nothing here.

He looked at the trees at the far end of the valley.

If this is the right place, then that is where Henry must have gotten knocked off his horse.

A chilling cry echoed across the valley, startling him. Not an animal, at least not any he had ever heard before. It sounded almost human. He looked toward the forest. It sounded like it came from there. Reaching into the ruck, he recovered a pair of binoculars and scanned the area.

Nothing.

The cry again. Closer this time on his left, which was soon followed by another on his right.

Kneeling next to the large bag, he picked up the pistol. He pulled the slide back far enough to ensure a round was chambered and free of water. He lay it on the ruck.

I'm being hunted.

He scanned the valley with the binoculars again. Something moved in the rocks to his left. Lowering the glasses, he reached down and flicked the safety off the pistol.

Sneaky bastards. Trying to flank me.

He pulled a large knife from its sheath attached to the side of the ruck and lay it beside the pistol.

They may not be hostile, he thought. Yeah, right. That's why they're sneaking up on me from both sides.

He lay down behind the rucksack, adjusting it to give him some cover.

"Hey! I don't want any trouble," he called out. "I see you out there. Why not come in and we can talk?"

He sat for a moment, waiting. Nothing.

Well, that's not good. So many damn rocks they could have moved halfway here by now.

Hal looked around for some place close to run where he could better defend himself. The problem was, if he moved to the rocks near the hillside, it would allow whoever they were to get behind him. At least here there was no way to reach him without breaking cover. Of course, that is assuming they don't have rifles.

Thud!

He looked at the nearly three-foot shaft of a quivering arrow sticking in the ground mere inches to the left of the rucksack. He sank as low as he could behind the bag, doing his best to keep it between him and the assholes who had just launched the arrow at him.

No rifles. He looked at the arrow. Not that they need them.

Another arrow struck, hitting the backpack and ricocheting to the side, not penetrating the nylon.

A figure suddenly appeared from around a rock less than fifty yards away and began to run towards him, carrying a long spear and screaming what he assumed was a challenge. He was closing fast and raised the spear, ready to throw. Hal aimed at the running man, but before he could shoot, another figure appeared and threw a spear at him, grazing his shoulder and embedding itself in the ground behind him.

The one that had thrown the spear pulled a huge sword from his belt and screamed a blood-chilling unintelligible cry as he sprinted towards him.

"Shit!"

He pulled the trigger.

CRACK!

The one with the spear was thrown backward, a hole appearing in his forehead. Hal quickly shifted his attention to the other man. He was almost on top of him. Jumping to his feet, Hal tripped over the ruck just as the deadly blade whooshed over his head. Rolling onto his back, he pulled the gun up and snapped off two quick shots.

The swordsman fell back, one black eye staring at the sky, a perfectly round hole above it, while a good portion of the other side of his head was a mass of mangled flesh.

Holding his gun at the ready, Hal scanned the area. Seeing no immediate threat, he approached the first man. Turning him over with his foot, he stared down at... at what?

What the hell?

He stepped to the other. The two were nearly identical. At least six feet tall, with long black hair, greasy and tangled, sticking out from under identical leather helmets. They had strangely elongated heads, flat noses, and eyes that were just a little too far apart. The color of their skin was nearly what was expected in a well-tanned Caucasian, but with a hint of something else. Something almost green. Dark beards extended down their chests, which lay on top of leather armor.

Trousers of what looked like coarse wool tied at the waist extending to just above the ankle, ragged and uneven. No shoes covered their bare feet. He looked closer. A big toe and three smaller ones. Four toes?

I'm not sure these things are even human. He looked around the valley again.

"God, Henry. I hope that storm brought me to your world."

The sound of a horse drew his attention to the eastern entrance of the valley. The approaching rider wore a chain-mail shirt similar to the one Henry had worn but dull silver. A long shield rounded at the top and pointed at the bottom extended from his left shoulder to the knee, the symbol of a red hawk painted on the surface.

He stopped about ten feet from where Hal stood and lowered a deadly-looking spear, pointing it at his chest. The rider looked at the two dead bodies and then back at him.

Hal slowly leaned down and placed the pistol at his feet. He raised his hands as he stood.

"Whence do you come, stranger?" The man on the horse asked.

"Uh, Maine?" Hal looked at the rider and gave a lopsided grin. "Would you believe I come in peace?"

CHAPTER 6

Treason

"Henry! Henry! Open the door. You must save me." Henry Lackland, Crown Prince of Cent, son of King John, dropped his quill and pushed his chair back. He nodded to the man standing next to him, who quickly stepped behind a large tapestry. The prince ensured it sufficiently concealed the man before calling out as he strode towards the heavy wooden door.

"I am coming, Edwenna. Stop banging, you are going to wake the entire castle."

Lifting the locking bar, he stepped back as his sister threw herself into the room and wrapped her arms around him, sobbing.

"There now, Winnie. What is so terrible that has distressed you so?"

"It is Father."

Pushing her back, he held her at arm's length. "What about Father?"

She broke free of his grip and marched to the open window. Without turning, she said with as much drama as she could muster, "He has told me I must marry."

Doing his best not to smile, Henry asked, "To anyone in particular?"

She turned. "That pig Oswald Kennington."

Henry chuckled. "Winnie, Oswald is only twelve summers. I do not think Father was serious."

"Oh, he was serious. He said he needed the duke's support. That Frisia was once again preparing for war. He said he needed Kennington's money and his soldiers and me marrying his son would give him both."

"And what did you say?" Henry asked.

"Well, of course, I told him I would not do it. I would never marry that skinny little brat."

"And what did Father say to that?"

She looked at her wrists covered by the long sleeves of her gown. Henry took her hand and gently pushed a sleeve up, exposing deep purple bruises.

"He grabbed me and pushed me against the wall. I thought he was going to kill me. Henry. I was so frightened. Father said I would do as I was told, or he would have no further need of me. That there was always Eleanor."

She trembled and Henry took her into his arms. "She is only nine, Henry. I am frightened. For us both."

"Your sister is ten, Winnie."

Henry stood quietly for a moment. Then he placed his hand on the back of her head and drew her to the well of his shoulder.

"It will be all right. I shall speak with Father, and we will work this out."

"But Henry. I fear if you anger Father, your very life may be in jeopardy. He has said terrible things. Things that frighten me."

Henry pushed her back to arm's length. "What kind of things?"

She hesitated and then looked down at the thick rug that lay on the stone floor. "Things about you. There are those in the palace that slink around him like the serpents they are. They have poisoned his mind with falsehoods. They say you seek the throne. That you plot to overthrow Father."

"And who are these serpents?"

"I could not see them all, but I could hear Duke Kennington's voice and that of Colby Three-Fingers, Father's sergeant-at-arms."

He thought for a moment. Kennington again.

Then he smiled. "I will be fine, Winnie. I am sure Father would not believe that I would ever plot against him. There is nothing to worry about, I assure you. Now you go pretty yourself. You do not wish to give Father the satisfaction of knowing he has frightened you."

"But Henry. He is drunk again. He is not himself. Something poisons his mind."

"He has been drunk before and I have been able to reason with him. Fear not, all will be well. Now go."

The pretty young woman nodded and turned to leave, stopped, and spoke without turning.

"Father has become crueler since the death of Mother. I believe she was the only person who could keep him from his basic nature. He is a monster, Henry. I hear in the marketplace that the people are restless. I fear for us all."

With that, she strode out, and Henry locked the door.

Sir Philip Huddleson stepped from behind the tapestry.

"Things are coming apart, Henry. If you do not take steps soon, I am afraid the people will do so for you. If that happens, you and your entire family will be in jeopardy. The kingdom would be as well. Your sister was right about one thing. The Frisians are again preparing for war. Hell, they are always preparing for war. They might see the unrest as an opportunity to cross the border in force."

"I do not believe it will come to that."

"Henry, I am your friend and as such I must speak the truth. In the last year, your father has changed. He tolerates no perception of disloyalty. He seeks no proof to strike out. People have disappeared based on rumors alone. Not just the common people, but those of the gentry as well."

"He taxes the people until there is little left. Certain nobles have had lands confiscated and redistributed to the likes of Kennington and his allies. These are dire times."

Henry turned to his friend. The closest thing he had to a brother. A man that would watch his back and give his life for him if he thought it necessary. But, most importantly, he gave honest counsel.

"I know. But what should I do, seize the throne? Father will never give up his power on his own. Should I commit regicide, patricide?"

Philip was quiet for a moment. "It need not be you, Henry," he mumbled.

Henry glared at him. "I will allow no harm to come to my father. Do you understand?" He hung his head. "If the time should ever come that it is necessary, I will do it myself."

"I am sorry, your highness. I understand he is your father."

"He is our king, Philip."

"A good king serves his people. A wise king knows that."

Henry walked to his chair and dropped into it. "I know." He sighed, then looked at his friend. "Do you have a list of those that would support me if it should come to that?"

"I do. But is it wise to write names down? Your father pays his informants well."

"No. Just tell me who I may count on if the time comes. For now, I must act as if all is well. I need to review these patrol assignments. And there have been reports of strange vessels coasting near our shores."

"Southlanders?" Philip asked.

"Most likely. But the boats do not resemble their drakkars, their dragon boats. They are larger. And they have landed no raiding parties."

"A trading vessel?" Philip asked.

"I suppose."

"Could it be Frisians?"

"I don't know," Henry said. "It is strange. No one has reported them coming to shore. It is as if they are sailing the coastline looking for something."

"Looking for a weakness in our vigilance, perhaps," Philip said. "The legions of Lantus will help you if you ask. They remain steadfast friends. To you, if not your father. Augustus looks to you as a brother."

"And I, him. I will need to ask if he has received similar reports. But I worry, Philip. Lantus supports us now, but my father has insulted the emperor more than once and has reneged on several trade agreements. If it was not for my intervention and the support of Augustus, we might already have lost our staunchest ally. I do not know how long it will be before they are forced to institute trade with the Southlanders or the Frisians."

"And the other thing?"

"What other thing?" Henry asked.

"The valley. Have you heard anything?"

Henry smiled. "Do you mean have I heard anything about the other world? Has anyone else been whisked away?"

"I have never said I did not believe you, Henry. Jamie told me of the storm and how you and Maggie disappeared. Your squire was beside himself when you vanished. John told me of the strange clothing you were wearing when they found you.

"It angered the king about the loss of your sword and spurs. The symbols of your knighthood, your princedom. I do not believe he accepted your story of losing them in the storm, and I know for certain he would not have believed the truth. The others in your party, your friends, and your loyal servants have maintained your confidence. They are good people. Despite that, he questions what actually happened."

"I am a fortunate man to have such people," Henry said.

"Their friendship and loyalty were earned, and it is given freely. As for me… I am one of but a handful today that believes that there is still magic to be found around us. Another world? Why not?"

"Magic? Maybe. I don't know." Henry smiled. "I think you may be as crazy as I, Philip. But I believe whatever took me to that place and brought me back did so for a reason. I cannot accept that there is not more to it. The reports of the storm in the valley beginning days after our return to Cyneburg cannot be a coincidence. No one has ever heard of a storm that sits in one place and lasts beyond a year. So, I will keep a watch on that valley. I have a feeling it is not done with us."

Henry raised his hand for silence when a knock at the door made them turn.

"Prince Henry. The king wishes you to attend him."

"Trouble?" Philip whispered.

Henry shrugged. "We shall see."

He lifted the latch and opened the door. "What is this?" he asked.

Colby Three-Fingers, his father's sergeant of the guard, and six of his men stood silent in the hallway.

"Is there something amiss, Colby, that the king should send armed men to escort his son to see him? Is there a threat to my person? Or to the king?"

Colby looked at him belligerently. "The king bade me bring you at once to the throne room. He ordered me to ensure that you were not armed."

Philip stepped forward, laying his hand on his sword.

"You will not address your prince in such a manner."

The guards came alert, and Henry placed his hand on Philip's arm.

"There is no need for that. I don't think Colby meant any disrespect, did you, Sergeant?"

He did not respond.

"Besides, I have no need of weapons simply to visit my father. You wait here, Philip. I will be back soon.

"Oh, and Sir Philip…"

"Yes, your highness."

"I feel like a hunt. I think I would like to leave tonight after I see my father. Please have James Longbow prepare for a trip. I think wild boar. And you know how crafty the beasts are. Tell him we may have to stay a few nights so ensure he arranges for sufficient supplies."

Philip looked at Colby and nodded his understanding.

"It shall be done, your highness. Will Princess Edwenna be joining us?"

"Not for this. I think men only. You know how she behaves when she is forced to go riding. And bring wine. I get a great thirst when I hunt."

"As you wish, My Prince."

"I shall return shortly." Henry turned to the sergeant-of-arms.

"Is that not so, Sergeant?"

Colby sneered. "If it is the king's will."

Henry smiled. "You know, Colby, one of these days you will go too far with your insolence, at which time you may find I am not as even-tempered as you may believe."

He strode forward, brushing the sergeant aside and causing him to quick step to catch up.

Osborn Kennington, the Duke of Sandford, leaned toward John deep in hushed conversation. Their whispering stopped, and they looked up as Henry was ushered into the room. King John stared at his son and the duke stepped back, the hint of a smile of satisfaction on his lips.

The guards stopped at the door and Henry stepped forward, bowed his head, and smiled.

"Your sergeant-at-arms said you wished to see me, your majesty?"

John leaned forward in the wooden throne. "Is it true?" he demanded.

"Is what true, Father?"

John jumped from the throne and rushed forward, almost falling as he descended the steps.

"Do you plot to kill me and take the throne?" he screamed, spittle striking Henry's shirt.

Henry stepped back in alarm and confusion. The crazed look in his father's eyes frightened him.

"Kill you?! You are my father, my king. Of course, I would not plot to kill you. I love you, Father."

"Love me! Love me! You don't love me. You fear me!" He looked at the duke as if for confirmation, then back at Henry, his eyes bloodshot, wild.

"As you should. I know you hate me for the power that is mine. That you desire it for yourself. You crave it! You can't wait for my death to assume the throne. I have heard the whispers. I know."

Shocked, Henry stared for a moment, then regained his composure. "Sire, that is not true. Who fills your head with such lies?"

John stepped so close Henry could smell the sour wine on his breath. His hands shook in fury.

"You will fail! I am too smart for you, boy! I have had people watching you. I know it all. They tell me you plot with our enemies. Those beyond our kingdom. That you have had secret meetings with your friend Augustus. They have told me of your plots to depose me."

"Who has told you such heresy, your majesty? Let me face my accusers."

"Oh, you shall. You shall. At your trial!" He spun around and threw himself onto the throne, screaming, "Colby!"

"Your Majesty?"

"Take this traitor to the dungeon and chain him up. Round up as many of his coconspirators as you can find. If they resist, kill them."

Colby tried to hide the smile of satisfaction that threatened to spread across his face. "As you wish, My King."

"Father, this is preposterous. You cannot possibly believe these lies. Please. Do not do this."

"Take him away. And shut him up." John's eyes rolled up and his head dropped as dark drool stained his shirt.

Kennington kneeled beside the throne and placed his hand on the king's chest.

"Summon the physician! The king is ill."

Henry lept forward. "Father!"

Slamming the hilt of his sword into Henry's stomach, Colby nodded to two of the guards.

"Take him to the dungeon. Chain him there while I seek the king's physician."

The guards grabbed Henry by the arms and dragged him from the room while he gasped to catch his breath. Regaining his feet, Henry walked between the guards quietly, scanning the shadows until he saw what he was looking for.

He offered no resistance as they worked their way to the narrow passage that descended to the storerooms, cistern, and far below, the dungeon. The stone walls of the stairway allowed only one man at a time to navigate the narrow passage requiring one guard to go ahead while the other followed their prisoner, pushing him with the butt of his spear.

Henry did his best to keep from falling, pushing his hands to the walls of the shallow passage. As the corridor opened onto the first level containing the storerooms, a man stepped out of the shadows, grabbed the guard's spear, and pulled forward, throwing him off balance. As the guard stumbled, the man grabbed him and ran a long dagger across his throat.

Henry jammed his elbow into the guard behind and ducked as a long sword passed over his head, removing the head of the second guard, which bounced down the remaining steps.

William Quick Arrow pulled the sword back and Henry stepped into the room, allowing the body of the dead guard to fall. Bruce-son-of-Bruce grabbed the body and dragged it from the stairs, then wiped his dagger clean on the dead man's tunic.

"The horses are ready, your highness," William said, handing Henry his sword belt.

"Thank you. As usual, your timing is impeccable," Henry said.

"Just luck we was down here, your highness. John Longbow suggested we might want to inspect the wine cellar." He smiled. "Just in case you might need help selecting a bottle to take with us on the hunt.

"But we must hurry. John and the others await at the far side of the postern gate with horses. Your squire and that of Sir Randel will follow and bring supplies and spare mounts. They will meet us where the charcoal burners ply their trade at Hamptons Wood."

Henry placed a hand on the shoulder of each man. "Thank you, my friends. Now let us flee before we are discovered. We have a hard ride ahead of us."

CHAPTER 7

SIR HAL

Jamie examined the strangely dressed man. He was tall with light brown hair cut short, no beard, and the physique of a warrior in his prime.

"You slew these creatures?" he asked without turning or lifting the spear.

"I had no choice. They tried to kill me."

"How did you kill them? I see no weapon."

Hal pointed to the pistol. "With that."

Jamie looked at the strange weapon. He upended his spear and drove the long-tapered head into the ground, and dismounted. Squatting next to one of the bodies, he turned its elongated head, examining the damage caused by the 9mm slug. He raised an eyebrow. The feet were bare and sported only four toes.

Jamie stood and signaled that Hal should put his hands down.

"Your appearance is a curiosity, stranger. The clothing you wear is… unusual." He looked at the green loafers. "Most unusual." He pointed to the pistol. "This is the weapon you used?"

"It is."

"Curious," Jamie said. "What is your name, stranger? And whence do you hail?"

"My name is Hal Bennet. I was in Maine before coming here. Not that I'm sure where here is."

Jamie raised an eyebrow. "Maine? You are Sir Hal of Deecee?"

Hal smiled. "Well, that's what Henry called me, so sure, I'm Sir Hal of D. C."

"Henry? You speak of Prince Henry?"

"Has a big cat he calls Maggie?"

"That is her name. A rather large longtooth. The prince is most fond of her."

"I know."

Removing his gauntlet, Jamie reached out and gripped Hal's forearm. "Forgive me, I am Sir Jamie Mercier, of Tilden. A friend of the prince. I was there the day the storm took him."

"Is he all right?"

"He is well. This is a most strange event. One I feel the prince must have foreseen. One I must admit I had not. When the prince returned and divulged the details of his adventure, I am ashamed to admit it was initially difficult for me to believe. But the prince is not one to tell fanciful tales. And there was little doubt that the clothing he returned to us in was irrefutable evidence that something beyond our understanding had occurred. Never had I witnessed such material, and the way it fastened was almost magical. We hid the clothes, and he swore us to secrecy, for fear some would think him mad, or touched by daemons. There are those within the kingdom who would welcome the opportunity to question the prince's sanity."

Hal took off his cap and ran his fingers through his hair and smiled. "I told no one either for the same reason. Insane, not touched by demons."

"Prince Henry believes that there was a reason for his time in your world. When the storm returned, he tasked us, his closest companions, to watch this valley. He did not explain why. But he cautioned us to never enter so long as the storm continued. It was as if he was waiting for something. Or someone."

"Does this place have storms like this often?" Hal asked.

"To the best of my knowledge, one such as this has never occurred before. The valley is known for its severe storms, true, but they normally last but a day or two. Never a full year."

Jamie noted the blood on Hal's shirt. "Are you injured, Sir Hal?"

"Just a scratch. I'm fine." He looked at the two dead beings. "Do you know who they are? Why they attacked me?"

"No. Nor do I know what they are. I have never seen their like. I have doubt they are even human."

"They sure as hell ain't friendly," Hal said.

Jamie smiled. "In this, I must agree. I believe these to be the same creatures that attacked two of my men last night."

Jamie looked around. "But Richard, my weapons master, believed there may have been more than two. I think it would be wise if we departed the valley and joined the rest of my party. We are too exposed here."

"You're not going to get an argument from me." Hal pointed to the pistol laying on the grass. "May I?"

"Of course. We are friends. Shall I assist you in collecting the rest of your belongings?"

"Thanks, but I'll get it."

"At least allow me to place your bag on my horse. It appears hefty."

"That would be nice, thank you. It is a bit...hefty."

They picked up the rucksack and while Hal held it in place, Jamie lashed it to the saddle.

Hal slipped the automatic into the holster attached to his belt. He recovered the long waterproof bag and tied it to the top of the ruck.

"May I inquire what is in that? Another of your strange weapons?"

"Swords." Hal stopped and untied the end of the bag. He pulled it partway down, exposing the hilts of three swords. One was a broadsword with a ruby in the pommel and a beautifully etched brass crosspiece.

"Is that the prince's sword?" Jamie asked.

"It is. Thought he might like it back."

"He will be grateful. That sword is important to him. You knew you would be returning it to him?"

"Not sure what I thought. I don't know why I brought the sword, just like I don't know why I needed to climb that damned mountain in the middle of a storm. I just felt I had to. I couldn't fight the need to do so." Hal looked at Henry's sword. "Maybe I did know, and just didn't want to admit it."

Jamie pointed to the other two swords. "And those?"

"They're mine. And before you ask, no, I don't know why I brought them either."

"I have never seen such a sword. May I?"

Removing the longer of the two swords from the case, Hal offered the weapon to Jamie. Griping the ten-inch handle, the young knight pulled the slightly curved thirty-inch blade free of the black lacquered scabbard.

"It is called a Katana. Its shorter brother is a Wakizashi."

"These are beautiful weapons. I have never seen blades such as these."

"They were a gift from a friend."

"A valuable gift and a story worth telling, I am sure," Jamie said. "And the silver wolf on the hilt. It means something?"

"The white wolf. A guardian."

Jamie ran his thumb over the image, then suddenly looked up at the distant forest.

Hal followed his gaze. "Shit!"

Several figures appeared from the trees at the end of the valley, racing toward them. The sound of a sliding rock drew Hal's attention behind them just in time to see three of the bearded men as they raised their spears. He pushed Jamie to the side and quickly drew the pistol, snapping off three hastily fired shots just as one of the long shafts penetrated the ground mere inches from where the young knight had been standing.

Jamie climbed to his knee and stared at the lifeless figures on the ground. He looked at the smoking pistol in Hal's hand.

"To your front!" Hal yelled.

At least two dozen of their assailants were almost on top of them. They had crossed the open ground faster than should have been humanly possible.

Jamie jumped to his feet and drew his sword. He reached down and picked up his shield.

Crack, crack, crack!

Jamie tried to ignore the frightening sound of Hal's weapon. He grabbed the reins of his frightened horse before it bolted.

Eight figures lay still in the grass, not more than a dozen feet from where they stood. The rest of the attackers stood silent, looking at their fallen comrades.

The slide of the automatic locked to the rear and Hal dropped the pistol and grabbed the katana. Pulling the blade free, he tossed the scabbard to the side. Jamie released his horse and stepped beside him, his shield forward, his sword poised above his head, the point towards the advancing threat.

One of the silent men lifted his head, snarled, then threw his spear. Almost immediately, he rushed forward with a sword in his hand. Hal smacked the spear aside with the flat of the sword, then swung the katana. A headless body fell at his feet.

Jamie blocked a sword strike with his shield while he thrust his blade down into the screaming mouth of another attacker.

Gripping the katana in two hands, Hal moved forward in a dance of death as he blocked, stabbed, and sliced with the katana, leaving six dead, or dying in his path.

Jamie pulled his blade free, allowing another of their attackers to slip to the ground, and carefully worked his way towards Hal until he felt his back touch the newcomer.

"Impressive swordplay," Jamie said between breaths.

Hal nodded at the men that lay at the knight's feet. "Not so bad yourself. So now what?"

Jamie smiled. "I expect that will be up to them."

The rest of the attackers milled about out of sword range and stared at the two men until one leaped forward, thrusting his blade at Jamie, who effortlessly smacked it aside with his shield and opened the man's throat with a backhanded swing.

"You must tell me the story of that magnificent sword and how you learned to wield it with such skill," Jamie said, as he waited for the next probe.

Hal took a breath and spat on the ground. "If we live through this, I promise." He chuckled. "I could use a drink right about now."

"As could I," Jamie said with veiled amusement.

Two of the enemy tried to pierce their defense at the same time. Before they could reach them, arrows appeared in their chests, driving them back. As the surprised enemy looked to see where the deadly shafts came from, Hal and Jamie took advantage of their confusion and stepped into them with fury. It was quickly over.

Hal turned towards the mouth of the valley as he heard a man call out.

"Are you all right, Sir Jamie?"

Jamie smiled. "Richard Ainsworth. I am well. Thank you."

"A friend of yours?" Hal asked.

"My weapons master. A finer archer never lived."

"Damn good shot with that bow. What was that a hundred yards?" Hal asked.

"I have seen him strike a bird in flight at twice that range."

Hal watched as the archer leaped onto his horse and trotted to them, keeping both the bow and a deadly-looking arrow at the ready while controlling the horse with his knees. He was a big man with huge shoulders. The bow he carried reminded Hal of an English Longbow.

"You are not injured, Sir Jamie?" Richard asked, looking down at the bodies.

"I am fine, Richard. Fortuitous timing."

"Two of these beasties tried to get to Master William. I was concerned they might try for you. Me thinking you being alone and all." He looked Hal up and down, then stared at the shoes.

"Was he hurt?" Jamie asked.

"No. It was strange. They just burst in, grabbed him, and attempted to drag him away. Franklin smashed one with a skillet and I rammed my dagger into the ear of the other."

Noticing Richard staring at Hal, Jamie nodded to him.

"This is Prince Henry's friend, Richard. Sir Hal of Deecee. The one he told us about after his return from the storm."

"Explains the footwear," Richard said. "Seen nothing like them. Interesting color."

He tossed a leg over the saddle and dropped to the ground. "So, you come from the other side."

Hal looked at his feet. "My boots were wet.

" Other side?"

"Of the storm," Richard said.

"I guess you could say that."

"I see."

"Does the other live? The one struck by the skillet?" Hal asked.

"No, Franklin has a powerful arm, and the skillet did him in."

"A shame. Would have been nice to interrogate one. Find out why they wanted us dead."

"And why they wanted William alive," Jamie added.

Richard walked around the bodies.

"Leather armor looks like they boiled it. Ain't too good." He kicked one of the spears. "These look heavy." He picked up a sword. "Almost like bronze, but stronger. Strange, I do not know what kind of metal was used to make the blade. It is heavy. No balance."

He squatted and examined the attacker. "No boots. By the looks of the bottom of their feet, I don't believe they have ever worn any."

Noticing a body felled by the pistol, he looked up at Hal, who touched the pistol.

"Makes a big hole," Richard said matter-of-factly.

It surprised Hal at how calmly he was taking everything. As if his arrival and guns were an everyday occurrence.

"It does," he agreed.

"Odd-looking thing," Richard said holding up the spear. "Looks almost like a pike." He turned to Hal. "Do you recognize it? Do these things come from your world?"

Hal shook his head. "Reminded me of something. Close, but not what I thought. And no, they are not of my world."

Richard glanced at the pack on Jamie's horse. "You should take my horse, Sir Jamie. No room on yours. I will walk."

"No. We will all walk between the horses. If there are any more of these things about, they will provide us some shelter." He turned to Hal. "Thank you."

"For what?"

"Jamie pointed to the spear that had almost struck him. "For saving my life."

Franklin looked up and reached for his spear. He dropped it when he saw Jamie. He turned back to William and wiped his brow with a damp rag. The young squire was wrapped in a blanket and, even from a distance, it was obvious to the others that he was shivering.

Jamie dismounted and strode quickly to them. He kneeled next to William. "How fairs the boy, Franklin?"

"Not well, milord. A fever came upon him soon after Richard departed. I covered him when he began to shake. Tried to give him water, but he won't drink."

"What happened to him?" Hal asked.

"One of those things attacked him," Jamie said. "I don't understand why he has not awakened. The wound did not appear serious."

"May I look?" Hal asked.

Jamie nodded, but when Hal tried to get near the boy, Franklin refused to move, staring at him menacingly.

"He is a friend, Franklin.," Jamie said. "Let him see. Richard will explain. Please see to the horses."

"And if you could bring me my pack, I would appreciate it," Hal said. "It's on Sir Jamie's horse."

"I will fetch it," Franklin said, staring at William for a moment. Then he turned and walked away.

Hal lay the back of his hand on the young man's forehead, then lifted an eyelid. Laying two fingers along the side of William's neck, he stared at the wounded boy. Jamie watched with interest.

"Pulse is strong. Where was he struck?"

"His back."

"Could you help me roll him over?"

Jamie removed the blanket, and the two men rolled William onto his side. Hal gently removed the bandages and probed the wound. He rubbed his fingers together, then smelled them.

"Did you put something on this?"

"I poured vinegar into the wound and covered it with honey."

Hal cleaned the honey from the wound with the strip of cloth that had been used as a bandage.

Franklin dropped the rucksack next to Hal.

"The bag is heavy."

"It is. I have a bad habit of over-packing."

"I need some clean water."

Richard looked at Franklin. "Bring one of the water bags."

Franklin hesitated.

"Now, Franklin, if you please," Richard said.

The old soldier walked towards the horse line.

"Richard, did you tell him who Sir Hal is?" Jamie asked.

"I have not had the time as yet, Sir Jamie."

"Well, you better do so."

"Aye." Richard walked away, looking back once as he went to speak with Franklin.

"Richard handles William's training. The boy is barely fourteen summers and small for his age. Richard looked at him as if he were his son. He has no children of his own. He did the same for me when I was a lad."

"He seems like a good man."

Hal unzipped the green nylon bag he had taken from the ruck while Jamie watched.

"The prince showed us a similar fastener. An amazing thing. What is in the bag, Sir Hal?"

"It's a first aid kit. A medical bag. And the name is Hal."

"I am sorry, Sir Hal. But when we are with others, you are Sir Hal, as I am Sir Jamie."

"Your world, your rules," Hal said, taking a bottle from the bag. "A cool rag across his brow would be helpful...Sir Jamie," he said with a grin. "This one is warm."

Jamie smiled. "I will get one."

He returned with a damp rag at the same time Franklin and Richard arrived with the water. Franklin looked at Hal like he was a boogeyman.

"You come from beyond the valley. From the world that took our prince?" he asked.

"Something like that." He glanced up at Franklin. "Weird, huh?"

Franklin smiled and nodded. "It is so."

"Let me have one of those bandages. The cleanest you have."

Richard handed Hal an unused piece of Jamie's torn shirt.

"Thanks. I need to get this cleaned out." He wiped the wound until all the honey was gone, then picked up the brown plastic bottle he had taken from the first aid kit. He poured a liberal amount of the peroxide along the wound. When it bubbled, Franklin gasped.

"It's all right. It's supposed to do that. It will clean the wound and help prevent infection."

"Infection?"

"I think he means corruption," Jamie said.

"Are you a sorcerer, Sir Hal? I have never seen a healer do such a thing." Franklin asked, staring at the bubbling wound.

"No, just a soldier that has had a lot of experience treating wounds." Picking up a tube of antibiotic cream, he worked some into the wound. Taking a curved needle from the pack, he tore open an alcohol pack with his teeth and wiped it down.

"Alcohol swab. It will help clean the needle," he explained, noticing the interest the men had in what he was doing.

Richard picked up the swab, smelled it, wrinkled his nose, and dropped it.

"He was lucky. Not too deep. The spine wasn't touched. Whoever did this either knew what he was doing and did not want to kill the kid or was piss poor with the blade."

When he finished stitching the wound, he cut the suture with his teeth and looked up.

"That should do it. He should be fine. Keep him covered. See if he will drink. If he will have him swallow these."

He handed Richard two gel caps.

"It will help with the pain."

Richard kneeled and offered the water bottle to William. As the cool liquid touched his lips, the young man gulped the water.

"Good. Put those in his mouth and make him swallow," Hal said. He opened another plastic bottle and handed two white pills to Jamie. "Give him these when he wakes."

"What is that?" Sir Jamie asked.

"It is an antibiotic. Something that will help his body fight infection. I think there was something on the blade. Something to keep him unconscious. I don't think they wanted him dead. Knocked him out so he would be easier to take with them."

"Do you believe they will return, Sir Jamie? For William?" Franklin asked.

Jamie looked back towards the valley.

"They've tried twice. I don't know what they want with him, but yes. If there are any more, I think they will try again."

CHAPTER 8

THE MAKING OF A KING

The setting sun cast long shadows over the small meadow as the weary riders broke through the trees of the dense forest. Henry held up his hand, halting those that followed as the silhouette of a man disengaged himself from a tree.

"All is clear, Bruce?"

"Yes, your highness. Peaceful it is. Ain't seen nothing bigger than a rabbit. And it was nothing to brag about.

"The charcoal burners are nestled next to their wives for the night with their doors locked tight. They been most helpful and wished to stay but I sent them home. Good people. I figured if we be discovered it's going be an ugly business. Best left to men trained for it."

"I agree and thank you. Your father would be proud." Henry dismounted and stretched his back.

"Happy to serve, as always, milord," Bruce-son-of-Bruce said with a quick nod.

Henry turned to Philip. "Send someone to watch our back trail."

"Already done. James Longbow and a few men dropped back an hour after we left the castle. He will let us know if we are being followed."

"They know to keep an eye out for John and Randolph?" Henry asked.

"They do."

"Thank you, Philip."

Henry pulled a gauntlet from his hand and slapped the leather glove against his thigh, causing a cloud of dust to rise.

"What was my father thinking? How could he believe this of me?"

"Snakes have been hissing in his ear," Philip said, climbing down from the weary horse.

"Snakes with designs on the crown," Henry agreed. "To accuse me of treason."

Philip lay his hand on his friend's shoulder. "Your father is ill, Henry. He does not know what it is he is doing."

"I wish I could believe that. But I'm not so sure. The hate I saw in his eyes will haunt me for the remainder of my days. What has happened to him? It is good my mother cannot see what her husband has become. I now fear for my sisters."

Henry turned to the men that had ridden with him.

"And I fear for you, my friends. You should return to your homes and your families. If you continue to ride with me, you will be outlawed. Hunted down and hanged."

Philip looked at the men, then at Henry.

"We are your men, Prince Henry. We follow you. Whatever is to come. Your enemies are our enemies. Your friends, ours."

Henry stood still and looked at the hardened warriors, all veterans from the most recent war with Frisia. His chest became tight, and he waited until his emotions were under control before he spoke.

"I know not what lies ahead, but I can think of no better company with whom to spend my remaining days. Thank you all."

Philip smiled at his friend, his prince. "And I have little doubt more will join us once word spreads what has happened."

"That is what concerns me. I do not want a civil war," Henry said.

"My Prince, the war began the moment your father ordered your arrest. You cannot stop it now."

"You may be right. But why? Why now?"

"The duke and those that support him seek to control the throne," Philip said.

Henry shook his head. "If it were only that simple. Kennington is ambitious but not smart enough to do this on his own. I believe there is someone else behind this."

"That may be true, and I did not say it was simple," Philip said. "But Kennington has men and coin. Two things your father desperately needs. He has taken advantage of the situation. And I say again, your father is ill."

"Ill? In what way?"

"I believe his illness lies within his mind."

Henry was quiet for a moment.

"I think you may speak true. I have denied what has been in front of me for too long. And now it has come to this."

He watched as the men unsaddled their exhausted horses.

"We must take care of these men, Philip. They deserve our best. We must gather their families. And we must do so quickly. Once the king identifies those who ride with me, he will go after them."

"I will. But where can we take them where they will be safe?"

Henry stroked his beard in thought.

"To the border of Lantus. I will ask Augustus to seek his father's permission to grant them sanctuary. They will be safe there. Even my father would do nothing to provoke the Legions of Lantus."

"And us?" Philip asked.

"I will not leave Cent."

Philip smiled. "That's why I asked."

"Riders approaching!" a voice called out from the dark.

Drawing their swords and reaching for their shields, the men formed a wall to either side of their prince.

"Hail the camp. Friends approach. Tis I, James Longbow."

"Approach the camp, friend," Henry called as he put his sword away.

James Longbow walked his mount into the field leading a line of riders and sumpters, packhorses laden heavy with supplies.

"It is our squires." Philip stepped forward and took hold of the bridle of his squire's horse. "Randolph, tis good you are here."

The rider, a young man of fifteen summers, lept from his saddle and kneeled in front of the prince. He was as tall as his knight and carried almost as much muscle. Henry bid him rise.

"We will have none of that here."

Randolph regained his feet.

"As you wish, your highness. We have brought weapons, food, and spare horses." He turned to Philip. "I have brought armor, my lord. Mail only, I am afraid. There was not enough time to retrieve plate for either of you."

He turned to Henry. "But we have your mail as well, Prince Henry."

"Good lad, thank you. And where is Sir Randel?" Philip asked.

"He did not come with us. He looks to rescue the princesses. He fears for their safety with the prince gone."

Henry stepped forward.

"Thank you, young Randolph. You have done well."

Another young man, older by three years than Randolph, approached and bowed his head. "Prince Henry."

"John. How fair you?" Henry asked.

"I am well, thank you." He looked around. "This is all that has arrived?"

"I am afraid so," Henry said.

"Others will come," Philip said. "You will see."

Henry took a deep breath and frowned.

"My father will not take kindly to any that breaks their oath."

"They will not be forsworn, for they swore to serve their king, to serve Cent," John said.

"I am not their king, John. I am their prince. Their oath is to my father."

John withdrew his sword and placed the point of the blade on the ground, gripped the crosspiece, and kneeled.

"It is you I serve. It is you I give my oath for you alone, are my king."

Philip looked around and smiled. "Your squire has said what needs to be said. He speaks true. I too swore an oath to my king. And I shall honor it."

He drew his sword and kneeled.

The sound of swords being drawn made Henry look up. All had kneeled. Taking a deep breath, he said, "Then let it be so."

James Longbow approached Henry as the others quietly rose to their feet and prepared their camp.

"Your high… your majesty. Bruce and William are setting sentries. Is there anything else you wish for us to do?"

Henry clapped him on the shoulder.

"Are you sure this is what you want, James? You have a family."

"I have always been your man. You are my king. Beth and the boys will be fine. Beth knows where my loyalties lie. Always has. She would skin me alive if I left you on your own. I will send for them. I feel sorry for any man that tries to stop my Beth from joining me."

"I am honored. But I am concerned for there will be trouble. We must take them to Lantus. And we must do so quickly."

"Aye, your majesty. That would be best. With your permission, I will tell the others and send someone to round them up."

"Thank you."

James Longbow gave a quick bow and walked to where two men were hobbling their horses."

"He is a good man," John said.

"He is that, John. I am a fortunate man to have such loyal friends."

"How many of us are there?" John asked, looking around.

"Until Sir Randel arrives, we are but one knight, ten men-at-arms, and a dozen archers. Sir Randel may have more when he arrives. I hope so."

"I know that Sir Randel has at least six men-at-arms with him. They will arrive soon with the princesses," Philip said.

"Not much of an army." Henry looked at John and smiled. "Two knights will not do." He drew his sword.

"Kneel, John Mercier."

CHAPTER 9
KYŪDŌ DA YUMI

As night settled, Franklin brought the horses nearer the fire where Hal and Jamie kept vigilance over William.

"The horses will give us fair warning of intruders," he said.

Richard threw a piece of wood into the fire. "We are too few to set a proper guard. I believe it best we stay together to better defend ourselves in case the beasties return."

"A wise decision," Jamie said.

Franklin sat beside Richard. "The horses are settled. I made sure the more skittish were nearest the trees. They will let us know if there is anything out there."

"Very good, Franklin. Thank you," Jamie said.

Hal noticed Richard staring at the deck shoes he had set aside now that his boots were dry. He picked one up and handed it to him.

"I keep them because they take up little room in the ruck. Besides, they're comfortable."

Richard examined the shoe and handed it to Franklin. "What are they made of?"

"The soles are rubber. I think the uppers are some kind of synthetic material. Maybe nylon."

"You use words that have no meaning to me, Sir Hal. These are mysteries of your world?"

Hal chuckled. "I suppose so."

Franklin handed him back the shoe. Hal picked up the other and slipped them into his pack.

"The colors of your clothing. Is there a purpose to the pattern?" Franklin asked.

"I was once a soldier. We wore clothing like this to help us hide from our enemies. Well, not hide, I guess. More like to make them less likely to see us before we saw them."

"So, you fought to ambush? You did not stand toe-to-toe with your foes?" Richard asked.

"Most fighting on my world is done with weapons that kill at a distance. We did our best not to get that close."

"Like with a bow," Richard said.

Hal nodded. "Something like that, but with far greater range. And every man carried one."

"How far do your weapons carry?" Richard asked.

Before answering, Hal pulled the automatic from the holster. He dropped the magazine and extracted the round in the chamber, catching it as it flew. He checked the chamber before handing it to Richard. "This is used at close range. It fires thirteen projectiles. Your chainmail will not stop a bullet fired from this. We have bigger weapons that fire at much greater distances."

"What distances?" Jamie asked.

"Weapons carried by men, some more than a mile. Larger systems much farther than that."

"Like a catapult or a trebuchet," Jamie said.

Hal thought about explaining the true destructive power of the weapons of his world. "My world has weapons that can travel thousands of miles and destroy entire cities, kill tens of thousands of people all at once."

They sat silently. Finally, Jamie handed the pistol back to Hal.

"I do not believe I would wish to visit your world."

"I can understand that. But it is not all about killing. There are wonderful things there as well."

For the next several hours, Hal tried to explain airplanes and cars, radios and telephones, electric lights, and trains. He thought about mentioning that man had landed on the moon but felt that might be going too far.

"It sounds like a world full of magic," Franklin said. "Words carried through the sky. Tis hard to believe all you tell us, Sir Hal."

"I understand, but it isn't magic, Franklin, it's science. Although some of it does sound like magic, I suppose."

Richard looked towards the east. "The sun will rise soon."

"Those things have not bothered us. I wonder why?" Hal asked.

"They may wait for daylight," Richard said.

"Or they may be afraid of your weapon," Jamie added, looking at the pistol.

"Maybe." Hal ran his hand over the handle. He looked up at Jamie. "Tell me about Glenlock. I have a lot to learn about this place."

And so they did. It was full light before they finished. Franklin rose to relieve himself. He stopped and listened, then rushed to grab a spear. "I hear horses."

"Our relief," Jamie said hopefully as he jumped to his feet. He drew his sword. "I hope."

Richard stood over William, a sword in his hand. Hal stepped beside Jamie and checked to ensure a round was chambered and flicked off the safety. They waited.

Six riders broke from the trees. Jamie returned his blade and walked towards the approaching men. The lead rider stopped and stepped down. He removed his leather gauntlets and smiled. He was older than Jamie, maybe in his mid to late thirties, strongly built with dark hair and a beard with just a hint of a few gray hairs.

"Sir Edwyn. Tis good to see you," Jamie said.

Edwyn handed the reins of his mount to his squire and gripped Jamie's arm in greeting. He looked back at the young man holding his horse.

"As Peter will attest, we would have arrived last night if not for being ambushed."

"Ambushed?" Jamie asked. "By whom?"

"I know not. They never showed themselves the cowards. Arrows and spears rained down from the rocks and trees on either side of the roadway. The arrows and spears grazed upon the hindquarters of one of the pack animals and wounded two of my men. We searched but found no one. Just several sets of odd-looking footprints."

"No boots and with only four toes?" Jamie asked.

"Yes, you know of them?"

"Unfortunately."

"Any idea who they are or why they would attack me?" Edwyn asked.

"I am afraid not." Jamie turned to Richard. "Will you please see to Sir Edwyn's wounded?"

"Yes, milord." Richard walked up to Peter. "If you will follow me, sir."

Edwyn's attention was directed to Hal when Richard led the new arrivals to their picket line. "And who is this?"

"Sir Edwyn Benton, I would like to present Sir Hal Bennet, of Deecee," Jamie said.

"Well met, Sir Hal," Edwyn said, gripping Hal's forearm. "I am not familiar with Deecee."

"I will explain," Jamie said.

"I am looking forward to it." Edwyn looked towards the valley. "The storm?"

"Gone yesterday. It seems to have signaled Sir Hal's arrival."

"Arrival. From the valley?" Edwyn asked, a little surprised.

"Not exactly," Jamie said. "That is where we met, but it is not whence he came."

"Interesting." Edwyn looked Hal up and down. "Such strange attire, Sir Hal. I do not believe I have ever seen the like."

"You should see his shoes," Jamie said in amusement.

"Shoes?"

Hal grinned. "My boots were wet, and I had to put on my deck shoes."

"Deck shoes?"

Jamie took Edwyn by the elbow. "Come to the fire. There is much to tell."

"I would say," Edwyn said as the two walked away.

Hal watched them for a moment until he felt a presence next to him.

"Sir Edwyn is a good man, Sir Hal. But he is...shall we say, conservative in his thinking. He sees the world with less wonder than Sir Jamie. His father is the Earl of Eudell. I do not envy Sir Jamie trying to explain what has befallen us in the last two days."

"You think he can?" Hal asked. "Maybe he can explain it to me."

Richard chuckled. "Knowing Sir Jamie as I do, he will try. He loves mysteries."

"Do you have to call me that? It seems weird."

"Weird?"

"Strange, uncomfortable."

Richard stared at him for a moment. "Are you not a lord from whence you come?"

"We do not use titles in my country."

Richard placed his hand on Hal's shoulder and, looking around, whispered, "It is best you keep that to yourself. Titles are important here, words are important. The prince has told us you are of the aristocracy in your world. A knight. It is best not to contradict him."

The earnest look on Richard's face was unsettling. "Thank you. I will remember."

"Richard, Sir Hal, will you join us, please?" Jamie called.

"Of course, milord," Richard said and turned to Hal. "One more thing you should know. Master William is Sir Edwyn's son, and his lordship was not with us the day the prince returned from the storm. Your story may not sit well with him."

As they reached the fire, Sir Edwyn stood and grabbed Hal's arm. "Sir Jamie has told me all. What happened to my son, what you have done for him. I am in your debt, sir. This shall not be forgotten."

Hal was about to tell him it was no big deal when he remembered what Richard had said. The rules here are different and words are important. "You are welcome, Sir Edwyn. I am just glad I could help."

"Jamie tells me you are acquainted with our prince. A friend, I understand. I am surprised he has never mentioned you. I have known the prince for many years. It is not like him to keep secrets from me. Where exactly is your home?"

I guess Jamie didn't tell him everything, Hal thought.

"He from an isle west of Lantus, Jamie quickly said. "Augustus introduced him to the prince. This is his first visit to Cent. He…"

"Come now, Jamie. I am no fool. Look at the man's clothing. The manner he administered to William. The color of his skin. He is not of Lantus. And nothing lies west of Lantus but the sea. Remember, my son was with you last year. He has told me of the prince's strange disappearance and return. And I have seen the storm. Sir Hal is not from some isle west of Lantus, or our world, I would suspect."

Hal smiled. "You're right. I am not from here. I'm surprised you guys accept all this otherworldly stuff so freely."

"And why not? It happened, did it not? So, how did you get here?" Edwyn asked. "I must warn you, Sir Hal, I do not believe in magic."

"To be honest, I don't know. The storm, or maybe something in it, brought me here. Just like it brought Henry to me last year."

"Why?" Edwyn asked.

"I have no idea."

"Perhaps you could show Sir Edwyn what our adversary looks like, Richard," Jamie said. "Take him into the valley and show him the bodies. Sir Hal and I have things we need to discuss."

"Father?" William said, sitting up. "What are you doing here?"

Clutching his son by the shoulders, Edwyn looked at him with tears in his eyes. "I am your relief."

"But you are not due till the marrow."

"You have been asleep for many hours, William. How do you feel?" Jamie asked.

"My back feels tight." He looked around. "Hours? What has happened?"

"You do not remember being attacked?" Jamie asked.

"Attacked? When? By whom?"

Richard spoke gently, like a father to his son. "It was the night before last, Master William. When you and Franklin went to ensure there were no wolves near the camp. You were injured."

"I… I do not remember. I…."

"Yes, lad?" Richard asked.

He shook his head. "I don't know. I don't remember going with Franklin. I thought I was still in camp. At the fire. That I had dozed off. But I have had such strange dreams. Something in the dark. Strange words being whispered."

"It's all right," Jamie said. "It will come to you."

William looked at Hal.

"This is Sir Hal. I believe he may have saved your life," Edwyn said.

"Sir Hal? The man from Prince Henry's story?"

"The same."

"I am glad to see you are feeling better. Any pain?" Hal asked.

"Pain? No. Just a stiffness in my back."

"It will come." Hal turned to Jamie. "Whatever they used to knock him out is still numbing the wound."

"Wound?" William asked.

"Just a nick," Richard said. "Nothing too bad. Just a few dozen stitches is all." William stared at him. "Stitches? A few dozen?"

"I would think whatever they used will wear off soon. I'll give him something for the pain when it does," Hal said.

Edwyn nodded. "That is kind of you, Sir Hal." He turned to Richard. "You were going to show me something?"

"'Tis in the valley. If you will follow me."

"I will go with you," William said.

"No, William. You stay with Sir Jamie. Richard and I will be fine on our own."

"But…"

"Stay with your knight, William," Edwyn said. He turned to his squire. "Peter, remain with him."

The boy nodded, and Edwyn turned and followed Richard.

"The storm?" William asked, concerned for his father as he watched them leave.

"Gone," Franklin said. "Strange happenings been going on, young master." He looked at Hal. "Unnatural things."

"You say they attacked Sir Jamie and Sir Hal?" Edwyn asked as he rode beside Richard.

"That they did. Had I not come along when I did, I am afraid one or both may have been slain. Came from the far side of the valley. From the trees, Sir Hal said."

"And they all had but four toes."

"They did. No shoes. Leather armor with pieces of metal sewed in. Helmets were leather, too. Dark hair and beards. Strange shape to their heads."

Richard pulled his horse to a halt, looking around in surprise.

"Here?" Edwyn asked. "Are you sure?"

Richard climbed from his mount and began searching the ground, pushing the grass around with his foot. "They were here, Sir Edwyn. More than a dozen of them." Spotting something in the grass, he reached down and picked it up.

"What is that?" Edwyn asked."

"One of them was an archer," Richard said, looking at the bow. "Sir Hal killed him with that strange weapon of his."

"Strange Weapon?"

"Sounds like thunder. Terrible thing."

He looked down the valley to the far side. "Someone took the bodies."

"Let me see that," Edwyn said pointing to the bow.

Richard handed it to him. It was nearly seven feet long. The grip was not centered as on a normal bow. The upper limb was almost half again what was normal.

"You are an archer, Richard. What kind of bow is this?"

"I know not, Sir Edwyn. I have never seen the likes. Seems a bit unwieldy."

Edwyn handed it back, then looked down the valley and up the banks on both sides.

"Mount up, Richard. I do not believe we are alone. Let us return to the others."

When they reached camp, Edwyn dismounted and handed the reins to his squire. "Have the men prepare to depart. We are leaving."

"Now, Sir Edwyn? We have just arrived. The men and horses are tired," Peter said.

Edwyn looked at the young man. "Tis better to be tired than dead, Peter. It is not safe here. Do as I say."

"Yes, my lord." Peter nodded and trotted away.

"Is something amiss, Edwyn?" Jamie asked.

"I believe our attackers may be on the move and heading in this direction."

"You saw them?" Jamie asked.

"Saw, no, felt, yes. And someone had removed the bodies from the valley. The only thing we found was that." He pointed at the bow Richard was holding.

Jamie looked at the older man, then turned to Franklin. "Anything we can't eat or fight with, leave. Get the horses ready."

Franklin gave a quick nod and rushed towards the picket line, where Sir Edwyn's men were preparing to leave. Hal walked towards them, wiping his hands on a rag. He looked at the commotion near the horses.

"Your men are going to be okay, Sir Edwyn. I cleaned their wounds and stitched those that needed it. Nothing serious."

"Thank you. Can they ride?"

"I don't see why not. Something going on I should know about?"

"The bodies in the valley are gone, and Sir Edwyn believes more of our foes are heading this way," Jamie said.

"Gone?"

"Someone removed them. The only thing we found was that." He pointed at the bow.

Surprised, Hal walked over to Richard, who had dismounted. "May I see that?" He asked, holding out his hand.

Richard handed it to him. Hal ran his fingers down the smooth wood.

"You recognize this?" Richard asked.

"Not sure. I know what it looks like. I just can't figure out how something like this could be here."

"Something like what?" Sir Jamie asked.

"This looks like a Kyūdōka Yumi."

"A what?" Richard asked.

"A yumi. A bow used by an archer from feudal Japan."

CHAPTER 10

DISCOVERED

"Horses," Philip said.

Henry picked up his sword belt and buckled it on. He took a few steps from the trees into the meadow. Philip stood beside him, his hand resting on the hilt of his sword.

"We have been here for more than a day and a half and have seen no one," Henry said without turning. "The road is being watched?"

"Of course, your majesty."

Several men stepped to either side of Henry, swords in their hands.

"Put your blades away. If these were foes approaching, we would have been warned."

A group of people appeared, leading their horses. One broke away from the others and ran to Henry, wrapping her small arms around his legs as she reached him. He kneeled and took her into his arms.

"Eleanor. Thank God you are safe."

The young girl looked up at him, her rust-colored hair spilling over her shoulders and onto her face. Henry brushed the hair from her eyes.

"Henry, what is happening? Sir Randel came to my chambers as I was preparing for bed and bid me to come with him. He said you had sent him. Two of his men tied poor Wilhelmina to a chair and told her it was for her own safety. Then they stuffed a dirty rag into her mouth. She was crying."

Henry looked up at Randel, who shrugged his shoulders. "She was making a lot of noise. I was afraid she would alert the guards. They were scrambling around the castle, searching for you."

Henry picked Eleanor up and kissed her forehead. "All will be well, little sister. I am sure no harm will befall your nursemaid. I was afraid you might be in danger, so I asked Sir Randel to find you and Edwenna and bring the two of you to me."

"From Father?"

"Well…"

Henry looked at Randel. "You did not tell her?"

"No. I thought it best to come from you."

"Henry, I am not a child. I know what Father is like and what that foul beast Duke Kennington has been telling him. That man is evil. A monster."

"I am sorry we frightened you. Father has… decided I pose a threat to him and the kingdom. He ordered me arrested and so I had to flee."

"You mean you were a threat to the duke," she said.

Henry chuckled. "When did you become so wise?"

"When you weren't looking. Which has been all too often of late."

Henry looked at Randel. "Edwenna?"

"She was not in her chambers. The castle was in an uproar looking for you, so I thought it best we leave with the little princess while we could. I am sorry, Henry."

"I understand, my old friend. It could not be helped. And thank you for bringing Eleanor to me."

"It was my honor, your highness."

Philip slapped his friend on the shoulder. "We now call him majesty."

Randel stared at Henry for a moment, then kneeled. "I am sorry, my king." He looked up and grinned. "And if I may say, it is about time." He stood and looked around. "This is all we have?"

"For the moment," Philip said. "I have sent messengers to our friends and hope they will join us soon."

Randel looked at Henry. "John did not take kindly to your departure. He will send men after you."

"I know, and I am sorry. I have placed you all in danger."

"Tis your father and Kennington that have done so, not you," Randell said.

Philip looked at the shadowy figures organizing the horses. "How many men did you bring?"

"I have my squire and twenty-three men-at-arms as well as ten archers."

"And your father?" Henry asked.

"I have sent a rider with a message explaining all. It will take time for him to call together his knights and their men. When he has, I am sure he will send help. I have also told those with families nearby to have them join us here. I do not believe they are safe."

"You think the Earl will defy my father?"

Randel smiled. "He will defy the Duke of Sandford. My father is no fool. He will figure out what is going on. And he is not fond of the duke."

"Your father is a good man and I wish him well," Henry said. "A wise decision about the families of your men."

"Where can they go where they will be safe? They can not stay with us. John will send men after us." Randel asked.

"They will go to Lantus. I will ask the emperor for sanctuary. They should be safe."

He looked down at Eleanor. "You will go with them. Tell Augustus what has happened. He will ensure your safety."

"I want to stay with you."

Henry kneeled and, taking her by the shoulders, spoke softly. "I need to know you are safe. I know you are brave, and I would be honored to have you fight at my side, but I need you to take care of our people in my absence. Those we are sending to Lantus. You will be my representative. When I can, I will send for you."

"You promise."

Smiling, Henry stood. "I promise."

Philip looked at the young girl. "And a promise made by a king is binding."

"What about Edwenna?" Eleanor asked.

"I will do all in my power to bring her to you," Henry said.

"Rider coming!" cried a voice from the trees.

They turned as a man drew his horse to a halt at the edge of the trees and lept from the saddle. He ran to Sir Randel.

"My lord."

"This is Mark, your majesty. I left him and five archers to watch the road." Randel said, then pointed at Henry. "Report to your king."

"King?"

"King Henry."

He looked at Henry, then dropped to one knee. "Sire, forgive me. I did not know."

"There is nothing to forgive. Now, rise and report," Henry said.

"Men come. Many men."

"How many?"

"I would guess close to a hundred, maybe more. It was hard to tell."

"Knights?"

"I saw four standards, sire. There were many horses. They are but a few miles behind and they are riding hard."

"Already," Philip said. "I would not think John able to organize a pursuit so quickly. Especially one of that size."

"Begging your pardon, Sir Philip. I do not believe they come from the king, ah, I mean King John. I recognized one of the standards. A rook pierced by an arrow."

"Ainsley. One of Duke Kennington's household knights," Philip said. "A nasty piece of work, that one."

"The rest of our men?" Randel asked.

"Right behind me, milord."

Henry turned to Philip. "Have the horses taken deep into the trees. Leave two men to watch them." He looked around. "Brian, tell James and William that I need them to assemble all the archers. Sir Randel has brought …"

"Ten."

He stopped and turned to the messenger, and smiled.

"Sixteen."

"Wait, have James do it. Tell William I wish to see him."

"As you wish, sire," Bruce-son-of-Bruce said, looking around for the other archers.

"Follow me," Mark said. "I will show you where they are.

"Do you think they will find us?" Philip asked. "I mean, we are some distance from the road. And it is getting dark."

"Many horses left the road," Henry said. "The ground is damp, and we have churned up the mud. There is still enough light. The path will be clear for any who look for it. They will come."

"They have many more men than we," Randel said. "Should we not flee?"

"Your horses are tired. We would not get far before they would catch us. I would rather fight them here than let them catch us in the open. We will use the trees to our advantage."

William Quick Arrow ran up and bowed. "You wished to see me, my king."

"William, take command of the archers. Bruce is assembling them as we speak. Set an ambush at the edge of the wood near the spot we left the road. The men coming are not our friends. If they leave the road, spring the ambush. I do not wish to lose anyone, so just a few flights then join us here."

Henry pointed to the trees at the end of the lea where he had sent the horses. "We will set up just inside the trees there. Place your archers on either side of the open ground and watch our flanks. But do not show yourselves. If they try to charge, take the lead horses. If any, try to enter the trees to flank us. Discourage them."

"Aye, sire."

"Remember, William, do not spring your ambush unless they leave the road. If it looks like they will ride past, do not expose yourselves. If they continue down the road, send word, but keep the rest concealed, in case they double back."

"I understand, your majesty."

"And William."

"My King?"

"Be careful. You are a valuable member of my household."

Glowing with pride, he bowed, then quickly ran off.

"That man would follow you into an arrow storm, naked and alone, if you asked him to," Randel said.

Henry strode toward the trees. "I hope he never has to. I have seen him without clothes.

"Okay, I want the men to gather at the edge of the trees facing the road. Have the squires bring spears. All we have."

"Your Majesty!"

Henry turned to see John running towards him while struggling with a heavy sack across his shoulder.

"Your mail, King Henry. And your helmet."

Henry smiled. "Thank you, but you are no longer my squire, Sir John. Have one of the men bring my shield and spears. Have you your mail with you?"

"I am afraid I did not have time to grab both. As it is, I was forced to leave your plate behind."

"You did well, thank you. You will stand behind me, John. Use a spear and stop those that try to take my shield. You will not stand in the front line. Not this time."

"But, sire, I am honor-bound to fight at your side."

"And you shall. But not today. Without mail, it would be suicide."

John stared at him for a moment, then nodded. "As you wish, my liege." He turned and trotted towards the chaos of men preparing for battle.

Philip whispered, "You believe there will be another time?"

"One can only hope."

Henry watched as the horses were led deeper into the trees and the men-at-arms lined up on either side, leaning their long-tapered shields against their knees. Many relieved themselves where they stood, while others emptied what remained in their water bags. Those with helmets pulled them on and fastened the chin straps. In their haste to leave, many stood without mail. Only Sir Randel's men-at-arms were all equipped with mail and helmet.

If we win this battle, we will strip the dead and take their mail, Henry thought. Or they will take ours. He looked at his small battle line. So few. He stepped forward and turned to the men, willing to give their lives for him. Do I deserve this degree of loyalty? I must never forget what these men do here today and spend my life proving that I am worthy of such sacrifice. And so too, to myself.

"Do not step from the wood line," he called out. "Make them come to us. If they have any sense, they will not face us on horseback in the trees, so I expect them to dismount. Work together in twos and threes. If they are foolish enough to remain mounted, attack from all sides with spears or pull them down and kill them. We will have no time to accept surrender. There will be no ransom. There can be no quarter. Our archers will do what they can to thin them out. Their knights may have plate, our arrows will do little damage. If that is so, leave them to those of us with mail. Remember, do not leave the safety of the trees even if they seem to be falling back."

He looked at the silent line of men. "It is my honor to stand here with you today. I could wish for no finer company."

As one, the men began banging their spears upon their shields. He stepped between Philip and Randel.

"We are all going to die, aren't we?" Philip said with a grimace.

Henry chuckled. "Probably. Shortest reign in history."

"You cannot stay here, Princess." Henry heard John say from behind him.

"Eleanor, go back with the horses," Henry said, turning. "If it looks as if we are about to fall, you must ride to Lantus and tell Augustus what has happened. Watch over our people.

"John, stay with her. Keep her safe."

"No, Henry. I will fight with you," she said.

He kneeled. "You are a courageous young woman, Eleanor, and I would be honored to have you by my side today. But it must not be. If I should fall, it will be up to you to carry on our fight."

"But, Henry," she sniffed away tears. "You cannot die. I need you."

He pulled her to him and hugged her. "I love you, little one. But I am your king and I command you to obey my orders. Now go."

An archer he did not know appeared out of the dark. "They have left the road. They come this way."

"John," Henry said. "I task you with the safety of the princess. Now take her to the horses."

John placed his hand on Eleanor's small shoulder, and she looked up at him.

"It is time to go, Princess."

She looked at Henry. "I love you, Henry. I will take care of our people. I promise." She straightened her back, turned, and strode back deeper into the trees. John followed.

Philip ran his hand across his nose. Henry looked at him and used the back of his hand to clear his eyes. He shook his head. "We are about to fight overwhelming odds where most of us will most likely die, and yet that little girl brings tears to your eyes."

"What tears?" Philip asked.

Bascom and Randolph, their young squires, both without mail, took their places beside their knights. Henry looked at Randel, who nodded.

"I believe it best if the two of you stand behind us," Henry said. "Be prepared to hand us a fresh spear if ours should break and watch that none grab our shields. I have no squire, so I am depending on you to serve the three of us."

The two young men reluctantly stepped behind them. Two of Randel's men-at-arms moved into their place.

The sound of frightened horses and screaming men broke the silence of the night.

"Seems William and James have introduced themselves," Randel said.

And then they were there. Two dozen riders walked into the open at the far side of the lea. Each man was armed with a lance and clad in mail, except for the knights. Three armored men with steel breastplates, pauldrons covering their shoulders, and greaves about their shins, mounted on destriers, the powerful warhorse which were clad in full bard.

"Those poor beasts must be exhausted. What kind of idiot uses a destrier for a pursuit? And in full bard," Randel said.

"A bit much, don't you think? Plate and horse armor," Philip said.

"Don't forget lances. It's like they think this is a tournament," Randel added.

"Works for us. Lances are too heavy to do them much good here," Henry said. "And they will be lucky if their mounts reach a gallop without dropping dead from exhaustion."

Henry called out to the men to either side. "Remember, do not leave the trees." He dropped his shield and stepped into the open.

"Henry!" Philip yelled. "What the hell are you doing?"

He started to follow but Randel grabbed his shoulder.

"He is buying the archers time to position themselves. And knowing our king, baiting the fools into a charge."

Henry walked ten paces from the trees and stopped. He stood with his hands on his hips and stared at the riders as they sat silently on their mounts, knee to knee, ready for a charge. The knight in the middle of the group moved a horse length forward and stopped. He raised the visor on his helm.

"I am here for Prince Henry," he said, his tone arrogant. "He is to be taken back to Cyneburg for trial on charges of treason."

"I am Henry."

"There need be no blood spilled today if you come with me of your own accord. These others may depart in peace. They are to simply lay down their arms and go."

"So, they can kill us without worrying about getting hurt," Philip said to Randel.

"On whose orders do you seek my arrest?" Henry demanded.

"King John and my master, the Duke of Sandford."

"So, that dog Kennington has made his move. It does seem strange, Sir Ainsley, for yes, I recognize you, that you should have such a force available to bring me back. And full plate armor. I mean, I was just accused less than two days ago. It is almost like you knew this was going to happen."

"Enough talk. Do you present yourself peacefully?"

Catching movement from the corner of his eye, Henry saw James Longbow's signal.

"Not today, Ainsley." He turned on his heel and strutted back to the trees.

"I only see three standards, Randel said. "Do you think the other knight is taking men to flank us?"

"If so, the archers will warn us. But I think not. He may be in command of the rest of Ainsley's men. Remember, they do not know how many we are. Perhaps they are being cautious."

"They are moving, sire," Randolph said as Henry returned to their line.

Henry looked up. Ainsley had rejoined the other riders who begin to walk their horses toward them.

"I think the idiot is planning to charge with that line alone," Randal said. "He isn't waiting for the rest of his men to clear the trees."

Henry smiled. "Good. Let us help him make the right decision."

He called out to the surrounding men. "Let them see you. Once they reach a gallop, hurry ten paces further into the forest. We will let them come to us. Let the trees break their line."

A single bang on shields signaled their understanding.

Knee-to-knee the horsemen brought their mounts to a trot and then a gallop. Their lances lowered as they aimed at their targets.

"Damn things are bouncing around like fishing poles," Philip said.

"What do we do about the knights?" Randel asked.

"Get them off their horses," Henry said. "Then kill them." He turned and yelled, "step back,"

The arrows began to fall, and so too, horses and men.

CHAPTER 11
TITLES COUNT

"Japan? What is Japan?" Jamie asked. "I do not know this word."

Hal stroked the upper limb of the bow. "I'm sorry. I'm letting my imagination run wild."

"Please share your thoughts, Sir Hal," Edwyn said.

"When I was a boy," Hal said after a moment. "I lived with my aunt in a place called Japan. Their people's history is filled with tales of skilled warriors called samurai. These ancient warriors were known to have used several uniquely designed weapons. My sword is such a weapon. Another was an eight-foot-long bow called a Nobi Yumi. It requires great skill to use properly. A skill I never attained. One of the unique aspects of the weapon was the location of the grip, below the centerline of the bow."

"This is a mighty tall bow," Richard said. "I would think the grip that low would make it unwieldy."

Hal smiled. "It was long. The arrows used with it were also long, the shaft being close to forty inches."

"You think what attacked us were these Japan people?" William asked. "From your world?"

Hal shook his head. "They were not Japanese. And they were not from my world. But the bow is remarkably similar."

"This is strange," Jamie said. "These things, I am reluctant to call them men, are not of either of our worlds and yet you say their weapons are of yours."

"I'm just saying the bow is similar. The swords are not."

"Well, whoever they are, they pose a threat," Edwyn said. "We should go. I would like to reach the village of Eldon before dark." He turned to his sergeant-of-arms. "Irwin, we ride out immediately. And I do not wish to ride into another ambush."

"I understand, Sir Edwyn. I will send riders ahead."

Franklin arrived leading three horses, two with saddles.

"Who is that for?" Edwyn asked, pointing at the sumpter, the saddleless horse used as a pack animal.

"It for Sir Hal, milord. It is the only extra horse we have."

"This is not seemly. Sir Hal cannot ride that," Edwyn said. He looked around and signaled to a boy securing the straps on another packhorse. "Bailey!"

The boy turned and, seeing Sir Edwyn, ran to him.

"My lord?"

"Sir Hal needs a horse. Bring him yours. Redistribute the supplies and take one of our sumpters."

The young boy's disappointment was obvious. "As you wish, your lordship."

"I don't need to take his horse," Hal said, watching the boy as he walked away.

"Nonsense," Edwyn said. "Bailey will not mind. He is a good lad. A little young. I bring him along to tend to the pack animals. His father, Ramsey, is one of my men-at-arms. Frisian raiders took his mother and sisters last year."

"Taken?"

"They take women and young girls. The boy has no other family and Ramsey asked that I bring Bailey with us. The lad works hard, and the men like him. Besides, the animal is too big for him. I am sure he will find the sumpter easier to ride. They are splendid horses. Unlike my friend Jamie, I only bring mounts that warriors can use."

"My lord." Bailey stood about ten feet back, holding the reins of a large gelding. Edwyn nodded toward Hal.

Slowly approaching, Bailey offered the leather leads to Hal, bowed his head, and whispered, "His name is Strongheart, sir. He will serve you well. Do not let him too near Sir Edwyn's stallion, however. They do not get along."

"Thank you, Bailey. I will remember, and I am sorry to be taking your horse."

"Oh, he is not mine. He belongs to his lordship. And he is a bit big for me right now. My father says I will grow into such a horse in a few years."

"I am sure you will." As Hal took the lead, he noticed a big man in a long chainmail shirt glancing up from checking the cinch of his saddle. His gaze focused on Hal."

"Your father?" he asked, nodding to the big man.

"Yes, sir. He is one of his lordship's men-at-arms. I hope to become such when I have grown. My Pa is going to teach me to wield a sword when I am strong enough. For now, I have this." He pulled a leather sling from his belt.

"I have seen the boy drop a pidgin in flight with that thing," Edwyn said. "Better than an archer."

Bailey straightened his back. "Thank you, Sir Edwyn."

"Now go along with you. Tell your father I wish to see him."

"Yes, your lordship." He ran towards the big man.

"A fine lad," Jamie said. "Reminds me a bit… I'm sorry Edwyn."

"He reminds me of Winslow as well. There is no need to apologize, Jamie. Perhaps the resemblance is why I agreed to take him with us."

"Winslow was my little brother," Edwyn explained, turning to Hal. "He was about two years Bailey's senior and my squire. He died three years ago in a skirmish with the Frisians."

"You wish to see me, Sir Edwyn?"

Bailey's father gave a quick bow. He was huge, a good six-two, and built like a professional linebacker. Hal guessed his age as late twenties, maybe early thirties. Ramsey's long dark hair tied with a leather thong in a ponytail trailing a good foot down his back. A scar ran the length of his face from his left eyebrow to his chin. Although he addressed Edwyn, he kept his eyes focused on Hal.

"I am gifting Bailey's mount to Sir Hal. I think it was a bit too much horse for a boy of but twelve summers."

"He will learn to master such a beast, your lordship, given time."

"I know he will, Ramsey, but I think the smaller horse will serve him better. At least for now."

Ramsey nodded.

"You have always served me well, Ramsey, as has your son," Edwyn continued glancing at Jamie, who gave a brief nod.

With a bit of hesitation, Ramsey responded, "Thank you, milord."

"I have a boon to ask. You may refuse, of course."

"A boon, Sir Edwyn?"

"Yes. Sir Hal saved the life of my son and I wish to reward him. I am considering releasing Bailey from my service and offering him the opportunity to serve as his squire if Sir Hal will have him. I know a boy of his age would normally begin his training for knighthood as a page…"

"Knighthood, milord?" Ramsey asked, surprised.

Edwyn smiled. "Yes, Ramsey. If Sir Hal wishes it. But I think it only fair I ask you as his father if you have any objections. He is, after all, still a boy."

Hal looked at Edwyn, dumbfounded.

"Will you accept young Bailey into your service if his father agrees?" Edwyn asked.

Before he could answer, Jamie said. "Of course he does."

Ramsey looked from Edwyn to Hal. "You would prepare him for knighthood, my lord?"

"I…" Hal started to say.

"Sir Hal is new to our ways, and it would be best if he had a man-at-arms to assist him in his squire's weapons training," Edwyn continued. "I was wondering if you would be inclined to pledge your oath to Sir Hal's service if I was to release you from mine. To help train your son and to be his sergeant-at-arms, to recruit and train men for his service and advise him in the ways of war."

"And until Sir Hal is settled with lands and income, I will provide for your pay," Sir Jamie added.

Hal's head spun from one man to the other, trying to keep up with what was happening.

Ramsey looked at Edwyn. "You would do this for him, milord."

Edwyn placed his hand on Ramsey's shoulder. "I would do this for you both. This is a posting I could not offer you for many years to come. No matter how deserving you may be."

Ramsey lowered his head. "Thank you." He looked at Hal. "You would have us, milord?"

Not knowing what to say Hal simply nodded.

Edwyn smiled. "Then it is settled. I release you from my service, Ramsey of Wairdell."

Ramsey turned and, drawing his sword, took a knee and offered it to Hal hilt first. Hal looked at Edwyn.

"Take the sword and ask him if he swears his fealty to you and your household."

Hal took the sword. He looked down at Ramsey. "Do I have your," he hesitated, thinking of the best word to use, "oath to serve me and those of my household?"

"I, Ramsey of Wairdell pledge …" He looked at Sir Edwyn.

Sir Jamie said, "Sir Hal of Deecee."

Ramsey bowed his head. "That I will give faithful service to Sir Hal of Deecee and all of his household. That I will never knowingly cause him harm and will serve in good faith and without deceit. I so swear."

He looked up and stared at Hal. "And I have never been forsworn."

Be careful what you wish for, Hal thought.

Jamie pointed to the sword. "Hand it back to him and accept his oath."

Hal handed the sword back. "I, Hal of," he did his best not to smile, "Deecee, accept you, Ramsey of Wairdell, into my service." He looked at Jamie to see if he had said the right words.

Jamie nodded, and Ramsey regained his feet, returning his sword to its scabbard.

"Now, with Sir Hal's permission, I think you should ask Bailey if he will accept the offer of becoming his squire."

Ramsey looked at Hal, who nodded.

As he turned to leave, Edwyn spoke louder than was necessary. "Sir Hal, I grant you the horse from my stables that the man Ramsey, who is no longer in my service, rode here today, and a sumpter for your squire in appreciation of what you have done for my family."

Without turning, Ramsey smiled and walked a little straighter to tell his son how their fortunes had changed. When he was far enough away, Hal turned to Edwyn.

"What the hell?"

"I owed you a debt. You are alone and without the means to hire men or purchase horses. You do not know our ways. You have no squire. And you are the prince's friend, as are we. I am a wealthy man and would be honored if you would accept my gifts as thanks for saving my son's life."

"I don't think I actually saved his life."

"I believe you did," Jamie said. "And until you can support yourself, I will provide funds until you have the means to support yourself." He chuckled. "Not my money, of course. My father's."

"I don't know what to say."

"Say you accept," Edwyn said.

Hal looked from one man to the other. "Thank you. But how do I earn the money to repay you?"

Edwyn smiled. "I'm sure the prince will think of something."

"I don't know the first thing about how to train a squire."

Jamie chuckled. "I will ask William to help prepare young Bailey."

"And Peter will help as well," Edwyn added.

"My lord," Bailey said, standing a discrete distance away. "My father says you wish me to serve as your squire." His nervousness was palpable. "Is this so?"

"Is this something you would be willing to do?" Hal asked.

Bailey dropped to his knees. He placed his hands on Hal's boots. "Thank you, my lord. My life and my sword are yours."

Hal reached down and pulled the boy to his feet. "Then, Bailey of Wardell, I accept you as my squire."

"You cannot swear on your sword when you have none. Draw a blade from my supplies," Edwyn said. "Ramsey, perhaps you should help him select one of a size that will suit him."

They looked at Hal.

"I think it best you do as Sir Edwyn suggests. I will speak with you both later."

"As you wish, my lord," Ramsey said. They bowed, and Ramsey placed his arm around his son as they walked away.

"I will never get used to being called that."

Edwyn laughed. "You will. But remember, there is a lot of responsibility that comes with the title."

"I know. I have had soldiers under my command before."

Richard stood nearby quietly and waited until Jamie acknowledged him.

"Yes, Richard?"

"All is ready, Sir Jamie."

"Have the men mount. We ride out immediately. I wish to reach Eldon before dark."

Richard turned and yelled to the waiting men. "Mount up."

"Until you have land of your own," Edwyn said." It would be best if asked you say you are one of Prince Henry's household knights. I do not believe anyone will have heard of Deecee"

"Land of my own would imply I will stay," Hal said.

Edwyn smiled. "You have a way to go home?"

Hal smiled. "Good point." He looked at Strongheart, waiting patiently.

"I never asked," Jamie said, noticing his gaze. "Do you know how to ride?"

"Saddles' a little different, but yeah, I think I can handle it."

He mounted and gently dug his heels into the side of the horse, who responded immediately."

Jamie looked at Edwyn. "We need to get him a pair of spurs."

Edwyn shook his head. "And some proper clothing."

Strongheart walked along the cobblestones of the road in an easy gait much to Hal's relief. The temperature was moderately warm and the humidity low. The sun glared through the nearly cloudless sky while birds flew overhead, calling to one another.

Oaks and pines, elms, and birch trees paralleled the highway with little underbrush reminding him of a manicured park. The grasses and flowers resembled those found on any country road on Earth. The birds that flew overhead were larks and starlings. It was peaceful and beautiful. But Hal reminded himself, this was not Earth. This was Tera and the land they traveled, Glenlock. How? A parallel world? Another dimension?

"Sir Hal?"

His reverie broken, Hal turned to the speaker. "Yes?"

Jamie looked at him with concern. "Are you well?"

"Sorry, I was lost in thought. Looking around, I realize how similar everything is to Earth."

"Earth," Edwyn asked.

"The world I come from. The trees, the grass, everything looks the same. He looked up as a hawk circled above, gliding on the currents of warm air. And yet I know I'm not home."

"Does this distress you?" Jamie asked. "Leaving your home?"

"It should. I mean, my sister and her family are there. My friends. My job. But I'm not. And I don't know why."

"Maybe you were meant to be here," Edwyn said. "It may have been destiny that you and Prince Henry met. That the storm took the prince to your world so you would follow him to ours."

"A rider approaches," Richard called out. Those behind urged their mounts forward, forming a line in front of the knights. Hal smiled when he saw William and Peter work their horses next to their knights, ready to defend them. And beside him, Bailey, his father taking a position in front of him, both ready to fight for their lord.

Back home he would be playing video games and riding a skateboard not holding a sword ready to fight, and possibly die. *For me.*

"It's Reid," Ramsey said.

The scout drew his sweat-covered horse to a halt and, catching his breath, blurted out, "It is gone!"

"What is gone?" Edwyn demanded."

"The village, milord. Eldon. Burned to the ground."

"And the villagers?"

"Dead."

"Everyone?" Jamie asked.

"I think so," the rider said. "At least all the men and women."

"And the children?"

"A few, milord. Older children. Found a boy near the village with an arrow in his back. He was maybe twelve. As for those in the village, best I could tell, none younger than him." He took a deep breath. "The bodies were mutilated. Most of the men had been beheaded."

Edwyn turned to Peter. "Spear."

Peter and William turned to retrieve spears from a bundle tied to one of the sumpters. Bailey turned his horse to follow, but Hal stopped him.

"Thank you, Bailey, but I don't need one."

Edwyn looked at him. "Are you sure?"

"Not sure it would do me any good. Used nothing like that from horseback." He laughed. "Not a skill required where I come from."

Jamie noticed Hal pull the pistol from the holster and check it. "He does not need one, Edwyn. Trust me."

Edwyn looked at the strange device in Hal's hand. Turning his attention back to matters at hand, he gripped the spear Peter handed him.

"Quickly. We ride to Eldon."

CHAPTER 12

Edwenna

John lept from the throne, almost falling down the single step to the stone floor. His tangled and greasy hair hung down in his glassy, unfocused eyes. He brushed the hair aside and squinted. "What do you mean, he is gone? Gone where?"

Colby dropped to his knee. "Escaped, your majesty. The watch on the curtain wall reported seeing riders outside the postern gate. They believe one may have been the prince."

"How could you let this happen!" he screamed. "You incompetent fool. I should have you beheaded."

"He must have had help, sire."

"Of course, he had help, you idiot!"

"Your Majesty," the Duke of Sanford said soothingly while stepping to his side. "This may well be fortuitous."

John looked at him, madness in his eyes. He shook his head and focused. "How so?"

"That Prince Henry fled the capital proves you were right in ordering his arrest. Why flee if not guilty?"

John was quiet for a moment, then climbed back to the throne. He picked up the goblet sitting on the arm and emptied it. He threw the cup, nearly striking his sergeant.

"Bring him back, Colby. Alive. His accomplices as well. Let him stand before me and explain his actions."

"Allow me, sire," Kennington said. "I have men standing by already."

"And why would you have men standing by?" the king asked accusingly.

"To prepare for my departure home, your majesty. The road to Sanford is long and can be treacherous."

John glared at him. "Then bring him back, Kennington." He pointed an unsteady hand at him, his finger quivering. "Nothing is to happen to my son, you understand. He is not to be harmed."

"I understand, sire." Bowing, the duke backed up three steps, then turned and hastened toward the door. As he passed Colby, he whispered, "Come with me."

The duke led Colby far enough away that the guards could not overhear them and grabbed him by the arm, pinning him against the wall. "You damned fool. How did this happen?"

"I don't know, your lordship. Everything had been arranged. My man was waiting with the poison."

"I think it was Sir Philip that helped him escape. He was in the room when I went for the prince."

"Too late now. Find Princess Edwenna. Bring her to me."

"Here?"

"No, you idiot. To my chamber. I don't want her speaking to the king right now. And don't tell her about Henry. I will send for my son. Once they are wed, no one will be able to stop me."

"And me, your lordship?"

"I am a man of my word, Colby. A knighthood and lands will be yours once my son sits upon the throne. Now go."

Nodding, Colby turned toward the south tower and Princess Edwenna's chambers. As soon as he left, Kennington signaled a man waiting in the shadows.

"Prince Henry has escaped. Find him."

"Yes, my lord."

"And Ainsley,"

"Your Lordship?"

"No one comes back. Do I make myself clear?"

The man smiled. "You do, my lord Duke."

They did not see the man that slipped from the dark recess of a doorway and headed for the stables.

Colby banged on the locked door. "Your Highness, your father wishes you attend him in the throne room."

"Go away, Colby," Edwenna called. "Tell my father that you could not find me."

"I cannot do that, Princess. I must insist."

"Insist all you want, but I will not come with you."

"Princess, please open the door or you will force me to break it in."

"You wouldn't dare! Now, go away!"

Colby threw his shoulder into the door only to rebound painfully as the thick oak failed to yield. He spat on the floor and, rubbing his shoulder, trudged his way down the hallway until he reached a guard.

"Get an ax. And be quick about it."

The guard ran down the corridor, returning with a large battle-ax. Colby led him to the princess's door and stepped back.

"Knock it down."

"But..." the guard said. "This is the princesse's chamber."

"King's orders. Now get that door open."

Edwenna backed to the wall. She looked around, terrified.

"Henry, where are you? I need you," she pleaded.

Stepping back as the door quivered from the first blow of the ax, Edwenna grabbed a small knife she had used to peel fruit and waited, tears streaming down her face, her hands shaking, her heart threatening to burst from her breast.

The ax finally broke through the thick wood and Colby reached in and lifted the latch. He pushed the door open while ordering the guard to return to his post, then stepped into the room.

"I am sorry, Princess, but you must come with me."

"Stay away, Colby." She lifted the knife, holding it before her with both hands. "I will not go."

Colby moved a step closer.

"Put the blade down, your highness. I will not hurt you."

"I'm warning you, Colby. Stay back." She swiped the knife back and forth, catching him on the forearm as he stepped forward.

Jumping back, he grabbed the wound.

"You bitch!"

"I'm sorry, Colby. I didn't mean to hurt you," she said, dropping the knife.

"Sorry!" Without thinking, he swung his arm up, striking the young girl in the face with the back of his hand. She stepped back and tripped, striking her head on the stone wall as she fell.

Colby rushed to her.

"I'm sorry, Princess. I didn't mean to strike you. You just surprised me.

"Princess?"

He kneeled next to her and stared at her unmoving form.

"Princess. Are you alright?"

He attempted to lift her head, then stumbled back when he felt the blood on his hand.

"No! No, no, no, no. Get up. Please, get up."

He crawled back to her and checked to see if she was breathing. Realizing she was dead, he picked her up. As he cradled her lifeless body in his arms, he looked around.

"What do I do? What do I do?"

He placed the limp form on the bed, then rushed to the door. Ensuring no one had seen what had happened, he pushed the damaged door closed. Picking up the small knife, he wiped the blood from the blade and placed it on the table next to the bed.

Trying to control his panic, Colby looked around until he spied the blood on the floor.

"Shite.

"Clean it up. Oh, God. Clean it up."

He looked about the room.

"With what, damnit?"

Colby looked at the body and reaching behind his back drew a long thin knife, then cut a piece of her gown. Getting on his knees, he scrubbed the blood from the floor, then his hands. He lay the soiled rag on her chest.

Turning quickly at the sound of voices coming from the corridors, he placed his hand on the hilt of his sword and stepped to the door. He held his breath until the sound faded.

I can't leave her here.

The body lay atop the blood-soaked coverlet. Noticing the cord that held the tapestry in place above the headboard of the bed, he grabbed them and cut two long lengths. Then he rolled her in the soiled blanket and tied it at both ends with the cord.

Opening the door, Colby checked the hallway. He sighed in relief.

Empty.

Rushing back to the bed, he lifted the body and tossed it over his shoulder. Checking once again that the hallway remained clear, he quickly carried his burden to Henry's chamber and dropped the young girl's body on the bed. Closing the door behind him, he hurried to tell the duke what had transpired.

"What!" Kennington demanded, trying not to scream.

"It was an accident, your lordship. She had a knife and…"

"And she should have gutted you, you fool." He took a deep breath. "Where is the body?"

"In the prince's chamber."

Kennington thought for a moment.

"That's good. No one will think to look for her there." Kennington stood silent for a moment. "No, wait. Take the body to the dungeon and put it in a cell. Lock the door. And cover that arm. Find Princess Eleanor and bring her to me when you are done.

"What do I tell the king?"

"Tell him you couldn't find her. You think she may be with her brother."

Colby nodded and rushed away.

A tall man wearing the robes of a healer stepped forward

"What now, your lordship?"

"That bloody fool almost ruined everything." He took a deep breath. "Thank God John has two daughters. All is not lost."

Osborn Kennington, Duke of Sandford, father of the future spouse of the queen of Cent, looked down at the king's physician.

"I believe it is time the king reaches the final stage of his illness."

CHAPTER 13

THE BLOODY MEADOW

Arrows glided unseen through the night sky, raining silent death upon the unsuspecting horsemen. Dozens of the narrow shafts bounced off steel plate, mail, and helmets or embedded themselves in shields, causing little to no damage. But not all. Some found purchase in flesh, for there was no armor on all but the three horses ridden by the knights.

Injured and dying animals fell on their riders, crushing or trapping them beneath their great bulk. Three horsemen died after being struck by the flying feet of panicked animals. Two more were thrown when their terrified mounts began to buck to escape the pain of the arrows embedded in their flanks.

The three enemy knights continued forward unscathed, outpacing their men.

"Stop them!" Henry cried. He rushed forward as the three riders' advance was halted at the edge of the trees, their confused and frightened horses refusing to proceed into the shadows that moved before them. Several of Henry's men rushed forward and, reaching the startled knights, pulled them from their saddles. Spears found purchase in the openings between cuirass and helm. Spikes were driven through chainmail while swords dealt death through the open slits of visors.

"Back to the trees!" Henry shouted.

His men stepped back into the shadows of the forest and waited.

The warriors of the new king allowed the enemy to enter the trees and then, working in groups of twos and threes, drove their spears into the attackers who could not defend themselves from the deadly shafts striking from multiple directions. It was over quickly. The dead and dying littered the floor of the forest, the grass and leaves soaked with blood.

They rescued the eight horses from the carnage and led them away. Those too injured were quickly relieved of their misery.

Pulling his bloodied sword free of a downed foe, Philip looked at the activity taking place at the other end of the lea.

"It seems they have learned the folly of a mounted attack."

"And that there are more of us than they expected," Randel added, cleaning his blade with a handful of grass. "They will be more cautious next time."

Henry wiped his blade on the tunic of a fallen knight, the black stag's head on his shield identifying him as a warrior of Sanford.

Henry turned to his friend. "Randel, see how we have fared."

"Aye, Majesty." The tall man disappeared into the shadows of the forest.

"What now?" Philip asked.

"That is up to them." Henry nodded toward the activity across the blood-stained meadow. Men moved about in the shadows of the trees, avoiding the open ground.

It surprised Henry when Randel rejoined them so fast.

"What is the butcher's bill?"

Randel smiled. "All stand."

"We lost no one?"

"Not one."

"And the attackers?"

Another pause as Randel scanned the carnage that lie around them. "Lord Ainsley alone survived. His exhausted horse stumbled and fell before reaching the trees. I believe it broke a foreleg. Ainsley lay trapped beneath, unable to free himself. Bascom stayed the hand of your man, Bruce, as he was about to slit the bastard's throat."

"Will he live?" Henry asked.

"Maybe. His injuries are severe. We had to pull him from beneath his horse. Beautiful animal. A shame. Bruce put it out of its misery.

"Ainsley's legs are badly broken," he continued. "One of his greaves was driven up into his thigh nearly severing his right leg. He is lucky Bascom reached him when he did, or he would have bled to death. If he lives, I have my doubts he will ever walk again. He may yet lose the leg."

"Bind him and have Bascom take him to the rear. Tell him I wish Sir John to see to his wounds. Have him searched; I do not trust that man."

"They come again, your majesty," Philip cried out.

"Someone with some sense has taken command. They come behind a shield wall," Randolph said. "Our archers will do us little good, I am afraid."

Henry smiled. "I do not believe you respect the skill of our archers, young Randolph. Their shields are not like those of Lantus infantry or the kites carried by our men. They are heaters, good on a horse but too short to provide adequate protection in a wall. If they raise their shields to protect their heads and torsos, they expose their legs and feet. If they lower them to protect their legs, then they will leave openings near their heads and shoulders."

"That is not much of a target. And there is little light, sire," the young squire said.

"It will be enough. Trust me." Henry turned to Randel. "Ensure all of our men have returned to the trees. Make clear they are to remain in the confines of the forest. Our only chance is to draw them in."

Henry watched as the enemy worked their way across the open ground in three groups of thirty men each. The center marched several paces ahead of the others, their shields locked tight.

"Fools think we will come out and meet them in open combat, allowing their center to strike while the flank formations encircle us," Henry said. "Whoever commands has learned his craft from tournaments and books, not war."

As the enemy reached the middle of the glen, the arrows fell, and the screams began. Men fell; openings appeared in the shield wall as more arrows found purchase. The formations faltered.

Three of Randel's men stepped from the shelter of the trees, screaming insults and challenges, one preparing to drop his britches and show them his bare posterior.

"Stay back!" Henry yelled. "Do as I say. Let them come to us. They cannot maintain the wall once they reach the trees."

The men disappeared back into the shadows.

"On my command, every man takes five paces back," Henry called out. "We will draw them deeper into the forest. Stay in your groups. I do not want us fighting ourselves."

The enemy had almost reached the edge of the trees when the arrows stopped falling. The survivors of the outer formations gravitated toward the center.

"Now!" Henry yelled.

Henry fell back, hoping the others had done so as well. As he did, he felt rather than saw someone approach from behind. He raised his sword and turned.

"Stay your hand, my king. Tis I, James Longbow."

"That stealth of yours almost cost you your life, James," Henry said, lowering his sword.

"Forgive me, sire. William wanted me to tell you the archers have fallen back. They stand ready between you and the horses with blades in hand."

"Have them choose their targets carefully. I do not need them slitting the throats of our own. And remind them they do not have shields or armor. I do not want to lose a bowman because he got too excited."

James chuckled. "You won't. They know their business."

"I know they do, James. That was an excellent piece of work on their flanks."

"Thank you, sire. I will tell the others."

With a rustle of leaves, the archer was gone.

And now we wait, Henry thought. He did not have to wait long. A cry to his right announced the arrival of the enemy.

The clang of steel and the crash of shields reverberated and echoed in the close quarters of the forest as the two groups of warriors, all men of Cent, once brothers in arms, did their best to kill one another. The fury of the battle intensified as the reminder of the foe entered the dark confines of the forest. Although less in number, the forces of the new king now had the advantage.

The sounds of combat, the screams of wounded and dying men. The smell of blood, vomit, and excrement filled the night air as the battle continued all around him. Henry gripped his shield, and braced himself, drawing his right foot back, preparing for the impact he knew would come. He waited.

Dark silhouettes moved to either side, blind to the presence of the king. As one came close, Henry struck, driving the point of his blade into his enemy's side. Feeling several links of mail give way, he pushed harder. The man screamed as the last of the links separated and the blade was driven deep into his body. Henry twisted before pulling it back, feeling the steel grate against ribs as the sword broke free. Catching movement out of the corner of his eye, he dropped to a knee and threw up the bloodied blade just in time to block the downward swing of a sword.

Pushing the steel blade aside, Henry rose quickly, driving his shield up under the helmet of his opponent. It struck with such force he felt the jaw shatter and heard the neck snap.

From behind, a blade rode across the mail below his raised shield, nearly severing his thick leather sword belt. Dropping his shield arm, Henry pivoted and jammed the brass crosspiece of his sword into his attacker's helmet, causing the chin strap to snap and the helmet to twist, blinding his opponent and breaking his nose. Grabbing his off-balanced foe by the chin and yanking the head back, Henry dragged the razor-sharp blade of his sword across the exposed neck. He stepped back quickly to avoid the blood as it pumped the man's life away.

"Philip! Randel!" he cried. "To me!"

"I'm here, Majesty," Randel said, stepping to his side.

"Philip!"

"Right here." He threw his shield down. "Strap broke. Damned thing is useless." He reached down and recovered the smaller shield dropped from the man Henry had just dispatched. "Not much, but better than nothing."

"Back-to-back, my friends. Let us wait for them to come to us," Henry said.

Time and again they blocked, slashed, and drove their blades and shields at and into the shadowy figures that stepped from the darkness. Their hours of training together allowed them to move as one.

The sounds of combat continued all around. Henry was concerned that the enemy had broken through. That they had reached the horses. That they had found Eleanor. Then suddenly it all stopped. No clang of steel, no shouts of challenge. Nothing, nothing except the cries of wounded and dying men pleading and moaning...for help...for family...for death.

"Are they gone?" Philip asked, gasping.

"I doubt it," Henry said. "Catching their breaths, most likely."

"And looking for us," Randel added.

John picked Eleanor up and sat her on a horse as the sounds of fighting grew closer. "Get ready to run."

"Not without you," she said.

"I will follow."

"John!" she screamed. "Behind you!"

He turned, drawing his sword as three men broke from the trees.

"Ride, Princess. Go to Lantus. Tell Augustus what has happened."

"But John…"

He slapped the horse, which reared, almost throwing Eleanor before leaping to a gallop. She turned in time to see John fall.

"We cannot survive much longer," Randel said, bending over to regain his breath.

The sound of a man screaming made the king turn. "They are all around us.," Henry gasped. "Philip, tell John it is time to leave. Stay with them. Protect Eleanor."

"I will tell John, but then I come back. If we are to die tonight, I will do so with my friend, my king."

Henry did not see as Philip was struck as he worked his way back to the rear. From the darkness, a war hammer flew, striking him in the side. Philip dropped to his knees. With his remaining strength, he tried to call out. To warn the others. But no sound escaped his lips as blackness overtook him.

"I hear nothing," Randel said.

"They are out there," Henry whispered. The snap of a twig warned him that someone approached from behind. He turned and raised his shield in time to stop the ten-pound hammer from crushing his skull, forcing him to his knee. His shield arm went numb from the power of the blow and, unable to maintain his grip, it slipped from his arm. He lifted his sword to defend himself, but no attack came.

William Quick Arrow, a bloody seax resting easily in his hand, stood over a nearly decapitated body. He nodded to his king. "Sneaky bastard. Seen him come up from behind, milord. Should have got here sooner. Sorry."

Henry regained his feet and smiled. "Thank you, William."

A horn sounded.

"What now?" Henry asked.

Several dark figures ran past them towards the meadow. "They are falling back, sire," William said. "The horn was a recall."

"What the hell is going on?" Randel asked. "They had us?"

"Who sounded the horn?" William asked.

"I don't know," Henry said, looking towards the open ground.

"Listen," Randel turned and took a few steps towards the edge of the trees. "There is fighting in the meadow."

"Another attack?" William asked.

"I don't think so," Henry said as he worked his way to the end of the trees. He stepped into the open and stopped, unable to believe what he was seeing.

Twenty mounted men rode around the fleeing warriors, cutting them down as they ran. It was over in moments. Those not already dead threw down their weapons and kneeled in defeat.

The circle closed. One man raised his hand and dropped it swiftly and the riders cut down those that remained. They gave no quarter. Two riders dropped from their mounts. They moved about and slit the throats of any found still breathing.

Henry moved towards the horsemen. To stop the carnage if he could. The survivors of his small force gathered around him.

The mounted warriors stood silent, watching the approaching men, their bloodied spears facing down, showing they did not intend to fight. The meadow was still, the only sound coming from the horses, as they panted and snorted, one or two pawing the bloodied ground.

A rider dropped from his mount and strode towards them with empty hands spread wide. When he was three paces from Henry, he removed his helmet and dropped to a knee.

"Prince Henry. I am sorry I did not arrive sooner."

"Sir Ealdwine, you are Duke Kennington's man, are you not?" Henry asked. "One of his household knights? I have seen you at Sandford."

Ealdwine rose. "I was your highness. But no more. He is a traitor to the crown. To Cent. He is a man without honor, and I can follow him no longer."

"Explain," Henry said roughly.

"I overheard Ainsley tell his squire that the king ordered you returned to him unharmed. But the duke did not want that to happen. He wanted you dead along with all your companions.

"When we discovered where you had abandoned the road, I held my men back. I told Ainsworth we would watch to ensure no man escaped. When we heard the fighting, I urged my men to hurry, but as you know, the forest is thick and it slowed our movement. I am sorry we did not arrive sooner."

"They are all dead?" Henry asked, nodding towards the field.

Ealdwine tilted his head as if he should not need to explain.

"It was necessary, your highness."

Henry was quiet for a minute while he studied the knight that stood before him. He turned to Randel questionably.

"He is right. Our only hope of survival is to avoid John's people. It is unfortunate, but it is an ugly truth. They were Kennington's men. We could not take the chance any would return and report our location. Not now. We are too few. I would have done the same."

Henry turned his attention back to Ealdwine.

"The men that stand with me today no longer serve King John. They have declared me their sovereign. I am at war with my father. Do you understand?"

Ealdwine smiled. He took a knee. When his men saw what was happening, they dismounted and did the same.

"That is welcome news, your majesty."

Henry turned as James Longbow skidded to a stop before him. Doing his best to speak while catching his breath, he said. "You need to come quickly. It is Sir Philip."

CHAPTER 14

ELDON

Smoke curled into the fading light, casting a shadow of despair over the small village of Eldon. Crows and other carrion gorged themselves on the bloated bodies that littered what once was the village square. In the distance, the howl of wolves brought tremors of fear to the exhausted horses.

Three lone riders picked their way through the piles of debris and death, scattering the scavengers as they moved until reaching the village center.

"I don't understand."

"What is it you do not understand?" Jamie asked.

Hal looked around. "Where are the rest of the kids? The youngest. They had to have had some."

Edwyn stared down at the mutilated body of a young woman. "That is what the others are trying to determine." He sighed. "But I do not believe they will find any answers."

"Raiders, you think?" Jamie asked.

"Southlanders dislike venturing this far from their boats. And Frisians would have taken the women. No, this was someone else."

He dismounted and squatted beside the body he had been studying, shooing the flies away. Pulling a dagger from his belt, he moved a piece of torn clothing.

"I do not believe they violated her."

He stood and surveyed the surrounding area. "They dragged brush to cover their tracks." He put his knife away. "But they missed this." He pointed to a partial footprint under the clothing he had moved. "No boots. Four toes."

"Do you think they are following us?" Jamie asked.

"I don't think so," Edwyn said. "This happened hours ago. Probably this morning."

"It must be another group," Hal said. "If they are afoot, I can't see how they could have got ahead of us."

"I agree," Edwyn said.

He remounted. "I think it wise we move back to that knoll for the night." He pointed to a high hill overlooking the village. "We have a better chance of defending ourselves there. Besides, I would rather not stay the night here."

"What about the bodies?" Jamie asked, looking at the villagers.

"They can wait until morning," Edwyn said. "It will be dark soon. We need to get settled before we lose the light."

Jamie whistled and pointed to the hill.

Richard nodded, then signaled that the search party should follow him.

Franklin stopped his horse a few feet in front of Jamie. "Richard says to tell you we have found nothing but trampled grass. The sheep, livestock, even the dogs are gone."

"Thank you," Jamie said. "Seek a stream and fill the water bags. I do not trust the water in the well. Have the archers find us something to eat. A deer would be nice. But they are not to travel far. I want them to remain within earshot. And tell them to conserve their arrows."

"Have the rest of the men collect firewood," Edwyn added. "Enough for several fires to last the night. But hurry. I want everyone on the hill before we lose the light."

Franklin nodded and rode to catch up with Richard.

"Enough light to prevent a stealthy attack?" Jamie asked.

"And to provide fagots to be tossed, providing light in which to fight."

"Cold rations, I am afraid," Jamie said, offering an oatcake to Hal. "The archers were unsuccessful. Even the rabbits seem to have fled."

Hal shook his head. "Thanks, but I have something." He pulled an MRE (meal ready to eat) from his pack and, tearing it open, set out its contents. Edwyn and Jamie watched, fascinated, as he poured a little water into the pouch and leaned it against a rock.

"Activates the heater," he explained.

"Heater?" Jamie asked.

"Yeah. Chemical heater. Warms it up. Cold chili is okay, but warm is better."

Edwyn moved closer. "You have this chili in that little bag? And the water somehow heats it? Without a fire?"

Hal realized this must seem like magic to them. He remembered a quote by Arthur C. Clarke. Something like advanced technology is indistinguishable from magic.

"The heat comes from a chemical reaction. Something like what happens when you add a pigment to water to make paint."

"I see," Edwyn said.

Hal knew he didn't but couldn't think of another way to explain it. He opened the crackers, broke one in half, and squeezed a little peanut butter on each piece. He offered one to each. Jamie took a tiny bite. He looked up, surprised.

"What is this?"

"It's called peanut butter. A staple in my life, that, and a little grape jelly. PB and J, basic food for a bachelor. And of course, coffee."

"These names are strange, but this butter is magnificent," Edwyn said, stuffing the rest of the cracker into his mouth. He reached for a water bag. "This peanut butter sticks to the roof of your mouth."

Hal laughed. "Yes, it does." He lay the back of his fingers on the plastic bag, leaning against the rock. "Almost ready." Picking up another bag, he ripped it open with his teeth and pulled out the plastic spoon. Noticing Jamie staring at it, he offered it for him to examine.

"It's made of plastic."

"So smooth, this plastic. It is not metal or wood. Of what is it made?"

Hal shrugged his shoulders. "Not sure."

Not sure I could explain how it is made.

Jamie offered it to Edwyn, who ran his fingers down it and then handed it back.

"Your world sounds like a wondrous place."

"It has its perks, I guess."

Picking up the bag of chili, he blew on the spoon and tasted it.

"Warm enough. Want to try it?"

Jamie took the spoon and carefully tasted the chili. Making a strange face, he offered it to Edwyn, who shook his head no.

"It is… very…spicey," Jamie said.

Hal laughed. "You should try some real Texas chili. Now that is some spicey stuff. He opened a tiny bottle of hot sauce and poured the contents into the chili.

The two men watched Hal eat while they chewed on dried mutton and oatcakes.

"May I ask you a personal question?" Edwyn asked.

Picking up his canteen and washing down the last of his meal, Hal smiled. "Not too personal, I hope."

"No," he said, returning the smile. "It is about your name."

"My name?"

"Hal. It means something?"

"No. Just a nickname. My full name is Harold James Bennet. But I always use Hal. It's what my dad called me."

Jamie stood and stretched his back.

"I believe Harold is a nobler name. It is a name fit for a knight. And it suits you."

"I agree with Jamie," Edwyn said. "Hal is a name for close friends and family."

Hal put the residue of his meal into the plastic bag and stuck it into a side pouch of the ruck. Habits. Never leave your trash for the enemy to find.

He watched as the shadows of the fire danced on the faces of his companions. He realized how serious they were about his name. He thought about what Richard had said. Titles count here.

"You think I should?"

"Sir Harold is a name one would expect of a knight," Edwyn said. "It may help to forestall questions."

When in Rome.

"Then Harold it is."

Edwyn smiled. "A name change is good; a wardrobe change would be even better."

Hal looked at his pants. He had to admit he leaned more toward functionality than style. A lot of it military issue. Fashion was never his forte, but they were right. He stuck out like a rube in an opera house. He pointed to the pistol and Katana. "And these?"

"I can explain the sword," Jamie said. "Somehow. The other... well, that I will admit could be a problem."

Edwyn looked at the gun.

"What exactly does that do?"

"It launches a projectile that kills people." He said as he picked it up and turned it in his hands. "No, people use it to kill people."

"Sir Hal?" Bailey and his father stood in the shadows of the flickering light, waiting to be recognized.

"Yes? Step closer. I can't see you."

Bailey stepped forward.

"William says that I should ensure your sword has a good edge and is clean. I should see if you require fresh clothing and prepare your bedroll. I have fed and brushed down Strongheart, and..."

Ramsey placed his hand on his son's shoulder.

"We are sorry for disturbing you, Sir Hal. The other squires are teaching Master Bailey what is expected of him as your squire."

"You are not disturbing me." He looked at Bailey and could see the boy was full of nerves. He smiled. "Thank you, Bailey. I will take care of my...bedroll tonight, and my sword is fine. It holds an edge well. Thank you for taking care of the horse. Have you two eaten?"

"We have," Ramsey said. "Is there anything we can do for you before we turn in?"

"No, thank you. I'm good."

Ramsey bowed.

"I will check with Richard and see what time my watch is. If you will excuse me, Sir Hal."

"It is best to use your master's proper name, Ramsey," Edwyn said. "It is Sir Harold."

Ramsey looked at Hal, then nodded.

"As you wish."

He turned and walked toward a distant fire. Bailey remained.

"Aren't you going with your father?"

"I am your squire, sir. My place is with you."

William and Randolph walked up to stand with him.

"Bailey is correct," Randolph said, placing his hand on the boy's shoulder. "A squire has to be the knight's shadows." He turned to Edwyn. "All is settled for the night, my lord. Horses have been brushed down and fed. I have put an edge on your sword, and your mail is clean and oiled."

"I have done the same, Sir Jamie," William said.

"How do you feel?" Hal asked.

"My back is a little sore, but I am well, sir."

"Do you need something for the pain?"

"I am fine, Sir Hal. I mean, Sir Harold. Thank you for asking." He turned to Jamie. "Is there anything else I can do for you?"

"No, thank you." He looked at Hal and Edwyn.

"We are good," Edwyn said. "Get some rest, all of you. It is going to be a long day tomorrow."

Edwyn rose and stretched his back.

"I think I will walk the perimeter and then seek my bedroll."

"Just a minute," Hal said. "I'll come with you." He reached into his rucksack and withdrew a small bag. Picked up his pistol and stuffed it into the back of his pants.

"Okay, let's go."

Jamie pointed at the bag.

"What is that?"

Hal smiled.

"A surprise. A bit of Deecee magic. Come, I'll show you."

The three men walked quietly around the perimeter of the camp, saying little except for the occasional hello to the warriors they passed on sentry duty. When they reached the edge of the hill overlooking the road, Hal stopped and opened the bag. He removed a pair of night-vision goggles and turned them on to the starlight setting. He offered them to Jamie.

"Take a look."

Jamie placed the binoculars to his eyes and took in a deep breath.

"This is truly magic, Hal. It almost turns night into day."

He handed them to Edwyn.

"You are truly a sorcerer, Sir Harold," Edwyn said before handing the NVG to Hal. He turned on the infrared setting and handed them back. As Edwyn looked down at a small copse of trees at the base of the hill, he dropped them from his eyes and whispered, "Daemons."

"What? Where?" Hal asked, taking the device.

"There," Sir Edwyn said, pointing to the trees. "There are beings in the trees that glow."

"In e trees was the heat signature of several men. Sweeping the base of the hill, he suddenly pushed Edwyn to the ground, reached behind his back, and quickly brought the pistol up.

Crack! Crack!

A body flew back and rolled down the hill.

"They're here!

CHAPTER 15

Lost Children

"Where is he?" Henry demanded.

"This way," James Longbow said, leading him carefully over the bodies of fallen warriors.

Henry whispered to Randel, "Stay here. Watch Ealdwine."

Randel nodded. Ealdwine started to follow. Randel grabbed his arm.

"The king needs time with his friend. They are like brothers and if Philip does not live, it is not seemly to witness the king's grief."

Ealdwine looked at his arm and then at Randel. He did not remove it.

"I understand."

Randolph kneeled next to Philip, loosening the mantel from his shoulders and removing his mail hood. He looked up when the king arrived

"He breathes, sire. It is shallow but steady."

"Thank, God. What wound has he suffered?"

"Yonder lies a hammer. I believe that was used to strike him."

"His head?"

"His helmet is intact. I fear it might be his back."

Philip's eyes fluttered, and he hissed, "It's my damn ribs, boy. Bastard broke my ribs."

"Randolph, see if Sir Ealdwine has a healer with him. If he does, bring him," Henry said. "Quickly."

"Hard to breathe," Philip gasped.

"Then shut up," Henry said in relief. "For once in your life, stop talking."

"You're enjoying this, aren't you?"

"Watching you suffer? No, Philip, I am not. Telling you to stop talking and having you listen to me. Yes, that I am enjoying. Wait until I tell Edwenna that a time finally came when you could not utter a word."

"You are a cruel man," Philip whispered and coughed. He cried out in pain.

"Let me through."

Henry looked up at the man who had spoken. He was a thin man, near middle age, with a shaved head and face, wearing a dark robe.

"You are a healer?"

"I am."

"You are the duke's man?"

"I was in the duke's employ. I am not under oath sworn to any. You are the prince?"

"He is the king," Randolph corrected.

The healer looked from Randolph to Henry, then bowed his head.

"I am Humphrey, your majesty."

"This is Sir Philip. He is the son of Baron Irwin Mercier of Tilden and my dear friend. I believe he may have sustained a broken rib. Maybe two. Please see if you can help him."

"And if there is nothing I can do?"

"Then you may go on your way in peace with my thanks for trying."

Humphrey stared at him for a moment, nodded, then set down his wooden box of medicines. He withdrew a hollowed cow's horn and placed it on Philips's chest.

"His heart is strong, and his lungs are clear. That is good." He turned to Randolph and pointed to the skirt of Philip's hauberk. "Help me lift his mail."

Randolph gently lifted the heavy metal shirt until Humphrey could get his hand under it. He probed and when Philip groaned, withdrew his hand, and nodded to Randolph.

"I was right. There are at least two broken ribs. Others may be cracked; it is hard to tell while he lay here. Those that are broken feel aligned and if we do not jostle him too badly, they may remain that way until I can properly bind them. But we must be careful. If a rib should move, it may puncture a lung. What struck him?"

GLENLOCK

"We think that." Henry pointed to the hammer laying near the nearly headless warrior.

"Then he's lucky the bones were not crushed. If that had happened, there would have been nothing I could have done." Humphry turned to Randolph. "We need to get your master on his feet and remove his mail."

"I will help," Henry said, kneeling next to his friend.

"It must be done carefully. You cannot pull on his arms. Place your hands behind his shoulders and his waist. Stand him. Do not lift him. Do you understand?"

Both men nodded and, as Randolph slid his hands under Philip's waist, Henry did the same to his shoulders. Humphrey placed his hands on Philip's knees and locked them in place.

"Now, keeping his body ridged, lift him to his feet."

Philip groaned as they pushed, but did not cry out.

"We must remove his mail," Humphrey said.

"How?" Randolph asked.

"If you hold him still, I will separate enough links to allow it to slide off," James Longbow said. He reached into his belt and removed a long, thin spike. "Good enough to shove through the mail. It should allow me to pry a few links free."

"Do it, James," Henry said.

"My mail," Philip said. "It cost me a fortune."

"It can be repaired in Tilden," Henry said. "Now shut up."

James pried the links of the mail until one side, from neck to sleeve end was free. Randolph pulled it to the side until the heavy shirt slid to the ground.

Humphrey examined the ribs again, then looked at Randolph and nodded to his bag.

"There is a roll of linen in the box. Get it and hand it to me."

Randolph retrieved the linen, and Humphrey wrapped it tightly around Philip's torso. When finished, he looked at Henry.

"That is the best I can do. It will take time to heal. He will not be able to lift a shield or sword for some time, and riding could prove quite uncomfortable."

"I thank you, Master Humphrey," Henry said. "please see to the rest of the wounded?"

"Of course."

"And if it so pleases you, we can discuss your future employment."

"It would be my pleasure … your majesty."

"James, please escort Master Humphrey."

James turned to the healer.

"Follow me."

Before they could leave, Henry touched James's shoulder.

"How many wounded have we, James?"

"Few, sire."

"And our dead?"

James hesitated.

"Many more."

Henry nodded and James left with Humphrey in his wake.

Philip watched as they faded into the dark forest. He turned to Henry and smiled.

"I was wrong. We live."

"A few of us anyway," Henry said.

"You know that if that man decides not to work with us, he cannot be allowed to return to Kennington."

"I know, Philip. We cross that bridge when we come to it."

"Where is the king?" A voice cried out from the darkness. "I must find the king."

"Over here, Sir John," Henry said.

John staggered as he worked his way to the king.

Seeing that the young man was injured, Henry asked with concern, "How fair you, John?"

"I shall live, Majesty. But Eleanor is gone."

"Gone? What do you mean, gone? I told you to watch her."

"I did, sire. I mean, I was until three of Kennington's men broke from the trees and ran toward us. Thinking the enemy had broken our lines, I threw the princess onto a horse and slapped it so she could flee.

"I slew two before the third struck me. I fell, but so did he. I got back up. He did not."

"And Eleanor?"

"The horse was heading west when last I saw her. I am sorry, my king. I have let you down."

Henry lay his hand on his former squire's shoulder and lay his forehead on his.

"You saved her life at nearly the cost of your own. You have not let me down, John."

Seeing the blood seeping through his fingers while he held his side, Henry asked.

"How badly are you injured?"

"I felt his blade grate a rib. Painful, but I will live."

"Go find James Longbow. He has a healer with him. He is somewhere in that direction. Can you make it there on your own?"

"I can. But Eleanor, your majesty."

"I will find her. Now go."

Henry turned to one of Randel's archers.

"Go to the meadow. Find Sir Randel. Have him meet me at the horses. Tell him to hurry."

The man nodded and ran towards the field.

"Randolph, help Sir Philip."

"You are going after her?" Philip asked.

"I am."

"I will go too."

"No, you will not. You need to wait here. When the families arrive, head towards Tilden. Stay away from the road."

He looked at Randolph.

"I hold you responsible for your knight. Keep him from doing anything stupid."

"I understand, your majesty," Randolph said, taking Philip's arm and leading him to the field holding the horses.

"Sire."

Randel nodded. Sir Ealdwine stood at his side.

"Eleanor has fled thinking us lost. She might travel to Lantus. We must find her before someone else does."

"I wish to help, Majesty," Sir Ealdwine said.

Henry looked at him for a moment and then at Randel, who nodded.

"We could use his help."

"Then get your horse."

As Henry settled in the saddle to wait for Ealdwine, he felt a tug on his trouser leg. William Quick Arrow looked up at him.

"Allow me to assemble a party to ride with you, sire. You should not go alone. You will need a scout."

"I appreciate your concern, William, but I will not be alone. I will have Sir Randel and Sir Ealdwine with me. The trail we follow should not require a scout. I need you to stay with Sir John and Sir Philip. Help organize what remains of our men. Tend to our wounded. Make sure Sir Ainsworth remains under guard. Have Humphry look at his wounds. I will wish to speak to him later.

"And watch for your families. We need them safe."

He turned to Ealdwine.

"You have a squire?"

"Yes. I instructed him to help Humphry."

"His name?"

"Kenneth."

"His family?"

"My sister's son."

"William. Find Master Kenneth. Tell him his master is with me and that he is to take control of Sir Ealdwine's men. They are to provide security for you and your families when they arrive. Take them to Tilden. I shall meet you there."

"Wait," Ealdwine said. He turned to Henry. "Kenneth is but a boy of fourteen summers. My sergeant would be a better choice"

Henry nodded.

Ealdwine signaled a man waiting with a group of his men.

"Abernathy, stay here and help keep these people safe."

"Aye, Sir Ealdwine."

"And let Kenneth know he is in charge."

Abernathy smiled.

"Of course, milord."

He turned and signaled that the others should follow him as he stepped back into the trees.

Ealdwine looked at Henry, who smiled understandingly.

GLENLOCK

"Excuse me," Henry said when he saw John. Around his waist was a bloodied bandage. He walked his horse over to him and, leaning down, He whispered, "I need you to stay here, John. Keep an eye on our new friends."

John glanced at Ealdwine.

"I understand."

"Sir Ealdwine, do you wish a fresh mount?" Henry called out as he walked his mount back.

"There is no need, King Henry." He patted the horse on the neck. "Daemon is a sturdy beast. He has many miles left in him before he tires."

"Then let us go. Lantus lies to the northwest and Tilden west. I know my sister. She will seek help in Tilden." He looked up. "There are no clouds. She will use the movement of the moon to guide her, so we ride west. She cannot be too far ahead."

"The sun will rise soon," Randel said. "Her horse will be tired. It should not be hard for us to catch her."

"I have never met the young princess," Ealdwine said. "But I have been told she has her father's strength and her mother's wisdom."

"She is a special person," Henry agreed.

"We cannot follow her tracks in the dark," Ealdwine said.

Henry nodded.

"I know. But it will be light soon. The forest ends in but a few miles and then there is nothing but open fields between here and Tilden. She should be easy to find once the sun is up."

"And if anyone is looking for us, we too will be easy to find," Randell said.

Henry looked at him.

"Then we best hurry."

By the time they reached the edge of the forest, the hint of dawn bathed the open fields in broken beams of light. A layer of fog floated low, casting pockets of dark shadow above the wheat and barley fields.

"It will burn off soon," Randel said, looking up. "It will be a clear day. We will find her, sire. Do not worry."

Henry dismounted and, leading his horse, scoured the ground looking for some sign that Elanor had come this way.

"We need to find where she left the trees."

Ealdwine leaned down and slowly walked Daemon while searching for the disturbed turf that would show a horse had recently passed.

The sun broke free of the horizon, casting its warmth into the fog and it began to lift.

Ealdwine dropped from his horse.

"Fresh manure."

Henry and Randel rushed to him. Henry dismounted and kneeled to examine the steam rising from the pile of manure. He ran his fingers across the dirt and smiled as he touched the light imprint of a small, booted foot.

"It's her. Well done, Sir Ealdwine."

Standing in his stirrups, Ealdwine looked out onto the waving stalks of grain, ready to be harvested.

"I do not see her."

"She is afoot. She cannot be far," Henry said and mounted. "We should spread out, but not so far that we cannot see one other."

Randel called out, "Eleanor!"

Henry turned to him.

"No! Do not call. We don't know who might be nearby. Others that may seek mischief."

"I am sorry, sire."

"There is nothing to be sorry for, my friend. This is a new world we find ourselves in. Where those who were once friends yesterday may now be enemies. We must be cautious."

Randel glanced at Ealdwine.

"I understand."

Henry saw smoke rising from where he knew a group of local farmers had settled.

"The people will soon come to their fields."

"Surely they pose no threat," Randel said. "There has been little time for word to reach them about what has happened at the capital. Perhaps Eleanor sought shelter with them."

"Perhaps," Henry said. "This land belongs to Baron Mercier, Jamie's father. The last stronghold between Cent and Lantus. His people are prosperous and content. Mercier is a good landlord. They know me here. If she sought shelter, they would not refuse."

GLENLOCK

Henry looked again at the smoke. Something was not right. He turned to Randel and saw that he too, was staring at the smoke.

"I do not like this," Henry said. "There is too much smoke."

A scream echoed from the field ahead of them.

"Eleanor?" Randel asked.

"I don't know. But we are going to find out." Henry drew his sword and urged his mount into the tall stalks of grain.

As they entered the field, something grabbed Randel's leg and pulled him from his saddle.

"Henry!"

The king turned his head to see what was wrong when he felt a blade rake across his mail, nearly knocking him from the saddle. Pulling his horse around quickly, he drove the huge animal into his attacker, knocking him to the ground. As the spearman tried to regain his feet, Henry leaned down and took his head.

More attackers appeared.

Ealdwine pulled on the reins and Daemon reared. As he came down, he drove his hoofs into the skull of another of the ambushers, crushing it like a melon.

Henry saw that Randel was unhorsed, and defending himself from three attackers, blocking their spear thrusts with his sword and armored gauntlet.

Urging his horse to action, the king rushed between two of those confronting his friend, knocking them aside.

Randel well used the distraction and slashed his blade into the shoulder of one, then turned quickly and removed the head from one of those Henry had knocked to the ground.

Dropping from the saddle, Henry raised his sword and hacked the arm from the other as he tried to regain his feet. Behind him, a figure raised his sword. Ealdwine rode the man down, then turned and allowed Daemon to crush him.

Henry looked around for more attackers. Seeing none, he ran to Randel.

"Are you hurt?"

"Just bruised. Landed on my shoulder. I'm fine." He looked at the bodies. "Who are these men?"

Ealdwine dismounted and dropped his reins. He rolled one of the dead men over. He moved the head from side to side with his foot, then looked at his feet. He walked over to the one Daemon had crushed.

"They have but four toes," he said.

Henry walked over and stared at the dead man's feet.

"Some kind of abnormality of birth?"

"I do not believe so. They all seem to have the same oddity," Ealdwine said. "And look at their heads. I have seen nothing like them before."

"What kind of man is this?" Randel asked.

The scream again. Henry rushed to his horse and leaped into the saddle.

"Eleanor!" he screamed while driving his spurs into the flanks of the horse.

Sir Ealdwine overtook the king and raced ahead. He drew Daemon to a sliding stop, almost striking a young boy that ran in front of the horse. In pursuit was another of the strange men. With a nudge of his knee, Daemon turned, and Ealdwine swung his blade, driving it from shoulder to chest into the man.

Henry came into a clearing of crushed wheat and dropped from his moving horse, driving his blade into the back of another of the strange man who was dragging a young girl by her yellow hair.

"Behind you!" the girl screamed.

Henry turned in time to block a spear thrust that near-opened his cheek. He backhanded his blade up and struck the man's leather cuirass, pushing him back but causing no actual harm. Quickly drawing a fourteen-inch dagger from the back of his belt, Henry faced his opponent with a sword and knife. Two more of the strange men stepped from the tall grain, each with a long spear. They suddenly turned and ran.

Ealdwine broke through the grass and shouted.

"I have them. They will not escape." He galloped after the fleeing men.

"Sire?"

Henry turned to see Randel step into the opening. He cradled a tiny body in his arms.

"An infant. I found her lying at the edge of the clearing."

"Does she live?" Henry asked.

Randel was silent for a moment.

"No."

The blond girl jumped to her feet and rushed to a group of children that stepped into the open. Two girls, maybe four summers, were being consoled by a boy slightly older as they held one another, tears flowing down dirty cheeks.

Four more children between the ages of five and nine dropped to their knees and stared at him, terrified. Henry walked towards them. The boy leaned back, holding the crying girls tighter.

Putting his weapons away, he dropped to one knee.

"I will not harm you. You are safe now." He looked around. "Are any of you injured?"

No answer, just the shaking of heads.

"Can anyone tell me what happened? Where are your parents?"

"Those things attacked them," came a voice from behind him.

"Eleanor!"

She walked towards him, a small child on her back, arms tightly wrapped around her neck. She lowered the boy, who ran to the others.

Eleanor fell into his outstretched arms. He hugged her tightly, then held her at arm's length and looked her up and down.

"I am uninjured, Henry."

He almost melted as she trembled, and a small tear appeared in her eye. He pulled her close and whispered, "I am here. You are safe."

Doing her best not to weep, she leaned her face close to his ear and stuttered.

"We...we are not. There are others."

Henry looked at the dead that lay scattered on the crushed grain.

"Like them?"

"Yes. There are many more. These stayed behind to watch us. I do not know where the others went or why they kept us alive. All the adults and any child over ten summers they slew."

"Thank God you were not one of them."

Henry reached for his sword at the sound of an approaching horse. Ealdwine dropped from the saddle as Daemon came to a halt.

"I dispatched two more, your majesty, but one got away. I did not follow, as I saw many men riding in this direction. I do not believe they saw me. It looks like they were heading towards the village."

"Stand where you are! You move and you die," commanded a voice from the field.

"I guess someone did see you," Randel said.

Henry lowered his blade when he saw stepping from the wheat, a dozen archers, they stood ready with arrows notched.

"Your Highness?"

Seeing a friendly face, Henry sighed with relief.

"Sir Marlowe. It is good to see you. Is your father with you?"

The tall knight nodded.

"He is your highness. He is on his way to the steading to check on the folks there.

"We saw movement in the field, and he sent me to investigate. We did not expect to find you here, my lord."

"I am sure you did not."

Marlowe looked at the children.

"What has happened?"

"I don't know." Henry looked at Eleanor. "But I intend to find out."

CHAPTER 16

DAEMONS

Hal jammed the night vision goggles into the cargo pocket of his pants.

"I'll stay here. Get the others."

A sudden shadow manifested itself behind Jamie. Hal pulled the pistol up and fired. The specter disappeared.

Edwyn stared at the gun, stunned. Jamie grabbed his arm.

"Come, we need to rouse the camp."

"I am sure the sound of that thing has alerted all," Edwin said, staring at Hal.

Someone from the camp called out, "What was that?"

"To arms, we are under attack," Jamie yelled, running back towards the fire. Edwyn followed.

Hal heard footsteps behind him and raised the automatic. He lowered it as he recognized the two men trotting toward him. Ramsey came to his side and raised his shield, keeping close to Hal.

"I brought your sword, Sir Harold," Bailey said, offering the sheathed Katana. In his right hand, he carried the naked blade of a short sword.

"Thank you, Bailey." He shoved the scabbard through his belt.

"Is it them?" Ramsey asked. "The one's from the valley?"

"I believe so." He reached into his pocket and withdrew the goggles. "I should have brought the headband." He scanned the slope down to its base. Three bodies lay a few yards downhill and were cooling rapidly. He could see nothing else on the hill. Switching to IR he searched the trees below.

"Damn, there's more of them huddled in the trees. At least another dozen."

"Are you a sorcerer, milord?" Ramsey asked. "That little box told you how many of those things are out there? Does it speak to you?"

Hal chuckled.

"No, Ramsey. Nor do I know magic outside of a few card tricks.

"Yes, the little box let me know how many are out there. It doesn't speak, but it allows me to see in the dark. Here."

He handed the NVG to Ramsey. "Look through this at the trees below. What do you see?"

Ramsey looked, then pulled the NVG from his eyes, looked again, then handed them back.

"Glowing daemons, milord."

Hal was amazed at how calm he was. He started to hand them to Bailey.

"No, Sir Harold. I beg you," Ramsey said.

"It is not magic, Ramsey. And those are not demons. It won't hurt Bailey."

"As you say, milord. But please do not have the boy look."

Hal stared at him a moment, then nodded.

"Have they moved?" Jamie asked, as he joined them. Richard and Franklin followed their lord, each with a flaming torch. Richard carried his bow.

"No. The sound of my gun may have scared them off. They are below in the trees."

Richard chuckled. "They are not the only ones concerned by that sound. Like to shite myself."

"Yeah, sorry about that. It is kinda loud."

"My ears are still ringing.," Jamie said. "But I thank you for saving my life."

"You would have done the same for me. Where's Edwyn?"

"Getting his sword and checking the other side of the hill."

An arrow thumped into the ground near Jamie's foot.

"Back up. Put those torches out!" Hal said.

"Shields!" Jamie yelled for the camp to hear. "Night arrows!"

"Night arrows?" Hal asked.

"Arrows fired in the dark. You cannot see them until they strike," Ramsey offered while holding his shield above Hal's head. "We need to get you a shield, Sir Harold. You and Master Bailey both." He tried to hand Hal his. "Take this."

"Better for us both if you keep it."

"As you wish."

Hal pushed the pistol into his belt.

Should have brought a sound suppressor.

Using the NVG he surveyed the area below until he spotted the archer standing with an arrow ready just at the edge of the trees.

"I'll be right back." He turned and ran back to his pack. Recovering the headband, he attached the NVGs. Then he pulled a knife and a black nylon holster from the bag. He clipped the holster to his belt and shoved the pistol into it. He rushed back to the others.

"I'm going to take out the archer." He pulled the sword from his belt and handed it to Bailey.

"I will go with you, Sir Harold," Bailey said.

"No," Ramsey said, gently placing his hand on his son's shoulder. "You are not ready. You would put Sir Harold at risk. I will go."

"There is no need, Ramsey."

"You may have your magic, Sir Harold, but only a fool goes after an enemy alone. I will watch your back. Begging your pardon, sir."

"Do you have a knife?"

"Yes, milord." He withdrew an anelace from behind his back, the long-tapered dagger looking more like a small sword than a knife.

Hal smiled.

"I guess you do." Reaching down, he attached the scabbard of the Camillus knife to his lower leg with two OD green straps.

"It was my grandfather's," he explained, seeing Ramsey watching him. "He used it in a war fought a long time ago. I kept it to remember him. Don't know why I brought it."

Jamie nodded.

"Maybe for the same reason you brought your swords."

Hal looked at the Katana and smiled.

"Curiouser and curiouser, Alice said."

"What was that, Sir Harold?"

He smiled. "Nothing, Bailey." He handed him his sword. "Hold on to that for me. I may need it later."

He pulled the NVG down over his eyes and flicked it on.

"Let's go."

The two men carefully worked their way down the hill. Hal split his attention between the archer, who lobbed a few more arrows into their camp, and the group hunched together in the trees. The figures in the woods started to move.

I guess the conference is over.

The archer let loose another shaft.

"He's the diversion so the others can get around the back of the hill," Hal whispered to Ramsey. "The bowman can wait. Follow me. I want to get ahead of the others."

Hal jogged along the edge of the trees, away from the archer. When he felt he had gone far enough, he entered the woods until he came upon a deer trail.

So that's what they are following. Good.

He signaled Ramsey, pointing to the trail. The big man nodded, and they melted into the brush where the path made a sharp bend.

"Stay here," Hal whispered. He crawled forward to the edge of the trail and then pushed the goggles up. Reaching down, he withdrew the knife and worked at calming his breathing.

It was not long before he heard whispering. As the first of the enemy passed, he began to count.

One, two, three… four… five. When he reached thirteen, he carefully worked his way to the trail and stalked his first victim. Just before reaching the bend in the trail, the man turned towards him, and Hal struck, driving the thin blade up below the ear and into the brain, twisting the blade before pulling it back. Carefully lowering the body, he listened to see if they had heard him. Nothing.

Ramsey watched until Hal had lowered the limp body before he made his way to the trail.

Three more times, Hal struck without being noticed. As he lowered his latest victim to the ground, he heard voices and froze. Someone whispered what he assumed was a name. He slid the knife back into its scabbard and reached for the automatic.

Ten rounds left. I should have brought a spare magazine. You're slipping, Hal.

He flicked the safety off and carefully pulled the hammer to the rear. A dark figure appeared around the curve in the trail and shouted.

"Shin'nyū-sha! Shin'nyū-sha!"

Surprised at the words, Hal hesitated and almost died as the man jabbed a large knife at his face, scoring a line across his cheek. He pushed the arm aside and slammed the pistol into the knifeman's temple. Ramsey rushed forward and drew his blade across the man's throat as he fell to his knees, stunned.

Hal nodded his thanks. He stood in the middle of the path and waited. He did not have to wait long.

As the first figure appeared, Hal pulled the trigger. He continued to fire. The enemy fell one after another to the crack of the pistol until the slide locked to the rear. Two of the enemy remained standing, staring at their fallen comrades in shock. Then the nearest man looked up and snarled.

Hal dropped the pistol and reached for his knife as the man charged, swinging a large sword over his head. Turning to avoid the descending blade, he spun around and ran his knife across his opponent's eye.

Screaming, the man dropped his sword, reaching with both hands for his face. Hal kicked him to the ground just as the second man lunged at him. Stepping back to avoid the blade, he tripped.

Smiling in triumph, the man raised his sword but before he could strike Ramsey threw himself into him, his knife held in both hands, driving it deep into his chest.

Hal rushed to the man whose eye he had slashed. He looked at him. The man held one hand over his eye while blood and fluid dripped down his cheek.

"Who are you?" Hal asked, holding his knife at the man's throat.

Suddenly reaching with both hands, the wounded man grabbed Hal's knife and pulled the blade deep into his own throat. Surprised, Hal jumped back to avoid the fountain of blood as it pumped from the severed artery. He watched dumbfounded until the hands slipped lifelessly to the ground.

"Why did he do that?" Ramsey asked.

"Because he did not want to be questioned."

"What was he trying to hide?"

"A good question. And thanks, by the way.

"Didn't I tell you to wait?"

"You did not tell me how long I was to wait, Sir Harold."

Hal chuckled.

"I want you to continue to selectively obey my orders. If they are stupid. Do what you think is best."

"As you wish, milord," Ramsey said with a smile.

"You are a remarkable warrior, Sir Harold. And that weapon that sounds like thunder is terrifying. I would like to know how it kills."

"I will explain. But another time. We need to find that archer."

What one of the strange men said troubled Hal as they worked their way down the trail. It wasn't possible. Not here.

"Is something troubling you?" Ramsey asked.

"Just letting my imagination run wild."

"It is my experience, Sir Harold. When your imagination speaks to you, it is often wise to listen to what it says."

"I thought I heard something that cannot be. A language that should not be found here."

"I do not understand. Language is language, Sir Harold. All speak Glenlockian."

"That's what troubles me."

CHAPTER 17

TILDEN

Henry lifted Eleanor onto his horse.

"That is the last of them, your majesty," Ealdwine said, lifting a pair of young girls onto his saddle.

"Where did you leave your mounts, Sir Marlowe?" Henry asked.

"Not far from here..." he looked at the other knights. "Majesty."

Henry slapped the big man on the shoulder. "Sticks to the tongue, does it not?"

"It is just, well, it is a bit confusing."

"I am the same person I was when you used to torment Jamie and me as children."

"You have not been that boy for many summers."

"When we reach your father, I will explain all. Until then, Prince Henry will do. Or Henry."

Marlowe smiled. "As you wish ... Prince Henry."

Henry looked at the bodies on the ground. "Have you any idea who these people are or why they attacked the village?"

"I do not. Nor can I explain their odd feet or misshapen heads. I believe they are human, but of a race, I am not familiar with" He looked at the children seated on the horses. "And I would like to know what their plans are for the children."

"As would I." Henry turned to Randel. "Sir Randel."

"Yes, My King?"

"I want you and Sir Ealdwine to take the children to the village. I am going to walk with Sir Marlowe. I shall meet you there. Tell the Baron all that has happened since we have entered his lands. But let me explain the rest."

Understanding what he was not to say, Randel nodded.

"Sir Marlowe, would you mind allowing a few of your men to accompany them? Elenore says there are more of these things about."

"Of course, your…"

"Highness, Marlowe," Henry said with an understanding smile. "Just a prince until we see your father. It is he that will decide if you should call me other than that."

"Thank you." He turned to one of the archers.

"Robert, take three men and escort these knights to my father. And be alert. There may be more of these men about."

The man knuckled his forehead in salute.

"Robert is a good man. He will make sure they arrive safely."

"Thank you," Henry said.

"You say they attacked you as you left the forest? May I ask why you are here? And why you did not follow the road?" Marlowe asked.

"I was looking for my sister. Her horse spooked last night and ran off with her."

Marlowe knew there was more to the story, but did not feel it was his place to pursue the issue. He assumed the prince kept his counsel for good reason. It would be best to let his father work it out.

"How did you see the smoke from the stead?" Henry asked. "The castle of Tilden is many miles distant."

"A messenger arrived yesterday reporting several Southlander longboats being discovered just this side of the land bridge to Lantus. They found the boats burned and there was no sign of raiders. If there had been bodies, they were gone. I sent a party to investigate. We had worked our way inland when we saw the smoke."

Nine figures lay still, listening as their quarry approached. Their leader rose to signal it was time to spring the ambush when suddenly he was struck. He cried out as six-inch razor-sharp claws tore him apart, his head crushed in powerful jaws, sporting two enormous canines.

"Maggie!" Henry called out.

The cat moved at a speed that allowed her next two victims no time to react before she tore into them.

Henry drew his sword and rushed into the carnage started by the enormous cat. Before Marlowe's archers could react, it was over. Marlowe stood beside Henry, his bloodied sword at the ready. At their feet lie three more of the strange men.

"Maggie, enough!" Henry cried as the cat continued to savage one of the would-be ambushers. She dropped the body, looked at him, then strode gracefully over and ran her head against his side. Henry stuck his sword into the ground and took her by the ears, laying his head on hers.

"I knew you would find me. Thank you, my friend."

The sound of the purr coming from the massive feline was more like the roar of a great beast than a contented cat. Henry pushed her away and Maggie dropped to her belly. She began cleaning herself, licking the gore from her paws.

"So, this is Maggie. The great long-tooth of Prince Henry," Marlowe said. "I have heard Jamie speak of her."

"This is she," Henry said with obvious pride.

"She is beautiful, my lord. And terrifying," Marlowe said, watching her in awe.

Noticing how Marlowe's archers stared at Maggie, Henry ran his hand down her great neck. She stood and leaned her shoulder against him, nearly knocking him from his feet. She yawned, exposing the saber-like teeth, then focused her attention on Marlowe's men. Her green eyes were unreadable.

"Maggie will not hurt you. Unless provoked, she is very gentle. My younger sister used to ride upon her back until she became too big."

Marlowe stepped away from Henry.

"As you say, your highness. It shall not be me that provokes her, I can assure you."

"Maggie, say hello to Sir Marlowe. He is a friend."

She slinked forward and rubbed her great shoulder against Marlowe, pushing him back. He hesitantly tapped her head.

"Hello."

Maggie looked up, dismissed him, and returned to stand beside Henry.

"We should go," Henry said. Maggie will make sure that none but friends remain in our path."

He pulled his sword from the ground, wiped the blood and soil from the blade with a handful of trampled wheat, then returned it to the scabbard. Kneeling in front of Maggie, he whispered. "Scout."

Thee-hundred pounds of tawny-colored cat lept forward, disappearing in the tall stalks of grain.

As they worked their way through the field, Marlowe could not get the sight of the saber-toothed cat from his mind.

"How came you to find Maggie, your highness?"

"When I was a boy, my father sent me with a conroi of his best men to the Valley of Storms. We were to explore the forest on the far side. He wished to debunk the superstitions that plague that valley and lay claim to the lands beyond.

"As we neared the forest, a great cry came from the trees, frightening the horses. No matter how much we insisted, they would go no further. That was, of course, none but mine. At the sound of a second cry, mine panicked and bolted in the wrong direction. As we reached the trees, he realized where he was and spun around, throwing me from the saddle and racing back to the others.

"I was dazed, and slowly climbed to my feet. As my eyes focused, I saw it. An enormous cat, a monster from a child's nightmare, so close I could smell her breath and feel the rumble that came from her throat burrow its way into my very bones. I could not move, expecting that at any moment I was to be torn apart. Then she placed her great head against my chest and sniffed."

Henry chuckled.

"I can tell you, Marlowe, I nearly soiled my britches. I knew I was about to die a terrible death. She turned her head and looked down the valley at the others, whose horses, including mine, continued their route.

"She looked at me again, huffed, then turned and melted back into the trees. I did not understand why she left, but I was relieved to be alive. It was then I felt something push against my leg. It was a kitten. A kitten the size of a large fox. It rubbed against my leg again and looked up at me. It was strange, but as I looked into her eyes, I felt something. A connection, I suppose. And affection I could not explain.

"Leaning down, I rubbed her head and looked back to the forest for the tigress, but she was gone. I waited for the kitten to leave, to rejoin her mother, but she just stood and continued to stare up at me. I tried to shoo her away, but she would have none of it. Finally, I decided to walk back to the others. I sensed she followed. I did not need to turn. I just knew she was there. From that time till now, we have never been apart."

"Upon your visits, I have never seen her," Marlowe said.

Henry smiled.

"She can be shy."

"Shy?" Marlowe said incredulously.

"And my father did not allow her within the walls of the castle. She made him…uncomfortable."

"I'm surprised," he said with a grin. "Did you explore the forest?"

"No. We only returned once, years later when Maggie and I…."

He stopped.

"Yes?" Marlowe asked.

"That is a story for another day."

Marlowe heard a horse snort.

"We are here, your highness."

Henry looked at the activity around him as they walked into what, at one time, had been home to the people that had worked the fields. Men worked to set up a camp away from the burning buildings while others labored with the grisly task of burying the dead. There was a mood of melancholy that seemed to have infected them all.

"Many of the men had friends here. Some family," Marlowe explained.

Archers surrounded the area facing out, watching diligently.

For what? Henry wondered. Men? Daemons? He watched as a soldier reverently carried a small body and gently laid it beside the line of covered figures.

These were innocent farmers. They posed no threat to anyone, Henry thought. Why kill them?

"Is everything all right, your highness?" Marlowe asked.

"No. What kind of people would do something like this?" He turned. "And why take the youngest of the children? What could they want with them?"

Marlowe looked at the burial party.

"I don't know. Perhaps my father has discovered something."

"I hope so," Henry said.

The two men walked towards a newly erected shelter where a banner with the golden horse's head on a field of green snapped in the breeze, announcing the baron's presence. Baron Mercier was kneeling in front of Eleanor and did not see their approach. But Eleanor did and jumped to her feet, rushing to her brother.

He took her into his arms.

"I am so happy you are safe."

"Sir Randel told me of the battle. I am relieved that John did not suffer a grave injury. I saw him fall and thought the worse."

"He is fine. He was more worried about you. Now, although I wish to hear your story, I must first speak with Baron Mercier."

"Sir Randel told me to say nothing. He said it was to be your telling alone."

"He was right. I am about to put the baron and his people in a difficult position. Accept me as his king or turn me over to Father."

"He could never support Father over you! Jamie and Marlowe are your friends, and John was your squire for years."

"That may be true, but the baron is a sworn servant of the crown and his son's friend is outlawed. If he sides with me, he will be in revolt. He has a grave decision to make."

The Baron of Tilden strode forward in greeting. Two of his sons, Brian, a tall youth of fourteen summers, and Walter, a man grown in his early twenties, followed closely, beaming. He took Henry's forearm and gripped it warmly. He was older than King John but, unlike him, was strongly built and fit. His dark hair had a hint of gray only at the temples and flowed around his shoulders like a mantle. His smile was genuine, but his caution was clear.

"It is good to see you, your highness. What brings you here? No one seems willing to tell me."

"It is good to see you, Baron." He turned to his sons. "Brian, Sir Walter, it is good to see you both. You look hail."

"As do you, your highness," Brian said, having trouble controlling his excitement having the prince in their camp.

"Find yourself a wife yet, Walter?" Henry asked.

"No woman will have him," Brian said.

"Maud says he isn't trying hard enough," Marlowe chuckled.

"And how is your wife?" Henry asked. "I am sorry I did not inquire earlier."

Marlowe puffed his chest.

"She is with child."

"That's wonderful. Congratulations."

"Thank you. She will be happy to see you. I take it you will join us for evening meal?"

"That will depend." He looked at the baron. "We must speak. Away from those not of your immediate family."

Irwin stared at him for a moment in obvious concern.

"As you wish." He turned to his youngest son. "Brian, please see to it we will not be disturbed, then join us."

"Yes, Father."

The baron waited until they reached the small pavilion before asking.

"What is it that requires such caution? Is the king ill?"

Henry sighed.

"In a way."

Brian returned and nodded at his father.

"It is done."

"Thank you." Irwin signaled Henry to take a seat. Randel and Ealdwine stood behind him as Eleanor leaned against his shoulder. The baron sat opposite. Brian, Marlowe, and Walter standing at his side. Irwin pointed to a beaker of ale questionably and Henry shook his head no.

"So, Prince Henry, what is so important? Why the mystery?"

"My father has ordered my arrest."

"He did what! What for?"

"Treason."

"Treason! That's ridiculous!" Walter said. "You are no traitor. And he is your father. Even John would not do this."

Irwin stared at his son, chastising him for his outburst. Walter lowered his head.

"Kennington?" Marlowe asked, knowing the answer.

"Yes," Henry agreed. "Duke Osborn Kennington." He almost spat the name. "He has taken advantage of my father's ill health, poisoned his mind with stories of plots and threats of invasion. He has offered money and troops if Edwenna marries his son."

"Oswald?" Walter scoffed. "That brat is not old enough to know there is a difference between the sexes. Nor is he smart enough to learn."

"That may be so," Henry said. "But Kennington is smart enough to know that by marrying my sister, his son becomes a legitimate member of the royal family. If something were to happen to my father and me, Edwenna becomes queen and Oswald, king. And you know who the power behind the crown will be."

"Surely the king has not fallen for this," Irwin said.

"My father is ill, Baron," Eleonor said. "He no longer has my mother to stem his insecurity or cruelty. He sees enemies everywhere. When Edwenna refused to wed Oswald, I saw my father throw her to the floor. He screamed she would do as he says, or he would no longer have any need for her."

"No. the king would not do such a thing," Irwin said.

Henry lowered his head.

"He did. I saw the bruises."

"There is more, Baron," Ealdwine said. "I was with the duke's men, sent to apprehend the prince. I overheard the knight commanding our force say that Duke Kennington did not wish the prince taken alive, even though the king had ordered he was not to be harmed."

Irwin jumped to his feet, tipping the stool.

"This is outrageous! What is wrong with the king? Who does Kennington think he is?"

Henry looked up at the baron.

"It is not who Osborn thinks he is, Irwin. It is who he thinks he is to become."

All were quiet until Randel placed his hand on Henry's shoulder.

"You need to tell all."

Henry took a deep breath.

"Tell him Sir Ealdwine," Henry said.

Ealdwine nodded.

"John declared his son to be outlawed. Anyone who gives him aid, shelter, or joins him will face trial for treason, have their lands confiscated, and have their and their family's lives forfeit.

"I find it hard to believe that John would do that! Execution! And their families?"

"I don't think that he did, Baron. I believe these to be Kennington's words. He cannot afford to have me return," Henry said. "Not alive.

"Those that ride with me know they can never return home as long as my father is king. For that reason, they have denounced him as their liege lord." Henry met Irwin's eyes. "They have declared me their king. I am at war with my father.

"I will not ask you for shelter. To do so would place you and your family in danger. If you decide to take me into custody, I will not resist. I just ask that you take care of Eleanor. Hide her. Do not let my father have her. And allow all that followed me here today safe passage to Lantus."

Irwin Mercier stared at Henry for a moment, then stood and reached for his sword. Randel and Ealdwine drew theirs.

"No!" Henry said forcefully, and they took their hands from the hilts of the swords.

"Father, no!" Walter cried while Brian stared at his father in disbelief.

Irwin drew his sword and turned it, offering the hilt to Henry before taking a knee. Walter looked at his brothers and smiled. As one, they drew their swords and joined their father.

Irwin bowed his head.

"I, Irwin Mercier, Baron of Tilden, accept you, Henry Langdon, as my liege lord, my sovereign, my king. I pledge my sword, my lands, my people, and my life to your service from now till perpetuity."

"Are you sure, Irwin?" Henry asked quietly. "You know what this means."

Irwin looked up.

"It means that I will finally have a king worthy of his people."

CHAPTER 18

The Battle of Eldon Hill

"There was no sign of the archer. The others are dead," Hal said. "So, anybody got an idea where these guys might come from?"

"If by guys you mean the daemons," Edwyn said. "No. I have never seen their like."

"Well, they seem hell-bent on killing us. Any idea why?"

"I do not," Edwyn said.

"They may have come from the far side of the valley," Jamie offered.

"Maybe," Hal said. "But if they did, why haven't you seen them before this? I mean, you've been to that valley."

"We have been to the valley, yes. Many have. But only the prince has ever ventured beyond the trees at the far side and returned. He tells the story of how, as a youth, his horse bolted and took him into the forest. Twas there he encountered a powerful beast. It was also where his cat first appeared."

"Maggie? The sabertooth?"

"The long tooth, yes," Edwyn said. "A magnificent beast. And terrifying. You have heard of her?"

"I have seen her," Hal said. "Aren't there more like her?"

"No. None, but the prince has ever encountered such a creature," Jamie answered.

Hal stared at the forest below.

"Why has it not been explored? The forest beyond the valley."

"Many years ago, history tells us, an attempt was made," Edwyn said. "A conroi of knights with many men-at-arms were dispatched by one of King John's ancestors to map the region. They did not return. They sent several rescue parties. They too were never seen again."

Jamie picked up the story.

"Every few years for a long time, small parties were sent to see what lay beyond the valley. The results were always the same."

"Has anything else come out of the forest? Animals, anything?"

Jamie shook his head.

"Nothing. Even the birds will not fly past the rocks at the end of the valley. And none has ever been seen exiting."

"Why is it called the Valley of Storms? Are there a lot of them?"

"Not the number, but the violence of the storms. That and the strange colors that dance in the clouds. They happen every few months and have for as long as any can remember," Jamie explained. "Usually lasting hours, never more than a day. And they stay within the confines of the valley itself. It has always been so. But that changed with the storm that took the prince to your world. It lasted but a day, but returned with a vengeance a week after we returned to Cyneburg."

About the time I left the cabin.

"Cyneburg?"

"The capital of Cent," Edwyn offered.

"That storm was unlike any seen before. It did not wain. It remained for nearly a year and only ended after you arrived."

"You said Henry sent you to watch the valley," Hal said. "Do you know why?"

"No," Edwyn said. "The prince never confided in us why he wanted it watched."

Hal scribbled in the dirt at his feet for a moment, then looked up.

"Do you think he was waiting for me?"

Before they could answer, a cry brought them to their feet.

"Alert! Alert!" a man yelled, running towards them.

"What is it, Wendell?" Edwyn asked, stopping the man.

"They come, milord. Hundreds!"

He pointed to a small rise not more than half a mile from where they stood. A long ridge of barren land rose above the grassy expanse that lay beyond the small wood below. Arrayed across the top of the ridge, silhouetted by the moonlight, stood more than a hundred shadowy figures.

Hal reached into his cargo pocket and removed the binoculars.

Edwyn shook his head.

"Another box."

Hal smiled as he handed them to him.

"They do not allow you to see in the dark, but it is light enough for them to work."

Edwyn lifted them to his eyes, and Hal was pleased to see he did not quickly return them.

"These bring them closer to the eyes. I know the Lantusians have talked about the possibility of such a thing. Their engineers are clever." He handed them to Jamie. "But I doubt even they have dreamed of something such as this."

"I would say there are close to a hundred of them," Jamie said, before handing the binoculars back to Hal.

Hal noticed Ramsey and Bailey patiently waiting. He signaled them forward, then handed the binoculars to Ramsey.

"Place them to your eyes and tell me what you see."

Ramsey looked through the binoculars. He lowered the glass momentarily and smiled. He put them back to his eyes.

"It is not what we can see on the ridge, Sir Harold, that concerns me. They are lightly armored infantry. It is what may lie beyond."

He lowered the binoculars, and after caressing them with his thumbs, reluctantly handed them back.

"Wondrous thing," Ramsey said.

Hal put them in his pocket.

"I agree." He turned to Edwyn and Jamie. "The horses are rested. Can we outrun them?"

"To where?" Jamie asked. "The closest castle is Tilden, and that is at least three hard days' ride from here."

Edwyn looked again at the ridge. Like an incoming tide, their foe began a steady advance.

"We will have to fight them here. We have no choice. At least the hill will slow them down." He pointed to the pistol in Hal's belt. "How many can that thing kill?"

"Not enough. And they would have to get close for me to use it."

"Within spear range?"

Hal thought for a moment before answering.

"A little beyond that if I take my time."

"Which I doubt they will allow," Jamie said.

Edwyn turned to Wendell.

"Have the men gather brush. Thornes if possible. Start here and build a barrier as deep as you can. At least waist-high along the edge of the hilltop. I want them off balance while we have solid footing. They carry no shields. That will help."

He turned to Hal.

"With your permission, Sir Harold, your squire has no armor nor a shield. It would be best if he stayed back. He can watch the horses."

"A suggestion, milord," Ramsey said.

Edwyn nodded.

"If Bailey were to take three or four horses, he could ride straight through to Tilden."

"And we would be without sufficient mounts to escape," William said.

Ramsey looked at the young man with a trace of sadness in his eyes.

"I am sorry, William," Jamie said. "I am afraid there is to be no escape for us. The horses can only carry us so far before they need rest. The beasts would be upon us before we got far. Assuming there are no more ahead of us. It is better for us to stay here than to be caught in the open. Our only hope is to hold out long enough for help to arrive. If we can keep the four-toes busy, Bailey might have a chance. If he succeeds, we might as well."

Jamie looked at Edwyn.

William noticed the unspoken question.

"I am Sir Jamie's squire, Father. I will stay and fight at his side."

Too proud to speak, Edwyn simply nodded.

William signaled Peter and the two young men walked to the far side of the hill to help collect brush. Edwyn watched them go.

"He is a brave lad," Jamie said. "He will make a fine knight."

"Thank you," Edwyn said, then turned to Hal. "Anything else in that magic bag of yours that will help see us survive this?"

Hal stared at the enemy aligning the ridge. "I wish I did. A few grenades would be nice."

"Grenades?" Edwyn asked.

Before he could answer, Hal was interrupted.

"Your sword, Sir Harold."

Bailey stood beside his father, the Katana in one hand and Hal's rucksack in the other.

"I did not know if you needed anything from your bag, so I brought it as well."

"Thank you, Bailey. Now, I have a difficult and dangerous task I wish you to perform."

"Yes, Sir Harold?"

"I need you to take four horses and ride as fast as you can to Tilden. You know the way?"

"I do, sir."

"You must not stop. I know it is a long way, but nothing can delay you. You must have them send help. We will do what we can to hold out until you return."

"But my lord. My place is with you."

"And I appreciate that. But you must do this. All our lives depend on your success. Do you understand? I am trusting you to do this for me. For all of us."

Bailey was quiet for a moment, then looked at Ramsey, who nodded.

"As you wish, Sir Harold. I will not let you down."

"I know you won't."

"Ramsey, will you please see that my squire is provided with sufficient food and water? See him on his way, then return. We have plans to make, and I will need your advice."

"Yes, milord. And thank you."

Once he was out of earshot, Edwyn whispered.

"You know he will not be in time even if he survives the ride."

"I know. But at least he will have a chance. Maybe William and Peter should take the rest of the horses and go with him. Increase their chances."

Edwyn smiled.

"Thank you, Sir Harold, but no. As William reminded me, he belongs with his knight. And we will need all our fighting men in what is coming. Besides, he is not mine to release, and I know my son. He would not go."

"I would let him go, Edwyn," Jamie said. "You need to simply ask."

"I know."

The three men watched while the others worked to build a ragged barrier around the edge of the hill.

They turned at the sound of horses trotting from the hill.

"God speed, Bailey," Jamie whispered.

They watched until he reached the apex of the next hill.

"No!" Ramsey cried when a dozen of the enemy rose from the tall grass reaching for his son. Bailey kicked one back as it reached for his stirrup. He urged his horse forward while gripping tightly to the lead of the other animals breaking free of the ambush. Ramsey watched in horror as the twelve figures ran in pursuit of his son at a speed no man should be able to achieve.

"He will make it, Ramsey," Hal said. "He was moving fast, and they were on foot."

Ramsey turned to him.

"You think so, milord. They were moving mighty fast."

"I do. Now, let us get ready to stop these people."

Ramsey watched the distant hill a moment. The enemy stood in a long line. Not moving. He nodded.

"As you wish, Sir Harold."

Peter lay a large leather bag on the grass.

"Your armor, Sir Edwyn."

Edwyn unbelted his sword.

"Thank you, Peter. Now help me with my mail, then ready yourself and bring me my shield."

Ramsey looked at the mail and helmet.

"You need mail, Sir Harold. Until you do, take mine."

"Thank you, but no. I'm good." He reached into the pack and recovered a box of 9mm ammunition. Ramsey watched closely as Hal ejected the magazine and fed fresh rounds into it. He freed the Katana from its scabbard and lay it on the ruck.

"You better get ready, Ramsey. You have your shield?"

"I do," he said. Ramsey walked to the edge of the hill where he had dropped it earlier.

Hal smiled.

"Do me a favor and watch my back."

William handed Jamie his shield, then turned to Hal.

"Sir Harold, you would honor me by using my shield this day."

"Thank you, William, but I think it better you keep it." He looked at the young man, barely out of puberty. "I have never used a shield and you need it to watch over Sir Jamie."

"I shall watch you both, my lord."

"They are moving, Sir Jamie," Richard called out. He had his bow and an arrow bag at his waist.

Jamie looked at the bag.

"How many?"

"Not enough."

Working their way slowly down the far ridge, the enemy began their advance. After a few yards, they separated into two perfect squares of a hundred men each. Then split again. On the back of the far-right man in each group of fifty, a long pole with a colored pennant was tied to his back. Hal grabbed his binoculars and focused on the flags. Each was a different color. Some solid, some striped. A horseman appeared on the hilltop.

"You've got to be shitting me," Hal said, lowering the binoculars.

Sitting proudly on the back of a beautifully decorated black horse was something that, to Hal's mind, could not...should not be possible.

"What is it, Sir Harold?" Ramsey asked.

"The guy on the horse. He looks like he is from my world. From centuries in the past."

"May I see?" Edwyn asked.

Hal handed him the binoculars. Edwyn scanned the helmet, and the red lacquered armor.

"He is oddly dressed, that is for certain. The mask is a nice touch." He lowered the binoculars. "I assume it is designed to frighten his opponents?"

"It is called a mempo mask. It is, and don't let the outfit fool you. If he is what he looks like, he is a formable warrior, and the armor is strong. The two swords he wears show he is a Samori, a knight."

"They have stopped, Sir Harold," William said.

"Look!" Jamie said, pointing to a man waving a red flag next to the horseman. The group of fifty with the red flag responded by running around the base of the hill to their right.

"He is controlling them with the flags. They will attack our rear," Hal said.

They waved the colored flags, and the groups moved until they surrounded the hill.

"They are going to come at us from all directions at once," Jamie said.

Hal put the binoculars back in his pocket.

"Seems that way." He turned to Richard. "When they get within range, can you take out the guys with the flags?"

Richard smiled. "That will be no problem, Sir Harold. The leather they wear for armor is no match for a good longbow."

"Maybe if we take out the leader, we might confuse them a little and slow them down. That could work for us."

"You have an idea," Edwyn asked.

"Maybe. It's crazy, but might buy us some time."

"I will welcome any suggestion that will help us survive this day," Jamie said.

"Okay, our best chance is to do something they don't expect. Throw them off balance."

"I am listening," Edwyn said.

"I think the guy on the hill is going to have everyone attack at once. He knows we can't stop them all, but we might not have to."

He turned to Ramsey.

"Have all the men gather anything that will burn, preferably something that will smoke. The more smoke, the better. Dump it in the brush on this side of the hill."

"Aye, Sir Harold," Ramsey called out as he ran back to the camp.

"Richard. Take two archers and place them on our right and left. I need you with us."

"And the rear, Sir Harold?" Richard asked.

"Leave it open. The rest of us will fall back there once the smoke is thick enough to mask our movement. When I signal, take out the guys with the flags."

"Once they are down?" Richard asked.

"You need to keep them busy until you run out of arrows. Then join us."

"And where will we be?" Edwyn asked.

"We are going to attack the group coming from behind. We don't wait for them to reach us. As soon as they begin to climb, we attack. Run right through them, killing as many as we can. Then we turn and do it again before they can organize. Hopefully, the rest will continue up the hill, not realizing we are no longer here."

"And what then?" Jamie asked. "Assuming we are still alive."

"We will back up a little and wait for the next group. The guy on the hill won't be able to signal them from his location, so with luck they will attack piecemeal, allowing us to fight them, one group, at a time."

Edwyn nodded.

"It is a good plan."

"It appears to be our only plan," Jamie said.

Franklin shrugged.

"If it is our day to die, let's take as many of these four-toes bastards with us as we can. I like this plan, Sir Harold."

"Then let's get to it."

Hal walked to the edge of the hill and watched as the enemy moved into position. They stopped just out of bow range.

"Why do they not attack?" Jamie asked.

"Probably waiting for the sun to rise," Hal said. "And I think the guy on the horse wants us to sweat a little. Strain our nerves. It will start soon."

"We should get torches ready," Edwyn said.

"Bring them here, but don't light them. And put out the fires," Hal said.

"We need a fire ready to light the torches," Jamie said.

"No, we don't," Hal said. "Trust me."

"More of your magic?" Edwyn asked.

"Something like that. Maybe let them think we have a wizard up here. Spook them a little."

"Your armor, Sir Edwyn," Peter pulled the heavy metal shirt from the linen bag. Edwyn tied the front of the padded gambeson and raised his arms. Peter slid the mail over his head. He recovered the leather arming cap and quaff from the bag and handed it to his knight. Edwyn put the cap on and pulled the mail hood over his head.

Hal watched while the squires donned their mail hauberks and picked up their shields.

This is not my kind of warfare, he thought. Or at least it wasn't.

He looked at the horseman on the hill and lay his hand on the katana.

None of this makes sense. Knights and Samurai, both warriors from the past, on my Earth. From different parts of the world. How are they here? And why am I?

"Are you well, Sir Harold?" Jamie asked.

Hal nodded while he continued to stare at the horseman.

"Just lost in thought." He looked around. "I think it would be best if all the men assembled around us. We form a circle. I want the horseman to think we are going to defend here at the top of the hill. We don't move until the smoke is thick enough to blind him to our plan."

Hal looked at Richard.

"As soon as they are in range, start shooting. When the arrows are gone, bring the horses down the far slope. If we live, that is where we will be."

"And if you do not?" he asked.

"Then take them and ride like hell away from here."

"If we survive, there are not enough horses for all of us," William said.

"I'm hoping we will not need them. If we do, we ride double," Edwyn said.

"To where?" Jamie asked.

"The next hill?" Hal looked at him. "I don't know. We sure as hell can't stay here."

"They are moving, Sir Harold," Ramsey said.

Hal turned to Franklin.

"Watch the far side of the hill. Tell me when they start to move."

Franklin looked at Jamie, who nodded.

"Sorry, not used to the whole who works for who."

"Those to our front are nearing the base of the hill," Ramsey called.

"Okay, some of you grab the torches and follow me. Hold them up. Make sure they can see that they are not lit."

Hal walked down the slope to the barricade. Ramsey followed with three of Edwyn's men-at-arms. When they reached the brush, Hal stopped and reached into his pocket. He raised his hands to his sides and yelled.

"Hey, you guys!"

Always liked that movie.

The one with the flag on his back raised his hand and the enemy troops stopped and stared at him.

"He's trying to figure out what we are doing," Hal smiled at Ramsey. "He can see the torches are not lit. Must think we are nuts."

"I am beginning to wonder as to our sanity as well, Sir Harold. Without a fire, how do we light the brush?"

Hal held up a blue BIC lighter.

"With this."

With a flourish, he touched the lighter to the first torch and spun the wheel. As the torch burst into flames, he was afraid the man was going to drop it as he jumped back. One at a time, he lit the others. The enemy watched but did not move.

"Light the brush and get back up the hill."

The wall of brush and debris began to burn. A slight breeze drifted up and over the hill. Hal smiled.

"Perfect."

While the others ran back up the hill, he stood and stared at the enemy. It was as if he had breathed the fire. None moved. They just watched as the fire grew larger.

"They are afraid of your magic."

Hal turned and found that Ramsey had not run with the others.

"I thought I told you to get back."

"I am your man, Sir Harold. I go when you go. I fight when you fight. I run when you run."

Hal chuckled. "Well then, I think it is time we run."

As they reached the top of the hill, he nodded to Richard.

"I think they are close enough."

GLENLOCK

Richard pulled the bowstring to his ear and released his first arrow. The smoke billowed. Hal waited until the smoke covered the top of the hill.

"It's time."

They drew swords and adjusted their shields. Hal looked at the men he was about to fight and probably die with. He took a deep breath.

"When I say charge, we run down the hill and hit them hard. Knock them down if you can. Kill any in your way. Push your way through them until we reach the bottom. Don't stop. If someone falls, leave them. When we reach the base of the hill, we turn and go at them again. Don't give them time to recover."

He drew the pistol.

Ramsey smiled.

"More magic to scare the devils."

"Hope so. Remember, do not move until I say to."

They removed the barrier and waited until the men below started to climb. The one Hal assumed was their leader, the one with the red flag attached to the back of his leather armor, looked up and then yelled. The word sent a chill down Hal's spine as the others repeated it.

"BONSAI!"

They rushed up the base of the hill. Their leader fell with an arrow in his chest after only a few steps. Without hesitation, the rest continued to climb.

The steep slope forced them to slow down, and their formation disintegrated. The arrows of Richard's archers continued to fall, reducing their numbers. But not by much.

The surrounding smoke grew thicker.

"It is time we moved to the back of the hill."

On the far side of the hill, Hal took the pistol and took careful aim.

Crack!

The figure with the flag fell back, part of his head missing, spraying the man behind him with blood and brain matter. The attack faltered a moment as they stopped and stared at the dead man.

Crack! Crack! Crack!

Three more fell while those on the hill, still not moving, stared up at the lone figure standing above him, smoke seeming to rise from his hands.

When the slide finally locked to the rear, nine of the enemy lie dead or dying, three more had wounds to their arms or legs. Still, they did not move.

"Now! Charge!"

Hal slipped the SIG into the holster and withdrew the Katana. In a ragged line, the defenders followed him as he ran down the hill. Five fell to the blades of the defenders before the enemy reacted. The knights and men-at-arms of Cent rushed past, leaving severed arms and heads or disemboweled figures kneeling in their own awful in their wake.

When they reached the bottom, everyone assembled around Hal. He smiled when he saw they all were there. He caught his breath as he looked at the carnage that lay on the slope of the hill. Those that survived the attack milled around in shock.

"We go again," he said, but stopped when he saw two more groups moving down the hill towards them.

Shit! No plan survives the first contact.

"Shield wall!" Edwyn yelled."

"Stay behind my shield, Sir Harold," Ramsey said.

"Thanks, but can't fight that way." He stepped to the side of the wall of wood and steel and, facing one of the flanking groups, waited; the katana poised above his head. Ramsey stepped beside him. They looked at each other. Hal nodded.

"Okay, let's do this."

A sudden shout and the enemy rushed towards them, a disorganized mob yelling and swinging their enormous swords in fury. When they struck the wall of wood and metal, they pushed some defenders back, but the wall held, and the killing began.

Striking over their shields, the warriors of Cent struck again and again while blocking the blows of the four-toes. All went well until two of the enemy warriors grabbed the top of a man-at-arms shield and pulled it down long enough to leap up and drive a blade into his shoulder and through his body. The wall was open. The defender's advantage was gone. The real killing began.

Hal didn't see any of this. He was too focused on those charging toward him. His blade seemed to have a life of its own as he parried, slashed, and stabbed in a rhythm developed during countless hours of practice in the art of the sword. The steel blade separated the leather armor of his opponents as if cutting paper, the exposed flesh falling victim to the razor-sharp steel. Repeatedly, he would block and strike, spin, duck, and leap in and out of engagements. He felt the sharp edge of a blade run down his arm and he slashed upward with one hand, opening the face of the man that had struck him. His arms and face dripped with blood. He forgot who he was, where he was, his only thought, where to strike next.

Ramsey quickly dealt with the two enemy warriors who had slipped behind him.

Edwyn turned his shield sideways and pushed, raking his sword across the neck of his opponent, nearly taking its head. He quickly swiveled to the side, taking a blade across his mail, then twisted and struck down on the head of the swordsman with the small spike on the hilt of his sword, crushing the man's skull.

Peter tripped over a body, losing his sword. He threw his hands up in horror as a four-toe raised his long blade over its head, a grin upon its misshaped face sensing an easy kill. Peter gasped when a bloodied blade appeared from its chest and the thing dropped its sword. Jamie kicked him from his sword and offered his hand to Peter.

"This is no time to rest, Peter. There is more work to be done."

The young man got to his feet and recovered his sword, and prepared to defend himself. But it was over. The survivors stood amongst the butchery that lie around them. The enemy had withdrawn. The fighting had been fierce; the bodies lay upon one another at their feet; the soil soaked in blood and gore.

Those that remained standing looked around as they tried to catch their breath. Jamie, Edwyn, William, Peter, Franklin, and the man-at-arms, Irwin, were the only men that still stood. Edwyn turned and stared. The others followed his gaze and did as well.

Sir Harold stood a few yards away, Ramsey nearby, leaning on his shield, gasping for breath. The man from another world looked like something from a nightmare. Covered in blood, his sword raised ready, frozen, staring ahead, his eyes wild. Bodies lay about him, ten, twelve, maybe more. They surrounded him, frozen in their final dance of death. Five others lay near Ramsey.

The sound of running feet made Hal focus. Two more groups, one on each side of the hill, rapidly approached, joining the survivors of their encounter. When they saw the man with the katana, they stopped.

Hal slowly lowered the sword and, in a snap of his wrist, flicked blood from the blade. He looked at the dead warriors on either side of him. Stepping over the bodies, he walked toward his foe, his Katana poised in his right hand, ready.

"Yameru!" He shouted.

The leader stepped forward and walked towards him, his sword held at his side. He stopped three feet from Hal and looked at the bloody katana, then raised his eyes.

"Anata wa dare desku ka?"

Hal stared at the figure before him.

"Watashi wa Shi desu."

The cold, unemotional words shocked the enemy leader. He looked at the bodies, then gave a deep bow. Putting his sword away, he turned and hurried back to the others. Another group had arrived from around the hill and watched the interchange. The leaders of each group approached the figure that had spoken with Hal.

As they spoke, the deep belt of a horn sounded from atop the next hill. Everyone turned towards the sound. Arrayed along the nearby ridge stood two silent formations. Long rectangular shields locked, spears held vertically.

A pair of horsemen trotted forward a few yards and stopped. The taller of the two rode stiff-backed and proud. His steel helmet adorned with a transverse crest of red feathers. A baldric lay across his intricately adorned cuirass, supporting a short sword.

The other rider was... Bailey.

Where the hell did the kid find a Roman Legion?

CHAPTER 19

Awakening

"Where is she! What do you mean, she is gone?"

"I am sorry, your majesty, but she is no longer in the castle," Duke Kennington said, doing his best not to back away from the fury of the king.

John grabbed him by the front of his shirt and drew him close. Forcing his face against the frightened man, he whispered.

"You will find her, Osborne. You will find her, and you will bring her to me. Unharmed. Do you understand?"

He shoved him back, and the duke stumbled.

"Unharmed!"

The king turned his back and stomped back to the throne. Turning, he pointed.

"Do not fail me in this, Duke. I am becoming tired of your excuses."

"Your Majesty, my men have scoured the castle and the grounds. We have searched every hovel within fifty miles. She is nowhere to be found. We believe she may have fled with Prince Henry."

"Henry! Henry is gone because you convinced me he was plotting my death. I should never have listened to you. I am awake now, Osborne. He is my son! And you turned me against him."

"I did no such thing, your majesty. I was only serving you, trying to make sure you were safe."

"Lies!"

John fell back into his chair and grabbed his chest, gasping for breath. The duke rushed to him while calling out.

"Guards! Bring the doctor. Quickly."

Kennington helped the king to sit up. He reached for the cup of wine that sat next to the throne.

"Here, your majesty, drink this."

John slapped the cup away.

"No more! I am not the fool you think me to be, Osborn. You may have your spies, but I have mine as well. I know what you have done."

He began coughing, then wiped the back of his sleeve across his mouth. A smear of blood stained the white cloth. John looked up. The burning hatred in his eyes made the duke shudder.

John wheezed out the words,

"I am not dead yet, Kennington. And your brat is not yet a part of this family. I still rule here."

The doctor rushed into the room and pushed the duke aside. Osborn stepped back and watched as the doctor examined the king. He turned and walked toward the open doors. He whispered as they closed.

"For now."

John lay propped up on several pillows as the doctor lay his head against the king's chest.

"There is fluid in your lungs, your majesty, and your heart beats not as it should."

"So, I am going to die."

"We all die, sire."

The king chuckled, which resulted in a fit of coughing. The doctor grabbed a cup and filled it with water. He offered it to John, who shoved it away.

"Enough. No more of your poisons. Leave me. I wish to be alone."

As the doctor opened the door to leave, he noticed a young man wearing the armor of a high-ranking Lantusian officer waiting just outside.

"The king is ill," the doctor said, addressing the young man. "He needs his rest. You may not enter."

"That is not for you to say, doctor," John yelled. "He is here at my bequest. Now, begone."

John gestured for the man to enter.

"Close the door."

The young man did as he was told and waited by the door.

"Well?" the king asked.

Felix Aurelias, the second son of Caesar, Emperor of Lantus, walked to the bed and looked down at the king. He was a tall man, young and fit, his deep brown skin straining against well-defined muscles.

"As you requested, I have sent a man to seek my brother."

"He carries my message?"

"He does."

"Your brother will provide an escort?"

"I believe he will. But I do not understand why you wish Lantus Legionaries to escort the prince to the capital. This is his land. These are your people."

"There are those of my people that may not wish his safe return to Cyneburg. I have been foolish, and pig-headed, Legatus. I have allowed myself to be led around like a fat hog waiting to be slaughtered."

He coughed and Felix reached for the cup the doctor had offered him a few moments before.

"No. Something from the cabinet."

Felix looked at the king questionably.

"I do not trust the doctor or what he puts in my drink. It has rattled my mind. I have seen him whispering with the Duke of Sandford. I believe they plot against me. Kennington seeks the throne."

"And you believe the doctor has been poisoning you?"

"I do. They both have been poisoning me. The doctor, my body, and Kennington my mind. I may not be a great father, I have been strict, but I love my children and I believe they love me. They would never betray me. Especially Henry. But I was not thinking straight. I have been ill, confused, easily influenced." He hesitated, then added, "And I have allowed the grape to control me."

"You believe the Duke of Sanford is plotting against you?"

"He and others. I do not know who to trust anymore. So many unfamiliar faces in the castle. The Chamberlin has recently allowed only a few servants that have been with me for a long time to bring me food and drink while disposing of what is supplied by the new stewards. It is he, the advisor I should have been listening to, that has allowed me to see what has been happening.

"It has allowed my mind to clear, but I fear he was too late to save my body." John gripped Felix's arm. "I am dying. My son trusts you and your brother. I am fortunate your father sent you to me as his ambassador. I need that trust."

"Lantus has always been a friend to Cent, your majesty."

"It is not Lantus that I trust. It is my son's friend."

"What do you know of what has transpired in the last few months?"

"Your Majesty…"

"Do not pretend your spies have not been reporting to you."

Felix smiled. "Well, I have heard rumors."

"I bet you have. Probably more accurate than what I have been fed. Kennington has convinced me that the Frisians are preparing for war. That there have been several probes along the border. People killed, farms burned, livestock stolen. He knows I do not have the money to raise a standing army and has offered to loan me what I need, money and soldiers."

"Soldiers are expensive," Felix said.

"Yes. In return, he proposes that my daughter Edwenna marry his son. That would give him a legitimate foothold on the crown. If something should befall both Henry and me, then Edwenna would become queen, and Kennington's whelp would be her king."

"I have heard whispers of such tales."

"Henry flees from me, and Edwenna has disappeared. Kennington believes she is with Henry."

"She is not."

"How do you know this?"

"The night that Prince Henry fled a man, one I trust…"

"One of your spies."

Felix smiled.

"A man I trust saw him depart. A short time later, several men left with a young girl. It was Princess Eleanor, but your elder daughter was not with them. My man overheard someone. He believes it was Sir Randel of Eudell, say that they could not find the princess."

"Then where is she?" John asked. "Kennington says she is not to be found. In this, he would not lie for he needs her."

"I do not know."

GLENLOCK

The door opened and Colby looked in.

"Get out and close that door!" John screamed.

Felix looked at the closed door.

"Someone you trust?"

"I did once, but no more. He is in this with Kennington, I'm sure of it."

"Does he normally look in the King's bedchamber without knocking?" Felix asked.

"He does not." John took a deep breath and shuddered as he released it. "We must hurry." He pointed to a trunk in the room's corner. "There is a dagger under my cloak. Please bring that to me."

Felix retrieved the long knife and handed it to the king, who slipped it under the covers.

"Do you believe you need that?" Felix asked.

John placed his hand on the hilt of the knife and smiled.

"I don't know, but I am more comfortable having it nearby." He coughed again, and blood seeped from the corner of his mouth. He wiped it with the edge of the pillow.

"You must go, Legatus. Colby has probably gone to tell Kennington you are here. I am sorry, but I may have put your life in danger."

"You believe they are so bold as to attack an emissary of the emperor?"

"I believe them willing to kill a king. It would not be difficult to make you disappear. Or place the blame of my death upon you. You need to go."

He pointed to the wall.

"Pull the wardrobe from the wall. Behind it, you will find a passage. It leads to the throne room."

"What should I tell your son when I see him?"

"That I was wrong. That I beg his forgiveness. Tell him his sister is missing. Tell him he is now king."

"Shall I tell him you abdicate?"

"No." He pulled the large ring with the seal of Cent from his finger and handed it to Felix.

"Give him this. Tell him that by the time he receives it, I will be dead."

The sound of footsteps echoed from the corridor outside the door.

"Go quickly. I thank you, Prince Felix. My son was wise to place his faith in you and your brother."

A tapping at the door signaled it was time to leave. Felix pulled the wardrobe a scarce way from the wall and squeezed behind it. Once in the passage, he pulled the cabinet back as the door opened.

The Duke of Sanford looked about the room.

"Who do you think you are barging into my chamber? Get out! Guards! Guards!"

Two men-at-arms rushed into the room.

"Escort the duke from my chamber and allow no one but the Chamberlin or my clerks to enter."

The guard bowed.

"As you wish, your majesty."

Kennington stepped into the hall, where Colby waited. The guards closed the door and took position on either side, observing the two men, their hands laying on their swords.

The duke whispered to Colby.

"Come with me."

When convinced he was out of earshot of the guards, he grabbed the front of Colby's tunic and slammed him against the wall.

"I thought you said that Lantus bastard was with him."

"He was your grace. That is why I sought you out. I thought you would want to know."

"Check with the guards. I want to know if anyone has left the king's chamber since that Lantusian Ambassador entered."

Colby strutted to the guards, doing his best to exude his authority.

"Has anyone left the king's chamber?" he demanded.

"Not since the sergeant placed us here."

Colby looked at the speaker.

"What sergeant?"

The guard answered cautiously, "Waxman. The Chamberlin assigned him today."

"Today?"

The other guard, not intimidated by Colby, added.

"With orders not to allow you or the Duke of Sandford to enter."

GLENLOCK

Colby stared at the two guards, then returned to Kennington.

"No one has left the king's chamber."

"Then Felix has left by other means."

"There is something else," Colby said nervously.

"What!"

"The guards at the king's door were assigned by a new sergeant. One selected by Sir George with instruction not to allow either of us access to the king."

"The Chamberlin?" Kennington looked around. "We must hurry. Find the Lantusian Ambassador and bring him to me."

"And if he resists?"

"He disappears."

"And Sir George?" Colby asked.

"I will take care of the Chamberlin."

Felix pushed the large chair from the wall and searched the throne room. It was empty. He stepped down from the dais and ran to his quarters, where two of his men waited.

"We are leaving," he said, entering the room. He grabbed his spatha, the long sword favored by the Lantusian cavalry, and draped it over his shoulder.

"We are no longer safe here."

"Something amiss?" Paulus asked.

"More than you could imagine. Do you know where my brother is?"

"Last I heard, he was conducting patrols along the land bridge to Tilden."

"Then that is where we are going.

"Lucius, tell the men to get ready to leave. You must hurry. We may not have much time. Bring the horses and meet me at the gate. Have the others wait on the far side of the bridge. And be careful. I do not want trouble if we can avoid it. There is something I need to do before we leave."

Lucius nodded and rushed from the room, keeping his hand on his sword.

Felix and Paulus hurried down the corridor, avoiding guards and servants alike until they came to the doors of the throne room. They were closed, and guards posted.

"What is it you need to do?" Paulus asked.

"Scratch an itch."

"An itch?"

"About the missing princess."

Felix nodded as the guards came to attention when they recognized the ambassador of Lantus. He and Paulus walked past and were nearly in the courtyard when someone called out.

"Halt!"

Colby stood at the top of the steps with two men.

"Shit," Felix said.

"Detain the Lantus emissary," Colby ordered. "By order of the king."

Felix turned and drew his sword.

"Paulus, tell Lucius to hurry."

Paulus ran towards the stables and Felix faced the two men.

"You would lay hands on the emissary of Lantus? I am the son of the emperor. If harm should come to me, it would be war. One I do not think your king wishes."

The guards turned to Colby for guidance.

"You heard me. I said detain him."

They drew their swords and approached cautiously. Felix lifted his blade, and they stopped.

"If you come any closer, you will force me to defend myself." He pulled the pugio from his belt and held the wide dagger in his left hand.

A crowd began to arrive drawn to all the activity.

Felix smiled.

"So, Colby, how do you intend to explain this? A mere soldier threatening the prince of a friendly nation. Think carefully. There are many witnesses now."

Felix heard the horses as they arrived behind him, followed by the sound of two swords being drawn.

"We are here, Lord Felix," Paulus said. "The others wait beyond the main gate. Let us go."

Felix backed slowly until he felt the heat of the horse behind him. He put his weapon away, turned, and mounted.

"We are leaving, Colby. Do not try to stop us."

Felix drove his heels into the flank of the horse and raced toward the main gate. Colby watched as they cleared the raised portcullis and fled across the drawbridge where the others of their party waited. As Felix rode past, the rest of his men fell in line and followed. When he could no longer see them, Colby turned and marched back into the shadows of the keep.

"We have little food and water."

"I know, Lucius. We will find what we need once we are clear of Cyneburg."

He looked behind him and sighed with relief that he could see no pursuit. But he knew it would come.

"We travel west to the coast and then north to the border. We will go by way of Tilden in case Augustus has stopped there to see Jamie. We must leave the road and use the hills and forests. It will take longer, but that cannot be helped."

"But why? What has happened that we need to flee from an ally?" Paulus asked.

Felix laughed.

"We are going to save Cent, my friend. My father is going to enjoy this. A Lantusian prince trying to save the court of Cent."

"And the itch?" Paulus asked.

"It still plagues me."

"And what causes this ailment?"

Felix looked at him.

"I have had one of my people listening at keyholes. I wanted to check with him before we left."

"And what is it you think he may have heard?"

"What has happened to Princess Edwenna."

CHAPTER 20

ELEANOR

Henry helped Eleonor dismount from a horse that was obviously too big for her.

"I miss Angel," Eleonor said as she patted the neck of the mare. But I thank you. You have been gentle. Perhaps I will grow into you."

Henry laughed. "By the time you are big enough for a beast such as this, she will be long in retirement enjoying sweet grass and quiet days."

"Maybe. But I am growing fast. Edwenna says it will not be many more summers before I am a woman grown."

"Do not rush such a thing," Henry said, mussing her hair. "I like you as you are. And are you really in such a hurry to be as your sister?"

"I will never be like her, Henry. I'm too smart."

He laughed again. "Yes, you are. A little too smart."

A stable boy took the reins of their horses while others escorted the remaining animals to the stables.

"Eleanor!"

"Marjorie," Eleanor cried when she saw the young woman rushing down the steps.

Her arms wide, the lady picked Eleanor up and spun her around.

"It is wonderful to see you. But why are you here? I was not told of a visit." Marjorie asked as she set her down.

"We are running from my father," Eleanor said, as if it was an everyday occurrence.

"You are what?" Marjorie asked, pushing Eleanor back and looking at her.

"We are outlawed. My father tried to arrest Henry. We had to flee. Then soldiers came and tried to kill us."

"Kill you? Whatever for?"

"Forgive my sister, your majesty," Marlowe said. "She really is a lady when she feels like acting like one."

Marjorie turned to Henry, and her cheeks reddened. She curtsied.

"Your Majesty?" she asked, confused.

Henry stared, appreciating her raw beauty. Marjorie was his junior by nearly ten summers, just approaching her eighteenth year. Her long red hair hung loosely around her slim shoulders against both fashion and custom. But Marjorie was never one who adhered strictly to the rules. Something he found alluring.

"A long story, Marjorie."

"One I look forward to hearing."

"Oh, Maggie!" she said, seeing the huge cat.

Maggie stepped around Henry and lay her enormous head against Marjorie's hip, waiting to have her neck scratched.

Randel shook his head.

"I do not understand what that cat sees in her."

"Maggie knows what she likes," Henry said. "Always has."

"Marjorie, allow our guests inside and arrange for food and drink," Irwin said. "They have had a trying day."

"Right away, Father."

Eleanor took her hand.

"I will go with you. Wait till I tell you about the monsters that stole me."

"Stole you? Monsters?"

Henry watched them, lost in conversation, as they climbed the steps to the keep. Marlowe smiled.

"Be careful, your majesty. My sister has had her eye on you for some years. You give her the slightest opportunity and she will own you."

"So John has warned me."

"And where is my brother?" Marlowe asked.

"He is with the rest of my men. He was wounded and couldn't ride with the rest of the men.

"Will he live?" Irwin asked, concerned.

"He will, Baron. He was not happy I left him behind."

"I'm sure he wasn't. A squire's place is with his knight."

Henry smiled.

"John is no longer my squire, Irwin. He has earned his spurs."

"He has been knighted?"

"Yesterday. I am sorry I could not wait until we could all be together."

"I understand," he said with a mixture of pride and disappointment.

"Which means, your majesty, you need a squire," Brian said hopefully.

"That is true, young Brian. I will need to look around and see if I can find someone with the proper skills and motivation." He said, grinning at his father.

Irwin looked at his youngest son and shook his head, warning him that this was not the time.

"Let us go inside," he said. "There is much we need to discuss. Marlowe, see that the gates are closed and double the watch. Then join us."

"The market, Father?"

"Must be closed for the day. Send the people home with my apologies. But leave the drawbridge down."

He bowed.

"I understand." He turned to Randel. "I am looking forward to hearing your story."

"We will wait for you before we tell our tale," Henry promised.

Henry noticed Ealdwine waiting and signaled that he should join them.

"Baron, have you met Sir Ealdwine?"

"You are one of Duke Kennington's household knights, are you not?" he asked coldly. "I believe I have seen you with him when last I visited the capital."

Ealdwine nodded.

"I was, Baron. But no more. I now serve King Henry."

Irwin looked at Henry with a little concern.

"Sir Ealdwine rode with Sir Ainsworth, allegedly to bring me back to Cyneburg to stand trial. He overheard Ainsworth remark that his orders from the duke were that I was not to be brought back alive. This treachery was something he could not accept. He has sworn his oath to me and has since proven his worth and loyalty."

He turned to Ealdwine.

"I have been remiss in thanking you for saving my life today. Not once, but possibly twice. I surely would have perished along with my friends had you supported Ainsworth's attack."

"What he tried to do was wrong, your majesty. I am a knight and have an obligation to do what is right." He smiled. "Besides, Ainsworth is a self-centered weasel."

"Is it not also your duty to stay true to your oath?" Irwin asked. "To serve the duke?"

Ealdwine glared at Irwin, then dropped his gaze.

"It should be, Baron. Never could I have fathomed that one day I would have to choose between the oath I took as a knight and the one to a man I pledged to serve. It was a most difficult decision." He looked at Henry. "One that I would gladly make again."

Henry slapped him on the shoulder.

"And I am glad you chose as you did you did."

Irwin noticed the way Randal watched Ealdwine.

So, not all are enamored with our new ally.

Marlowe presented his goblet to a servant to refill. "So, who or what are these things that attacked you and destroyed the village? And why take the children?"

"These remain questions with no answers," Henry said.

"Could your father or the duke have sent them?" Marlowe asked.

Henry set his goblet down and placed his hand over it showing he wished no more.

"I do not believe so. The attack on the village gains them nothing. And I have never seen or heard of these four-toed creatures before. No, something else is going on."

"But what?" Irwin asked. "My people have been attacked, killed by an enemy no one has heard of before. Their children stolen. Why?"

"I do not know," Henry said. "But I intend to find out."

"How, your majesty," Ealdwine asked. "You are a wanted man." He looked around the table. "We are all wanted men. The king will send soldiers to find you. And the duke will send men as well." He leaned on the table. "And Kennington will hire men to kill you. Assassins. Those that poison and murder in the dark. We must be alert for such things. I do not see how we can take the time to investigate these creatures. It is our responsibility to protect our king. It is not the time to hunt monsters."

Randel slammed his fist on the table.

"Damn him!" He looked at Henry. "Sir Ealdwine is correct, sire. You must hold up here until this situation with your father is sorted out. To leave these walls is too dangerous."

"I appreciate your concern, all of you, but that is not going to happen. Whoever these strange men are, they are a threat to all of Cent. I cannot allow that. I must seek them out. To make them answer for what they have done."

"But, your majesty…" Randel started to say when he was interrupted by one of Baron Mercier's guards rushing into the chamber.

"Rider's approach, Baron."

Irwin rose, followed quickly by the others.

"Have they been identified?"

"Not as of yet, your excellency. But they appear to have wounded with them. And there are women and children."

"You say there are women and children?" Henry asked.

"Yes, your highness."

"He is no longer your prince, Barle. He is your king," Irwin said.

"I am sorry, your majesty," Barle said, bowing.

"There is nothing to apologize for," Henry said, smiling. "I doubt many know of my change in fortune."

"Keep the gates closed and call out the guard," Irwin told the man, who bowed, turned, and rushed from the hall.

"Could it be the duke's men?" Irwin asked.

"I do not see how," Henry said. He turned to Ealdwine. "Were men sent to notify the duke that Ainsworth had found us?"

"No. If Ainsworth sent a rider, he would have had to pass me. I saw no one. I believe he wanted to keep the glory of killing you to himself."

"Thank God the egocentric fool did not succeed," Randel said.

"I believe it time to see who our visitors might be," Irwin said.

Brian ran ahead as the others worked their way up the stone steps to the curtain wall.

"It's Philip," Randel said. "Thank God. But who are the women and children with him?"

Henry concentrated on the party as it approached. Several of Sir Ealdwine's men walked beside horses carrying wounded. Henry identified those he could: John, Bascom, Randolph, Bruce-son-of-Bruce, William Longbow, and John Quick Arrow, all walked in front. William Longbow led a horse carrying Sir Philip.

"They are our people," Henry said. "At least the warriors are. I do not know who it is that follows them. Surely, their families could not have arrived so soon."

Irwin leaned down from the parapet and shouted,

"Open the gates. Help those people and send for Priscus. Tell him there are wounded." He turned to Brian. "Run and tell your sister people are arriving. Have her arrange for them to be fed. And tell her there are children."

As Brian eagerly ran to find his sister, Irwin turned to Henry.

"Since the death of my wife, Marjorie has become the lady of the castle. She will know what to do."

"Thank you, Baron. I remember your wife fondly. She always made me feel welcome when my mother brought me here as a boy."

"She loved you and your sisters as she did your mother. They were close since childhood."

"I remember."

The first of the new arrivals reached the bridge over the dry moat where they were met by members of Irwin's household. Henry descended the stairs and waited as John handed the reins of his weary horse to a groom. Henry took his forearm and noticed a deep cut above the right eye of his former squire.

"That's new. What happened?"

"We were ambushed as we left the forest. Two of Sir Ealdwine's men were killed."

"Were you able to identify the ambushers?"

"No, sire. But they used unusually long arrows. John and William said they had never seen their like."

"Who are the women and children?"

"They are my father's people," John said. He looked at Irwin. "It is Robert the Miller and his family and many from surrounding farmsteads. They tell of strange men attacking farms."

"How came they to survive?" Irwin asked.

"They were in the fields and hid when they first heard the screaming."

"And the mill?" Irwin asked.

"Gone. Burned to the ground."

John looked at Henry, exhaustion evident on his face.

"I could not leave them, sire. They are our people. I have known many of them my entire life."

"You were right not to leave them, Sir John," Henry said.

Irwin smiled and slapped his son on the shoulder.

"The king has told me. A knight. I am proud of you."

John lowered his head.

"Thank you, Father."

Henry pointed at Philip, who was being helped down from his horse.

"How is he?"

"Doing well, your majesty. Angry that I insisted he ride."

Henry chuckled.

"I'm sure he tried to pull rank."

John smiled.

"Many times. William helped me keep him in the saddle. He threatened to tie him to it."

Irwin bowed.

"If you will excuse me, sire. I will see to my people. And then I will ride out to see if I can find these things that have invaded my land."

"I will come with you," Henry said.

"As will I," John said.

"No, John," Henry said. "I think it best you remain here. We have many wounded and I need someone I trust to take care of them."

"Aye, your majesty. If you think it best."

"I do. And thank you, John. For bringing them. You have proven yourself a good and trusted knight.

"What of the families of our people?"

"Richard, one of Sir Randel's archers, and five of Sir Ealdwine's men wait for them with instructions to bring them here."

Henry nodded.

"Good."

"With your permission, I would like to see to our people," John said.

"Of course," Henry said and watched as John walked away."

"A good lad," Irwin said with pride.

"Yes, he is."

Irwin bowed.

"If you will excuse me, your majesty?"

"Of course."

Irwin turned and strode towards the villagers, signaling that the guards should follow.

Henry and Randel watched as Marjorie and Elanor moved about organizing the people, separating the families from the warriors, and directing Pricus's healers to those in greatest need. They smiled as Eleanor chastised Philip as he tried to come to Henry, and Marjorie signaled two men to take him inside.

"He will not be happy about that," Randel said.

"Maybe not. But he was smart not to argue with those two ladies."

"Do you think it wise to venture from these walls?" Randel asked. "I mean, we are not just talking about these four-toed things. Kennington and your father will have troops looking for you."

"What kind of king would I be to allow these atrocities to go unpunished? I will ride with the Baron and his men."

Randel bowed his head.

"Then I will see to fresh horses. For us both."

CHAPTER 21

Legionaries

Hal stared at the soldiers along the ridge with their long red shields linked like a wall.

"Where are they going?" Ramsey asked, pointing to the enemy as they turned and moved back around the hill.

"I'm not sure," Hal said then looked at the ridge. "Maybe they don't like the odds."

Bailey broke away from the other rider and rushed towards them. The Roman-looking soldier followed at a leisurely pace.

The long line of soldiers on the ridge marched down the hill, their formations unaffected by the slope.

Hal looked at Jamie.

"Friends or foe?"

Jamie smiled.

"Friends. Although I don't know what they are doing so far from home."

Baily jumped from his horse.

"Sir Harold."

"Bailey," Hal said. "I see you brought help."

"I did, my lord. As I was riding towards Tilden, Lantusian riders stopped me, scouts. They took me to their camp and their commander asked me where I was going in such a hurry. I had heard that the prince of Lantus is a friend of Prince Henry, so I thought it was best to tell him what was happening. He ordered some of his men to follow me back here. He has come to help. Did I do right, my lord?"

Hal smiled.

"Take a breath, Bailey. Yes, you did right. You have saved us all." He slapped him on the shoulder. "Thank you."

Ramsey reached for his son and pulled him into an embrace.

"I am so proud of you." He pushed him back and with a small bow bellowed, "Sir."

Riders appeared on the hill, stopped for a moment, then split into two groups in pursuit of the four-toed warriors.

The rider that arrived with Baily brought his horse to a halt a few yards away and lifted the feathered helmet from his head. Unlike the soldiers behind him who wore the armor of metal slats around their torsos called lorica segmintata, this man wore an ornately decorated cuirass of gilded metal, armor normally reserved for senior officers of a Legion. His dark red cloak signified someone of importance.

Hal shook his head. Just like in the history books. Roman soldiers except for one significant item. Rome allowed no black Africans in the legions.

The man's skin was the deep brown of polished mahogany. He was tall, maybe six foot two, with broad shoulders, his hair shorn short. He reminded Hal of the pictures he had seen of Mohammad Ali in his prime.

"Your Highness," Edwyn said with a bow. "A most fortuitous arrival."

The man stepped from the horse and gripped Edwyn's forearm.

"Augustus, Edwyn, please. We have known each other for many seasons. It has always been as friends since the days that you, Henry, and I played stag and hounds together in the gardens of Orn."

Edwyn smiled.

"It is good to see you, Augustus. It has been a while. How is your father?"

"The emperor is in good health. He enjoys a bit too much food and wine, but after all, he is Caesar. Besides, his fighting days are over."

"That is good to hear."

Augustus turned to Jamie and reached for his arm.

"Jamie, well met. I meant to drop in and see your father, but circumstances prevented the opportunity."

"Not as good as it is to see you, sir. Another five minutes and we all would have been nothing but a memory."

"There did seem to be a lot of them," Augustus said with a grin. He turned and looked at Hal questionably.

"And who is this unusually attired gentleman?"

"I'm sorry," Edwyn said. "Augustus, this is Sir Harold Bennet of Deecee. A friend. He is not from around here."

Augustus looked him up and down in amusement. Then smiling, offered his hand.

"It is a pleasure to meet you, Sir Harold. And I can see you are not from around here. Or anyplace else I know of by the looks of things."

Hal took an instant liking to the tall man and gripped his forearm.

"The pleasure is mine, sir. And thank you for the rescue."

Augustus looked at the dead that littered the field.

"I am sorry I did not get here sooner. I will have your wounded tended to."

"Thank you," Edwyn said.

A soldier wearing the standard armor of a Roman soldier and a helmet with a red horsehair crest approached. He slapped his arm across his chest in a salute and made a slight bow. The baldric draped across his shoulder held the famous short sword of Rome, the gladius.

"Your orders, Imperator?"

"Wait on the far side of the ridge. Place centuries along the apex of the hill and send out scouts. When the others arrive tell them I want a fortified marching camp set up in the valley before dark."

"As you wish." The man smiled. The gap between his teeth obvious.

"Sure, were a lot of the bastards. Would have been fun to take them on. Been chasing them long enough."

"You will get the chance, Celsus," Augustus said with a smile. "But not now. We would need a full legion to take on that many."

"I could do it with a single century."

Augustus shook his head and turned to the others.

"Gentlemen, may I introduce my senior centurion, Centurio Primus Pilus Celsus Aelius."

A Roman commander of the first cohort of a legion, Hal thought. The senior centurion of the legion. This is nuts.

They nodded, and he gave a slight bow.

The sound of horses drew their attention to the ten riders appearing from around the hill. Nine stopped, and the tenth rode forward. He leaped from his horse and saluted Augustus. His armor was different, a sleeveless mail shirt called hamata rather than the slats of metal worn by the infantry.

"They have fled, Imperator. Beyond the woods. We did not pursue."

"A wise decision, Antonious. Now go with Celsus. He will tell you what he needs."

The soldier saluted, mounted, and rode back to the other scouts.

"I will take my leave, sir. The rest of the cohort should be here shortly," the Centurion said.

"Thank you, Celsus. Tell the men they have done their Legion proud."

The man retreated, and Augustus turned to Edwyn.

"So, what happened here? You piss in their porridge?"

"Our first contact with them was near the Valley of the Storm. They attempted to take my son and attacked Sir Harold and Jamie. Not knowing how many there were, we hastily departed the valley wishing to reach the village of Eldon before dark only to discover the village destroyed and the people slaughtered.

"Deciding the hill would be easier to defend, we set up camp. It is there they attacked us in strength. I lost some good men today, friends."

"Whose idea was it to charge them?"

"Sir Harold," Jamie said.

Augustus looked at Hal.

"A wise and courageous move. Worthy of a legionnaire"

He turned back to Edwyn.

"I am sorry for your losses, my friends. It is never easy to lose men. Especially if they have been with you for a long time.

"If you don't mind my asking, Edwyn, why were you at the valley? Not a place to visit for pleasure I have been told."

"Waiting for him I think," Jamie said pointing to Hal.

"We believe that Sir Harold is the man Prince Henry met last year," Edwyn explained. "The prince has had us watching the valley for close to a year. He did not say why."

"I thought Henry's story was just that, a story," Augustus said. "Something to amuse his friends over a flask of good wine."

Edwyn smiled.

"When my son told me of Henry's encounter, I had my doubts as well. But no longer. I have seen Sir Harold do things that if I was not an educated man, I would consider magic."

"Magic? Really? And the storm?"

"Stopped when Sir Harold arrived."

"Fascinating. You are from the valley?" Augustus asked, turning to Hal.

"It is where I arrived."

"Arrived?" Augustus laughed. "This should make for some wonderful entertainment over dinner. I am looking forward to your story, Sir Harold. And hearing about your magic." He laughed again. "Arrived."

"My friends call me Hal."

"And I am Augustus."

"Augustus, how is it you are here?" Jamie asked. "Not that I am complaining, but this is far from Lantus. And with so many men. What did my father say when you asked to pass through his lands?"

"I am sorry to say I did not seek his permission."

"You did not?" Jamie asked, his tone becoming serious.

"I am not here to create tension between our two countries, Jamie. I did not seek your father's permission because, well, to be honest, I did not expect to still be here, or to have traveled so deep into Cent."

"I think you should explain yourself, Augustus," Jamie said.

Augustus took a deep breath.

"I was afraid of what would happen if I did not stop whoever was killing our people. Yours and mine. If it were brigands from Lantus, I wished to catch them before they created a political situation that could affect us both.

"Unfortunately, their trail drew me deeper into Cent than I had planned to go. I intended no slight on your father, Jamie."

Edwyn turned to Jamie.

"You know Augustus, Jamie. He would not do such a thing unless there was a good reason."

"We should go," Augustus said, not wishing to further aggravate Baron Mercier's son. "The enemy might return, and I would rather surround myself with the rest of the Cohort. We will talk more then."

"A wise decision," Edwyn said, then turned and looked at the dead littering the field.

"I will send a party to retrieve the bodies of your men," Augustus said. "They will be treated with honor, I promise."

"Thank you," Edwyn said.

"Sir Harold, take my horse," Bailey said, offering the reins.

Hal placed his hand on Bailey's shoulder.

"See if any of the wounded need it. I will walk. Thank you, Bailey. And again, thank you for bringing help. We live because of you."

"Take mine as well, young man," Augustus said. "I too will walk." He looked at Jamie. "I think we should talk."

As they climbed the gentle slope, Augustus turned to Jamie.

"For the last several days, we have been receiving reports of villages being attacked along the land bridge near the border. I set out with the First Cohort to see what this was about.

"We came upon a fishing village near the border, the buildings burned and the people slaughtered. The only survivor was a shepherd boy that had been in the hills at the time of the attack. He spoke of monsters that came from the sea and killed his family. The lad was but 10 summers and was in shock, so I paid little heed to his claim of monsters.

"I sent a healer to see to him before sending him back to Ome. The capital has a wonderful school for healers. There are some that study ways to heal the mind. I believe he will get the best care there."

"The only direction they could have gone was east. I decided to follow, I will admit my ire was up after what I had seen, and I sought justice for what they had done to the villagers.

"Shortly after crossing the border, my scouts reported smoke near the coast. We went to investigate, wondering if they had attacked another village. It was not."

Augustus continued. "The smoke was from the remains of several burning ships. Southlander drakkars. The remains of many of their warriors littered the beach. The bodies had been mutilated.

"We followed their trail inland when we came upon a group of Southland warriors. Survivors of the massacre. They surprised me when they did not put up a fight.

"I questioned them about what had happened. They claimed they had come ashore simply to get fresh water when they were attacked.

"They spoke of monstrous men with strangely shaped heads that babbled words that had no meaning. I did not believe them at first, for there was no sign of such monsters amongst the dead."

"I have never heard of a Southlander leaving home without sufficient supplies," Jamie said. "They should not have needed to refill their water barrels."

"My thinking exactly," Augustus agreed. "I had them secured for later questioning and continued my search for who, or what, had destroyed the village and attacked the Southlanders.

"We picked up their trail near to the Great Highway." He looked at Jamie. "I sent a rider to Cyneburg to report my intentions. I should have done the same to Tilden. My only excuse was that I did not wish to lose my prey. I am sorry, Jamie"

Jamie shook his head.

"No need to be. I would have done the same."

"Were you able to capture any of these men?" Hal asked.

"Men. Well, I suppose they are, although I have seen nothing like them before. We saw them many times but never got close enough to make contact. These things can move fast. They would disappear when they saw us leaving strange tracks in the dirt."

"No boots and four toes?" Edwyn asked.

"Yes. Celsus counseled me they might lure us into an ambush, which is why I kept my men in the open and away from villages and large pockets of forest land. I was not avoiding your father, Jamie."

"I wonder if they were leading you here. There were a lot more of them on the other side of the hill," Hal said. "This valley would make a great spot to trap an army. Kinda like what happened to Custer."

"Custer?" Augustus asked.

"A general on my world that was led into a valley like this. No one survived."

"Then I am glad we did not meet the same fate as this general," Augustus said. "Although I doubt whoever he fought had ever faced Legionaries," he said with a grin.

Hal chuckled.

"No, probably not."

They reached the top of the hill and stopped, looking down at the activity taking place on the plane below. Engineers scurried about laying out the camp, placing stakes where each tent was to be pitched, the location of latrines, and supply areas, while dozens of others labored digging a trench while building a wall with the excavated soil around the whole of the encampment.

"Impressive," Hal said, amazed.

An additional two hundred troops were marching towards the camp, escorting a steady stream of wagons. One wagon, in particular, caught Hal's attention.

"Who is in the caged wagon?" Hal asked.

"The Southland survivors," Augustus said.

"Why are they imprisoned?" Hal asked.

"They are Southlanders," he said, as if that explained everything.

Deciding to change the subject, Hal asked.

"How many men do you have with you?"

"Five centuries. The entire First Cohort of the Second Legion. Close to five hundred men and one turma of cavalry. Another thirty."

"You brought an entire cohort into Cent. Without the king's permission?" Edwyn asked, surprised. "Risky don't you think? Some might think that many men a precursor to war."

"I had no intention of bringing the First. My father insisted I take it because of the reports. When we came upon the Southlanders, I was going to send all but one century back and pursue those that had attacked the village across the border with just them and one turma of cavalry. I sent a rider to King John to let him know what I was doing and why. Celsus reminded me we did not know the size of the enemy force we were tracking. I decided it prudent to bring the First, knowing that I had informed the king of my intentions. I thought he would appreciate the help."

"With King John, one never knows, but I think you made the right decision," Edwyn said.

Augustus led them to a large tent in the center of the camp.

"Let us refresh ourselves, and then we can share our stories. Your men will be shown quarters and provided with food and drink. Do you wish your squires to remain?"

"I think it best that we four speak alone for now," Edwyn said.

"As you wish." Augustus signaled a nearby legionnaire. "See to these men. They are to be treated as honored guests."

CHAPTER 22
A Wedding

The door flew open, and Duke Kennington strutted into the king's bedchamber. John sat propped up with pillows and stared at the intruder.

"A bit forward of you, Osborn, entering the king's bedchamber without seeking an audience. I thought I instructed the guards that I was not to be disturbed," he said, clutching the dagger beneath the blanket.

"Forgive my rudeness, your majesty, but I have good news. Your daughter has been found."

"Edwenna? Where?"

"Near Hampson Wood, near to the mill."

"Found? What do you mean, found?" John demanded.

She was injured, sire. We believe she was thrown from her horse. The miller's wife has been tending to her. They did not send word as they did not know who she was."

"Thrown? Edwenna is a fine horsewoman. That is unlikely. And how could they not know who she was? You speak in riddles, Kennington. Where is she? I wish to see her."

"She is with the doctor, sire. He has given her a potion to help her sleep. He feels rest is the best course of action."

"How badly was she injured?" John asked, showing unusual concern over the health of one of his children.

"I was told she struck her head. She was unconscious when the miller found her and remains so."

"All this time? Will she live?"

"The doctor believes she will recover. In time. He has bled her and says her heart beats strong. That is a good sign."

John started to rise then fell back. Kennington rushed forward and helped him sit back, resting on the pillows.

"You should not try to stand, sire. The doctor says it is not wise for you to be about. You have been quite ill."

John looked at him and sneered.

"Ill. My illness is not the result of anything natural."

"What do you mean, sire?"

"You damn well know what I mean. But I'm not dead yet, Kennington. And it may shock you to learn I am feeling stronger."

The duke looked down at the king. Concern showing in his eyes.

"Yes, Duke. You are right to be afraid, for I know what you and that bastard of a doctor have been doing to me."

"I do not know what you mean, your majesty."

"The hell you don't. Now get out of here and send in Sabinus."

"Not your doctor?"

"I said Sabinus. The Lantusian ambassador brought him, and he is reported to be one of their best healers. I trust him. Now go!"

Kennington stepped from the room. He spied Colby waiting down the hallway and signaled to him. The two walked away from the king's chamber, whispering.

"I don't trust that snake," one of the guards at the door said, watching them as they walked away.

The other agreed with a snort.

"Nor our ex-sergeant, if truth be told. He be too friendly with the duke. I think he has forgotten who he serves."

"Maybe. Or he has a new master."

As Kennington and Colby turned the corner, the duke stopped and grabbed the front of Colby's shirt.

"Why are those men guarding the king? Who are they?"

"The Chamberlain placed them there. He has also forbidden the doctor to enter. I no longer have the king's confidence he said. There is to be a new sergeant of the king's guard."

"The King is regaining his strength," Kennington said.

"The doctor says not to worry. It is too late; nothing can save him. He will die soon."

"He had better be right. The king wishes the Lantus healer to see him."

"He's not here. He fled with the others," Colby said.

"I am aware. I believe the king is as well. I think he was trying to see if I knew about the ambassador's flight.

"Where is my son?"

"He is in the stables."

"Get him and bring him to the throne room. And get the doctor."

"May I ask why, your grace?" Colby asked.

"We are going to have a wedding."

"A wedding. Who is getting married?"

"Oswald and the Princess Edwenna."

Colby looked at the duke as if he had lost his mind and then his face developed an evil grin.

"Exactly," the duke said. "Now hurry. It needs to be done before John dies. He must acknowledge the union."

Colby turned to leave.

"Wait."

"Your grace?"

"Before you do, find Sir Robert and send him to me. There is something I need him to do."

Colby bowed and rushed to do as he was told.

Kennington sauntered toward the throne room. "Soon, you bastard, your kingdom will be mine."

Sir Robert Beckett approached and gave a short, cursory bow.

"You wish to see me?"

Duke Kennington looked at the knight. A ruthless man, known for his cruelty when dealing with women. Not one of his household knights, a man for hire, one that would do almost anything for money.

"I have a job for you."

"To do what?"

"Do I pay you and your ruffians well, Robert?"

"You pay enough. What do you want doing and what is in it for me?"

"How would you like to become a baron with your own lands and property?"

Eying Kennington with suspicion, Beckett asked.

"And what would I need to do to attain such a thing?"

"Not too much. I think you might even enjoy the assignment. I need you to take your men along with mine and find Prince Henry. I know the two of you have had issues in the past."

Kennington was aware of the thrashing Henry had given him when he discovered Beckett had nearly killed a prostitute at a nearby tavern. He threatened to take his spurs if it happened again.

"And what do I do once I find him?"

"Kill him."

Beckett stood for a moment.

"And the title?"

"I believe Tilden will soon require a new lord. Of course, it must be done in such a way that no one can accuse you of murder."

Robert smiled.

"Or you, of course. It will be done." He stared at the duke. "I will hold you to our arrangement, Duke Kennington. I would hate for you to find yourself in a similar situation as our prince."

"You threaten me, Beckett?"

"Just stating a fact, my lord duke. I do not make threats."

He turned on his heel and strutted away just as Colby arrived with Oswald and the doctor. Colby watched Beckett until he stepped into the courtyard.

"That is a dangerous man," the doctor said.

"Dangerous men have their uses," Kennington said.

"And when you no longer have need of them?" the doctor asked.

"Then they become expendable."

"Why have you sent for me, Father?" Oswald asked, stepping around Colby.

"You are going to get married."

"Married? To whom, Father? When?"

"Now. To the Princess Edwenna. Come, let us go to the throne room. After all, you are about to become a prince. What better setting."

GLENLOCK

As they stepped past the guard that Colby selected for the post, Kennington stopped and spoke to him.

"Make sure no one enters."

The guard nodded and the Duke of Sandford closed the door.

CHAPTER 23

Ambush

Seeing a column of smoke ahead, Felix held up his hand to stop the five Turmae of cavalry.

"Lucius, see what is causing that. But be careful. I'd rather not have those villagers know we are here."

The senior decurion nodded.

"Marko, come with me. The rest of you remain with the Legatus."

The two men shifted their oval shields from their backs and, while resting the hilt of their lances in the small leather boot near their right foot, galloped towards the rising smoke.

Paulus leaned toward Felix.

"Trouble?"

"I don't know. That fire seems to come from Acher."

"Raiders?" Paulus asked.

"More likely brigands. Far from the river for raiders. We will wait and see what Lucius finds." He looked at the nearby trees and nodded toward them.

"Clear those woods. I am in no mood to become the victim of an ambush. My mother would scold me to death if I were to get myself killed."

Paulus laughed.

"And I do not even wish to think what she would do to me, cousin."

"It would not be pretty," Felix said, grinning as he stepped down from his horse. "I believe she even frightens my father."

"A wise man, your father," Paulus said.

Felix withdrew a water bag from his saddle and drank deeply. He looked up.

"The sun is strong today. We will need to find water soon."

Paulus turned to the second in command of the fifty-man cavalry squadron.

"Brutus, clear those woods."

Brutus saluted and signaled to the ten members of his turmae. He pointed to the trees, and they sped off.

"There may be a well in Acher."

"May well be. We will see what the scouts find before we consider risking entering the village," Felix said as he watched the scouting party gallop away.

"That Brutus is a good man. Won't be long before he is elevated to senior decurion. Which will surely annoy Lucius. He just got the man broken in."

"Maybe so, but Lucius deserves more than the command of five turmae. It is time he commanded more," Paulus said.

Felix nodded.

"I will speak to Augustus and see if there is an opening."

Paulus pointed.

"Lucius is coming back. He is riding hard."

Felix lept into his saddle.

"Something is wrong." He drew his three-foot spatha and shifted his shield to his left arm.

Paulus followed suit and shouted,

"Skirmish line, now!"

The remaining horsemen split to either side of the officers and readied lance and shield.

Lucius skidded to a halt.

"The village is burning, and dead lie everywhere."

"Did you see anyone?" Felix asked.

"No one alive."

Felix turned to the trees and the sounds of a battle.

"What now?" He looked first in the village's direction and then at the trees. Deciding the threat lay in the forest, he turned his horse.

"Paulus, watch the road."

"Your highness," Lucius said. "Let me take one turmae. You should remain here."

Paulus reached for Felix's bridle.

"Let him do his job, Felix."

Felix listened to the sounds of combat, then looked at the decurion.

"Go!"

"Aurtorous, bring your men!" Lucius shouted. He galloped towards the trees, the ten men of the Turmae following close behind.

Felix looked down the road. The ground was flat grazing land to their right.

"We will make a line here at the edge of the road. Three horse-holders twenty yards behind. The rest of you dismount and form a shield wall." He looked at Paulus. "I do not know what is out there, but I want someplace Lucius can fall back to if need be."

Felix called to the horse-holders.

"Be prepared to bring our mounts forward." He turned to Paulus. "We may need to run."

"Look," Paulus said, pointing at a riderless horse appearing from the trees. It trotted towards them. Paulus grabbed its bridle. There was blood on the saddle.

"We will advance forty paces," Felix called out to the others. "Titus, call the step."

"The second rank prepares to volley with plumbatae. Third rank ready lances. First rank hedgehog."

The first rank lowered their eight-foot spears, pointing them between shields facing the trees, the butts jammed into the ground at their feet. The second stepped back a pace while the third stepped back two. The men of the second rank jammed their lances into the ground and removed one of the six deadly throwing darts from the back of their shields. The third shifted the grip on their spears and prepared to launch them on command.

Suddenly, a group of horsemen broke free of the brush, pursued by dozens of men on foot wielding long, deadly swords. The riders split to either side of the Lantus line as they neared it. Once the last man cleared their front, Felix yelled.

"Throw!"

Five of the spears found purchase, while ten of the weighted darts came streaming down onto the heads and shoulders of their advancing foe. The enemy never slowed as they continued in a disorganized rush, leaping over their fallen comrades.

They drew their long swords and hastened forward, placing their shields in the backs of the men to their front and leaning into their forward leg after launching the missiles.

The enemy crashed into the line of shields, three impaling themselves on the lances of the defenders while they pushed the wall back a few inches. Two attempted to leap over the shields and the blades of the second rank stopped them.

"Forward!" Felix called, and the line took one pace forward, pushing the enemy back inch by inch.

When they could go no further, Felix yelled out.

"Yield!"

"The line of legionaries retreated two paces, causing the enemy to lose their balance.

"Advance!" Felix shouted, and the line stepped into their off-balanced foe.

The men of Lantus quickly dispatched those that had fallen and pushed again.

A strange horn sounded from the trees and the enemy stopped, then turned and fled, leaving their dead and dying strewn about the bloodied field.

Felix called out as several of the legionaries started to pursue.

"Hold!"

They stopped and reformed their line, watching as the enemy disappeared into the trees.

Paules leaned on his shield, catching his breath.

"I do not think they will return."

"Maybe," Felix said. "Sabinus, check the wounded.

"Lucius, are you alive?"

"I am, Legatus," a voice from the rear called out.

"Can you ride?" Felix asked.

"I can."

"Take two men and see if they have truly departed. And be careful. I do not wish to lose you."

"I shall, Legatus." Lucius pointed to two of his scouts. "You two come with me."

The three men strode back to the horse line and mounted. They walked their horses slowly towards the trees, expanding the distance between each other as they moved.

Paulus was talking to the survivors while Sabinus did what he could for the wounded.

"How bad?" Felix asked Brutus.

"We lost three men in the trees. Attackers pulled them from their horses and butchered them before we realized we were under attack.

Felix signaled Sabinus.

"How are they?"

"Nothing a few stitches can't handle."

"And them?" Felix asked, pointing to the enemy's bodies.

"Do you want me to treat them?"

"I want to make sure they are dead," Felix said.

Sabinus moved carefully, drawing a pugio from his belt as he stepped over the bodies that lie before the Lantusian line. He leaned down and examined one of the fallen.

"What in the name of my mother's shade are these things?"

Felix walked forward to see what Sabinus meant.

"I have never seen men like these. They all have the same deformities," Sabinus said.

Felix turned a head from side to side with his sword. "Strange."

Paulus kneeled beside the body.

"His facial features appear human. Two eyes, a nose, two ears. And he has five fingers and a thumb on each hand. But the skull." He looked up at Felix. "These things are not human."

Felix pried the sword from the hand of the dead man. He rolled it in his hand.

"The balance is off. Well, off for one of us. Maybe not for them. I don't know what metal this blade is made of. It is not bronze or iron."

He dropped the sword and turned to his healer.

"Sabinus, how is it they could all have the same deformity?"

"I do not believe that is possible, Legatus. I must agree with Paulus. These are not human. At least not any human form I am familiar with."

Felix turned when he heard Lucius draw near. The young cavalry officer dropped from his saddle and saluted.

"Well?"

"They are gone, Legatus. They left six of their dead."

"And our men?"

"They remain where they fell."

"See to their burial."

"As you wish, Legatus," Lucius saluted and remounted. "Brutus, let us go get your men."

Brutus signaled the rest of his turmae. Those that were wounded mounted and followed to retrieve the bodies of their comrades.

"And Lucius," Felix called before he could join the others.

"Sir?"

"Fine job."

The young man smiled, saluted, then urged his mount to a gallop.

"Good man," Paulus said.

"They all are," Felix agreed. He turned and looked at the trees. "Where did these… things… come from? And why attack us?"

Paulus watched as the horsemen returned, carrying the dead legionaries strung across the front of their saddles. He turned to Felix.

"Should we not warn the emperor of these monstrosities? They may well find their way to Lantus."

"Yes, my father needs to be warned. But so does Augustus."

"And Prince Henry?"

"I am no longer concerned with the affairs of Cent," Felix said." I shall keep my promise to their king, but only after I have sent word to the emperor and found and warned Augustus."

He looked up and watched as a hawk slowly circled above them.

"Have two men return to Lantus and warn Caesar. They are to avoid trouble. I want them to ride hard. Take an extra mount each." He turned to the men digging the graves. "We will depart as soon as we have said farewell to our fallen."

"And where do we ride?" Paulus asked.

"West. To Tilden. They may have word of Augustus."

CHAPTER 24

THE KING'S CHAMBERLIN

John lay in the soaked bedding, the sweat from his shivering body making it impossible to keep dry. William and Bartholomew, two loyal servants, the king's clerks, men that had served him for many years, stared at their king frightened, not knowing what to do to ease his suffering.

John's eyes shot open, and he called out in pain.

"Henry!"

Sir George Williamson, the King's Chamberlain and closest friend, reached for his hand. John attempted to focus his bloodshot eyes as he squeezed the hand.

"It is I, sire. George."

At first, confused and then with relief, John gasped,

"George. Thank God it is you."

"You are safe, your majesty. I have trusted men at the door. They will admit no one without my permission."

"Kennington?"

"I have not seen him since he demanded I officiate at the wedding."

"What wedding?"

"Between his son and Edwenna."

"She has recovered?" John asked hopefully.

GLENLOCK

"Recovered, your majesty?"

"Kennington said she was hurt."

"I have not seen the princess since Prince Henry left. To the best of my knowledge, no one has."

"But you said there was a marriage."

"No, sire. I said the duke wanted me to marry them. He wanted me to declare them wed in absentia. I refused. I told him that without the presence of the bride, it was not a legal union."

"The bastard is after my crown. With Henry gone, his road to the kingdom is a union between Oswald and Edwenna. I should never have listened to that snake."

"What about Colby?" The king asked.

"He is no longer a threat."

"And the doctor?"

"I have people I trust looking for him. When found, he will join Colby."

John gave a weak smile.

"That's good." He closed his eyes and sighed.

"Sire?" George whispered, concerned.

The king whispered.

"I am still here, old friend. But the poison has won. I do not know how much longer I will be with you." His eyes fluttered open, he whizzed, and he tried to sit up. George gently pushed him back.

"You must conserve your strength, John."

"George, you must leave. It is no longer safe for you in Cyneburg."

King John looked at the two frightened men waiting near the door.

"William, you and your brother must go with him. Get your families. Seek my son. I fear for your safety when I am gone."

"We will be alright, your majesty," the Chamberlain said. "Even Duke Kennington would not attack loyal servants of the crown."

"Do not underestimate him as I did, George. He is dangerous. The man was willing to commit regicide, for God's sake. And he has people throughout the capital. I should have seen what he was doing. Your only chance, the kingdom's only chance, is to find Henry. I have sent my seal with the Lantus Ambassador to find him. To keep Kennington from getting it."

He looked up at the two clerks.

"William, I want you to write this down."

The young scribe struggled to get pen and parchment. When he signaled he was ready, John nodded.

"I, John Lackland, King of Cent, lord of all that lie within its borders, commander of its armies, servant to its people, declare that my son, Henry Lackland, the one and true heir to the crown."

He reached out.

"Now give it to me."

He took the quill and signed it, then handed it back.

"The three of you sign it as witnesses. When you find the ambassador, use the seal. Show it to the barons. We cannot allow Kennington to seize control of Cent. You guard that with your lives. Take men you trust and leave immediately."

"But sire?"

"George, thank you, my friend. You have always provided me with wise counsel, even when I did not listen to you. You warned me of the danger Kennington posed. I should have listened to you."

"You were not yourself, your majesty. I believe the doctor poisoned not only your body but your mind."

John gave a sad smile.

"That may be. But I allowed it to happen. So, here is my last command as your king. Take that document to Henry. He is your sovereign now. It falls to him, and to you, to save this kingdom. And, George, tell him I'm sorry. I did not know what I was doing."

"I cannot leave you, sire."

"I am dead already, George. I will not live beyond the hour. I can feel it."

George Williamson, Chamberlin to the king, squeezed the hand of his friend for the last time. He leaned down and kissed the brow of the man he had served most of his life. A man he loved as a brother.

Without another word, he tucked the document into his jersey and walked to the door. The two servants took one last look at their king and then the three men left. The last thing John heard as the door closed and before the darkness took him was George telling the guards to follow him.

"How many men can we trust?" Sir George Williamson asked Francis Appleby, one of Henry's senior men-at-arms, as he looked around the courtyard.

"Twenty men are waiting in the village. I have directed them to bring horses for their families as well as yours. But we must hurry. The castle is teaming with the duke's men."

"Before we do, send for John Waxman's family. They will accompany us."

"And the Sergeant?" Appleby asked.

"He volunteered to stay. When we return, we will need people we can trust inside the castle. He volunteered. Asked we take his family with us just in case."

"Colby knows he is loyal to you."

"Seems the king's former sergeant had an accident. Word is he was drunk and fell from the tower," George said with a wicked grin.

Appleby smiled, then looked up.

"I hear men approaching."

"Then we must go," Williamson said, mounting.

A group of men wearing the livery of the Duke of Sandford rushed across the yard.

"Halt! Stay where you are."

"Go!" Appleby yelled, drawing his sword.

The two guards that had followed the Chamberlain from the king's chamber turned their horses and drew their swords. They took a position on either side of Appleby.

Appleby slapped George's horse upon the rump, and it bolted towards the gate. William and Bartholomew followed quickly.

"Stop them!" The leader of the approaching men screamed. "Close the gate!"

Appleby used the flat of his sword and knocked the man from his feet. He turned and the three men drove their horses into the others, scattering them, and then raced after the Chamberlain. They cleared the gate before it could be closed and quickly crossed the drawbridge. Six men waited, swords drawn. A crossbow bolt struck the wood of the bridge. One of the waiting riders called out.

"What did you do this time, Francis?"

Appleby laughed.

"You know, Billy. The usual."

Another bolt flew past, nearly striking his horse.

"We need to go. Everything ready?" Appleby asked Billy Thatcher, his second in command.

"Everyone is gone. I told them to take only what was necessary. They will meet us at the wood. We waited in case you needed help."

He suddenly raised his shield, and the bolt that struck it penetrated the wood and almost impaled his arm.

"Let's get the hell out of here before they find someone that knows how to use one of those things."

The small party continued down the road, constantly turning to see if they were being followed. By the time they reached the bend in the road that led to Hampton Woods, the sun was setting and it cast the world in shadow.

Appleby raised his hand, and the group came to a halt. He rode forward alone and slowly approached the dark silhouette of a mounted figure standing in the middle of the road. He could see the crossbow aimed at him. He stopped.

"How goes it, Dick?"

"Francis. Damn. Call out next time you approach someone in the dark. I almost shot you."

"Sorry. Everything all right?"

"Not much time to get ready, but we have all the women and children. Had to leave the animals except for the dogs and a few goats and chickens. Grabbed what supplies we could. We are good for maybe two or three days."

"Anyone attempt to stop you?"

"Some questions asked by the villagers is all. I don't think they know what is going on. Shite, I don't know what is going on."

"Where are the others?"

"Moving down the Kings Road. That clerk, William, said we were to head towards Tilden. I stayed back to wait for you. What's going on?"

"I'll tell you more once I know. For now, the king has sent Sir George to find Prince Henry. We are to keep him safe. Seems the Duke of Sandford is trying to take the crown."

"Shite."

"You better believe it. And we need to find the prince before he does."

"I heard the king outlawed him."

"Was, I guess. Isn't now according to Sir George. Don't know the details. But we have fallen into it I can tell you."

"Anything else I should know?"

"Sir George says that King John is dead."

CHAPTER 25

ASTRID

Hal set down his goblet and leaned back, almost falling before remembering the chair had no back. He stretched his legs and stifled a yawn to cover his embarrassment.

The goat hide command tent was large, a good fifteen feet wide, and another eighteen long. It stood eight feet in height, allowing a grown man to stand even at the corners. The scent of incense drifted from oil lamps hanging from the center beam.

"You are tired, Sir Harold," Augustus said, standing.

"A little. It has been a tough couple of days. Haven't had much time to sleep." He stood and stretched his back, lifting his knees one at a time to his waist, trying to loosen sore and stiff muscles. He rubbed his hands down the back of his trousers.

"And I am not used to riding."

"I will have a salve provided for your thighs if you wish," Augustus said, controlling a grin. "I remember when I began my training on horseback. Never could decide if my thighs or ass hurt more."

Hal chuckled.

"Ass. And I would appreciate the salve."

Augustus picked up a goblet and poured from a nearly empty ampere. He held it up and Hal shook his head no.

"Anymore, and I'm afraid I will doze off."

"I find your story fascinating, Sir Harold," Augustus said, taking his seat, leaning forward, his elbows on his knees. "I have heard of the Valley of the Storms, of course. But did not know it was a gateway to other worlds. Those that speak of it tell of ghosts and demons challenging any who enter. I always believed them to be stories designed to frighten children. Henry never told me the full story of his time on your world."

"Few of us knew," Jamie said. "The prince was worried that those that did not know him well would think him mad."

Augustus nodded. "Probably a wise decision. I have often heard our philosophers speak of the possibility of different realities but like most young men forced to listen to their lectures, I thought them nothing but fairytales.

"These things that attacked you. You say they are not of your world?"

Hal gingerly sat back down.

"No. I have no idea who they are, where they come from, or what they are doing here. Nor do I understand why they tried to kill me when I first arrived."

"They ambushed me on my way to relieve Jamie," Edwyn said. "I do not believe they were seeking you alone."

"I agree," Jamie said. "They attacked two of my men the night before I discovered you in the valley. They tried twice to take my squire."

"I wonder why they tried to take him?" Hal asked.

"A good question," Jamie agreed.

"Hal?" Augustus asked.

"A nickname. What my friends call me."

Augustus smiled.

"Well then, Hal, I understand you told the others that you thought you recognized the strange bow these barefoot monsters used. And that you used words when you spoke to them that had no meaning to us."

"The bow reminds me of one I saw when I was a kid. A group of warriors used it from my world's past. In a land called Japan. The man I saw on the hill today was dressed as one of those warriors. They were called Samurai. Fearsome warriors known for their prowess with the bow and the katana."

"Katana?" Augustus asked.

"A sword. Like mine."

Picking up his sword, he handed it to Augustus, who withdrew about four inches of the blade and examined it.

"A beautiful weapon. A stiff spine. Unusual. It is sharpened on only one side."

"I have seen him use that sword," Edwyn said. "It is deadly in the hands of one trained to use it. And our friend here is well trained. His skill is something to behold."

Augustus pushed the blade back and handed it to Hal.

"I studied the technical use of the sword since I was seven. But until today, I have never used it to kill a man."

"Then why did you bring it with you?" Jamie asked. "The other weapon, the gun, is one you say you have used on your world to fight your enemies. Why bring the sword?"

"I don't know. Probably for the same reason I climbed that mountain, I guess."

"This place, this Japan," Edwyn asked. "You say the man we saw on the hill looked like one from there?"

"He did, but that would be impossible. Samurai warriors like that have not existed in my world for centuries. And the men he commanded, the ones with the oddly shaped heads and feet. There is nothing like them anywhere on my world."

"The strange words you used. Were they words used by these Japan people?" Jamie asked.

"Yes."

"Why did you use them?"

"I took a chance because of the horseman. And I thought I had heard a word yelled out by the attackers. One I recognized."

"Which was?" Augustus asked.

"Banzai," Hal said. "It has often been used by warriors of Japan when they attack."

"Does it have meaning?" Augustus asked.

"Literally, it means to live ten thousand years. But in the past, warriors that attacked in the name of their emperor used it. Usually suicide attacks."

"Suicide?" Edwyn said.

"Yeah. Very dedicated warriors."

"I would say," Edwyn agreed.

"This is all so strange," Jamie said. "Even the armor this Samurai wore. It was very colorful. And it looked to be cumbersome."

"He carried no shield," Edwyn added. "Seems a little foolish."

"They did not use them as far as I know," Hal said. "And it would surprise you how light that armor is. And how strong."

"Can you use a shield with that sword of yours?" Jamie asked.

"Never tried. I learned to use the sword in a fencing sport called Kenjutsu. No one used a shield. Many movements require both hands."

"This sport has taught you well. Your skill is remarkable," Edwyn said.

Hal was quiet for a moment, reflecting on the beings he had killed. Unable to think of anything else to say, he simply muttered.

"Thank you."

"What did the words mean you used when you spoke to those things?" Augustus asked.

Jamie laughed.

"Tell him, Hal. I will never forget the look on that daemon's face."

Hal remained silent.

"Well," Augustus asked. "What did you say?"

"I told them to leave."

"And then," Jamie insisted. "Come on. Tell him the best part. The one that almost made him soil himself."

"He asked me who I was," Hal said a little sheepishly.

"And who did you say you were? Go on, tell him. Tell him. Scared the hell out of him."

"I said I was the messenger of death."

"Of course, he was surrounded by the bodies he had just killed with that Katana of his when he said it," Jamie explained gleefully. "You should have seen him. I have never seen a man move so fast or with such control."

Augustus smiled. "I think I like you, Harold Bennet of Deecee."

"None of this makes sense," Hal said.

"What does not make sense?" Edwyn asked. "Besides you coming from another world, of course."

"All of this," Hal said. "You, them, the language. It makes no sense. I mean, look at me. I came here, dumped by a storm from another world, and you act like it happens all the time. My clothes, my equipment, you accept it all without hesitation. I would think you would be concerned that I was some kind of witch or something."

"Are you?" Augustus asked.

"Of course not. I don't believe in witches. Or the supernatural, for that matter."

"Nor do I," Augustus said. "I believe in engineering and science. Hocus Pocus is for the weak-minded."

Hal stared at him.

"Well, okay. What about the language? You claim that everyone here speaks one language and yet you use words that are from others."

"I do not understand," Edwyn said. "What words?"

"Words like segmintata and centurion. Those are Latin."

"I beg to differ, Hal," Augustus said. "They are Glenlockian."

"On my world, they are an ancient language that is no longer used. How is it they are a part of yours? It makes no sense."

Edwyn stood.

"What you are saying is what makes no sense. Words are words. All know them, all use them. Until these things showed up, I never even considered that words existed except for what we use."

"And why would you? Why would you consider another language would exist if you never heard one?" Hal asked.

They were interrupted when, from outside the tent, Celsus called out for Augustus.

"What is it?" Augustus asked.

The Centurion pushed back the flaps and saluted.

"Imperator."

"You have something to report."

"Two of our scouts report the enemy is leaving."

"Follow them. I want to know where they go."

"Already done, sir. And I have doubled the guard in case this is a ruse."

"Very good. Are they using the road?"

"No. They head east beyond the road."

"Do you think they are heading for Cyneburg?" Edwyn asked.

"Unable to tell. But there are a lot of them. More than a legion," Celsus said.

"Cavalry?"

"None reported, Imperator."

"The ones we fought must have been an advanced guard. Scouts or something," Jamie said. "Why are they here? What do they want?"

"Whatever it is their intentions are not peaceful," Edwyn said.

"An invasion?" Jamie asked.

The room remained quiet until Augustus turned to Celsus.

"Thank you, Celsus. I wish to leave at sunup. Break camp and have the Cohort ready to move by then."

Celsus saluted.

"As you wish, Imperator." He turned and left the tent.

"Go where?" Jamie asked.

"First to Tilden. I would like to see you safely home, Jamie, and warn your father of this new threat. Then I need to get back to Lantus and brief my father."

"And what of Cent?" Edwyn asked.

Augustus walked to the closed tent flap and flipped one side open. He looked at the torches lining the encampment.

"That will depend upon King John." He started to turn when he was stopped by a legionary.

"Imperator,"

"Yes?"

"I apologize for the interruption, but a prisoner demands an immediate audience."

"Demands? One of the prisoners? Which one?"

"The woman, sir. She is quite insistent."

"Bring her here. I will speak with her. Only her, you understand. Watch the others closely."

"As you wish, Imperator." The man saluted and ran off.

"Prisoner?" Edwyn asked.

"I told you we came across a group of Southlanders. Said they were fleeing monsters. I have not had the time to properly interrogate them. I almost forgot we still had them."

"Raiders?" Jamie asked.

Augustus shrugged.

"Said they weren't. But then what else would a Southlander say when captured?"

They all turned to the tent opening when they heard a struggle and the growl of an angry woman.

"Keep your hands to yourself, you piece of pig filth, or I will gut you like a fish and feed your innards to the dogs while you watch."

The flap flew open, and the guard threw his prisoner to the floor. She rolled, saw Augustus, and lunged at him. The guard pulled the rope around her neck and forced her back. She spat at the guard, then turned to Augustus. Her long auburn hair flew like flames, her blue eyes boring into him while she fought to gain her feet.

"Let her stand," Augustus said, seeming unaffected by her fury. He smiled. "But keep her on a short leash."

The young woman climbed to her feet and glared at him, ignoring the others.

"You wished to speak with me?" Augustus asked politely.

"This is the way you treat your guests. I came to you in peace."

"You did not come to me. I found you roaming the countryside of Cent after your boats had been destroyed. Probably looking to steal one to return home."

"If I intended to steal another boat, I would have done so and been long gone before you or any of your toy soldiers would have been aware of my presence. I came seeking you, or someone like you."

"Really," Augustus said. "And why would you do that?"

The fiery young woman fascinated Hal. She was slim, athletic, her long red hair tangled and wild, falling below her waist. He guessed her age as late teens or early twenties. She wore leather trousers dyed a deep green under a long blue dress split on either side and held in place by a thick, ornately tooled leather belt. On her feet were tall gray boots made of something other than leather. An intricately embroidered vest lay open over her white linen blouse, the green and gold thread depicting mythical beasts and… runes. Viking runes.

"What is your name!" Augustus demanded.

"I am Astrid, daughter of Aeric of Ingibjörg."

Augustus smiled and gave a brief bow.

"Princess. If I would have known I was entertaining royalty, I would have had you join us sooner."

She glared at him with a fury almost alive.

Augustus waved a hand towards Astrid.

"Gentlemen, may I introduce Princess Astrid Leofric. Daughter of Aeric, the king of Southland."

Edwyn walked to the soldier holding the rope. He took it and stepped toward the girl.

"I will not hurt you." He gently removed the rope.

Jamie lay his hand on his dagger.

"Do you think this is wise?"

Edwyn took her hand and led the young woman to his seat while Augustus gazed at her with a grin, amused about the whole thing. Hal found the smile disturbing. It reminded him of a lion eying its latest prey. He spied the naked blade of a pugio lying next to the Lantusian commander.

Augustus gave a slight nod, and the guard retreated from the tent.

"Why were you in Cent, Princess?" Jamie asked pleasantly, but with an undertone of menace.

Astrid never took her eyes off Augustus.

"My father sent me with a message for King John."

"A message?" Jamie asked.

Astrid was silent for a moment.

"A warning. And…"

"And what?" Edwyn asked gently.

"And, and a request for aid."

"Aid? Help from Cent? For a Southlander?" Augustus asked, astounded. "Now I know you are lying. What on Tera could so frighten a Southlander that they would seek help from anyone, let alone the king of Cent?"

"Mares," she said.

"Mares?" Hal asked.

"Daemons," Edwyn explained.

Astrid turned to Hal, wondering why the man would need an explanation. She looked at his strange clothing. She stared at him for a moment, then turned back to Edwyn.

"They first appeared about two weeks ago. At first, it was just reports of strange ships cruising along the southern coast. Huge vessels, four times the length of a fifty oar drakkar and more than twice its height."

"Drakkar?" Hal asked.

"A craft of war. Sometimes referred to as a dragon ship. The Southerners use them to raid the coast of Cent," Edwyn explained.

"And that of Lantus," Augustus added, staring at Astrid.

The Southlander princess turned to Hal. Who is this strange man? Why does he ask such odd questions?

Augustus cleared his throat and waved his hand impatiently. Continue."

She turned her attention back to him, the tension between them palpable.

"My father," she nearly spat the words, showing her contempt for the Lantusian general. "Sent men to investigate and discovered several of our fishing villages destroyed, the people slaughtered."

She hesitated.

"Something else?" Edwyn asked kindly.

"In each case, they piled the bodies in the village square. Several of the men had been beheaded, the women butchered."

"Did they take the heads? Or mount them on spikes?" Augustus asked.

"It was not Frisians. The heads lay next to the bodies. But there was something else."

"What?" Hal asked, feeling he knew the answer.

"They found no young children. The bodies of the older children were with their mothers, but the youngest were nowhere to be found."

"Why ask for help? Your warriors are strong and fierce," Augustus asked. "All your fishermen are trained warriors. Even your women are trained to fight."

"That is so," Astrid agreed. "But the decision was made because of what happened next."

"Go on," Edwyn said.

"My father sent several ships to seek those that would commit such atrocities. They found nothing along our coast except destroyed villages until a fishing vessel reported seeing several large craft lying off the coast of the Forest of the Dead.

"Six drakkars set off to find the monsters that killed our people. When they found the boats lying off the coast, they boarded them and searched. No one was aboard. Several smaller craft were sighted laying on the beach. They, too, seemed abandoned. Our warriors went ashore."

"Did they find anything?" Hal asked.

"They saw nothing at first. The beach was deserted. Suddenly, many thousands of the devils rushed from the trees. There was no time to return to the boats, so the warriors formed a shield wall. The commander of the fleet knew they could not stop the attackers, there were too many, and to turn their backs and run would be suicide.

"Knowing they were in a hopeless situation, he ordered one crew back to their boat to flee and to tell my father what they had found. Most of them made it to the boat while the others fought to give them time to escape.

"They stayed close to the shore, just out of arrow range, until it was over. Then set sail. It was the only boat to return. Nearly four hundred warriors remained on the sands of the cursed place."

"Where is this forest?" Hal asked.

"The Forest of the Dead lies beyond the Valley of Storms on the southern tip of Cent," Jamie said. "Few have ever entered the forest from either the valley or the shore. Those that have never returned."

"Your people never pass through the forest?" Hal asked.

"A strange question. How do you not know?"

"Sir Harold is not from Glenlock," Edwyn explained.

Augustus laughed.

She looked at him and then back at Hal.

"Not from Glenlock? How can this be?"

Augustus interrupted.

"Sir Harold's story is one for another time. Right now, I want to know why your father would want to warn Cent. And why send his daughter? Why not your brother?"

"It was Knute that commanded the warriors on the beach. He remains there with the others."

"What happened to your boats?" Edwyn asked. "I can't imagine your father sending you with only a single crew."

"He did not. The devils attacked us as we came ashore. Three longboats of warriors accompanied ours. One hundred and fifty of us left Southland. Now we are but thirty."

Augustus was silent for a moment. Then he stood and called out, "Sentry!"

The guard entered the tent.

"Free the prisoners and find them accommodations."

"Their weapons, Imperious?"

He looked at Astrid, and then at the others. Edwyn nodded.

"Return them. It seems we have a new ally."

CHAPTER 26

The Messenger from Cyneburg

Henry left his horse with a groom and followed Baron Mercier up the stone stairs to the keep where Marjorie waited, her arm around Eleanor. Irwin stopped when he reached her. His eyes told the story, his despair was clear.

"Nothing but two more burned homesteads. I have sent riders to bring everyone to the castle. Please make arrangements to accommodate them."

"And the younger children?" Eleanor asked.

"We found none," Henry said.

Marjorie waited until her brothers and all the squires had entered the keep before turning to the steward of the castle.

"Edward, please see that my father and his guests are provided refreshment. Then begin preparations to receive the people. Best prepare for a siege. Use the barracks and the stables."

He bowed.

"It will be done, my lady."

She watched as he scurried towards the kitchen, his lean frame threatening to fall at the slightest breeze.

"Edward has been with us since my father was a child," she said. "No one knows his actual age." She smiled. "He is family."

"Come, Eleanor. Let us see what occurs beyond the wall." They climbed to the curtain wall and watched the activity below. Marjorie sighed.

"It is a shame," she said. "I have known these people my entire life. I see them every day. The merchants and shopkeepers. They are friends."

"What is a shame?" Eleanor asked.

"What must happen. As the town grew, my father allowed them to build their homes and their shops nearer to the castle wall than they should. If it looks like we will come under siege, they will have to be destroyed."

"Why?"

"No wood, no stone. Nothing can remain for an enemy to use as shelter this close to the walls."

"Those poor people," Eleanor said, watching them move to and fro." She looked up at Marjorie. "Do they know?"

"They do. But I am not sure they believe it will come to that. The idea of soldiers of Cent laying siege to Tilden is unimaginable. And few know of the other threat."

"Do you think those things would attack the castle?" Eleanor asked, concerned.

"I don't know. From what I have heard, they do not seem to want to fight armed men. They simply attack those that cannot defend themselves."

"They attacked John."

Marjorie looked at her.

"They did, didn't they?" she said.

"What do you think these things want?" Eleanor asked.

"I do not know."

Eleanor leaned on the wall and stared out toward the horizon.

"They are not human."

"Not human?" Marjorie asked.

"They are misshapen daemons with deformed heads and only four toes on their feet. They say words that have no meaning. They are creatures of nightmares."

"If that is so, how did they get here? And what do they want?"

Henry dropped into the chair and nodded his thanks to the servant that offered him a glass of wine. He sipped the cool liquid, then ran his tongue over his dry lips. He turned when a messenger rushed into the room.

"You have a message for me?" Irwin asked.

"I am sorry, my lord. My message is for Sir Randel. Is he here?"

"I am here, Wendell," Randel said, stepping from the shadow of the wall.

Henry stood and walked to the exhausted man and lay his hand on his shoulder.

"I am Henry. What is your news?"

"Your Highness," he said, nodding his respect. "Sir Randel tasked me to remain after you left and seek the Princess Edwenna. I was to bring her to the woods of the charcoal burners if I could find her."

"Did you find her?" Henry asked.

"No, my lord. Many of King John's men and those of Duke Kennington have searched as well, but there has been no sign of her."

"Do they continue to search?"

"No, your highness."

"Why did you leave if she has not been found?" Randel asked.

"I have grave tidings, Sir Randel. Events have developed that I felt you needed to know. And it was no longer safe for any that serve the crown in the capital."

Henry pulled a chair from the table.

"Rest. Drink. Then tell us all."

The weary man gratefully dropped into the seat and nodded thanks to the servant that offered him a goblet. He smiled when he realized it was ale. Wiping his mouth with the back of his hand, he took a breath.

"For days I watched as more and more of Duke Kennington's men entered the walls of Cyneburg while forcing the king's men to leave until only they remained.

"In the evenings I visited the White Pony, an alehouse. I knew the servants of the palace often visited hoping to get word of the princess."

He looked at Henry, who smiled.

"I know the place. Go on."

"They spoke of strange happenings within the palace."

"What kind of strange happenings?" Henry asked.

"Some said they had not seen the king since the night you left, your highness. I heard tell the king remained in his bedchamber, too ill to venture out.

"Others spoke of guards at the doors to the throne room and the hall to the kings' quarters. They were placed there by the duke and none but those loyal to him could pass. Another spoke of seeing the Lantus emissary enter the king's chamber but never came out. Then they were seen fleeing the castle."

"Fleeing?" Henry asked.

"Fleeing from whom?" Philip asked.

"From Duke Kennington's men."

Henry turned to Irwin.

"Baron, send men to find Legatus Felix and bring him here."

Irwin nodded to his son.

"Marlowe, find him. Keep him safe."

"As you wish, baron," Marlowe said and rushed from the room.

Henry turned to the messenger.

"Anything else?"

"The Chamberlain has not been seen for days. Some say the duke has detained him. Others that he has been killed."

"Killed. Why?" Randel asked.

"I know not, my lord. I was lucky to escape the castle. The walls are patrolled by the duke's men. The gates are closed to all but those that serve him. The duke's men arrest or slay any that resist."

"Where are the king's soldiers?" Irwin asked.

"They look for you, your highness," the messenger said, turning to Henry.

"All of them?"

"All that remain free...or that still live."

"To arrest me?"

"I do not believe they seek to arrest you, your highness," Wendell said. "But the duke has sent a large force to find you, Prince Henry. I discovered where you were from those that follow that army.

"An army?" Randel asked, shocked.

"Yes, sir. I saw over two hundred men leave a camp near the castle walls. They were the duke's men all, and I heard they were about to meet more. One of the boys that prodded the cattle said they were to meet many more."

"Did you hear who led this army?" Randel asked.

"I did, my lord. I overheard the duke tell him to ensure you do not return alive. It is Sir Robert Beckett, curse the name."

"Beckett," Henry said. "I know him. He is a cruel man. Kills for sport. Enjoys hurting women. Loves gold and will do practically anything for it."

"He is a powerful knight. I have seen him in tournaments. He is ruthless," Philip said.

Irwin looked at Wendel.

"You say the duke ordered the king slain?"

"King?"

"We serve Henry now."

Wendell started to rise, and Henry placed his hand on his shoulder.

"Do not get up. You did not know."

"Where is the duke getting all these men? Surely he did not bring that many with him," Philip said.

Irwin slapped his hand on the table.

"The border, damn him!"

"He would need to strip it clean. Even Kennington is not that foolish," Philip said.

"Unless he has made some kind of deal with the Frisians," Randel added.

Henry was silent as he walked to the door and looked out at the activity taking place near the gate. He turned to the rider.

"I wish to thank you, Wendell. You have served us well. Now seek a place to rest."

Wendell looked up at Randell, who nodded.

"And something to eat. You have earned it."

The young messenger left the hall and Henry sat at the table. Suddenly, he slammed his fist on the thick wood, causing the goblets to topple.

"What the hell is Kennington playing at?"

Irwin looked at the others and then at his king. "I think it is obvious, your majesty. He seeks the throne."

CHAPTER 27

SIR GEORGE

Sir George sat silently, watching as two riders cautiously approached. "Any sign of pursuit?"

"None, milord. Me and Patrick watched for near on an hour. They closed the gates, and no one has gone in or out," Steven Longarm said.

George smiled.

"Kennington has boxed himself in. He has sent most of his troops in pursuit of the prince. What he has left, he needs to ensure his control of the capital. Barring the king's men from the city has left him with too few men to commit to a proper chase."

Patrick Allgood looked back down the road.

"Not all the king's men are gone. More than a few have taken Kennington's coin."

"Damn them for that," Longarm said. "Traitors all."

Sir George looked at him.

"How many do you think remain loyal to the crown?"

"Depends, milord."

"Depends on what?"

"Who wears the crown. Folks ain't too keen on King John," Longarm said.

"What about Prince Henry?" George asked.

"That be a different story. Most men I know would follow that man into the Valley of Storms if he asked them. A right honorable man, our prince."

George looked at the two men.

"What if I was to tell you John is dead? That Henry is king."

"If that be true, I almost feel sorry for the duke. Most people would welcome Henry as their king."

It was nearing midnight when Sir George and the guards reached the clearing in the forest outside of Milltown. It was crowded.

"Who are all these people?" The Chamberlain asked as William reached for his bridle and he dismounted.

"Mostly the king's men and their families. Soldiers. Every time we were stopped and explained what had happened, they would send someone for their families and join us."

George looked around.

"Have you been keeping a tally?"

"Bartholomew and I are doing what we can, Sir George, but the numbers grow so fast. It is like half the capital is fleeing."

"Give me an idea."

"We have close to fifty soldiers, a dozen archers and men-at-arms, and near a hundred of their women and children, as well as an equal number of servants, stableboys, farmers, and cooks and their families. And we have three farriers from the town and a blacksmith."

"Do the farriers and blacksmiths have their tools?"

"Aye. In a handcart."

"Good. What about horses?"

Bartholomew chimed in, trying to help his brother.

"I have counted sixty-two horses, my lord. Most belong to the soldiers."

"Two are plow horses that followed their owners as they fled their farm. Seems they did not wish to be left alone. We are using them to carry supplies."

"What about food?"

Bartholomew sighed.

"That is a problem. Many of the people brought what they had wrapped in blankets or dragged along in small carts. But it is not much. The soldiers had only what was in their saddlebags. It is not enough for more than a few days."

"What do we do, Sir George? Where do we go?" Bartholomew asked.

"We head for Tilden. It is the closest place Henry could seek sanctuary."

"Do you think the duke's men will have come to the same conclusion?" Allgood asked.

"Most likely. We will have to avoid the road. Go south for a few days then head west," George said.

"How will we feed these people?" William asked.

"We will seek game, fish. When possible, we get what we can from the farms we come across. It will not be easy, but we have no choice." He looked at the two guards. "And we must get to Tilden before the Duke's men."

"And if the people cannot keep up?" Allgood asked.

George was quiet for a moment.

"Then we leave them behind."

He was awakened when a guard called out a challenge to an approaching rider.

"A scout, Sir George," William said.

George Williamson rose slowly, then rolled his shoulders and stretched his neck as he walked towards the rider. They had been traveling for days, making cold camps to avoid being seen. It had been many years since he had slept on the ground. It was taking its toll.

"What is it?" he asked.

"A large force, Sir George. More than a thousand men on the road to Tilden."

"A thousand men! Where would Kennington get a thousand men?"

"I do not know, milord, but I watched them join with the five hundred that came from the castle. I saw the standard of Sir Robert Beckett. He seemed in charge."

"All those men just to catch the prince," Bartholomew said. "Why would he need so many?"

"Because Duke Kennington wants more than to simply capture the prince." George looked at Steven Longarm, who had just arrived, eager to see what news the rider brought. "How far are we from Tilden?"

"Maybe thirty miles as a bird flies. But that would bring us too close to the road. By keeping forest and hills between us and the road, it is closer to fifty. Normally I would say we could make it in a day, two at the most. But with this lot, it is going to take a lot longer. They will eventually spot us. I don't believe the duke's men could miss a group this size, nor would they allow us to continue towards Tilden."

The Chamberlin was quiet for a moment, then pointed to a ridgeline not more than a mile away.

"What lies beyond that ridge?"

"A small forest next to the Epotix River and an old fort about a mile west that was used to warn to local villages of raiders on the river," Steven said.

"Is it defensible?" The Chamberlin asked.

"It could be, I suppose. With some work. It has been abandoned for years. But there are too many of us. The fort could never hold the people we have. And we could not hold it for long against the force Beckett has."

The Chamberlin smiled.

"We won't have to. Bartholomew, bring my horse. Steven Longarm, send riders to Eudell and Burke. Tell Earl Benton and Baron Huddleston that their king needs them at Tilden. That his life depends upon their support and time is short. Let them know John is dead and Henry now rules.

"Send a rider to Tilden and let Baron Mercier know we are on our way. Ask him to seek the prince if he is not already there. Tell him his life is in jeopardy. He must keep him safe behind his walls until we arrive. I will explain all when I get there."

"Yes, milord," Steven said.

"Once that is done, get your horse and show me this fort."

Steven nodded and ran towards the picket line where the soldiers had hobbled their horses.

The Chamberlin looked at William.

"Bring my sword. I wish you two to remain here. Make sure the people stay in the trees until my return. No fires."

"Yes, Sir George."

George Williamson, Chamberlin to the king, stretched his shoulders, trying to relieve some of the tension that lingered there. He smiled as he thought,.

John, it is like when we were young. Powerful warriors facing impossible odds. I wish you were here.

"Your sword, Sir George."

He took the hand-and-a-half broadsword from William and withdrew a foot of the shining steel from the ornate leather scabbard. He read the words etched in the blade.

"Truth and Honor" The words of a knight of Cent.

"We are ready, Sir George," Steven said as he rode up. He had three armored warriors with him. "I get lonely," he said with a smile.

Bartholomew handed him his reins and a shield with the golden lion of Cent. He slung the shield over his shoulder and climbed onto the saddle.

I am a warrior again.

He turned to Steven.

"Show me this fort."

CHAPTER 28

WHAT TO DO WITH THE WOUNDED?

Felix looked at the line of horses as they made their way along the grassy lane far from any trees. The wounded, with heads drooping, their bodies swaying to the rhythm of their horse's gait, made him sigh. Legionaries on either side rode close, ensuring they did not fall.

Too many, he thought.

Twice now the four-toes, those disciples of Hades, had ambushed them. Each time their arrows struck, more of his men fell. No longer could he take a path designed to keep them hidden from Kennington's men. They now rode in the open, as far from the forests and the trees as the terrain allowed.

Eleven men he buried in the last two days. Eleven friends. Men with families.

How many more, Felix thought. Will any of us make it home? Will I ever see Julia again?

The thought of Julia made him look away. He intended to ask for her hand upon his return to Ome, his father's capital. He knew the emperor would not approve of their joining, but that did not matter. They would marry with or without his permission.

Their meetings had always been in secret. Her father was a senator that did not approve of the power of Caesar. Only Augustus knew of their affair. Not an affair of the flesh but one of the soul, for they had never once done more than touch fingers, intertwining with gentle caresses. Hers were so small. So delicate.

"Legatus?"

Felix turned, his revere broken.

"Yes, Lucius."

"Titus reports that one of his scouts has spotted a large force two miles north along the road to Tilden."

"Was he seen?"

"Of course not, Legatus."

Felix smiled.

"I apologize for even asking. So, how large a force, and does he have any idea who they are?"

"He reports maybe a thousand infantry and another five-hundred horse. There were several banners. At least ten knights."

"More than a thousand infantry?"

"Yes, sir. Moving slowly along the road. Their supply train is more than a mile long, trailing the army with little security. Whoever they are, they fear no threat of ambush. They do not even have outriders, just a few forward scouts."

Felix was quiet for a moment while he considered the news.

"How long until we reach Tilden?"

"Two days. If we maintain this pace," Lucius said.

Felix looked at the wounded. Several did not try to lift their heads when the column halted. Those able to do so offered them water. Too many did not try to drink. Felix knew they would not all make it to Tilden. If they needed to fight, there was no way he could protect them.

He looked at a hill covered in tall pines less than half a mile from their position. He nodded towards it.

"Take the wounded to that hill. Make them comfortable. Leave six men to guard them. Send for Sabinus. I wish to speak to him."

Lucius saluted and turned his horse to speak with his Subaltern, his second in command.

Paulus brought his horse next to Felix.

"We are going to leave them?"

"I have no choice. It is their only chance. If we continue at this pace many will die in the saddle. They need rest and their wounds tended to. If we have to run…"

Paulus nodded in agreement, knowing how hard the decision was for his friend to make.

"It is for the best. And the rest of us?"

"We make our best speed to Tilden. If Henry is there, then so too might be Augustus."

"You believe the Centian prince is there?"

"It is the closest place he could seek refuge. Baron Mercier's wife and Henry's mother were close. I believe he would find safe haven at Tilden. And I believe my brother knows that. If he has received word of what has happened, I have no doubt he will offer the prince his help. They are close."

"You believe the army on the road is a threat to him?"

"I do."

"The Duke of Sanford?" Paulus asked.

"It can be no one else. What I cannot figure out is where all the men come from. They had to be nearby to respond so quickly, and I know John did not send them. Kennington must be getting help from someone." He looked at the distant hill. "Someone from outside Cent."

"Are they a threat to us?"

"I have little doubt. They did not afford us a fond farewell when we left Cyneburg. I don't believe that they are actively seeking us, but they would not be averse to insuring we did not find Prince Henry."

"They would risk war with Lantus?"

"It sounds insane, I know, but I do not believe that has even crossed their minds."

Felix thought of his father. Had he made a deal with Kennington? Is that where the help was coming from? But to threaten me. It makes no sense. Besides, Lucius said nothing about legionaries.

"There is more going on than we know, that is for sure. But for now, we need to save as many of our men as we can, and we need to find my brother. Then I need to get to Lantus and speak with my father. He must be warned about these creatures."

Paulus watched as Lucius prepared the wounded and the little supplies they had left for movement to the woods.

"Do you believe they will be safe there?"

Felix did not answer, thinking of the strange men that had attacked them.

"Cousin? Are you alright?"

"I am concerned, Paulus. I do not believe any of us are safe. And the frustrating thing is, I don't know why."

Lucius walked towards them, leading his horse.

"All that can be done has been, Legatus. The wounded, with what little supplies we had left, will settle in those trees. I have instructed that no fires are to be built."

Lucius handed the two senior officers a small bag each.

"A day's ration. It is all we have."

"How much did you leave them?" Felix asked.

"If they are careful, maybe three or four days."

Felix stared at the hill. His men. His friends. Would he see them again? Was he leaving them to die? For what? To save the life of a foreign prince. He turned to Lucius.

"Prepare the others. We leave immediately. I wish to be in Tilden by tomorrow."

Lucius saluted.

"As you wish, Legatus."

Sabinus walked toward him, leading his horse.

"You wished to see me, Legatus?"

"I know you wish to stay. I cannot allow it."

"But Legatus."

"You have done all you can for them, Sabinus. And I need you with me in case we meet these monsters again." He did not mention the army along the road. "When we reach Tilden, I will send help. I give you my word."

Sabinus stared at him, then nodded. He saluted, then lept onto his horse and moved to the back of the column.

Paulus watched him go.

"A good man."

"He is. And I know he is not happy with my decision. But it must be done."

Felix mounted and trotted towards the remainder of the force that had accompanied him to Cent. Twenty-three men out of a force of fifty.

Paulus drew up beside him.

"Do you think the things that attacked us are gone?"

Felix looked towards the hill.

"I hope to Jupiter that they are. Come, we have a long road ahead of us."

Felix walked his horse down the column. He noticed the wounds on several of the men wrapped in bloody bandages.

Strong men. Loyal. Fearless. What an honor it is to ride with such warriors.

He looked around.

"Lucius!"

The senior decurion trotted to him.

"Legatus?"

"Where is Brutus?"

Lucius looked at the hill.

"With what remains of his turmae."

Felix watched as the six men he had left behind helped the wounded. Brutus looked back. Felix started to wave but stopped and took a deep breath. He turned his horse and rode to the head of the column and raised his hand.

"Forward."

Paulus and Lucius took positions on either side of him. He turned to Lucius.

"Send two men to Ome and report to the emperor what has occurred. Tell him I am on my way to Tilden. That an army approaches I believe intends to kill the king of Cent." He hesitated a moment and looked back at the hill. "And tell him of the monsters."

"Yes, Legatus." He pointed to the first men in line and signaled he wanted to speak with them.

"Do you think your father will send help?" Paulus asked.

"To Cent, I don't know. He likes Henry. But I don't know if that will be enough."

"And what if we get trapped in Tilden by Kennington's army?"

"Then we fight."

The two Lantusian messengers slowed their horses.

"I don't see anyone," the first rider said. "We need to slow down. The horses are tired and will not last much longer at this pace."

"I know," the second rider said. "As soon as we reach those trees, we will walk for a while. Let the horses catch their breaths. We won't get far if they drop dead between our legs."

When they reached the trees, they dismounted.

"Wait here," Cassius said. "I need to use a tree."

Cassius untied his breaches as he walked towards a large birch when he slumped back, his eyes staring blankly at the clear sky as he came to rest on the grass, an arrow protruding from his chest.

Julius lept into the saddle and kicked his horse to a gallop as another of the deadly shafts buried itself in the ground he had just occupied. Cassius's horse closed the gap and ran beside him. He reached down and grabbed the reins, then dropped between the two animals, pushing a foot in the stirrup of each. Riding between them, he galloped northwest.

"Shit, shit, shit."

"Do you think we will make it?" Paulus asked.

Felix smiled.

"If we don't, I will never hear the end of it from Augustus. You know how he is."

"Felix, you never finish anything you begin. Someday that will be the death of you." He laughed. "Could be he was right."

"I really did not need to hear that," Paulus said.

Felix was quiet for a moment.

"I believe we will make it, Paulus." He looked behind him at the tired troopers. "We have to." Reaching into his pouch, he withdrew the ring John had given him.

"But in case something happens to me, you must take this to Tilden. Show it to Baron Mercier and tell him he must find Prince Henry and give it to him."

He put it back in his pouch.

"We are errand boys now for those of Cent?" Paulus asked.

"No. We are loyal servants of Lantus doing our best to prevent a civil war in a friendly nation. One that could hurt the Empire. Duke Kennington is no friend to Lantus."

He raised his hand and stopped the line of men. Dismounting, he led his horse.

"We will walk for thirty minutes every hour. We will keep going until the horses can go no farther."

"And then?" Paulus asked, offering a water bottle to his friend.

Felix shook his head.

"Save it. I don't know when we will find more."

"Well?" Paulus asked. "What do we do when the horses give out?"

"We walk."

CHAPTER 29

PLAN OF ATTACK

Hal flipped back the flap of the goat hide tent and stepped out into the morning sun. Squinting, he placed his hand above his eyes until they adjusted to the light. Looking around, it surprised him to see that most of the camp was gone. A group of legionaries stood a few yards from the tent, apparently waiting for him.

"Good morning, Sir Harold," Augustus said, doing his best not to laugh.

Behind him stood Edwyn and Jamie and their squires, all sporting enormous grins. The only ones not smiling were Bailey and his father, although Ramsey was having difficulty controlling his.

"I was afraid I was going to have to have these men strike your tent with you inside."

"I'm sorry. I didn't realize I was so exhausted."

"No need to apologize, Sir Harold. You have been through a great deal in the last few days." Augustus said. "Do you not find the clothing satisfactory?"

Hal looked down.

"Not what I'm used to."

"The Imperator felt it wise to provide clothing that would help you blend in," Edwyn said. "Although I am not sure he has been totally successful."

"Thank you, Imperator," Hal said, realizing it was time for titles. "I appreciate it. The pants are a bit short."

The brown wool trousers stopped close to a foot above his ankles. The red sleeveless tunic fell short of his knees, held tight around his waist by his web belt sporting a black nylon holster. Below the hem of the trousers, the red stripes of a pair of white athletic socks peeked out from the top of his tan desert combat boots. He had fastened the Camillus knife around the calf of his right leg with a pair of OD green straps. He carried the katana in his right hand, the baseball cap in the left.

"I prefer my own boots. Kinda used to them. Besides, I could not figure out how to tie those things." He pointed to the caliga worn by the legionnaires.

Augustus shook his head.

"I suppose from a distance you might be confused to be one of us."

"I doubt that," Jamie said.

Augustus snapped his fingers, and a trooper stepped forward, carrying a scaled metal vest.

"Sir Edwyn was concerned that you lack armor. The Lorica Squamata is what the offers of the turma wear. I hope it meets with your approval."

Hal undid his belt, and the legionary slipped the scale armor over his head.

Not as heavy as the vest I wore in Afghanistan. But then I doubt I will have to worry about it slowing down a bullet.

He buckled his belt and pushed the katana through.

"It is good armor and will hold up against most blades, although it will hurt like hell when you receive a blow, may even break something, but at least you won't bleed to death," Augustus said.

"And arrows?" Hal asked.

"It will deflect or even blunt an arrow. They should not penetrate. Even the ones the daemons use," Jamie said.

"And if they are using bodkins?"

"Bodkins? Edwyn asked.

"The arrowhead designed to penetrate armor."

"I have never heard of such a thing," Edwyn said.

"Let me show Richard what I'm talking about later. He is an archer. See what he thinks. Maybe something you might find useful."

He turned to Augustus.

"Do you have a blacksmith?"

"I do."

"I could show him if you'd like."

I would appreciate that.

"And you will teach Richard?" Jamie asked.

"Of course," Hal said, realizing why he asked. Lantus was not Cent.

"If they do as you say," Edwyn said. "They would have been useful in the last war."

"Last war?" Hal asked, doing his best to settle the metal shirt on his shoulders.

"Against the Frisians. Lantus was our ally," Edwyn explained.

"Many perished. On all sides," Jamie said.

Remembering the story of Edwyn's brother, Hal remained quiet.

"The Frisians are a threat to us all," Augustus said. "If they had taken the north of Cent, our borders too would have been in jeopardy. The bastards have raided our shores even more than the Southlanders. We did not need to give them a land bridge to Lantus."

"Your legions stopped them," Edwyn said.

"And your cavalry sent them running home. We indeed have strong infantry, but we mostly used our horsemen as scouts or to secure our flanks. We have but one Alae to a legion."

"Alae?" Hal asked.

"Three hundred horsemen," Augustus explained.

Hal pulled on the Detroit Tigers baseball cap.

Edwyn shook his head. He turned to Augustus.

"He needs a helmet."

Augustus laughed, then signaled to a pair of waiting legionaries.

"Collect Sir Harold's belongings. Place them in my wagon. I want a guard on them at all times. They are not to be touched."

He turned to Hal.

"We do not wish any of your things to disappear. You have yet to show me all the wondrous items you carry in that bag. I especially wish to see the device that allows you to see in the dark. Sir Edwyn has told me of it. As well as the weapon that strikes down a foe with a crack of thunder." He pointed to the holster. "That is it?"

"Yes."

"It kills daemons," Jamie said.

William and Peter handed their knights their sword belts.

Sir Harold," Bailey stepped forward. "I saddled your horse. I will fetch it when you are ready."

Hal looked at Augustus, who nodded.

"I'm ready."

Bailey turned to go when his father placed a hand on his arm.

"I will get it, Master Bailey."

As Ramsey ran towards the horses, Edwyn whispered,

"I believe your young squire is finding his change in status a bit hard to accept."

"I'll speak to him."

"No, Sir Harold," Edwyn said. "He and his father must work this out on their own. Bailey is a squire. Someday he may become a knight. A position his father can never hope to achieve. He knows this and is proud of his son. It is Bailey that is having difficulty accepting that he is no longer just Ramsey's son. He is now his superior."

Titles matter, Richard had warned.

Hal remembered a time when his team was waiting in England to deploy on a training exercise. They were playing cards. It was hot, and no one was wearing a shirt. A sergeant from the British SAS asked to join the game. As the cards were being dealt, one of his team referred to him as sir. The SAS sergeant asked if he was an officer. When one of the other man said yes, the sergeant got up and left without saying a word. In their world, officers and NCOs did not fraternize. Ever.

"I appreciate the advice."

"Your men are efficient, Imperator," Hal said as he looked around. The camp was gone. Even the trench had been filled in.

"I have never seen a camp come down like this."

"They are legionaries, Sir Harold. That is what they do."

Celsus stepped forward, leading both his and Augustus's horse.

"The First Cohort of the Ninth Legion is prepared to march, Imperator," the man said. "Scouts are out, and the way is clear."

"Very well, Celsus. We will be with you shortly."

Celsus mounted and rode toward the assembled soldiers.

"We should go, gentlemen," Augustus said, leaping into the saddle ignoring the stirrups. We have a long march ahead of us."

Hal, using a stirrup, carefully swung himself onto the saddle and immediately regretted it.

Yep, the ass still hurts. And my thighs feel like all the skin has been rubbed off.

Augustus noticed his distress and smiled. "I will have a healer see to you when we halt, Sir Harold. He will have a salve that will provide some relief."

"I would appreciate that."

They walked along the column. They arranged the formations of eight men wide and ten deep, with ten paces separating each century. Six wagons pulled by mules stood at the rear of the formation, a half-century of legionaries providing security.

When he saw the command party nearing, Celsus leaned down from the saddle and spoke with the man carrying the standard, a brass eagle, wings spread above a red banner displaying a bull's head and the number IX embroidered in gold thread.

The ninth legion, Hal thought. *The Lost Legion of Rome. This is crazy. I know it can't be them. Rome never allowed Black Africans in a legion throughout its history. And the Ninth disappeared in Britain centuries ago.*

Two deep, bellowing calls on a horn drew Hal's attention to a soldier carrying a large horn looped around his body.

He looked up when, all along the column, commands of attention echoed. Augustus rode to the front and was about to give the command to advance when someone called out. Astrid along with four men galloped towards them.

Augustus turned. "Damn that woman.

"Celsus!"

"I've got it, Imperator." Celsus turned his horse and intercepted the Southland group.

"I am sorry, Princess. You and your people need to ride with the wagons."

She looked at him and then at the small party from Cent.

"I will ride with the strange one." She pointed at Hal.

Celsus looked at Hal, who shrugged his shoulders, not knowing what to say. Jamie leaned over.

"Good luck, Sir Harold. I think you are going to need it. That woman has an interest in you."

Astrid stopped her horse next to him. Bailey gave her a nasty look and moved forward.

"It's all right, Bailey," Hal said.

Bailey looked at his father. He shook his head, but Bailey noticed that his hand lay upon his sword.

Astrid turned to her men.

"Oelig, you and the others ride with the boys."

Oelig was an enormous man. His blond beard and mustachios were braided and draped over his massive chest. Stuck in his belt was a long-handled ax, a massive broad sword was slung across his back.

Vikings. This place just keeps getting weirder and weirder.

"As you wish, Princess," the Southland warrior said, his deep voice barely a whisper, his anger clear.

Oelig rode past the squires and drew his horse beside Ramsey. Although taller, Ramsey matched Oelig's build pound-for-pound. The two stared at each other, then Oelig reached down and undid a bag from his belt.

"I do not ride with boys." He offered the bag to Ramsey.

Ramsey took a deep swig. He wiped his lips with the back of his hand and then nodded his thanks as he handed the bag back.

"I have not had decent mead for a long time."

Oelig smiled.

"No finer drink exists for a fighting man."

"Wait until we get to Tilden," Ramsey said. "I will find us some whiskey. Something new. Burns like hell going down. Best stuff I've ever tasted."

Oelig gave a deep laugh and patted his stomach.

"I look forward to it."

Hal turned at the sound of Oelig's laugh.

"Seems they are getting along."

"Oelig respects warriors," Astrid said. "But do not misunderstand. He may not like it, but a warrior's bond will not stop him from doing his duty. He will kill your man without a second thought if he feels it is necessary."

Hal smiled.

"He may try."

She ignored his comment.

"He and the others are my Huskarls, my bodyguards. Oelig has been at my side since I was a child." She explained.

Sir Jamie brought his horse to Hal's left and Sir Edwyn on Astrid's right, keeping her horse between him and Strongheart.

"It seems your friends are concerned I may do you harm, Sir Harold," Astrid said with a grin. One Hal felt unsettling.

"They're just being friendly," he said, relieved they had done so.

She looked at his boots and smiled. It surprised him she said nothing.

Augustus lifted his hand, palm open, then quickly dropped it. Celsus turned his head and called out.

"Advance march!"

The Imperator walked his horse forward while six riders broke from the formation and rode to their left and right flanks. Hal remembered Celsus mentioning that riders were already ahead, ensuring the way was safe. These were the flank guards. He squirmed in the saddle, attempting to find a comfortable position.

Astrid chuckled.

"You are not accustomed to riding, Sir Harold?"

"No. And I'm not sure I ever will be."

"It will take but a few days in the saddle and you will be fine. My father insisted I ride every day as soon as I could walk. He said I would not always have a ship to take me where I needed to go, and like a sailor learning to train his stomach to the roll of a ship, the inside of one's legs needs to do the same to the saddle."

"Your father sounds like a wise man."

"He is. And a powerful leader. It took courage for him to send his remaining child to those that fear us."

"These things took your children?" Jamie asked.

"And killed everyone else they encountered."

"Did you see one?" Edwyn asked.

"That attacked the villagers, no. Those that attacked our boats, yes. They were not men. They screamed words with no meaning and their heads were those of beasts from Helheim."

"No boots, four toes?" Edwyn asked.

"You know of them?" she asked.

"We have come upon them."

"Sir Harold spoke with them," Jamie said. "He understood their words."

She looked at him in surprise.

"You understood their gibberish?"

"They spoke a language I'm familiar with," Hal said, wishing Jamie had kept his mouth shut."

"Language? What means that?" she asked.

"Language is the words we use to communicate," Hal explained.

"But all in Glenlock use the same words," she said.

"Where I come from, many people use different words that mean the same thing. The words used by your demons were Japanese. But how they know it is beyond me."

She looked at him as if he had sprouted a second head.

"What do you mean, where you come from? No one in Glenlock uses other words. What you say makes no sense."

"Sir Harold is not from here. His world is far away."

"World? Beyond the Great Sea? No one lives beyond the sea. You use untrue words, Sir Harold."

"He comes from beyond the Valley of Storms," Edwyn explained.

Astrid stared at him.

"I have never heard of anyone living on the other side of the valley. You are from The Forest of the Dead?"

"I don't exactly come from beyond the valley. I mean, I don't live there."

"He is not from Tera, Princess," Jamie explained.

She stared silently at Hal for a moment.

"You are a curious man, Sir Harold. I think we should speak more."

Just like the others, he thought. She just accepts that I am from another world.

Astrid looked at the katana and then at the holster on his belt. "I have never seen a sword such as that."

"It is called a Katana."

"What is that thing hanging from your belt? And what is it made of?"

Hal lay his hand on the handle of the pistol.

"A weapon of my world. And the holster is made of nylon."

"Nylon? Some kind of animal pelt?"

"No. Plant-based; I think. To be honest, I don't really know what nylon is made of."

"May I see the weapon?"

Hal pulled the pistol from the holster, ejected the magazine and the round in the chamber, then handed it to her. She took the pistol as if it were a deadly snake and examined it. She pointed to the bullets.

"And what is it you took from it?"

"Bullets. The weapon… launches them?"

"Something like those used by slingers," Edwyn said.

"Those little things kill?" she asked.

"I have seen the results of one of those bullets striking one of your devils," Jamie said. "Believe me when I tell you they are deadly."

She handed the pistol back.

"Alarm! Alarm!"

They looked up at the rider galloping towards the column. Celsus turned his horse and shouted,

"Form line! Form line. First eight of the first century to the Imperator."

The rider reached Augustus.

"Those things have turned and are but a mile ahead, Imperator."

"How many and what is their disposition? Calm yourself, trooper. I need an accurate report."

"Sorry, Imperator. There are at least six or seven hundred less than a mile ahead blocking the road. I saw more along a ridgeline, but they continue marching north."

"How many going north?"

"I would guess at least a legion, Imperator. Maybe more."

"Very well. Report to Decurion Antonius."

The rider saluted and rode off as eight legionaries formed a wall of shields in front of Augustus.

"It appears that our friends do not wish us to continue along this path," he said, turning to them. "They have left six centuries of warriors behind to intercept us. The rest of their force continues north. Suggestions?"

"To the west are steep hills and the sea. We do not want to find ourselves with our backs to the sea. If we go east, it will add several days to our journey," Edwyn said. "That is assuming more of these things are not there waiting."

"Then I suppose we have no choice but to remove the obstacle that lay ahead of us," Augustus said.

"We fight?" Astrid asked with a smile.

"We fight," Jamie agreed.

"Good," Astrid turned and called to Oelig. "The daemon spawn lies ahead. Get the others."

Oelig smiled. He spoke to one of the Southlanders who turned and rode back towards the wagons. Oelig rode forward, pushing Sir Edwyn's horse aside to sit beside Astrid.

"No Oelig. I shall ride with these people. I am curious to see how they fight. Assemble the men and ride with those of Cent."

"But Princess."

"Do not fret, my loyal guardian. I will be safe. I have an Otherworlder to watch over me."

"Otherworlder?" he asked.

"Is it not exciting?" she asked.

Oelig stared at Hal, making him very uncomfortable. Ramsey moved forward, and Hal shook his head. Ramsey stopped, but his hand remained on his sword.

"Have I interrupted something?" Augustus asked.

Edwyn stared at Oelig.

"No, Imperator. Just sorting out where our allies are to ride."

"Well, I need you all to ride together. With your men, Sir Edwyn, the Southlanders, and my riders, we have close to eighty horse-mounted warriors.

"May I assume your people are familiar with fighting from the back of a horse, Princess?"

"The deck of a drakkar, the dirt of Tera, or the back of a horse, are all the same to my warriors."

Augustus smiled.

"The answer I expected." He turned to Jamie. "I apologize, Sir Jamie, for speaking as if Sir Edwyn were in charge. It was simply that he is… uh, more experienced."

Jamie stopped him before he could continue.

"Although we have not discussed it, I would naturally bow to Sir Edwyn's– experience."

Edwyn laughed.

"You two calling me old?"

"Not at all…just more seasoned in the art of war," Jamie said, trying to keep a straight face.

"Seasoned," Edwyn said, stroking his beard. "That's good. I like the term seasoned."

Augustus chyckled.

"Now that it's settled, let me explain what I would like you to do."

Jamie, Astrid, Ianuarius, and Augustus lay next to Edwyn and Hal, looking down on the enemy formation. The rest of their forces waited on the far side of the small hill.

Hal handed the binoculars to Augustus.

"They have selected a good spot," Augustus said. "The road turns as it runs through the saddle of these two hills. If we had not had scouts out, we would have run right into them. No way to go around with the marsh on their left and heavy forest on the right." He reluctantly handed the binoculars back to Hal. "These are amazing."

Decurion Antonius, the commander of the scouts, crawled up next to Ianuarius.

"The flanks are secure, sir."

"Thank you, Antonius." Ianuarius smiled. "Ready for a cavalry charge?"

The young man could hardly control his excitement.

"Yes, Decurion. Finally, an opportunity to show those dirt grinders what cavalry can do."

Augustus turned and looked at him. Antonius quickly worked his way back down the hill.

"They have no shields," Ianuarius said, wishing to redirect his commander's attention from the young warrior.

"But they have archers. I can see them arrayed behind the formation," Jamie said.

"I don't know how good they are with those. The Yumi bow is difficult to master," Hal said.

"And a charging horse is not an easy target," Ianuarius added. "Without shields, they will be sitting ducks to a cavalry charge."

Edwyn turned to him.

"Do not underestimate these things. Those pikes they carry are long enough to stop a rider before he can get close enough to strike. Horses will not ride into them."

"Richard and his archers could help. There are few, but they could open a hole in their line," Jamie offered.

"Their bows are too long to be used from the back of a horse," Edwyn said.

"Then they will have to dismount as we charge."

Edwyn thought about it and then shook his head.

"No. We need all our riders to break that line."

"I think I can open it," Hal said.

"Can you use that weapon from the back of a horse?" Edwyn asked.

"Use it, yes. Hit anything, probably not. I'd have to dismount."

Edwyn looked at him, waiting for more.

"Maybe a couple of us ride towards them while everyone else stays hidden behind the crest of the hill. We dismount, confuse them. Maybe they will think we came to talk."

"And if they use their bowmen against you."

"Whoever comes with me will have to use their shields to cover me."

"I have sent Celsus with a full century through the forest on their right to flank them," Augustus said. "When they are in position, they will make a good deal of noise to draw the enemy's attention away from us. Hopefully, those below will think we attack from their rear and turn their pikes. If that does not work, we will have to go with Sir Harold's plan."

"Oelig and I will go with Sir Harold," Astrid said.

"Thanks, but I will take Ramsey and Bailey." He looked at Edwyn. "That is their job, and I would not wish them to think I do not trust them. Besides," he looked at her shield. "Their shields are bigger."

Astrid stared at him for a moment, then nodded.

"I understand."

"Now that is settled, let us talk about how we will do this," Edwyn said. "We will attack in a wedge. Jamie and I and our squires will form the point with our longer spears followed by Ianuarius and the Southlanders.

"Richard, you will lead our men. Follow the Southlanders.

"Sir Harold, you will ride with them as well," he smiled at Astrid, who returned it. "If it is you that has to open their front, however, wait until we pass you before mounting."

Hal nodded.

"We will keep him safe," Astrid said.

Edwyn looked at Hal, who shrugged his shoulders.

"As you wish," Edwyn said. "But a warning, Princess. That weapon of his barks like thunder. If he uses it, be careful it does not frighten your horse."

"All the more reason someone needs to watch him," she smiled at Hal. "It may be his horse that panics."

Smartass.

Augustus continued to watch the men below.

"Celsus should be ready shortly."

Fifteen minutes later, the rhythmic banging of pila on scuta, the long rectangular shields of the Lantusians, rose from behind the enemy line.

"Celsus will move his men forward over that small rise and deploy the century in line," Augustus explained. "Hopefully, they will think the greater threat lies beyond the rise. With luck, they will turn their pikes.

"Celsus will make a lot of noise. Banging on shields, yelling insults, and sounding the horn. That will be your signal. Hopefully, that will mask the sound of your charge. I will follow with the rest of the infantry."

"If they turn, you will not need to use your weapon, Sir Harold," Edwyn said. "We must be ready either way. If Sir Harold's plan is necessary, only his man and squire will advance. When we hear his weapon, we will move up the hill.

"Either way, we will advance at a walk down the slope. Once we all are on the plain, we will trot until one hundred yards of their line, then spur to a gallop and strike their center. Do not stop. We drive through reform and charge again. Questions?"

There were none.

CHAPTER 30

THE FORT

"There it is, Sir George," Steven Longarm said, drawing his horse to a halt.

The Chamberlain looked at what had once been a small wooden fort. No Ditch remained around the mostly dismantled wall. The lookout tower was little more than a pile of rotting wood, having fallen in on itself many years ago.

"It has been abandoned for more than ten years," Steven said. "I do not know what it is you hope to use it for, Sir George. It will not provide much protection."

"It will not need to," Sir George said.

He turned to the six men Frances Appleby had sent as a guard. Appleby, his man-at-arms, did not accompany him, taking command in his absence.

"Before we left, I asked Frances Appleby if there were men that I could count on. He selected you. There is something that needs doing. Something important but dangerous. If you agree, I cannot guarantee your survival. I am asking, not ordering, you to do this. If you decide not to no one will think the less of you. Only those of us here will know. But if you succeed, it will buy precious time for me to get everyone safely across the river and eventually behind the walls of Tilden."

One of the six looked at the others, who all nodded.

"My name is Harry Millerson, Sir George. My wife Betsey, my boy, and two girls are back with the others. All of us have family waiting. I knew Francis was up to something. He said this would be dangerous. He gave us a choice. If this will help get our families safely to Tilden, whatever you have in mind will be worth the risk."

George stared at each man as if it was to be the last time he would see them and wanted to memorize their faces.

"I want you all back, but if that does not happen, I give you my word that your families will be taken care of. I will see to it myself."

"Thank you, milord," Harry said. "What is it you need us to do?"

Sir Robert Beckett was tired of the meandering pace required to accommodate the foot soldiers and the supply train. He turned and looked at the long line of men marching along the road.

"I should never have agreed to take the infantry. Their pace is such that the seasons may change before we reach Tilden. Damn the Duke."

The young knight riding next to him tried in vain to see the end of the column. The dust raised by the horses made it all but impossible. Seeing the dust, he was glad to be at the head of the column.

"I believe that the duke was concerned that the prince might be behind the walls of Tilden, Father. If we need to lay siege to the castle, the infantry will be needed."

"I know, Billy. But if we had sufficient horse, we could have prevented him from reaching the damned castle."

The sound of a fast-approaching horse from the rear of the column made them stop and turn.

"A dispatch rider from the capital?" Billy asked.

His father watched as the man rode to the side of the troops crowding the road, his tired horse almost falling as it hit the damp grass of the sloping edge of the roadway. Seeing Beckett, he worked his way toward him. He slipped from the saddle and walked swiftly from the panting animal to the two riders and nodded his respect.

"Sir Beckett, a message from Duke Kennington."

Beckett looked at the unbroken seal.

"Do you know what this says?"

"No, sir. I was just told to deliver it as quickly as I could. This is my third horse. I have been in the saddle for two days."

"Sir William, take this man to Captain Ringwald and see he is taken care of. Then return."

Billy nodded and turned to the exhausted rider.

"Come with me."

The dispatch rider took the reins of the sweat-coated horse and stroked its neck.

"You can rest now. I will get you water and a bag of oats. You have earned them."

Beckett broke the seal and unfolded the paper. As he read, he smiled.

"You wily bastard." He folded the paper and placed it in his shirt, then dismounted, enjoying the opportunity to stretch sore muscles.

"Ringland has taken the man in his charge, Father," Billy said when he returned. "You have read the dispatch?"

"I have. King John is dead. Kennington's whelp Oswald has wed Princess Edwinna. With the death of the king and her brother being outlawed, she will take the crown. The duke will act as regent until Edwinna reaches her majority."

"But you told me that Edwenna is dead."

"She is. That idiot Colby killed her. But few know this, so the duke simply announced that she and Oswald had wed with the blessing of the king. Who is to dispute the claim? I'm sure he has some plan to explain her death in the future. Upon which, Oswald becomes king."

"Do you think he will get away with this?" Billy asked.

"He already has. With the announcement of their joining, his claim is irrefutable. The other nobles will have no choice but to accept Edwenna as their queen, and Oswald as their king."

"But won't they be suspicious?"

"Maybe. But trust me, Kennington will deal with that."

"Was there anything else?"

"Yes. Sir George has fled the capital and may have in his possession a message from John to Henry. We are to intercept him before he reaches Tilden."

"So, what if he does? There is nothing he can do."

Beckett leaned towards his son and whispered. "Kennington believes he carries the king's seal and a letter from John declaring Henry his heir. That is something he does not want the nobles to see.

"Find Sir George. He must not reach Tilden. If he has the letter, burn it, and bring me the ring."

"And if others follow him."

"None are to reach Tilden."

Sir George looked at the mass of people as they secured their few belongings. Men, women, children, mothers with babes in arms, and the elderly, some so frail they had to be carried.

There must be two hundred families here and less than a hundred soldiers to protect them.

"We are ready to move, Sir George," Appleby said.

"Is Thatcher sure we can safely cross the river?" George asked.

"Billy grew up not far from here. He says there is a ford that never exceeds three feet and that the current becomes lazy, as he puts it, due to a nearby bend in the river."

"And the men at the fort?"

"Await your signal."

Sir George took a deep breath.

"I hope this works. Let's get them moving, Captain."

"I'm not a captain, Sir George. I'm simply a man-at-arms sworn to serve the crown."

Williamson smiled.

"And I, as a representative of the crown, have decided you will be my captain."

Appleby stared at him for a moment, then smiled.

"As you wish, My Lord Chamberlin. And thank you. The misses will be pleased with the extra pay."

"We need to sort all this out before anyone gets paid, I'm afraid."

"But think of my back pay."

Williamson laughed.

"We should go."

"As you wish, Sir George." Appleby turned when the man standing beside him slapped him on the shoulder.

"Congratulations, Frances. Need a sergeant?" Steven Longarm asked.

"Thank you and ask me again once we have everyone across the river. Now get these people moving. Make sure we have a rear guard. A large one. Have some of the other men flank the civilians and their animals and keep them in line."

"Rider coming!" someone shouted.

The three men waited until the scout reached them.

"What is it?" Sir George asked.

"Several horsemen have broken off from those on the road and are headed this way, milord."

"Were you spotted?"

"No, sir. But it will not be long before they see us if we remain here."

"Kennington must have sent word to stop me. We need to get across the river as quickly as possible. Signal the fort. It is time."

Appleby waved at a waiting archer.

"Now!"

The archer dipped the tip of the arrow into a bucket of pitch, then touched it to the small fire he had been maintaining. Aiming high and pointing the bow to the northeast, he pulled the string back to his ear. With a twang, the arrow rose into the sky, trailing a thin line of black smoke.

"That's the signal, boys," Millerson said. "Light er up, Thomas. Get the horses, Johnnie. Run them around and churn up the mud. I want them to think everyone had headed southeast.

"Freddie, you be the sentry. Make sure they see you, look surprised to have been spotted, then frightened. Then lead them back here."

Thomas Clinton threw the torch into the remains of the tower. Earlier, they had trimmed pine boughs from nearby trees and soaked them in water. Once the fire was high enough, he threw the boughs onto the flames to make as much smoke as possible.

Millerson looked to the west. God speed, Betsey. Take care of the kids.

"Look, Sir William," his sergeant said, pointing. "Smoke."

William Beckett held up his hand, and the two hundred men of his conroi stopped.

"What is it?" he asked.

"Not sure, but it is a lot of smoke. Either a bunch of fires or something big is burning."

William looked around, then back at the smoke.

"It has to be them. Take twenty men and see. We will follow."

"As you wish, sir."

Freddy galloped into the clearing and drew his horse to a halt near Harry.

"Here they come. A bunch of 'em. We best be going."

"Mount up," Harry said. "We head east away from the river, then south. Use the trees. We play hide-and-seek with them. But don't lose 'em."

"We ain't going to see the signal to leave in all the trees," Johnnie said.

Millerson smiled.

"You didn't really think we were going to get out of this, did you?"

Johnnie shrugged his shoulders.

"A fella can hope."

"Yes, he can," Millerson said. "So, let's not get caught. Arrow or no arrow, if we keep them busy till dark, we will sneak across the river and join the others. If not, don't allow yourselves to be questioned."

Everyone knew what he meant.

For the next two hours, Harry led his small group of volunteers down deer paths, ducking under branches while galloping recklessly, hoping to remain ahead of the pursuing men. Twice they slowed as they broke from the trees, making sure they were still being followed.

"I don't hear them," Johnnie Casher said as they stopped to catch their breath.

Harry looked around. Seeing a small rise, he pointed to it.

"Up there."

"Sort of makes us easy to see," King said.

"That's the point. We got some time till it gets dark. Don't want to lose them too soon."

They climbed the hill and scanned the terrain they had just traversed. Less than half a mile away, they saw them, close to a hundred riders working their way through the forest. Millerson waited until the lead element finally broke from the trees. One rider pointed at them and called to the others.

"Guess they saw us," Johnnie said.

"Looks to be," Millerson said. "Now the real game begins. Make sure they see which way we are heading, then ride to the next tree line. We lose them in the woods for a bit, find a lea, let them see us, then we run again. Let's go."

Francis Appleby stood waist-deep in the water, anchoring the chain of soldiers stretched across the river, helping to ensure no one floundered. The water was swifter than they expected because of the recent rains. An adult or older child carried or helped some of the children as the water was too much for them.

A boy, no more than ten years old, swam up to Appleby and grabbed his leg.

"You all right?" Appleby asked.

"Just catching my breath, sir. Waters cold."

He chuckled. "It is that. You going to make it?"

"Yes, sir. Been swimming since my pa tossed me in the pond when I was a kid."

Trying his best not to smile, Francis Appleby nodded to the many working their way through the water.

"Some of the older folks ain't so lucky. You tall enough to stand?"

The boy looked up at him, the water touching his chin.

"Yep."

"Well, why not make sure the other children are doing okay. Urge them on."

"Yes, sir. Be glad to."

"What's your name, boy?"

"Sam. Sam Millerson."

"I know your father."

"He's helping make sure we make it to the other side. Said he would see me tonight."

"He's a brave man."

Beaming with pride, the young boy pushed away and swam toward a group of children fighting their way through the water.

"Think he will?" Sir George asked, watching the boy.

Startled, Appleby turned. "Sorry, Sir George. I did not see you."

"I was downriver, speaking with one of the scouts. It seems the plan is working. They have seen no one so far. How are we doing?"

"This is the last of the families. Most of the men are either in the water making sure we don't lose anyone or are on the other side helping get people out of the water. Mud is getting to be a bit much over there."

"Almost all the horses have crossed. Only things left are the carts. Might be a challenge to get them up the other side in that muck."

Sir George looked at the people struggling through the mud.

"Cut some grass and brush. Put it on top of the mud. We can't afford to have any of those carts break free and float downriver."

Something bumped Appleby's leg, and he looked down. A small brown terrier was doing its best not to be swept downriver. He reached down and grabbed the dog. Tucking it under his arm, it stopped struggling, exhausted.

"I've got you, fella. Just stay still."

"How much longer?" Sir George asked.

"Maybe an hour. Maybe a little more."

"We need to hurry. It will be dark soon and I want to make the far side of the hills before we stop. Get the high ground between us and the river." The Chamberlin looked back down the river.

"Do you think Millerson and the others will make it?"

Appleby watched Sam Millerson swimming toward a group of children.

"No."

The six men stood beside their tired mounts. Harry Millerson stroked the neck of his horse and then placed his hand over her muzzle.

Johnnie did the same while they listened.

"You think we lost them?"

"Hope not. Not dark yet. Got to give Sir George the time he needs."

"Horses are tired, Harry," King said.

"I know. As are we. But we ain't done yet. Mount up."

Slowly, they walked their horses into the open. Harry was surprised when he almost bumped into a rider.

"It's them!" The rider yelled as he drew his sword. Four others suddenly appeared, swords already in their hands.

Harry drove the shoulder of his mount into the horse of the man that had shouted, almost knocking it from its feet. The off-balanced rider dropped his sword. Harry quickly drew his blade and drove it deep into the man's throat, nearly taking his head.

Seeing another rider trying to unhorse Fredric, he rushed forward and sliced down on the man's shoulder. Although his blade did not penetrate the mail, the crack of bone told him he had broken something. The injured man fell from his horse, screaming.

"Break and run!" Harry screamed as he turned his horse towards the relative safety of the trees. "Go! Go! Go!"

After thirty minutes, they stopped and listened.

"Think we lost them?" Fredric asked.

"Not likely," Harry said. "Everyone all right?"

"I think Thomas is hurt," Johnnie said.

Harry dismounted and walked over to his friend.

"You okay, Thomas?"

Clinton smiled, and a trickle of blood leaked from the corner of his mouth.

"Caught a mace. Stove in some ribs, I think. Hurts like hell, hard to breathe, but I'll live."

"Can you ride?"

"I think so."

"Time to head for the river."

"Sounds good," Clinton said, and then coughed up more blood. He took a rasping breath.

"I hear them," Johnnie whispered. He nodded in the direction they had just come. "They ain't far."

"Fredric," Harry said quickly. "Stay with Thomas. Head for the river. The rest of us will lead them away. Now go. Get across the river and wait for us."

Fredric took Thomas's reins and led him away.

"We got to go, Harry," Johnnie Casher said.

Harry jumped into the saddle.

"We head north, then shake them and head for the river. Let's go."

Two hours later, the four men worked their way through the brush and scattered water birch, leading their exhausted horses, their way lit as occasional rays of moonlight made their way through the foliage. A horse nickered.

Johnnie shrugged.

"Sorry. She smells the water. Do you think we lost them?"

"I think so," Harry said. "Haven't heard them for close to an hour now. I think they continued north."

He led his horse carefully to the end of the trees and stepped onto a rock ledge overlooking the river. The rushing water lay ten feet below.

"Going to be difficult getting across that," Johnnie said, looking at the drop and the rapids below.

"We'll look further downstream. There has to be a way across," Harry said.

"Going to be tricky in the dark," Johnnie said.

"I know. But we have to try."

… … … … … … CHAPTER 31

The Chamberlin's Message

Henry leaned on the granite wall of the barbican, watching as the last of the local farmers slowly crossed the drawbridge. He felt someone step beside him. Without turning, he asked, "Still no sign?"

"They just disappeared," Philip said. "Nothing. Not even footprints."

"Any more farmsteads attacked?"

"No. And before you ask, still no sign of the missing children."

Henry sighed.

"At least you didn't find their bodies."

"What do you think they want with them?" Philip asked.

Henry turned and stared at the keep.

"I don't know, but I thank God we found Eleanor when we did."

"And the other children that were with her. All orphans now," Philip said.

"The baron will take care of them. He's a good man."

"He is," Henry agreed. He looked towards the east. "I wonder if Edwenna is all right. I should have looked for her and brought her with me."

"If you had, you would be in irons or dead."

"I suppose. But I promised I would take care of her. Keep her safe. She is just a child."

Philip smiled.

"She has not been a child for some time, Henry. You were just not paying attention. I can assure you; others were."

Henry turned to him.

"And you, Philip. Did you notice?" he asked, stifling a grin.

"Your Majesty. I am but a simple man and she is a princess."

Henry laughed.

"There are times, my friend, when you can be such an ass."

"Your Majesty?"

Marjorie appeared at the top of the stair, stopped, waiting for permission to join them.

Philip bowed.

"With your permission, sire, I need to... uh, check on the squires. They should be training."

Henry looked at Marjorie.

"I think that would be prudent. Thank you, Sir Philip."

Philip waited until she stepped onto the fighting platform before approaching the steps. He bowed.

"My lady."

"Sir Philip," she said with a thankful grin.

He winked and ran down the steps.

Henry offered his hand.

"What brings you to this lofty place, my lady?"

"Why, your majesty, it is you, of course."

Henry smiled as she gently took his hand. Her fingers were so delicate and warm. He looked down into her deep brown eyes. No khoel highlighted them, nor paint to redden her cheeks. A beautiful young woman with no need for such things. The wind blew her hair, which hung freely about her shoulders, exposing the delicate skin of her slim neck. Henry found the sight intoxicating.

GLENLOCK

Henry escorted her to the edge of the battlement. The two stood, their hands interlocked, as they gazed upon the land that lay beyond the castle walls.

"It is beautiful," she said.

"It is not the only thing I find beautiful in this land."

Blushing, she squeezed his hand.

"I have not seen you much this last year. Not at all, actually. Have I displeased you in some way?"

Turning, he took her other hand.

"You could never displease me. I'm sorry. My father has kept me busy." Thinking of the valley, he added, "And I had some things I had to sort out."

"Such as?"

He hesitated and then smiled.

"You, among other things. I mean my feelings for you. How I was to tell you how I felt and fearful you might not feel the same. To speak to your father about… us, in case you did."

"I do. And he knows," she said shyly.

Henry laughed.

"Of course he does."

"And what else was on your mind?" She asked, drawing closer. "Besides me."

He looked down into those captivating eyes and did not step back.

"Something happened to me," he almost whispered the words, as if someone else might hear.

"In the Valley of Storms?"

Somewhat surprised, he stepped back, dropping her hands.

"What have you heard?"

"I am sorry. I did not mean to…"

Reaching down, he took her hands as he shook his head.

"No, it is I that am sorry. It is just it was not to be spoken of. To anyone outside of a few trusted friends who were there. Too many ears attached to men who could use what I claimed happened to do me harm. Who told you?"

"No one," she said. "I overheard Jamie and his squire William speaking. They have not spoken of it to any but each other that I know of. I do not believe they even told my father."

Henry was quiet for a moment.

"Jamie is a good man. A good friend. I know he would tell no one without asking me first."

"May I ask what happened?"

"You may think me mad."

She stepped a little closer.

"I could never think that."

And so he told her. He told her of the storm, the cabin, and of Hal. Of how he lost his father's sword and found Maggie only to be returned home. When he finished, he asked,. "Still think I am sane?"

She chuckled.

"Your best friend is a long tooth. How could I doubt anything you say?" She looked around. "Where is Maggie?"

"Hunting. She enjoys her independence. You know how cats are."

She chuckled.

"Does she also play with balls of yarn?"

"Not that I've noticed. But I have seen her play with…"

"Rider coming in!" A sentry yelled.

"Where?" Henry asked, looking up at the tower.

The sentry pointed. "From the northeast."

"Is he alone?"

"I see no other riders, sire. His horse stumbles. I do not know if he will reach the castle."

"Who do you think it is?" Marjorie asked.

"I don't know, but he comes from the direction of Cyneburg. I doubt he brings good tidings." He stepped to the edge of the parapet and yelled down. "Bring my horse."

He turned to her.

"Stay here. I will return."

She nodded and turned to look between the arrow slots of the crenelations in time to see the rider's horse stumble and fall, throwing him.

"You must hurry, Henry. He has fallen from his horse."

The king started towards the steps, hesitated, turned, and, hurrying back, took Marjorie by the shoulders and placed a gentle kiss on her lips.

"Go, see who he is," she said, lowering her head, trying to hide the flush that adorned her cheeks.

Baron Mercier met Henry as he reached the bottom of the stairs.

"What is happening?"

"A lone rider from the east. He may be from the capital."

"I will go with you." Irwin turned to a man-at-arms that had accompanied him from the keep. "Get my horse and six riders. I want the walls manned. If it looks like trouble, close the gates."

"The people, my lord?"

"Hurry them along. But if something does not look right, close the gates and raise the bridge."

"But what about you, your lordship? And the king?"

Irwin looked at Henry, who nodded.

"If it appears we will not make it back in time to close the gates safely, do not wait for us."

"Trouble?" Philip asked as he joined them, buckling on his sword belt.

"I don't know. A rider approaches. From the direction of the capital."

"From your father?" Randell asked, joining the small group surrounding their king.

"Maybe," Henry said.

"Perhaps your father has regained his senses," Irwin said. "Maybe he wishes you to come home."

Henry shrugged.

"One can only hope."

A small group of the baron's guard approached with several horses in tow. Henry walked to his and climbed into the saddle.

"Let us go find out."

Without waiting for the others to mount, Henry spurred his horse to a gallop as soon as he cleared the gate.

Marjorie watched them go and smiled when she saw the large cat break from the forest, running to join Henry.

The king threw his left leg over the saddle and dropped to the ground before the horse had stopped. Maggie stood over the man and sniffed, occasionally pushing him with her nose. She gave a low, deep-throated growl. Henry scratched her behind an ear. She purred with the tremor of a tame lion. Kneeling beside the cat, Henry turned the man over.

He wears the Lion of Cent. The livery of the king.

"Does he live?" Irwin asked, his horse dancing nervously while staying a respectful distance from Maggie.

"He does," Henry said. "But for how long I cannot say."

Philip kneeled beside the fallen horse. It was white with salt. He stroked its neck as it puffed out its nostrils, seeking oxygen.

"It has been ridden hard. Neigh on to death, the poor creature. What is so important that he would drive a horse so hard?"

Irwin turned to his men.

"Dismount and get this man on a horse. Tend to the rider's mount, and if it lives, bring it to the castle. It has earned our respect."

Philip joined Henry while the others remained a respectful distance from Maggie.

"He wears your father's livery. A messenger or a scout, you think? But how would they know to look for you here?"

"Many know of my mother's relationship with Baron Mercier. This would most likely be one of the first places they would look for me."

The soldier tasked to look after the rider's horse kneeled beside the animal and called out.

"There are broken arrows embedded in the saddle."

Philip looked at Henry.

"A good sign?"

"Depends on who was shooting at him."

"Baron," called the soldier helping the unconscious rider onto a horse.

Irwin turned.

"Yes."

"This fell from his shirt as we lifted him," he said holding out a rolled paper.

"Let me see that." Irwin unrolled it and glanced at the writing. Surprised, he handed it to Henry.

"It is a message from Sir George addressed to me."

"The Chamberlin?" Philip said.

"I think it best you read it, your majesty," Irwin said. "It concerns you."

"He asks for you to seek me out and provide me shelter," Henry said as he read.

"Why would the king's man wish that of me? I thought your father outlawed you?" Irwin asked.

Henry looked up.

"The only reason I can think of is that my father is dead."

CHAPTER 32

CARNAGE

Celsus ordered the eighty men of the century forward. The legionaries began to sing and beat their shields in cadence as they marched down the gentle slope. Thinking they faced the full force of the Lantusian warriors, the enemy shifted their pikes.

"They have turned," Edwyn called, running to his horse. He gave the signal to advance, and the eighty horsemen urged their mounts over the crest of the hill. It must have been the vibration of the heavy beasts that alerted the enemy, for one began to yell and point at the oncoming wave of the cavalry. But it was too late to turn the pikes.

"They have seen us! Forward!"

The wedge of horsemen urged their mounts to a full gallop. William and Randolph pushed forward until they were riding boot-to-boot with their knights. The four lowered their spears.

Flanked on the right by Ramsey and Bailey, and on the left by Astrid and Oelig, Hal withdrew the katana and held it out to his side.

The knights of Cent slammed into the enemy, the weight of their horses tossing the defenders left and right. Their spears broke in bodies and they discarded them, then reached for their swords.

The hammers and axes of the Southlanders swung down, crushing and hacking flesh, while those with swords slashed as they drove into the opening created by Edwyn.

Hal swung his blade from side to side across his horse's neck, taking heads and limbs with each blow as he pushed his way through the throng of bodies.

When they reached the far side of the enemy formation, the horsemen split, Edwyn leading the riders from Cent and Southland to the left while Ianuarius led the legionaries to the right. As they reached the flanks of the enemy, Augustus's infantry arrived and halted less than fifty yards away. They launched two hundred javelins. Another sixty were thrown by Celsus's men. The deadly shafts climbed high over the formation of the enemy and, reaching their apex, fell, driving their weighted points into flesh.

The horsemen reformed. Only three men were missing, their mounts struck by pikes, the riders hacked to death as they fell. Six more men swayed in their saddles, clutching wounds, unable to continue.

Edwyn watched as the horse of a wounded legionnaire stumbled onto its forelegs, then fell to its side. Panting desperately, the poor beast's eyes rolled back as its lifeblood spilled onto the soil. The injured rider crawled to his knees and, drawing a dagger, slit the poor beast's throat. He then collapsed onto its neck, joining it in death.

Ianuarius looked at the melee taking place.

"Too dangerous to mount another charge with the infantry engaged. Dismount. We will fight on foot."

Edwyn saw what the legionnaire was doing and dropped from his horse, sheathed his sword, and reached to the saddle to unhitch a ten-pound mace.

"Dismount!"

Jamie stepped beside him, a war hammer in his right hand and his shield on his left arm, a long dagger in his hand.

The squires gathered behind their knights along with the rest of the men from Cent and Southland. Bailey and Ramsey took their place on either side of Hal. Bailey gripped a short sword while his father pulled a massive war hammer from across his back.

Looks like Thor, Hal thought.

"Swords are too long for the kind of fighting that lies ahead, Sir Harold," Edwyn said.

"The katana was made for this." Hal reached down and made sure the pistol was secure in its holster, afraid that using it would cause panic by both friend and foe.

"Stay behind us, Sir Harold. You have no shield," Edwyn said.

Astrid pushed Bailey aside and withdrew a long dagger from behind her back. She hefted her round wooden shield.

Bailey reached for her when a beefy hand landed on his shoulder.

"I wouldn't do that, lad. The lady is quick with that blade and no one, not even the king, tells her what to do. Stay with me and we will watch their backs together."

Bailey looked at Oelig and then at Ramsey, who nodded.

Lifting the smaller heater shield given him by Sir Edwyn with the crossed swords of Burke painted on its surface, Bailey took his place next to the big man from Southland. He gripped his short sword and focused on what lay ahead.

"Shield wall!" Edwyn called. "Let us push the bastards into the legionaries."

Edwyn saw the Lantus cavalry as it stepped into the chaos, their long oval shields overlapping as they pushed the enemy flank into the waiting infantry.

Edwyn locked shields with Jamie and the squires.

"We will punch our way in and trap them between us and the Ianuarius. They have no shields, but they are inhumanly strong. Do not underestimate them."

Hal turned to Astrid.

"Give me room to use my sword."

"That may not be up to me, Otherworlder, but I will try to heed your words." She looked at the long blade.

"With a single edge, Sir Harold, you will have no backswing."

"With luck, I won't need one," he said.

"Together, march!" Edwyn called out, and they moved.

The wall struck the disorganized and frantic enemy and quickly dissolved into the chaos of individual bouts of combat.

Hal drew the wakizashi with his left hand and rushed into the fray. He blocked a blow with the short sword, then pushed his katana forward, easily slicing through the leather armor and into the stomach of the first foe he came to. Twisting the blade, he pulled it up and out, eviscerating the man.

The sound of steel striking wood made him turn in time to step aside and swing the blade of the wakizashi across the neck of the enemy, whose sword had been deflected by Astrid's shield.

Hal nodded his thanks, then quickly turned as he caught movement out of the corner of his eye. He swung the katana upward, taking an arm at the shoulder. Pivoting with a speed he did not know he had, he blocked another strike with the katana while drawing the razor-sharp blade of the wakizashi across an exposed throat.

And then he was alone, swinging, slicing, and stabbing at all that came near him. Step by step, remembering all his sensei had taught him on the floor of the kendo dojo and the fields of grass where he learned Kenjutsu with the wooden bokken.

Feel the enemy, deliver the blow where he least expects it, see the next target before you complete the last, then be aggressive. Strike, block, stab. Dō, Men, Kote, and Tsuki. Head, body, wrist, and throat. Don't think, act.

And then it was over. Exhausted men fell to their knees. Some clutched wounds while others cried out for family members, many with their last breaths.

Bodies lay all about. Hal searched for his friends and was relieved to see them all still standing. Edwyn and Jamie directed their squires and remaining men to tend to the wounded.

Hal watched in amusement as Oelig slapped Bailey on the back, nearly driving the boy from his feet. He saw Ramsey approach his son, holding his arm, blood seeping between his fingers, pride gleaming from his eyes.

He looked for Augustus and was surprised when he saw him sitting atop a horse on the hill where Celsus had brought his century.

How did he get up there?

"Sir Harold?"

He turned to find Astrid staring at him. She was covered with blood, but he quickly realized that it was not hers. He started to respond when he realized that it was not him she stared at, but what lie around him. The remains of more than a dozen bodies.

What have I become?

Without thinking about what he was doing, he flicked his wrist, freeing the blood from the katana, and returned it to its scabbard, then did the same with the wakizashi.

A horn sounded and Hal looked up at the hill. Augustus was waving frantically and pointing at something behind him. He turned, surprised to see a rider galloping towards them. It was the samurai.

Without slowing, the warrior lept onto the piles of the dead, his horse slipping in the gore almost falling. It quickly regained its balance, and the rider urged it towards Hal. Ianuarius rushed him and the samurai drove the shoulder of his horse into the Decurion, knocking him from his feet.

Warriors stood stunned as the rider continued towards Hal, who reached for his sword. But the man shifted his track and, leaning down with one hand, grabbed Astrid by the hair and lifted her onto his saddle. She dropped her shield and dagger, reaching for her hair as he slammed the hilt of his sword on the back of her head, rendering her unconscious. His horse reared and he pointed at Hal.

"Oka no ue de Watashi ni au. Ichi hito de kuru ka, onnanoko ga shinu."

Then he turned and galloped back the way he had come.

Hal jogged toward their horses. Jamie grabbed his arm.

"What did he say?"

"To meet him on the hill. I come alone or Astrid dies."

He shook Jamie's hand off and climbed onto Strongheart.

"I'm going too," Oelig said. "She is my princess. I am her Huskarl."

"As am I, Sir Harold," Bailey said as his father rushed to join him, still holding his wounded arm.

"You can not. If you do, he will kill her. I need to go alone."

Jamie stepped in front of his horse.

"Let me get Richard. He can drop him with an arrow."

Hal shook his head.

"Not with that armor, not without a bodkin. This is the only way."

"You are going to fight him one-on-one?" Ramsey asked.

"If I have to."

"And if you do not come back?" Jamie asked.

"Then find him and kill him." He turned the horse's head and drove his heels into its sides.

"Sir Jamie, what should we do?" Bailey asked.

"Run and get Richard."

Oelig watched the young man run back towards the carnage, then turned to Jamie.

"And then what?"

"We follow him, of course."

Strongheart snorted and Hal pulled the horse to a halt. He looked up and on the hill that he and the others had recently defended stood the samurai, his horse standing calmly at his side.

Where is Astrid?

He dismounted and cautiously approached the warrior, his hand on the hilt of the katana.

"Koko ni. Onnanoko was doko ni iru?" (I am here. Where is the girl?")

"She's safe," the man answered in perfect American English.

"You speak English?"

"I do, although my brethren do not, and they don't know that I do. I would like to keep it that way."

"I don't understand. Who are you?"

"My name is Miyamoto Musashi." He smiled. "Not that one. He died centuries before I was born." He glanced at the two swords Hal carried. "You have studied his style of Nitōjutsu, the art of two swords. Impressive." He chuckled. "Especially for a gaijin. May I ask where you learned?"

Hal hesitated. He looked around for Astrid. Not seeing her, he turned back to the man that had abducted her. He decided not to antagonize him until he knew what was going on.

"I lived most of my life in Japan. The man next door was a master of the sword. He took me under his wing after the death of my father. He taught me."

"And the swords?" Miyamoto asked.

"A gift. His father's father made them. Enough of this. Who the hell are you and what do you want?"

"I told you. I am Miyamoto Musashi, but my friends at school called me Mike."

"Mike? What school?"

"UCLA, of course."

"You're kidding me."

"MA in business." He chuckled. "And you are?"

"Hal. Harold Bennett."

Mike looked down the hill.

"We have little time, Hal. Your friends will join you soon. And I can't let the Shogun know I am speaking with you."

"Shogun?"

"It's what Sato calls himself. Arrogant bastard."

He withdrew his swords from his obi, still in their scabbards, and sat on the ground, his legs crossed, and lay the swords beside him.

Not knowing what else to do, Hal followed suit.

"You going to tell me what the hell is going on?"

"I'll try. As I'm sure you noticed, I'm not from around here. I too am from Earth. Based on your hat, I assume you're new here. You'll stop wearing it soon. I've been here a bit longer by maybe a few years, I would guess. It's hard to tell. Time is a bit screwy. Years are hard to calculate. Where we are from months are calculated differently."

He looked at the pistol on Hal's hip.

"A SIG?"

"Yes."

"I would love to take a look at it, but this is probably not a good time." He smiled. "By the way, thanks for not using it."

Hal squinted, looking closely at the symbol on Mike's helmet. It was not the demon he had seen before. It was a chrysanthemum. This was not the same man.

Mike looked over his shoulder and then back at Hal.

"When I saw the hat, I knew you were from home and had to talk to you."

"Nice boots, by the way. I wish I had mine."

"You served?"

"Two tours in Iraq. You?"

"Afghanistan."

"Listen, Hal, there is much we need to discuss, but now is not the time. I will seek you out when I can, and I will tell you what I know. For now, understand that I am not your enemy. I will do what I can to help. I don't like what Sato is doing."

"Is he from Earth?"

"He was born here."

"Glenlock?"

"Nihon."

"Japan?" But you said…"

"It's what he calls his island. I'll fill you in later," Mike said, picking up his swords.

"Who are those things down there?" Hal asked, recovering his and standing.

"They are called Brusshers. They are not from here either."

"You mean Glenlock? Or Nihon."

"I mean Tera."

Mike tucked his two blades back into the obi.

"I must go." He offered his hand. "Until we meet again, Hal. It is good to find another American in this crazy place."

Hal hesitated, then took it.

"American?"

"Born and raised. California." Mike turned and leaped onto his horse.

"Later," he said, then rushed down the far side of the hill, never looking back.

Hal watched him go, stunned.

"Sir Harold?" Astrid stumbled from behind the remnants of the brush he and the others had recently used as a defense.

He rushed to her, helping her to steady herself.

"Are you alright?"

"What happened?" she asked, rubbing the back of her head.

The sounds of horses made him look down the hill.

Of course, they didn't listen.

"I will explain what I can. When we are all together."

Yeah. Like I know what is going on.

Baily surged ahead of the others and lept from his horse, stumbling but remaining on his feet.

"My lord, are you injured?"

"I'm fine, Bailey." He looked down the other side of the hill at the retreating horseman. "Just a little confused." He turned to Astrid, who held tight to his arm to maintain her balance.

"The Princess needs to use your horse, Bailey." He turned to Astrid. "Do you think you can ride?"

"My head hurts, but I can still sit a horse." She looked around. "Who was that?"

"A friend. I think."

CHAPTER 33

REVELATIONS

Marjorie walked into the hall, drying her hands on a towel. She handed it to a servant.

"He is awake. It is a wonder. The poor man has not been out of the saddle for two days. He has gone without food and with little water."

"Did he say anything else?" Henry asked.

"I think it best you ask him yourself, your majesty. I told him you were here, and he was quite insistent that he speak with you, alone."

Philip started to rise, and Henry placed his hand on his friend's shoulder.

"I will go alone." He looked at Marjorie and smiled. "I assume he poses no threat?"

"None, your majesty."

Henry gestured she should proceed. He followed. As they entered the chamber, the messenger tried to stand. Marjorie rushed forward and pushed him back onto the bed.

"You must stay where you are. If you try to stand, you will fall."

"Do as the lady suggests," Henry said gently. "It will do you no good to try and do otherwise."

"Prince Henry," the man said.

"I am he."

"I have a message."

"I have read it."

"There is more," he said.

"More?" Henry asked.

"Yes, your highness. I was to tell the baron that Sir George is on his way along with many others?"

"Others?"

"Soldiers and their families. Those that have fled Cyneburg. They should be here in two to three days if they are not discovered first."

"Discovered? By whom? And why flee the capital?" Henry asked.

The man tried to get up again and Marjorie placed her hand on his shoulder, pushing him back.

"Duke Sanford controls the capital. It was not safe for those loyal to the crown to remain. He has sent an army seeking you, your highness."

"Do you know the size of this army?" Henry asked.

"More than a thousand men, both horse and infantry."

"That many men to find you and bring you back to Cyneburg?" Marjorie said, confused.

Henry looked at her.

"They were not sent to bring me back."

Marjorie lifted her hand to her mouth in shock.

"They wouldn't dare."

"I am afraid our dear duke is that bold." He looked at the messenger. "What path does the Chamberlain travel?"

"Along the Keisby River. I was to tell the baron that he intended to cross the river and approach Tilden from the south."

Henry turned to Marjorie.

"Please ask your father, Sir Philip, and Sir Randel to join me?"

"Of course, your majesty."

As she left the room, Henry turned back to the messenger.

"There were arrows in your saddle. How came them to be there?"

"We were set upon shortly after leaving Sir George. Bobby fell. I grabbed his horse and rode with all speed. My horse went lame. I left it and rode Bobby's."

"I am sorry about your friend. Was it the duke's men that ambushed you?"

"I'm not sure, your highness. Never saw the archers."

"You weren't pursued?"

"No, milord."

"We no longer serve John," Irwin said as he entered the room. Henry is our king."

"I beg your pardon, your majesty."

"No need to apologize," Henry said. "I want you to tell Baron Mercier where he can find Sir George."

"Irwin, I think it best you send wagons to help move the families. This young man will explain." He turned to Philip and Randel and with a nod indicated he wished to speak to them alone as he walked to the door.

"Kennington has sent an army to find me. They travel the road from Cyneburg. I believe they are at least three to four days out. Longer if we are lucky. Take James Longbow and William Quick Arrow. Find them. Confirm their strength and, if possible, see if you can identify who leads them. But be careful. Do not let them see you. Then return with all haste."

Randel nodded. Henry reached for his arm and stopped him before he could leave.

"Sir George sent two riders. They were ambushed. This one does not know by whom. Be extra careful. I need information, but I need you four back even more. Now go."

They turned and nodded politely towards Marjorie, who waited just outside the door.

"You heard?" Henry asked.

"I did," she said.

"As the lady of the house, you have been instructed how to prepare for a siege?"

"You think they will attack the castle?"

"Once they find out I am here, then yes, I do. Do you have sufficient supplies?"

"I will have my brother send men to gather what they can from the local villages and farms and ensure no cattle remain outside the walls. We have two wells within the castle, so water will not be a problem. The storerooms are full. My concern is the number of people that are with Sir George. We are crowded as it is. I do not know where we will find space for more."

"We will have to send them on towards Lantus. I have directed that families of the men that came with me are to travel there as soon as they arrive. Eleonor will go with them as my representative. I am sure the emperor will provide them sanctuary."

"I will make the arrangements." She squeezed his hand, then quickly withdrew it when she saw her father approach. She nodded towards him, turned, and left.

"She is so much like her mother," Irwin said.

Henry watched her as she walked away.

"She is a fine lady."

Irwin smiled.

"Yes, she is. And she knows her business. The castle will be ready by the time the army arrives."

"And the defenses?"

"I will have the mote flooded. The two scorpions we purchased from Lantus have just been installed and every man of the barony not in the guard gives me four days a month of archery training. That will give us close to a hundred archers. Their hunting bows do not have the range of a war bow, but they should help keep people from the walls. I will have to check with my Castilian, but I believe we have no shortage of arrows. And of course, every shepherd boy is deadly with a sling."

"And trained soldiers?" Henry asked.

"Counting the people you brought with you, we will have seven knights, about a dozen men-at-arms, and maybe a hundred trained soldiers."

"And whatever Sir George brings with him," Henry said.

"Depending on their condition," Irwin added.

"With such a force, we should have no difficulty holding the outer walls. Especially if Sir George has trained warriors with him."

"And the people he brings with him? The women and children. We will be hard-pressed to take care of my people, let alone what he brings."

"The families will not stay; they will have to continue to Lantus."

"That is asking a lot, considering how far they have traveled," Irwin said. "And they will need soldiers to protect them. Soldiers we could use here."

"I know. But it can't be helped."

"Do you honestly believe Kennington has sent an army of a thousand men just to find you? Where would he get that many?"

"Sir George's messenger seems pretty sure of the numbers. Where he got them, I don't know. And that troubles me."

"Send messengers to Eudell, Burke, and Lydell," Henry said. "Let the barons and the earl know you seek their help. Tell them you are under siege by forces unknown. Do not mention that I am here."

"Do you think they will not come if they know?" Irwin asked.

"I believe they will do what they feel is right for Cent. However, if word reached them that the king has outlawed me… I don't know. To support me against my father would lead the country to civil war. That is a lot to ask. But I believe they will respond to your plea for help."

They reached the end of the hall and looked out into the courtyard. Henry caught the sight of James Longbow as he raced to catch the others as they crossed the drawbridge.

Never was good on a horse.

Marjorie was waiting when they returned to the hall.

"I heard a rider leaving."

"I sent men to see how far the army is from Tilden," He explained.

"Do you think they will attack?" she asked.

Henry sighed.

"I don't know. I hope not, but a lot of what is going to happen will depend on who is leading that army. I need to speak with Ainsley. Maybe he will know. And where Kennington got so many men."

Marjorie lowered her head.

"What troubles you?" Henry asked.

"I'm sorry. With everything going on, I forgot to tell you."

"Tell me what?"

"There was little the healers could do. He is gone."

Henry was quiet for a moment.

"It could not be helped. He brought this upon himself."

Irwin laid his hand on her shoulder.

"Marjorie, please send for your brothers and have them come join us. Also, I need to see Captain Hill and Frank Henson."

He turned to Henry.

"Hill is my Castilian and Henson commands my men-at-arms."

Henry nodded, then turned to Marjorie.

"Do you know where Sir Ealdwine is?"

"I believe he is in the stables. Do you wish me to send for him?"

Henry smiled.

"That man loves his horse. Yes. I would appreciate you sending someone to fetch him. Perhaps he can enlighten me where the duke got these men. And who may lead them."

Marjorie nodded and turned to a nearby servant.

"Send for my brothers. And have one of the stableboys ask Sir Ealdwine to come to the hall."

The girl ran off.

"Should I prepare food?" she asked.

"Not now. Perhaps later," her father said.

She bowed and left the room. Irwin watched as Henry followed her with his eyes, a thin smile crossing his lips. When Henry pulled a chair from the table, he waited until the king sat down, then pulled one out for himself.

"I am curious. What can Ealdwine offer? I am not sure I trust the man. After all, he was one of Kennington's men."

"I believe he is sincere, and he has sworn fealty to me. I'm hoping he will give me an idea who may lead the approaching army."

"Father! Rider's approach." Marlowe said, rushing into the hall. He stopped when he saw Henry.

"Forgive me, your majesty. I did not realize you were here."

Henry stood.

"There is nothing to forgive. Riders, you say?"

"Yes, sire. They are but a mile away. They ride across the fields from the northeast."

"But the messenger said we should not see the army for at least two more days," Irwin said. "And Williamson is coming from the south."

"Army, Father?" Marlowe asked.

"An army approaches from Cyneburg."

"These are not men of Cent. They are Lantusians."

CHAPTE 34

An Ally

"Who was the rider that took the princess?" Augustus asked, using a stick to stoke the fire the four men sat around.

"And why did he not kill her?" added Edwyn. "Or you."

"His name is Miyamoto Musashi," Hal said, not looking up. "He took Astrid to make sure I would follow him."

Augustus poured wine and offered the goblet to Hal before pouring one for himself.

"And what did he want with you?"

"To talk."

"Talk?" Jamie asked. "Talk about what?"

"About letting us know we had an ally. One in the enemy's camp."

"In the camp of the four-toes?" Edwyn said.

"He called them, Brusshers."

"He is one of those Japan people, is he not?" Edwyn said. "The one's leading these things, these Brusshers?"

"He is not the same warrior we saw on the hill yesterday. And he spoke English. Without an accent."

"English?" Augustus asked. "What is English?"

"Sorry. Glenlockian."

"He was quite concerned that the others might see him speaking with me. And he said something else. Something odd."

"Odd?" Augustus asked."

"He said that he arrived not too long ago."

"Arrived? Like you?" Jamie asked. "In the storm?"

"Not the one that brought me here. I got the impression this happened a few years ago. And not in the Valley of Storms. But yes. He is from Earth."

Edwyn cocked his head.

"There is another such as you?"

Hal stood and walked a few paces from the fire and stared out into the darkness. The sounds of the camp were all around. He watched as one of the Lantusian sentries walked along the dirt wall.

"I think so."

"But where? I mean, where did he… cross over?" Jamie asked. "The only place in Glenlock that has ever seen a storm such as the one that brought you here have been in the valley."

"He did not arrive in Glenlock," Hal said, sitting back at the fire.

Augustus put his goblet down.

"That is impossible. No land exists beyond the Great Expanse or the Daemon Sea. Sailors have tried for as long as records have been kept, and not one has ever returned. The waters consumed them. No land lies beyond those waters."

"That is true, Sir Harold," Astrid said, stepping from the shadows. At her side stood Oelig, a long ax dangling from his hand. His eyes scanned their surroundings.

"Southland has the finest sailors in the world. Many times, powerful men, adventurers with sound vessels, set sail never to be seen again. Something within the waters beyond Glenlock takes them," she said.

"Has any wreckage washed ashore from these boats?" Hal asked.

Oelig answered for her.

"None. No wreckage, no bodies, nothing. My brother set sail five years ago with a crew of forty experienced sailors. Nobody has heard from him since. It is as if they never existed."

Astrid sat on the log next to Hal. Oelig took position behind her and lifted the ax, holding it across his body.

"There is no life beyond Glenlock, Sir Harold," she said.

Her hip brushed his and Hal tried not to look at her. At those deep blue eyes, that strong, proud, beautiful face, that firm athletic body. A small breeze brushed past her, engulfing him in the fragrance of sandalwood. He had a hard time focusing on the others.

"Then where do the Brusshers come from?" Edwyn asked, saving Hal from an embarrassing moment.

"I don't know. Could they have come from the land beyond the forest at the end of the valley?"

"It is unlikely," Jamie said. "Many ships have traveled around that coast. They have never reported any signs of life. No villages, no boats, no smoke."

"Has it ever been explored?" Hal asked, looking first at Jamie, then Augustus, avoiding looking at Astrid.

"Not for a long time. The only person I know of to enter the far side of the valley and return is Prince Henry, the day he found Maggie, and he did not venture deep into the forest," Edwyn said.

Jamie snickered.

"I think Henry said that she found him."

"The cat is real?" Oelig asked.

"Oh, she is real," Jamie said.

"Why not?" Hal asked. "Why has no one gone beyond the valley?"

Augustus reached for the jug of wine.

"It has been many years since the last man ventured into that accursed place. No one has ever returned. Something lies beyond the trees and the rugged coastline that does not want to be disturbed. The forest protects it on one side and the other by the valley. No one ventures into that land anymore."

"My lord?"

"Is that you, Bailey?" Hal asked. "Step into the light."

The young man stepped forward. Behind him, partially covered in shadow, stood his father.

"How is the arm, Ramsey?" Hal asked.

"Just a scratch, Sir Harold."

"Sir?"

"Yes, Bailey?"

"I went into your tent to prepare your bedding and I found this laying on your swords. No one saw who placed it there. There are strange markings on it. My father thought you might know what it means."

He handed the small piece of yellowed parchment to Hal, who unfolded it and leaned into the firelight.

道路ははっきりしています。あなたは急ぐ必要があります.

Astrid leaned over and looked at the paper.

"What are those strange marks? Do they mean something to you?"

"It's from Mike. It says the road ahead is clear for now. It also says we must hurry." He turned to Augustus. "I think he means there are no Brusshers between us and Tilden at the moment."

"Who is Mike, and how did he get that note into camp?" Augustus asked. "And how did he know which tent was yours?"

Hal smiled.

"Mike is Miyamoto Musashi and I think our friend has studied Ninjitsu. The art of the shadow man."

"I do not understand?" Augustus said. "What does that mean?"

"Ninjitsu is the art of stealth. If he is a master of the art, I don't think any of your guards could have seen him enter or leave. As for knowing which was my tent. I would guess he has been watching us."

"He uses magic?" Oelig asked.

"No, although it may seem that way. Just many years of training," Hal said.

And he sure as hell didn't learn that in the States.

"That he could get into camp and out again without being seen is unnerving," Edwyn said. "And I think dangerous. To us."

"If he had wanted me dead, I would be," Hal said.

"Do you believe what it says? That the road is clear?" Augustus asked.

"I do. I'm not sure why, but I sense we can trust him."

"Then we should leave immediately," Augustus said, standing. "I will make arrangements." He threw the last of his wine into the fire and walked away.

"Do you think the Brusshers are on their way to Tilden?" Jamie asked.

"Looks like they may be," Hal said.

"My family is there. My father, my brothers, and my sister. We must warn them."

Edwyn turned to Astrid.

"What are your plans, Princess? Will you try to find a way home?"

"No. I will travel with you." She looked at Hal. "We shall fight at your side. It seems we have a common enemy. One that threatens all of Glenlock." She turned to Jamie. "When we reach Tilden, would it be possible to send a boat to Southland? I wish to tell my father that I am safe. And warn him of the threat these Brusshers pose to us all."

Jamie nodded.

"I think that is possible, Princess." He turned to Hal and smiled.

"What?"

"Nothing, Sir Harold."

"What would you have me do, Sir Harold?" Bailey asked.

Not realizing the two men were still standing behind him, Hal jumped when he spoke. Before he could answer, Edwyn took charge.

"Please tell Peter we are leaving."

Astrid turned to Oelig.

"Have the men prepare to move. We ride with Sir Harold."

Jamie slapped Hal on the shoulder.

"I think you are in it, my friend. Good luck."

CHAPTER 35

THE ROAD TO TILDEN

Sir William Beckett watched as his men searched the remains of the fort. His sergeant walked toward him.

"Anything, Samuel?"

"No, sir. The fort is empty."

"How many were here?"

"Difficult to say. The ground is muddy and is churned up quite a bit. That could mean many riders or a few that made it look like many."

"And they headed southeast?"

"My scouts discovered riders heading that way. I sent people after them. I don't know if they were the last to leave the fort, left behind to burn it, or a decoy. We found no other tracks."

"Is it possible that the Chamberlin crossed the river?" Beckett asked.

"If he did, it was not here. The river is wide, and the water is too swift. I have sent men to search for another way to cross. A bridge or a ford. This land is not known to us."

"Have you tried to ask one of the locals?"

"We have found none. Every village and homestead in the vicinity is deserted. No people, no animals."

William spat on the ground.

"The bastard must have taken them with him." He followed the bank of the river with his eyes until it disappeared as it bent along the forest to the west.

"If he has families with him, they will slow him down. Stay here until your scouts return. I will have another patrol follow the river upstream. If they report seeing the Chamberlin, send a rider. I will continue on the road to Tilden with the army."

"Yes, my lord."

Sir George watched as the last of the animals were herded away from the river. He looked westward.

"We will let them rest for an hour. Then we must push on. Have men cover our trail as best they can on both sides of the river."

"And if they discover we have crossed here?" Appleby asked.

Williamson took a deep breath.

"I will take twenty men and the families with me. You remain here with the rest of our warriors. If they try to cross, do your best to slow them down."

"Shortest promotion ever," Appleby said with a smile.

"I am sorry, Francis. But I must reach Tilden. The future of Cent depends on Henry learning that he is king."

"I understand, Sir George. We all do. Besides, they may not find us."

"You are a brave and honorable man, Frances. One that it would be an honor to call friend." He offered his hand.

Appleby looked at it for a moment, then gripped it firmly.

"The honor is mine, Sir George."

Appleby looked at the retreating people, and seeing Billy Thatcher called out. "Billy!"

He walked his horse over and nodded in respect to Sir George.

"What's up, Frances, Uh, sorry… Captain." He added with a smile.

"I want you to go with Sir George. Take twenty men with you. Have the others join me here."

Billy looked at Sir George, and realizing what was happening, shook his head.

"You go. I'll stay here. You need to keep the Chamberlin safe. You're his captain."

Appleby grinned.

"Thanks, Billy, but this is my job. I'm trusting you to keep him safe and get these people to Tilden. That's an order."

"But…"

Frances placed his hand on his friend's shoulder.

"You're the only man I trust to watch over my family. Please, Billy. I need to know they will be safe."

Billy Thatcher stared at him, then turned his horse.

"You're a bastard, Frances Appleby. You get yourself killed and I'll kick your ass." He spurred his horse and galloped back to the main body.

"Why not take him up on his offer? You have a family," Sir George asked.

"So does he. And his wife is with child."

"How much farther do you think?" Paulus asked.

"With luck, we should reach Tilden by nightfall." He looked at the exhausted legionaries, then raised his hand. "Dismount. We continue in fifteen minutes. Do what you have to do and see to your mounts. Then we walk for a while."

"They need rest, Felix. If we keep this pace, I'm not sure any of us will make it to Tilden. The men haven't eaten since we left the wounded."

"I thought they had a day's ration."

Paulus shrugged his shoulders.

"Seems there was some misunderstanding, and they left what they had."

Felix smiled.

"They saw you give yours to Brutus."

"We need to find water. For the men and the horses," Paulus said changing the subject.

"I know. But if we don't keep moving, Kennington's people will find us. There are too few of us left to put up much of a fight. Our only chance is to get to Tilden."

He pulled the water bag from the saddle and shook it. Pouring a little onto his hand, he wetted his lips, then stepped in front of his horse. He removed his helmet and poured the remaining water into it, and offered it to the animal. He pulled the soaked arming cap from his head and wiped his brow.

Paulus looked at him.

"Are you alright?"

Felix looked back in the direction they had traveled.

"I'm concerned about the wounded?"

"We will go back for them," Paulus said.

"By the time we get to Tilden, there will be an army between us and them. I wonder how long they can survive without help."

"They will survive as long as they have to. They are legionaries," Paulus said.

Harry Millerson dropped to the ground and crawled to the edge of the trees. Johnnie Casher inched his way forward until he lay beside him.

"Think we lost them?" he asked.

"Looks like," Harry said.

"Just hope Thomas and Freddie made it across the river."

"Get the others. I think we have done all we can here. Let's go find Sir George."

They threw Thomas Clinton to the ground, and he screamed as his broken ribs shifted.

"Who's this?" Samuel Whitham asked.

"One of the riders that fled the fort," the soldier who had thrown him down said.

"Was he alone?"

"No Sergeant. Another rode with him. He resisted."

Whitham looked down at the injured man.

"What is your name?"

"Thomas Clinton."

"You serve the Chamberlin?"

"I serve the king," Thomas spat.

Whitham smiled.

"Then we do not have a problem. I too serve the king. King Oswald."

"Who the hell is that?" Clinton groaned.

Samuel Whitham kneeled next to Thomas.

"Watch yourself. Insulting a king is punishable by hanging. Do you want to hang, Thomas Clinton?"

Thomas glared, but said nothing.

"Where is Sir George?" Whitham asked.

Thomas looked away.

The sergeant stood and placed his foot on Thomas's chest. He slowly added pressure and Thomas screamed.

"I can grind these ribs into powder or push a little more and sink one into a lung. Or I can get a healer and have him bind your ribs. Up to you. Now, where is Sir George?"

Thomas shook his head, sweat and tears spraying the ground. Witham lifted his foot and Thomas attempted to take a shallow breath, but the pain was too great, and he passed out.

"Wake him. And get a healer. I need this man alive."

One of the soldiers ran to get the healer as another tossed water onto Thomas's face. He came around and for a moment, forgot where he was.

"Where are the others? The ones you rode with?" Whitham asked.

"Gone," Thomas gasped. "You will never find them."

"Start a fire. Put a dagger into it. I will get my answers."

CHAPTER 36

A Meeting on the Hill

The Sun was casting a red glow over the exhausted column. The men from Cent, Hal and Astrid, and her remaining warriors stood in the grass next to the road and stretched their backs while waiting for the command to continue.

"Is the river dangerous?" Hal asked.

"It is deep and swift," Jamie said. "But there is a bridge. A good one built by Lantusian engineers. It's stone and wide enough to cross four abreast. There is also a ferry run by Glenn Rider and his family. Nice people. We should be able to get everyone across in less than an hour."

"How far is this river?" Astrid asked.

"Not far. Less than two miles," Jamie said, his attention drawn to a rider galloping toward the lead element of the column.

Augustus signaled him, and the man quickly responded, halting in front of his commander. After a few moments, Augustus turned and signaled Celsus, who was speaking with Ianuarius. Celsus mounted and trotted forward.

Augustus pointed east, and Celsus nodded. He turned and signaled that Ianuarius should join them.

"Something is wrong," Edwyn said as he mounted.

The others followed him as he rode to join Augustus.

"Something amiss?" Edwyn asked.

"The bridge has been destroyed. They somehow brought down the center span. I do not have the material to repair it. We cannot cross here."

"What about the ferry?" Jamie asked.

"The raft lies on the far bank. Someone cut the rope, preventing us from bringing the raft across. The water is too swift, or I would send a man to retrieve it."

"What about the ferryman?" Jamie asked.

"Dead. They slaughtered the whole family. Even the children."

"They were good people. Kind," Jamie said. "Bastards!" He took a deep breath. "There is another way."

"Another way?" Augustus said. "To cross the river?"

"Oak crossing is about ten miles downriver. There is a large sandbar that lies just a few feet under the water that can be forded even when the river runs high."

"Is it easy to find?" Augustus asked.

Jamie shook his head.

"Not really. You have to know where to look. With the bridge, it is not often used."

"What about horses? Can they cross?"

"If you walk them single file. Men can cross three abreast, but I would recommend two. Safer that way. The water on either side is deep and treacherous. There are sharp rocks that lie beneath."

"Can you show Ianuarius where it is?"

"I would be glad to. But it will take us over twenty miles out of our way. We will not reach Tilden today."

Augustus looked around and then at Hal.

"Do you think your friend knew about the bridge?"

"I don't think so. If he did, I think he would have warned us."

"Did the scouts report any Brusshers?" Edwyn asked.

"None. Not even tracks showing they came this way," Augustus said.

"Then maybe they didn't," Hal said. "Maybe the main body crossed somewhere else, and another group destroyed the bridge. Or they may not have crossed at all. We have no idea how many of those things there are."

"They seem to be heading towards Tilden," Jamie said. "I need to warn my father."

Augustus looked at his tired troops.

"Ten miles to the ford, then another thirty to forty miles to Tilden. If the road is safe. Longer if we have to navigate through forests and fields. We will be fortunate to reach your father by tomorrow late afternoon."

"Then I will ride ahead," Jamie said. "I know the land and can get there in a day."

"Assuming you don't run into those four-toed bastards," Edwyn said. "You cannot go alone, Jamie."

"And he won't. I will go with you," Hal said.

"I do not wish to pour vinegar on your enthusiasm," Augustus said. "But without a guide, none of us could see Tilden in time to warn them. I have traveled these roads, Sir Jamie, and I emphasize the word roads. I am unfamiliar with the terrain beyond them. I think it best you remain with us."

"I will leave my squire with you. He can guide you."

Augustus thought for a moment.

"Then be on your way. And may Jupiter watch over you. I will do my best to reach Tilden tomorrow. If the Brusshers intend to attack your father's castle, we will support our allies in the fight. You have my word."

Jamie bowed.

"Thank you, Imperator."

"We will come with you," Astrid said.

Jamie nodded, then signaled William. The young man ran to him, leaving his horse with Peter and Bailey.

"The bridge and ferry cannot be used. I am going to ride ahead to warn my father of the Brusshers. I wish for you to lead the legionaries across Oak Ford and then cross-country to Tilden. Avoid the roads."

"But Sir Jamie."

"I need someone I can depend upon to guide them. That man is you."

William looked like he was going to argue, then nodded.

"I will not let you down."

"I know you won't. Tell the others we move out immediately." Jamie looked at Astrid. "And let the Southlanders know their princess wishes them to accompany us."

As William ran back, Jamie turned to Edwyn.

"He is a brave young man. I have learned to rely on him."

Edwyn nodded.

"Thank you. His mother will be proud to hear that."

"His mother?" Jamie chuckled.

Edwyn smiled.

"When I tell her how proud of him I am. Yes."

Sir George looked back the way they had come as they loaded the families onto the wagons and carts sent by Baren Mercier.

"Do you think they will make it?" Thatcher asked.

"I don't know what I will tell their families if they do not," Sir George said." He turned as a rider approached. Sir Marlowe reined in and gave a quick nod of respect.

"My Lord Chamberlin, the last of your people are about to be loaded. I will have some of my men help herd the animals, but we should not tarry. If what you have told us is true, I do not know how much time we have before Kennington's army will reach the castle."

Sir George gave a quick nod.

"I understand." He smiled when he saw Appleby and the others appear out of the forest.

"Looks like we gave Beckett the slip, your lordship," Billy Thatcher said.

Sir George smiled.

"What about Harry and the others?" Billy asked. "Any word?"

"Nothing I am sorry to say."

"Shame," Francis Appleby said, looking down. "I'll tell his family."

"No," Sir George said. "I will do it. But first I must keep my promise to them and get their families safely behind Tilden's walls."

Sir Marlowe cocked his head in acknowledgment, not wishing to explain the king's plan to send them on to Lantus.

"Do you wish me to leave men behind to wait for them?" Marlowe asked.

Sir George sighed, shook his head, and, turned his horse towards the wagons.

"No. They know where we are going. If they are coming, they will meet us there."

Harry lay at the edge of the wood and watched the far bank.

"Where are they?" Johnnie asked. "I mean, they should be here yesterday."

"I know."

"Think they got caught?"

"I hope not. We will know soon if they were."

"What do you mean?"

"If Kennington's men show up on the far bank, we will know they were caught."

"I know these men. You do too. They're our friends. They would never give us up," Johnnie said.

"Any man will talk if tortured," Harry said.

Johnnie looked shocked.

"You think they would torture them?"

"These are Kennington's men." Harry looked back at the river. The false dawn approached, covering his face in shadow, so Johnnie did not see the tears that filled his eyes. Harry suddenly pushed Johnnie further into the grass.

"Look."

Two riders appeared from the trees on the far bank. They neared the river, stopped, and looked around. One dismounted and walked to the edge of the water, studying the ground. He leaned down and lay his hand on the mud, then stood. He said something to the other rider, who rushed back into the trees.

"They have found us," Harry said.

"Who found us?" A small voice asked behind him. Harry turned.

"Sam! What are you doing here, boy?"

"I come to find you. Ma's worried, so I promised I'd find you and bring you home."

"She let you go?"

Sam looked down.

"Not exactly. While everyone was loading the wagons, I just slipped away."

"Wagons?" Johnnie asked.

"Yes, Uncle Johnnie. The Baron sent them. To take us back to the castle. There were soldiers too."

Johnnie smiled.

"They made it."

"They will," Harry agreed, relieved that his wife and daughters were safe.

"Wow," Sam said. "Look at 'em all."

Harry looked across the river.

"Damn! There's more than a hundred horse over there."

"So, what do we do?" Johnnie asked.

Harry Millerson worked his way back deeper into the trees, dragging his son with him. He stood when he was sure they could not see him.

"We run."

"What about Clinton and King?" Johnnie asked.

Harry looked at the riders milling around the far bank.

"They're not coming."

Taking his son's hand, he ran to the horses. When he got near, he called to the others.

"Mount up!"

Harry lept into the saddle and reached down, taking Sam's small hand. He tossed him up behind him and the boy wrapped his arms around his father.

"How long did it take you to get here, Sam?"

"Most of the night. You been gone close to two days, Pa. I was worried. I know Ma was too. Once I knew she was safe, I slipped from the wagon, and I come looking for you."

"You should have stayed with your ma," Harry said, driving his heels into the flanks of his horse.

I can't let them find the others before they get to Tilden.

"We head south," he said.

"South? Johnnie asked.

"We need to lead them away from Sir George. Give them a chance to get to Tilden." He felt Sam's arms tighten around him. There was no way he could send him back now. He had to come along.

The sun rose to its full glory, bathing the world in the warmth and light of a clear day. Harry stopped and turned his head, squinting to see if they were being pursued. As he did, he could make out several horses as they broke from the trees. One rider pointed at them.

"They've seen us! We cut left and head for that hill. We will try to confuse them in those pines."

"Confuse them?" Patrick Allgood asked. "Confuse them how?"

"Once we get there, we split up. I'll go south with Johnnie. You two go east. When you find another copse of trees split up. We'll do the same. Make sure they see you. Just don't go west."

"And then?" Johnnie asked.

"Once night has fallen, work your way to Tilden. Our families should be safe by then." He looked at his friends. "Good luck to you all. It has been an honor to ride with you."

"Brutus."

"What is it, Gaius?"

"Riders in the valley. They appear to be headed this way."

The Decurion lay down the bowl that held his meager ration and rose to his feet, reaching for the baldric that held his gladius as he did so.

"Legionaries?"

"No. Pretty sure they are from Cent."

"Show me."

Gaius led him to the edge of the trees, staying in the shadows so as not to be seen.

"Four of them," Gaius said. "Make that five. I think one is riding double."

"Look," Brutus said. "More riders. Lots more."

"The four are running from them. What do you want to do?" Gaius asked.

"How many men have bows?"

"Three. All wounded. But only two could draw one, and one of those may not be able to stand."

"As many as the others that can stand need to pick up shields and pila. Collect all that we have as well as plumbate. Have them lock shields here, at the edge of the trees. Stay out of sight. We are about to have company."

The tired horses struggled to climb the steep hill. Harry's horse slipped and nearly threw him and Sam. As they neared the top, a figure stepped from the trees. He held up his hand, and they stopped.

What the hell? Harry thought.

The dark-skinned man lowered his hand and lay it on the hilt of his sword. He wore the armor and helmet of a Lantusian legionary.

"Hold where you are," the man called out. "What is your purpose here?"

Harry stepped from his horse and handed the reins to Sam. He held his arms out to his sides, showing he held no weapon.

"We mean you no harm." Harry looked behind him. "But I cannot say the same for them."

"Who are you, and who are they?" Brutus asked, pointing to the oncoming horde.

"I am Harry Millerson. I serve Sir George Williamson, the Chamberlin of the king. Those men that pursue us are in the service of the Duke of Sanford. I believe they have orders to stop Sir George from reaching Tilden. They believe we will lead them to him."

"The Duke of Sanford's men?"

"Yes." Harry looked back at the rapidly approaching horsemen. "I do not know why you are so far from Lantus, friend, but I fear you are in as much danger as we find ourselves."

"And where is Sir George?" Brutus asked.

"With any luck, nearing Tilden."

Brutus looked at Harry with newfound respect.

"You are luring them away from your lord? Dangerous work."

"We are and it is. We were six."

Nodding toward Sam, Brutus asked.

"And the boy?"

"My son." Henry smiled up at him. "Little bugger ran away from his mother thinking he could help me."

Brutus grinned and slapped his arm across his chest in a salute.

"A hero, huh?" He looked at Harry. "It looks like it runs in the family. "Follow me."

Leading their horses, they followed the Lantusian into the trees. As they entered the shadow of the small forest, a wall of four-foot oval shields stopped them from proceeding. Brutus flipped his hand, and the wall opened, allowing them through.

Harry turned to Brutus.

"How came you here?"

"We were part of Legatus Felix's party."

"The Lantusian ambassador?"

"Yes."

"Why leave Cyneburg?"

"We fled the capital. Your King John tasked him with finding his son, Henry. To tell him his father is dead, and he is now your king. The Duke of Kennington does not want the Legatus to succeed."

"Sir George is on a similar quest." Harry looked at the wounded men lying in a small clearing at the apex of the hill. "What happened?"

"You have not seen them?"

"Seen who?"

"Not who, but what. Strange men with misshapen heads. They have shadowed us for days. More than a dozen legionaries lay beneath the ground, never to return home. They left six of us to stay with the wounded until the Legatus reaches Tilden and sends help."

"We have not encountered such things."

"Fortunate you are."

"Brutus, they come," Gaius called out.

Brutus turned away from Harry and walked back to the line. He watched the riders as they worked their way up the hill. He stepped from the trees, and they stopped. A man dismounted and removed his helmet.

"I am Sir William Beckett, and I demand to know what Lantusian Legionnaires are doing here," he yelled, not approaching.

"I am Brutus Milos Antilles. I serve Felix Arrelious, son of Caesar, Legatus of Lantus, to the court of King John."

"John is dead. His daughter Edwenna now rules with her husband, King Oswald, son of the Duke of Sanford. You have not answered my question. Why are you here?"

"I do not answer to you. Be on your way and there will be no trouble."

"Where are the riders that entered these woods?"

"Under my protection. I will take them to Tilden."

"They are outlaws. Turn them over," William demanded.

"No."

William Beckett stared at the man, unable to accept that he had refused.

"Present them, or I will be forced to take them."

Brutus smiled.

"You may try." He turned and as he walked back, he heard a horse rapidly approach from behind him. He turned swiftly, drawing his gladius just in time to see the rider tumble from his horse. An eight-foot javelin quivering in his chest. William lept into the saddle and, yanking the reigns, turned his horse, and galloped back to the rest of his men.

Brutus stepped through the shield wall.

"Who threw that pilum?"

"I did," Gaius said. "The bastard was going to run you down."

"Nice throw."

"It was the boy that unhorsed him," Gaius said.

Brutus looked at Sam, who was returning the sling to his belt. He smiled and tapped him on the shoulder.

"I owe you one, young warrior."

Sam beamed with pride.

Harry stepped forward.

"What now?"

"Well, I suppose they will try to take this hill."

Harry looked around.

"You have barely two dozen men able to stand. You can't stop a hundred men on horse."

Smiling, Gaius handed Brutus a shield.

"Then I guess we need to get them off the beasts."

From the shield wall, someone yelled. "They come."

Brutus stepped into the wall of shields and a man handed him a pilum. Harry tapped him on the shoulder.

"Mind if we help?"

Brutus smiled. He nodded to the men lying on the ground.

"Grab one of their shields."

Picking up the shields, the four men worked their way into the line of legionaries.

Harry felt someone tug on his shirt. Sam stood looking up, a Lantusian dagger in his hand, defiance and fear showing on his face.

"Sam, I need you to watch the horses. If things go bad, we may need to leave in a hurry. Stay with them. I am counting on you, son."

"I'll keep them safe, Pa."

Harry smiled.

"I know you will. Now go." He watched as Sam ran back to the horses.

"You have a fine son, Harry Millerson," Brutus said.

"Thank you."

"If things do not go well. Take the boy and run. Tell the Legatus what has happened here."

Harry drew his sword. He said nothing. He looked down at the approaching enemy and took a tight grip on the handle.

Johnnie looked at him.

"One of us will make sure he gets home, Harry."

Harry nodded.

The horses of a dozen riders struggled as they climbed the steep slope. A couple of dozen yards behind, another eighty. They moved quickly, a mob trying to be the first to reach the top of the hill. Brutus thought it odd that their leader was not one of them.

"Stupid," he said. "No cohesion, no discipline. "Ready pilum."

He waited until the lead riders were in range.

"Throw!"

CHAPTER 37

SACRIFICE

Henry helped Felix as he dismounted.

"What has happened? Why are you here?"

Grasping his forearm in greeting, Felix reached into his shirt and withdrew the signet ring with the King's Seal.

"Your father bid me give you this, Henry. I am sorry, my friend, but I do not believe he still lives."

"I have heard that is so. But why send you?"

"He felt there were few he could trust in his own court."

Henry looked at the wounded men. "What has happened?"

"Let me see to my men and I will tell you all."

Marjorie stepped forward.

"I will see to your men. Go to the hall. Food and drink await."

Felix bowed.

"Thank you, my lady."

"It is Marjorie. I am the Baron's daughter. I know your brother. He and the king visited here often. Augustus is a friend."

Felix smiled.

"He has spoken of you fondly. He did not do you justice. Your beauty exceeds his description."

Marjorie blushed, then hurried towards the keep.

Felix turned to Henry.

"You say you already knew."

"A messenger from Sir George arrived telling me of my father's death."

"So now it is official. You are the King of Cent. Although I am not sure you have a kingdom to reign over. Kennington has plans of his own."

"I have heard."

"You must prepare. The duke has sent an army to find you. I do not believe he intends to take you alive."

"I have heard this as well. Now come. You need to rest. You can tell me all that has happened once you have eaten."

Felix turned to Paulus, who was waiting with the rest of his men. He turned to Henry.

"You know my cousin Paulus?"

Henry smiled.

"We have met. Good to see you"

"And you ... your majesty."

"Paulus, see to the men and then join us," Felix said.

"Riders coming!" a guard called down from the wall. "It is the relief party."

Hearing the sentry, Marjorie hurried back to the courtyard. She stepped beside Henry, who was looking up at the sentry.

"Please ask Sir George to see me as soon as he arrives." He looked at Felix's men, who were being taken care of by Priscus and the women of Tilden.

"More come, Marjorie. Women and children. Can you cope with all this?"

"I am the lady of the castle, your majesty. And as you can see, I have help. The women of the villages and the staff. All will be well." She brushed her hand across his and smiled. Felix looked at the two and shook his head.

"It appears there are a few things my brother left out."

Henry, Felix, Paulus, George, Irwin, and his sons, as well as Randel and Philip, sat around the large wooden table used for banquets. The squires leaned against the stone walls and waited at the edges of the room in case they might be needed. The remains of a meal littered the table while a half-empty jug of ale was passed from one to the other. Marjorie entered with three girls and signaled they should clear the table.

"Do you require more ale?" she asked.

"No thank you, dear," Irwin said." He looked at the squires. "They might though." He smiled. "But just a little. Please make sure we are not disturbed. And thank you. You would have made your mother proud."

She curtsied and, after checking on the squires, shooed the girls out.

"Quite a lady, Baron," Sir George said.

"She is that," Henry agreed as he watched her leave.

The Chamberlin raised an eyebrow and Irwin nodded. He smiled.

"You said you were attacked," Henry said to Felix. "And you say they were not men?"

"Ghastly beasts. Followed us for days. I lost many good men and had to leave the most severely wounded on a hill a day's ride from here."

"I will organize a rescue party to recover your wounded," Irwin said, sipping at his ale.

"I thank you, Baron, but I do not think it will be possible. Between here and there lies an army of Kennington's men."

"This is my land, Legatus," Irwin said. "My men know it better than any invader. They will find your men under the very noses of this renegade army and bring them back to you. Besides, an army such as approaches will remain on the road. My men will not take the road."

"You say these things that attacked you had four toes?" Henry asked.

"And elongated skulls."

Henry nodded.

"We know of them. They have been attacking local villages, slaughtering all but the youngest children."

"They let them live?" Felix asked. "Why?"

"They take them. We hope they keep them alive. We don't know why," Peter offered.

"I need to return to Lantus and warn my father about these things," Felix said. "And tell him what is happening in Cent. I am concerned the Frisians may feel this is an opportunity to test our borders."

"And ours," Henry said. "You said you were hoping to find Augustus. You believe him to be in Cent?"

"The last I heard, he was patrolling the land bridge. He may have crossed into Cent hoping to see you. I don't know. I was hoping the baron had seen him."

"I have had no word of him," Marlowe said. "He surely would have let us know if he intended to cross our lands."

"I'm sure he would," Felix said, looking at Henry.

Marlowe turned to Sir George.

"You said you left six men behind to misdirect Kennington's men. Would you like me to send a patrol to see if they can find them?"

Sir George looked down.

"I am afraid it would do no good. If they still lived, they would have been here by now." He sighed. "I will need to tell their families. It will be the hardest on Harry Millerson's wife. Not only is her husband lost, but her ten-year-old son is as well. He disappeared as we were loading the children onto the wagons. One of his friends said he was going to find his father. He was a brave lad. Helped the other children cross the river."

"But how could he find him? I mean, they went in the opposite direction," Marlowe asked.

George chuckled.

"You don't know the boy. If there was a way, he would find it."

There was silence for a moment, then Henry looked up.

"So what do we do about this army?"

Hal turned in his saddle at the sound of laughter behind him. Ramsey rode between Richard and Oelig, who had just, very loudly, recited an off-colored story about an alewife and a sailor.

Astrid chuckled.

"He heard that one from my father."

"He seems a good man. I'm glad he is getting along so well with those two."

"They are warriors, Sir Harold. Brothers, in a way. They share a common view of the world. Of course, that would not stop them from killing one another if it came to that."

"Let's hope it never does."

She looked at him for a long moment. "Let us hope."

"Do you think your friend was telling the truth?" Jamie asked. "That there are no Brusshers between here and Tilden?"

"I think that is what he believes," Hal said. "On the road, at least. He seemed sincere enough to risk his life to get that message to me."

"That was some spooky stuff," Jamie said. "I have never seen Franklin so worried. He sees these shadow warrior people everywhere now." He laughed. "Richard even caught him looking under all the horses before we left."

"If Miyamoto has truly mastered the art of Ninjitsu, I'm not sure he would have seen him. Or survived if he did. There are few left in Japan that have truly mastered the art. Many people around the world study it and claim mastery, but in truth, they know but a fraction of the skill. Ninjas are not just masters of close-quarters combat, but weapons, stealth, poisons, and explosives. I knew one while in Japan. His name was Manaka. He was taught by his grandfather, who began his training when he was four years old. I think he was in his late twenties or early thirties when he completed his training. Big deal when it happened. Took place in their capital city. He was also knighted as Samori by their emperor."

He chuckled. "I remember a demonstration he gave to a bunch of guys from a nearby military base. He had one of his students lay on the ground without a shirt. Then he placed a watermelon on his belly."

"Water melon?" Astrid asked.

"A big fruit about the size of Oelig's helmet. I guess you don't have them here. Shame. Anyway, the guy lay on the ground and Manaka stood over him with his Katana sheathed. He gave me a Kleenex."

He stopped and held his hands apart about six inches.

"A very light piece of parchment. He made me hold it above my head and said I should drop it when I was ready. When I did, he drew the blade, swinging it up over his head and then down, cutting the melon, and returned the sword before the paper hit the ground. Never saw anything like it. He was so fast. Then he leaned over and touched the melon, which was split in the middle and rolled off the student's belly. Not a mark on him.

"It's funny. When I told him I was amazed at his skill, he told me that the true discipline was the students. If he had moved, he explained, the blade would have opened the young man's stomach."

"Sounds to me like the student was frozen in fear," Jamie said.

Hal chuckled.

"It's true he did not get up right away."

Jamie laughed.

"I do not wish this man as an enemy."

"I just hope he is not training anyone else," Hal said.

Four riders fell as an equal number of the long shafts of the Lantusian javelins struck, penetrating their mail.

"Throw!" Brutus yelled, and they launched six more of the deadly missiles into a sloping arch. One struck a horse in the neck, and it went down, crushing its rider while the other five found purchase in the bodies of men. Two fell lifeless to the ground while the others turned away, all but one slouching in their saddle.

Their leader, the one that had first spoken to them. The one that stayed behind was screaming and waving his arms frantically.

"Looks like he ain't happy they came back down," Gaius said.

"They will be back. Ready plumbatae," Brutus called out.

"What's that?" Harry asked.

Gaius pulled one from the back of his shield and handed it to him to examine.

"Big dart. Weight just behind the head and fins at the end of the shaft. Throw them high and when they come down, they do so point first and whap! Into the head or shoulder of a man or a horse. Nasty thing. Good for about thirty yards. I love 'em."

Harry examined the deadly weapon, about a foot and a half long with a weighted barbed point. He smiled.

"Got any more of these things?"

Gaius snapped his head to the rear and one of the uninjured legionaries went back and collected a few from the discarded shields. He looked at Brutus and shrugged.

"Sorry, Brutus. Saved a few." He handed six to Harry, who gave one to each of his friends.

"Here they come!" One of the wounded men in the line called out. His head was bound with a bloody bandage and a splint covered his left leg.

"Wait for my command and launch two, then tighten the line. Not sure they will stop this time," Brutus said.

The horsemen came up the hill in a loose formation, six wide and three deep.

Only eighteen men, Harry thought. He tried to see what was happening at the base of the hill, but could not see past the approaching horsemen.

"Throw!" Brutus called.

Seventeen of the small missiles rose high in the air, their deadly points vertical, fell and struck both men and the animals they rode.

The sound of gladius being drawn did not blot out the screams of man and beast just below the crest of the hill. Several horses bucked or reared, throwing their riders while they cried out in pain. Three men lie dead, two with darts sticking out of their heads, while the third lie still, a dart in his shoulder and his head lying at an odd angle.

Two horses in the second line tripped over those that had fallen, throwing their riders. The others slowed down to navigate through the chaos that lay before them.

"Finish them!" Brutus yelled as he rushed forward.

Only six men from Lantus followed, as well as the four warriors from Cent. The wounded watched, plumbate in their hands, unable to follow.

The ten men grabbed riders fighting to control their horses, dragging them from their saddles quickly driving their blades through necks and faces.

"Grab the uninjured horses and take them to the rear!" Brutus said.

Harry looked down the hill.

"Brutus, we have a problem."

The Lantusian commander turned, and Harry pointed. Two groups of dismounted men were running to either side of the hill while a larger force began climbing directly to their front.

"They are going to come up the center and, on our flanks," Johnnie said.

Brutus watched for a moment, then turned and walked back to his waiting men.

"Back to the wounded. We make a turtle around them."

Henry looked at him.

"They cannot ride, and I can't leave them," Brutus said. We stay together."

Harry stared at him for a moment.

"I understand."

Brutus placed his hand on Harry's shoulder.

"You and your boy should take the freshest horses and leave."

"You should as well, Brutus," Gaius said. "Someone needs to tell the Legatus what has happened."

Brutus turned and looked at the two dozen wounded men.

"I will not leave them."

"Then I suppose today is the day," Gaius said.

Brutus gripped his forearm and smiled.

"To die with friends is the best way to die." He looked at the approaching men. "But let's take as many of these sons of whores with us as we can."

Harry turned to Johnnie.

"Take Sam and find Sir George. Tell him what has happened."

"I don't think so."

"Would you two stop!" Patrick demanded. "They are almost halfway up this damn hill." He turned to Harry. "Take the kid and run."

"I doubt we could get through. Not now. Maybe if we beat them back, we can go while they regroup."

"If you are staying, grab a shield," Brutus said.

Several of the wounded fought their way to their feet and offered a hand to those unable to rise on their own. Picking up shields, the Lantusian warriors formed a circle around those unable to stand. A legionary crawled from man-to-man, ensuring those who remained conscious had either a pugio or gladius. Several dragged themselves to those unable to move and lay beside them. Gaius saw a man working his way to the line, missing his left arm.

"Priscus, what in Jupiter's name do you think you are doing? You can't fight like that."

Priscus laughed and looked at the man to his left who carried a shield with his left hand, his right arm hanging limp, the shoulder obviously broken.

"Me and Julius add up to one man. He is my shield, and I am his sword. He blocks, I kill. We ain't about to die lying on our asses."

The sound of screaming men came from three directions.

"Brace!" Brutus called out.

They came at them piecemeal. No formation, just angry men intent on killing. But they had never faced the war machine of Lantus before.

As the attackers crashed into the wall of linked shields, gladii darted in and out between shields into legs, groins, and armpits. Those in the second row reached over the first and drove their short swords into the faces and shoulders of those they could reach.

Every time a legionnaire fell, the man behind him would step forward and take his place while wounded men in the center would crawl forward and pull the dead and injured back, allowing those still standing to fight.

Harry pushed with his shield and then drew back, causing his opponent to lose his balance. As he stumbled, Harry drove his blade into the man's neck above the mail and pushed until the armored vest bulged in the chest.

Back-and-forth warriors pushed, stabbed, and hacked; the attackers were trapped against the shield wall of the legionaries while those behind continued to push forward. In some places, the enemy wounded could not fall. In many places, the dead still stood, the men behind packed so tight.

One after another of the Lantusians rested their arms, as their opponent could not continue forward. The dead and wounded blocked their advance.

"Fall back!" someone shouted, and the enemy retreated.

Several of the legionaries fell to their knees in exhaustion. Brutus staggered back and Gaius grabbed him before he could fall.

As he lowered his friend to the ground, he felt the warm flow of blood under a torn piece of his armor.

"Links snapped and opened just under my arm. The bastard used a dagger and drove it deep. I think he missed the lung, but I cannot raise a blade."

Gaius looked around. Not a single legionnaire escaped without a wound. Many would not be able to fight again. Only ten men remained standing. Around them, lie over fifty dead or dying of the enemy.

"We can't stop another attack, Brutus. We're done," Gaius said.

"I know," Brutus said. "You need to go with Millerson. Tell the Legatus that Lantus can be proud of those that stood here today."

Gaius removed the scarf from around his neck and stuffed it under Brutus's armor. He turned to Harry.

"Take him and go while they lick their wounds. I will buy you some time."

"No!" Brutus said.

"You can do no good here, and Lantus needs to know what has happened. The emperor needs to know that this was Duke Kennington's doing, not their king." He chuckled. "Besides, you know I hate riding. The only reason I joined the cavalry is that I didn't have to carry my kit."

Harry wiped the blood from his brow, a blade drawn across his hairline nearly scalping him, and held out his hand to Gaius.

The Lantusian hesitated for a moment, then took it. He nodded.

"Take care of Brutus."

"I will," Harry said, then turned to Johnnie. "The horses safe?"

"There is a deep cave on the far side of the hill. Impossible to see unless you're right on top of it. I told Sam to stay there until you came for him."

Gaius placed his hand on Harry's shoulder.

"You must hurry."

Harry looked at the small group of men preparing their weapons. They know they are going to die and yet, not one complaint. He raised his knuckled hand to his injured forehead in salute. "It has been an honor to fight alongside you."

"Go. Get to the cave before it is too late," Gaius said, picking up his helmet.

CHAPTER 38

Arrival

Hal scanned the road before them with the binoculars. He handed them to Jamie.

"Who is that?" he asked.

Jamie looked, then passed them to Edwyn.

"I don't know. They are on the road from Cyneburg. A lot of them."

"Must be a thousand men," Edwyn said.

"What is that thing?" Astrid asked, pointing to the binoculars.

"Binoculars. Allows you to see things at a distance," Hal said as Edwyn handed them to her. "Take a look."

Lifting them to her eyes, she quickly pulled them down with a gasp. She looked again, then reluctantly handed them to Hal.

"This is a wonderful device, Sir Harold. Are you a Galdramenn?"

"A what?"

"A wizard," Edwyn explained.

Hal chuckled. "No."

"He has another that sees in the dark," Jamie added. "Those are spooky."

"I wonder who they are," Edwyn said, bringing them back to the matter at hand. "Why so many men on the road to Tilden? And where did they all come from?"

"Do you think they have heard of the Brussher's army?" Hal asked.

"I doubt it. That army must have been traveling for days. There is no way the king could have reacted with such a force in the time we have been gone."

"Why head toward Tilden?" Jamie asked.

"A question that maybe your father can answer," Edwyn said. "At the pace, they are moving, it will take them several days to reach Tilden. A Lantusian Legion may march all night, but by the looks of those men, they will be lucky to make it another hour without resting."

"Then let us go. We can reach Tilden by this evening if we cut cross-country. The road does not run straight," Jamie said. "I know not what the purpose of this army is, but I must warn my father it is coming."

"A small party of horsemen, Sir Beckett," the scout reported. "They watched for a short while, then met up with a few more waiting beyond the hill."

"Could you see who they were?"

"No, sir. At least, not for certain."

"And what does that mean?"

"It was strange, my lord. They looked to be riders of both Cent and Southland."

"Which way did they go?"

"Towards Tilden."

"Is it possible to overtake them?"

"Not before they reach the castle."

Beckett looked down the road and considered what a mixed party of potential antagonists could mean. He turned to the scout.

"There's nothing for it now. If Henry is there, we will know soon enough. If he tries to run, well…" he smiled. "He won't."

"He won't, Sir Robert?"

"An honorable man, our prince. If he thinks we pose a threat to his friends, to their families, to the people of Tilden, he won't abandon them. No, if he is there, and I believe he is, he will not leave knowing we are coming."

The cave was damp and the horses restless. One of the captured horses nickered and pawed at the slivers of rock that lined the cave floor.

"Keep her quiet," Harry whispered.

"It's been an hour since we have heard anything, Harry," Johnnie said. "They must be gone by now." He looked at Brutus laying on the floor of the cave, his eyes closed, shivering. "If we don't get to Tilden soon, he isn't going to make it."

Harry looked at the legionary. They had dressed his wound as best they could, but he could see that it still seeped.

"Alright. Help him on a horse and let's go."

"We need water, Harry," Johnnie said after nearly two hours of riding.

"I know. We will stop there." Harry tilted his head towards the small stream of rushing water.

"Father! Sam yelled as Brutus slipped from his saddle and fell unconscious to the grass.

Johnnie dropped from his horse and kneeled beside Brutus. He looked up.

"He's burning up, Harry. I don't know how much longer he will live if we don't get him help."

"Can you burn it?"

"I've only seen it done."

Henry looked at Patrick Allgood, who shook his head.

"We will rest for ten minutes," Harry said. "Patrick, refill the water bags. Johnnie rebind his wound. If we have to, we will tie him to his horse. But we need to keep going." He looked up at the sun. "I think we should reach Tilden by evening. They will have a healer. It's his best chance."

"Father, look," Sam said, pointing at a small party of riders standing atop the next rise.

"How did they get in front of us?" Patrick asked.

"I don't know," Harry said, laying his hand on his sword but keeping it in the scabbard.

Two of the riders slowly worked their way toward them.

"We can't run," Johnnie said. "The horses are exhausted, and Brutus would never make it."

Harry watched the riders.

"I know." He held his hands out to his sides, hoping the approaching men meant them no harm.

"Keep your hands away from your swords. Sam, get behind me."

The riders stopped when ten yards from where they stood.

"I am Sir Jamie Mercier of Tilden. Do you need help?"

"From Tilden," Harry asked, relieved. "Did Sir George make it?"

"Sir George?" Edwyn asked.

"Sir George Williamson, the king's Chamberlain."

"Why would King John's Chamberlain go to Tilden?" Edwyn asked.

"King John is dead, my lord. Henry is king. Sir George believes he may be at Tilden. He goes there to find him."

"Dead? How, when?" Jamie asked.

"I do not know all, my lord, but from what I have heard, his death was not natural. Duke Kennington has seized the crown. He sends an army to find King Henry. Sir George believes he means to kill him."

"The men on the road," Edwyn said, looking at Jamie. "That must be the army."

"What about him?" Jamie asked, nodding towards Brutus. "Where did you find him?"

"He was a member of the Lantusian Ambassador's escort."

"Felix?" Edwyn asked. "What happened to him?"

"I don't know, my lord. We came upon a group of wounded Lantusians while running from Duke Kennington's men." He hesitated, then looked at Brutus.

"He is their sole survivor. The duke's men killed the rest."

Sir William Beckett rode slowly to his father.

"What happened?" Beckett demanded. "Where are the rest of your men?"

"We ran into a problem."

"What kind of problem?" Robert Beckett demanded.

"We believe those we chased were a diversion. We tried to capture them, thinking they might know where Sir George was, but they found refuge with a group of Lantusian legionnaires."

"Legionnaires? The ambassador's men?"

"We believe so. About two dozen. Many of them had been wounded. I do not know by whom. I demanded they turn over Sir George's men. They refused."

"Was the ambassador with them?"

"I do not think so."

Beckett's tone was enough to freeze the blood in his son's veins as he asked. "What did you do?"

"We tried to take them."

"You fought Lantusian Legionnaires?"

William looked down.

"Yes."

"And what happened?" Beckett demanded.

"They are dead."

"All of them?"

"I think so."

"You think so!" Beckett backhanded his son, knocking him from his saddle. He screamed down at him. "You slaughtered Lantusians, and you are not sure there are no witnesses! You fool! You may have well started a war."

Breathing deeply to control himself, Beckett finally turned to the man next to his son.

"Sir James, have someone show you where these people are. Make sure they are all dead. Get rid of any evidence." He hesitated and then stared at his son.

"And make sure the ambassador was not among them."

"The knight nodded and turned his horse, calling for men to follow him.

Beckett looked down at William as his son regained his feet. He spat and whispered.

"Get out of my sight."

Henry looked out over the countryside, leaning on the stone crenellation of the curtain wall. The sun was beginning its descent behind him and cast deep shadows on the land below. He turned as he felt a small hand take his.

"Why, Henry?"

"Why what, Eleanor?"

"Why did the duke send these people to kill you? What does he want?"

Henry picked her up to sit on the wall.

"Some people spend their lives seeking power. Not just riches and land, but to dominate others. The control over the very lives of those that fall under their rule. It makes them feel powerful. The duke is such a man. I should have seen this coming. He has always been ambitious. But like Father, I was blinded by my faith in the way things have always been. That all were loyal to the throne. It was he that protected our northern border with Frisia. We had faith in him. We were wrong."

"And now Father is dead," she said.

"Yes. I'm sorry."

"There is nothing to feel sorry about. Father was a cruel man. He never showed affection for me or Edwenna. It is she I miss." She looked up at him, a tear in her eye. "Do you think she is all right?"

Wiping the tear with the back of a knuckle, he smiled.

"Sir George says that she is wed to Oswald. I know she is not happy about that, but I don't think the duke would harm her. Not now. This may be the best thing to keep her safe. He needs her to attain any legitimacy to the throne."

"Poor Edwenna. She so despised that boy."

Henry laughed.

"I know."

"Marjorie thinks you are special."

"And I think the same of her."

"She has not said, but I think she desires you."

Henry chuckled.

"And what do you know of desire?"

"I'm not a child, Henry."

"Of course you aren't. But…."

"Riders!"

Henry turned to the lookout. "Where?"

The guard pointed to a distant hill. Henry set Elenore on the fighting platform and stared in the direction the man pointed. Along the crest of the hill stood five riders.

"Elenore, go get Baron Mercier. Quickly!"

As she ran down the stairs, she saw Philip.

"Riders come," she said.

"The army?" he asked.

"I don't know. They come not from the road. The king wishes me to get the Baron."

"Then go."

She ran past him, and Philip took the stairs two at a time.

"Friend or foe?" he asked as he stepped beside Henry.

"I don't know. They are just standing there."

"What should we do?"

"I'll wait until Irwin gets here and then we will decide."

"Should we sound the alarm?"

Henry watched the riders. They had not moved.

"Not yet. Let's see what they do. There is no telling what lies beyond that ridge. There could be a thousand men."

Irwin and Marlowe rushed onto the platform, the Baron stopping to catch his breath.

"This used to be a lot easier twenty years ago."

"Father," Marlowe said. "There are few men alive today that have the strength that you display. Do not fault yourself for a shortage of breath after the pace you set. I need a moment."

Irwin slapped him on the shoulder.

"Lier." He smiled. Turning to Henry, he asked, "What is it, your majesty? Elenore said there are riders?"

Henry pointed.

"On the hill."

"They just sit?"

"They do," Henry agreed.

"Why do you think they do not approach?" Irwin asked.

"Maybe they are trying to determine who controls the castle," Marlowe said.

Henry looked at him.

"You mean they are trying to determine if the duke's men have arrived first."

"The thought has crossed my mind," Marlowe agreed.

"What do you wish me to do, sire?" Irwin asked. "Should we man the walls?"

"Not yet. Let us see who these visitors are and what it is they want before we panic."

"I will take ten men and ride out, sire," Marlowe said.

"No. He looked at the ring Felix had delivered as it rested on the index finger of his left hand. "I will go."

Philip took hold of Henry's wrist.

"You cannot. It is too dangerous." Henry looked at his hand and Philip released it.

"I am sorry, my king. I forget myself."

Henry slapped him on the shoulder.

"You do not. For I count on your council, my friend."

"He's right that you should not go, your majesty," Irwin said. "You are king now. You cannot place yourself in danger, willy-nilly?"

Henry laughed.

"Willy nilly?"

"You know what I mean."

"I do, my friend. And thank you."

"I will go, sire," Marlowe said.

"As will I," Randel said, stepping onto the platform. Sir Walter stood at his side.

"I will take ten men," Marlowe said, looking at his father. "With your permission, sir."

"You have it, go. And be careful."

"As always, Father."

The three knights ran down the steps. Walter looked at Irwin. He smiled.

"Go."

Walter rushed to join the others.

"Is he always careful?" Henry asked.

"He's, my son."

Henry chuckled. "Yes, he is. That is why I asked."

The fourteen men trotted forward over the lowered drawbridge, not wishing to show aggression. The riders on the hill walked their horses down and when they reached the bottom, dismounted and waited for the men from Tilden.

Sir Marlowe stopped the party fifty yards away and dismounted. He, Walter, Randel, and Philip left their mounts with the rest of the men and walked toward the newcomers. It shocked Henry when Marlowe and Walter suddenly rushed forward and embraced one of them.

After a few minutes, one stranger signaled and more riders appeared on the hilltop.

"It looks like they may be friends," Irwin said as he watched them approach.

"But who are they?"

"Let us go see," Henry said.

"Who is it?" Eleanor asked as she and Marjorie joined Henry and Irwin at the gate.

"I am not sure," Henry said. "But Sir Marlowe feels safe bringing them here, so I will assume they are friends."

Over two dozen riders walked their horses toward the castle.

"Who is Marlowe talking to?" Irwin asked.

Marjorie suddenly brought her hands to her mouth.

"It's Jamie!"

"It is," Irwin said. "But who has he with him? The woman looks like a Southlander. And I think that is Sir Edwyn."

Henry stepped forward as he stared at the man in a strange hat walking next to the woman. Maggie suddenly appeared from nowhere and ran at the stranger. Seeing the enormous cat, the man froze as Maggie bumped against him. He cautiously ran his hand down her neck.

Henry walked across the drawbridge. The man with the hat looked up as he approached.

"Hello, Henry? Been a while."

EPILOGUE

The Beach at the edge of the Dark Forest

The Kraken wrapped its massive tentacles around his torso, squeezing the air from his lungs. He pushed down, frantically fighting to get away, his hands sinking into the sticky mud on the floor of the sea. Finally, finding some purchase, he heaved until his body rose a few inches, releasing the pressure from the deadly arms of the beast. Gasping, he drew in the putrid air into his tortured lungs.

Knut slowly opened his right eye, unable to lift the lid from his left as it was plastered to his face with dried blood. Seeing nothing but darkness, he was afraid he was blind, or that maybe the beast had swallowed him. He tried to roll to his side and cried out as the nearly unbearable pain brought him back to this world, causing him to fall back, gasping for breath.

Some figure, shadowy and faint, moved above. It was screaming something. Something important. He tried to focus.

"Frigg?"

Atop the pile of bodies, the image of a blood-soaked woman turned her head.

"Knut! Is that you?"

Hearing the muffled call, Knut's mind began to clear.

"Here," he groaned.

Frigg Daggerblood dropped to her knees and pulled at the bodies that covered her prince.

"Knut, hold on. Stay with me."

Three and then four fallen warriors, she pulled from the pile of the dead and rolled them to the side until she saw him move.

Light. Blessed light. "Frigg?" Knut whispered. "Is that truly you?"

"It is I, my lord. Do not move. I will have you free in a moment."

Pulling the last of the fallen warriors from the pile of the dead, she worked her way down until she was standing next to him. She reached under his arms and pulled. He screamed. Frigg stopped.

"I am sorry, my lord. Give me a moment. I need to remove the others from your legs."

She pulled the bodies of two more of her friends, hesitating when she recognized Sibbe Brodirsson although half his face was missing. Gripping him by his lifeless arms, she pulled until able to roll his body to the side.

Carefully, she again reached down and tried to lift him.

He cried out.

"I am sorry."

"Get me out of here. And for Oden's sake, stop apologizing."

She smiled and pulled him to a sitting position. Squatting down, she wrapped her arms around his waist as she placed her shoulder into his stomach. She slowly lifted with her legs until able to roll him onto the bodies above.

"Damn!"

"I believe your left leg to be broken."

"Really," he grimaced. "What was your first clue?"

She laughed as she examined him. "You're winning like a babe for one. That your foot looks to be facing away from you the other."

He looked at the surrounding carnage. "Any others?"

Running her fingers down his leg and not looking up she whispered, "None but us. Until I heard you groan, I thought myself alone."

He looked at the bloody mound of bodies that were his people, his friends. Then he looked at the woman that kneeled before him.

"How badly are you injured, Frigg?"

She smiled. "Not nearly as bad as you. I can walk."

Seeing her wipe the back of her hand across her brow to clear the blood seeping down into her eyes, he asked again as he gently ran the back of his hand down her bloodied arm.

She looked at him. "A few cuts here and there. Took a blow to the head. Must have knocked me out. I came to with Beorn's shield atop me. He laying across it."

"He saved your life."

She was quiet for a moment. "He did." She looked at the pile of bodies she had pulled from him. "As they did you."

They were both quiet for a moment. She took a deep breath and nodded towards the trees.

"I think they are gone. I believe it is best we move to the trees."

"Did you see if Leif made it?"

"No. I was a little busy."

Helping him stand, she said, "Now, hang on to me, and let's get off this cursed beach."

Once in the shade of the trees, she lowered him and fell exhausted to sit next to him. They sat there for a moment, not speaking, filling their lungs with the clean air.

From deep within the dark forest, they heard a monstrous roar.

Frigg rose and walked slowly to the wall dead that lined the sands of the bloody shore. After a few minutes, she returned with two swords and an ax. She handed a sword to Knut and took a grip on the ax.

"I'll cut some wood for a fire and see what I can find to fashion a splint."

"Frigg."

"Yes, my lord."

"Be careful. And thank you."

She looked at him and smiled.

"I'm always careful."

Watch for book two in the Riddle of the Storm series coming soon:

The Riddle of the Storm
Book Two
The White Wolf

Definitions

Conroi: A group of fighting men.

Gambeson: A padded tunic worn under chainmail to help cushion a blow

Chainmail: Metal armor consisting of metal rings.

Coif: Chainmail hood

Kite shield: large, almond-shaped shield, rounded at the top and pointed at the bottom carried by horsemen. It was long enough to cover the left side of the body while mounted from shoulder to foot.

Heater shield: A shorter version of a kite shield.

Lance: A long heavy spear often associated with jousting

Anelace: A long dagger or short sword sharpened on both sides often carried in the small of the back.

Surcoat: Tunic worn over armor often with a crest identifying allegiance

Destrier: A warhorse

Sumpter: A pack horse

Imperator: Supreme military commander

Legatus: An ambassador

Centurion: Commander of a century (usually eighty men)

Optio: Second in command of a century

Centurio Primus Pilus: Commander of the First Cohort of a Legion

Hamata: Sleeveless chainmail shirt
Squamata: Scale armor
Lorica Segmintata: Armor consisting of metal strips formed into circular bands
Pugio: Wide dagger
Gladius: Short, wide, lightweight sword, about twenty-seven inches long and almost three inches wide.
Spatha: A long, straight sword carried primarily by cavalry
Plumbatae: A throwing dart with a heavy barbed head
Pilum: A six to seven-foot javelin with a twenty-eight-inch iron shank
Turmae: A squadron of thirty cavalrymen divided into groups of ten
Decuriones: Commander of ten horsemen in a Turmae
Drakkar: A warship with sail and oars often associated with Vikings
Knarr: A merchant ship
Seax: A short sword
Galdramenn: A wizard
Huskarl: A bodyguard

Authors Note

Writing is my opportunity to escape, even for a little while, from the demands of the real world, so I thank you for taking the time to read Glenlock, the first in the Riddle of the Storm series. I would appreciate it if you could take a moment to share your thoughts by leaving a review. This is something that will allow me to continue my writing journey as I look to provide the escape that you and other fantasy readers desire. Also, if you could take a moment to recommend Glenlock as a worthy read to your social media followers, I would be thankful.

Glenlock is a creation of my imagination. Obviously, nothing like this exists in our world today. We all wish that society had no strife, no crime, and no power-hungry individuals seeking to expand their influence in the world, but unfortunately, we all know this is not the case.

Many very smart people have said that most of the conflicts in history are in one way or another linked to things like organized religion, language barriers, racial differences, and oftentimes, superstitious responses to things that are hard to explain.

So, what would happen if a world existed where there was no organized religion, no racial discord, no language barriers, and no cultural hatred? Would the world be a more peaceful place? Something to think about. I can tell you Hal is thinking about these things. When he has a chance, of course.

You can keep up on what I am doing, ask questions or leave comments on what you have read or what you would like me to consider in future stories by visiting my website at:

https://www.robertsnyderwrites.com

Looking forward to hearing from you.

R. L. Snyder

Milton Keynes UK
Ingram Content Group UK Ltd.
UKHW020626050324
438776UK00006B/1080